CONGAI
Mistress of Indochine

CONGAI

Mistress of Indochine

by

HARRY HERVEY

Foreword by
Pico IYER

Edited by
Kent DAVIS

Featuring

Through a Woman's Eyes:
Congaies, Heroines & Harry Hervey

by

Harlan GREENE

DatAsia Press

MMXIV

About the Cover

Award-winning cover artist Yuehui Tang is widely recognized for his stunning depictions of Asian women. His artistic vision captures the allure, secrets and ultimate power wielded by women who embody feminine perfection in the eyes of men who desire them—the most powerful of whom become powerless in their thrall.

www.HarryHervey.com

DatASIA Press

www.DatAsia.us

Copyright ©2014 DatASIA, Inc. Holmes Beach, Florida

Production Credits

Editor – **Kent Davis**

Hervey Biographical Consultant - **Harlan Greene**

Cover Artist – **Yuehui Tang**

Cover Design – **Becca Klein**

Text design – **Surendra Gupta** & **Daria Lacy**

Literary Consultant – **François Doré, Librairie du Siam et des Colonies**

With special thanks to the **Georgia Historical Society** (www.georgiahistory.com) for maintaining the Hervey archive and for use of the author's portrait.

Additional blessings to **Sophaphan Davis, Jon Dobbs, Meng Dy, Tom Kramer, Jessie Liu** and **Duffy Rutledge** for their special contributions and encouragement.

ISBN 978-1-934431-88-7 (paperback)

Library of Congress Control Number: 2012947977

Printed simultaneously in the **United States of America** and **Great Britain.**

First Edition

The last time I saw her was at the Continental in Saigon, where Frenchmen listening to the latest music from Paris are able to forget for a moment that sun-weary land of exile.

She swept out of the café "like the Queen of Sheba," as the estimable Malardier put it, and into her waiting motorcar.

And after she passed, a gentleman, in one of those preposterously large felt hats which Frenchmen persist in wearing even so near the equator, laughed and said: "I wonder how long that will last!"

Perhaps, *Madame la Panthère*, you will accept this inadequate testimonial of my belief in the integrity of your cleverness....

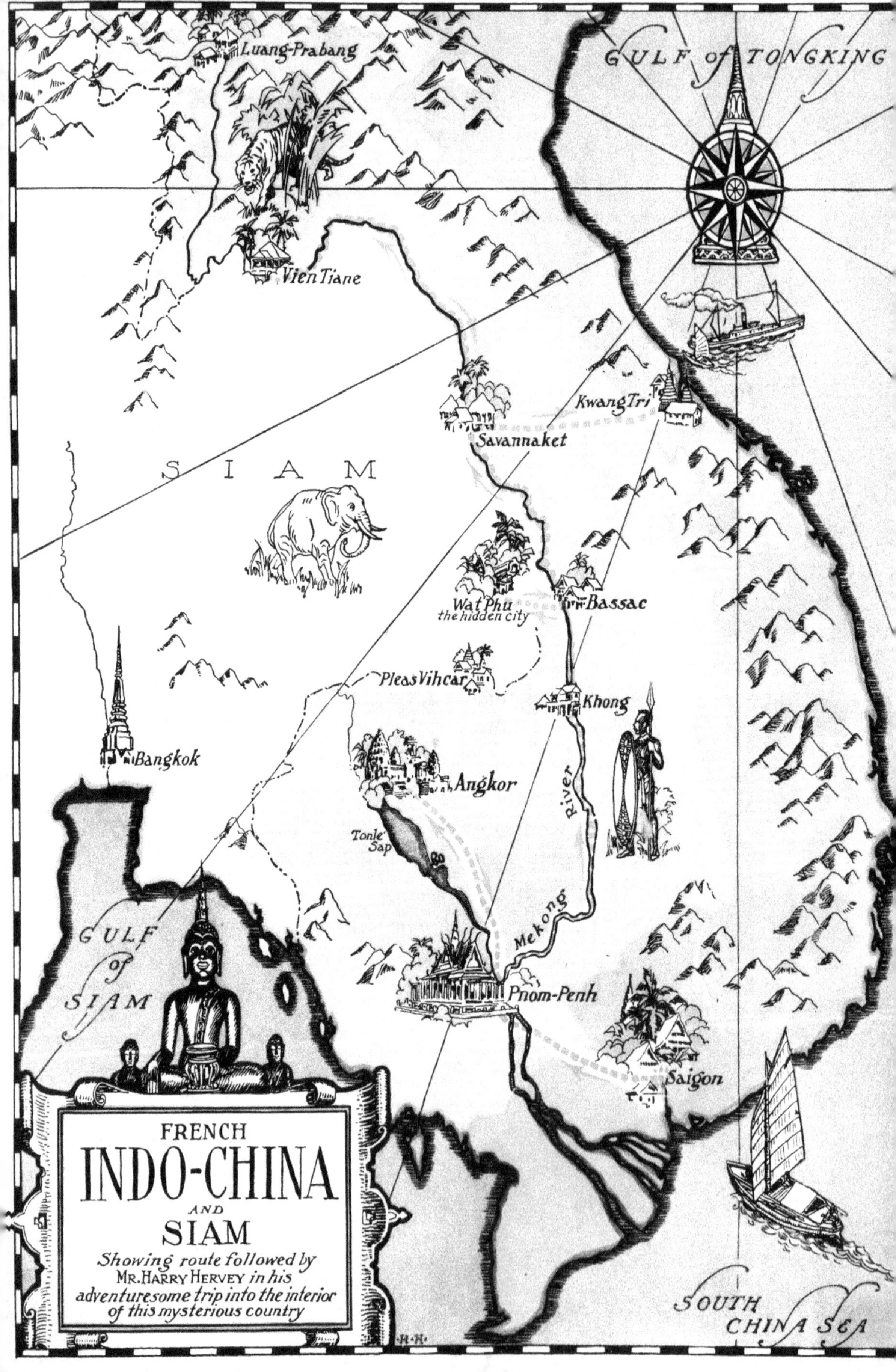

GULF of TONGKING
Luang-Prabang
Vien Tiane
SIAM
KwangTri
Savannaket
Wat Phu
the hidden city
Bassac
Pleas Vihcar
Khong
Bangkok
Angkor
River
Tonlé Sap
Mekong
GULF of SIAM
Pnom-Penh
Saigon
SOUTH CHINA SEA
FRENCH
INDO-CHINA
AND
SIAM
Showing route followed by
MR. HARRY HERVEY in his
adventuresome trip into the interior
of this mysterious country

Table of Contents

The Book that Launched
a Thousand Ships

By Pico Iyer

Be patient when you enter Harry Hervey's humid, sometimes overwrought early novel, *Congai*. And be aware that one of its main themes is that things in French Indochina are seldom what they seem.

It's true that at first you may feel you're trudging through a very heavy jungle on a horribly steamy day and being concussed by low-hanging fruit at every turn. By page 3, you're reading of the "pitiless incandescence" of the heat, by page 4 you're surrounded by a "silent brown mystery" and very soon you'll notice that the young author never met a noun ending in "-ness" that he didn't like, generally accompanied by an over-ripe tropical adjective.

We're not accustomed to such smoldering and febrile eventfulness in the 21st century—"sultry brooding" and "exquisite frailty" in the same sentence—and when a Frenchman starts talking about "beautiful savages" on page 3, we're taken aback: you're not supposed to say things like that! Indeed, the Frenchman himself is advised that soon he won't be calling any locals "savages"—and may come to wonder whether he's not the real savage himself.

"Everything is paradoxical—particularly here," says a nearby priest, giving us our first intimation of what a connoisseur of secrets and fictions our young author really is. *Congai* is about to prove a lot more supple and unexpected than it appears, as will both the French colonial presence and the indigenous Vietnamese population that are its central subjects.

What I love about this book is how constantly it proved me wrong, and how deliberately it overturned my every expectation, the first time I read it. To take perhaps the most obvious example, it begins with a young Frenchman in Indochina in the 1920s encountering a sultry local girl and slowly surrendering to her charms. *Madama Butterfly* revisited, I thought—or any of Pierre Loti's famous romances (such as *Madame Chrysanthème* on which *Madama Butterfly* was based) updated a little, to tell the story of a carefree Western romancer and bewitching, if ultimately abandoned, dark-skinned nymph. When, early on in the book, the wandering French writer actually publishes a novel about his local love—titled *Une Fille d'Annam* (*A Girl of Annam*), no less—I was sure that I was simply reading a thinly-veiled account of Hervey's own romance with some local beauty. Everything seemed thinly-veiled in *Congai*.

How wrong I was! The writer turns out to be just one of several amours his heroine will encounter, and Hervey had a much more intriguingly complex and equivocal relation to his subject than I'd guessed. At a central dinner party in the novel, the characters actually start discussing *Une Fille d'Annam*, and even as various French officials downplay its value, it's the "half-caste" Vietnamese girl—its subject and dedicatee—who defends it. At that same party, the guests go on to talk about Loti, as if to show that Hervey was acutely conscious of the tradition in which he was working and of the stereotypes he was invoking. Yet again, it's the Frenchmen who dismiss the French chronicler of exoticism even as the Vietnamese woman finds much to praise in the traveler's depictions of native beauties.

Loti was "able to catch the nostalgic beauty of Asia," she says, while entertaining reactions that are "undeniably Eastern." Emotionally, for her, he's a "strange blending of both Oriental and Occidental." She might almost be talking about her own creator, the 27 year-old American Harry Hervey—or, in truth, his alter ego: herself.

Harry Hervey first arrived in Indochina in 1925, at a time when very few Americans had set eyes on it—he came out with six rich travel-books and novels. In every one, he is scathing about colonialism and more than ready to go native—even as he never begins to assume the native culture is either easy or uncomplicated (when a Frenchman walks through her garden with the heroine, Thi-Linh, he registers "roses mimosa, agaves, acacias, palms…with just enough thorny growth to make it interesting").

By the time Hervey arrived, the French, after 60 years or so of occupation had, inevitably, compiled a whole library of books describing their local loves and losses—as their American counterparts would do in Vietnam and Japan and the Philippines. In 1911 Jean d'Estay published *Thi-Sen: la petite amie exotique* (*Thi-Sen: The Exotic Little Girlfriend*), and by 1919 Roland Meyer released his controversial epic tale of cross-cultural love, *Saramani, Danseuse Khmer* (*Saramani, Khmer Dancer*). In 1920 the prolific Jean d'Esme came out with *Thi-Ba, fille d'Annam* (*Thi-Ba, Girl of Annam*), and Henry Casseville followed with *Thi-Nhi, autre fille d'Annam* (*Thi-Nhi, Another Girl of Annam*). The year after Hervey released *Congai*, noted author and Cambodian expert George Groslier published his novel of East-West romance, *Le retour à l'argile* (*Return to Clay*), which later won France's Grand Prize for Colonial Literature.

But in English literature, the topic was much less familiar. Hervey effectively threw open the door for dozens of later travelers to consider what could be called the hidden sales-tax, the night-time subversion of colonialism. By day, after all, many westerners imagined they were ruling the people they were in charge of; by night, in all kinds of ways, the empire struck back.

Six years after *Congai*, Andrew Freeman brought out his anthology, *Brown Women and White*, and then the floodgates really opened: Somerset Maugham's stories of westerners giving themselves over to the lure of the East; Jack Reynolds's still celebrated *Woman of Bangkok* in 1956; Richard Mason's *World of Suzie Wong*, in 1957; Paul Scott's unforgettable *Chinese Love-Pavilion* three years later. Soon even Ian Fleming was giving James Bond his only love-child, courtesy of Kissy Suzuki.

If you step into a Bangkok bookshop tomorrow—or one in Phnom Penh, Hong Kong, Saigon—the books on the place written in English by foreigners will, almost to a one, be the grandchildren of *Congai*. I should know; I wrote one myself.

Hervey also stands up impressively when you consider some of the best-known fiction of his time trafficking in Asia. As soon as I entered the ripe, thunder-heavy world of *Congai's* Vietnam, I couldn't help thinking of the acclaimed young American novelist, Frederic Prokosch, who published a fantastically vivid and evocative account of a journey from Beirut to Hanoi in *The Asiatics*. But Prokosch's book came out in 1935, eight years after *Congai*, and the most startling thing about it was that its author had never been to the countries he described; he wrote the whole thing in New Haven, simply drawing upon the descriptions of other travelers, Hervey perhaps among them.

Two years after *Congai*, Somerset Maugham brought out his enduring travel-classic, *The Gentleman in the Parlour*, still one of the first works I recommend to travelers headed to the Asia where I've been living for more than a quarter of a century. But where Hervey dives fearlessly into the intensity of East-West relations in his works, Maugham simply observes them from a safe distance and in a sedan-chair being carried by local bearers. The 1920s marked a great explosion of writing about exotic corners of the world that suddenly became available to fortunate Western travelers, and it's no wonder that the years between the wars are now seen as a Golden Age of writing about far-off cultures, thanks to such masters as Graham Greene, Evelyn Waugh, Peter Fleming and Robert Byron. But all of them, of course, were privileged Brits; Hervey was the relatively rare American of his time to go much farther than a Fitzgerald or Hemingway and to plunge into the intricacies of colonial dramas that were not his own.

Not every reader knows about all these precedents; I didn't know any of the French ones until the publisher of this volume, Kent Davis, pointed them out to me. But Hervey surely did, and so he at once joined a grand tradition and subverted it by bringing the French stories into a new language and by challenging their premises. Of course there is a lot in *Congai*—maybe too much—about "white" and "brown." In describing one French character, Hervey goes on about "pathetic whiteness" so obsessively, and with so many incantatory repetitions, that I wondered if he'd just emerged from a heavy ingestion of D.H. Lawrence ("Oh, the excruciating whiteness of him as he stood there!").

There's also a lot about young and old: Thi-Linh finds Saigon "ancient and inevitable…{with} an oldness that had nothing to do with actual years," and we see that the same applies to her. But at heart Hervey is discerning enough to realize that old and young can coexist in the same culture—or person. And as it develops, his book turns out to be as much about the struggle between Thi-Linh and her culture as it is about the struggle between Europe and Asia. As we follow his Annamite version of Madame Bovary, first torn between a local childhood lover and a Frenchman she's drawn to, later divided between her restless longing to try a different kind of life and the changelessness that is part of her inheritance, we clearly see the division that defines Asia today: in India, in China, in Thailand and in the Japan where I live, many are perpetually wondering how to take in the best of the modern, affluent West without losing the Eastern values that have guided and steadied them for millennia.

Yes, you have to wade through a lot of "gurgling brownness" and "fluid drowsiness" in *Congai*; to absorb plenty of "insuperable brutality" and "shuddering ecstasy" as you tramp through its torrential dramas. Hervey's description of emotions is often as feverish as a Harlequin romance, and there's always a "savage splash of hibiscus" adorning his prose. But there's no question that he inhaled Southeast Asia deeply and with tremendous vividness.

Look at the "dart and glide of two rickshaws beyond the low iron fence"; listen to the "chirp of scissors and ring of sandaled feet; voices and the droning tear of silk." Again and again, "a sense of suppressed drums" in the background makes us feel the languor and the heat. Deeper than that, Hervey always makes the reader aware that, just beneath the gossamer delicacy of the culture he's describing is something hard as steel: Thi-Linh sinks her nails into one French cheek until she draws blood; and, as Hervey explains, the limber dancing beauties of Phnom Penh have their joints broken so they can perform with greater flexibility.

XIII

What took me aback, at every turn, as I went through his story, was how wisely Hervey cuts through simplistic explanations and, much like his heroine, penetrates to something more complex and riddled. The French here are often patronizing and crude, but, just as often, they're more sensitive and open than we might imagine; Thi-Linh is never just a silly girl—or a calculating minx—but a confounding mixture of the two. At one point, we read, she "had learned enough about her Frenchman to understand his needs and desires." But then Hervey goes on, "If she had known more…undoubtedly they would have had many arguments."

The whole novel, as it develops, turns into a celebration of "fluidity," the new, post-national consciousness that allows Westerners to go native to some extent, to keep setting down roots in different places and, at times, to carry the locals they meet somewhat into their own culture: in other words, just the mobile, global culture we know today, then in its first stages. And this is a matter not just of circumstance and movement but of inner movement and sensibility. Hervey, after all, enters the spirit of a distant continent and a different gender with great sensitivity and passion, as if to remind us that most borders exist only in our heads.

Notice, too—wonderfully, and quite plausibly (it's almost the story of the East right now)—how it's the Frenchman Justin who explains to the Vietnamese woman the classic Buddhist metaphor of how a flame is passed from candle to candle as a soul moves from life to life. Notice how the book's constant, furious dramas play out against a backdrop of calm acceptance, as if the eventful tales of Thomas Hardy (or an eager Hollywood melodramatist) were placed within a Confucian frame. There are flashes from the Catholic confessional here, and quite a lot of Buddhist realism and tolerance about impermanence, but in the end we move past all religions to follow a flow as all-enveloping and unceasing as the river in Hermann Hesse's *Siddhartha*, published just five years earlier.

Reading the book, you may not be surprised to learn that Hervey, with his gift for twisting stories and for swooning local color, found his way very quickly to Hollywood, where he had a hand in such Orientalist classics as Marlene Dietrich's *Shanghai Express*. You may flinch a bit at the "clouded, half-wistful intensity" of his prose (to borrow the phrase he uses for a young American's eyes), or descriptions of a local girl wanting "to burn her lips in the soft rim of fire" on an American's hair. But you will also surely note that Hervey was prescient enough to write about an American presence in French Indochina thirty years before that became the stuff of worldwide headlines.

In fact, my deepest astonishment in reading *Congai* came with seeing how much it anticipates perhaps the greatest and most evergreen foreign novel about modern Vietnam, *The Quiet American*, by Graham Greene—a book that urchins outside the Metropole Hotel in Hanoi still tout to visitors (in pirated editions), and the one that every wise newcomer to the country still consults. For here in *Congai*—twenty-nine years before Greene's classic—Hervey gives us a Vietnamese woman, coolly judging her prospects with a variety of foreign suitors. He gives us another Vietnamese woman who's even more pragmatic about the market value of beauty and exoticism. Here is a young American who sounds like an Englishman and whose sovereign quality is "innocence." Here are scenes on the Rue Catinat, the evocative center of Greene's novel, and memorable moments of Europeans spilling out onto the hot tropical streets at night after *thé-dansants*. Even the dedication page of *Congai*, with its unorthodox form and tone, is so strikingly similar to Greene's that it's hard not to believe that the English novelist took in Hervey's novel when he spent time in Vietnam during the last days of the French.

So maybe it's no coincidence that Greene's heroine is called Phuong—which means "Phoenix," as he tells us on his opening page; the symbol of the phoenix plays a central part in Hervey's novel. And again and again—in Thi-Linh's trips to the cinema, in the French Prefect of Police calmly reflecting on a murder (on the Rue Catinat), in the descriptions of plowmen working the fields immemorially, in an American who may wear a "stupid, grinning mask," but is something much more inside—Hervey seems to be anticipating Greene and so opening the door to the way we would be seeing Indochina, on the page and in our heads, well into the 21st century.

For those who weary of the account of the young American—or get distracted by the "wistful luxury of feeling in his eyes" and his "suavely muscular being"—I simply recommend pressing on to the very end.

When you get there, you'll find that the novel's central discussion of Pierre Loti has implications for the plot as well as for the theme you may not have foreseen. You'll realize that Thi-Linh's ability to see the merits of a French perspective of Vietnam will help a Frenchman see the merits of a Vietnamese perspective on France. East and West are so mixed up—so all over one another—that all notions of black and white, of right and wrong, dissolve. In that way, *Congai* is an unexpectedly invaluable guide to the Asia that is waiting to take in millions of new visitors next year. Those of us who write on the continent almost ninety years later are often, more unconsciously than not, following in the footsteps of an intrepid latter-day Lafcadio Hearn who intuited more than he knew. Even in his wildest moments, Hervey caught something true that those of us more than twice his age can only bow before.

Pico Iyer

Nara, Japan — August 2013

Pico Iyer has been called "arguably the greatest living travel-writer" by *Outside* magazine and "one of 100 visionaries worldwide who could change your life" by the *Utne Reader.*

A traveler since birth, he has ventured throughout Asia for more than 30 years, as chronicled in his books including *Video Night in Kathmandu, Falling Off the Map* and *Sun After Dark.*

He has also, as mentioned here, committed at least one book about a visitor from the West and his romance with a woman of the East (*The Lady and the Monk*). Since 1987 he's been based in western Japan, though often making forays from Laos to Bali and Ladakh to Bangkok.

CONGAI

Mistress of Indochine

Where a shaft of sunlight falls,

the shadows seem the darker

just beyond its radiance:

Gloom follows at the heels

of those too vivid to be pure.

The Beginning:

Portrait of a Frenchman

he stood by the edge of the river, her slender legs and thighs sheathed in rust-brown mud, her sarong rolled about her hips, and a rattan basket held against her side. Behind her, the oozy bank ascended to the jungle which, in the melting heat, seemed to lose form and contour and become a depth of fluid green in which the few native huts floated like bits of cork on green wine. Her body was so nearly the shade of the bank that Justin Batteur, watching from the deck of the passing river boat, wondered, drowsily, if she were not an illusion sprung from the soil.

Father Mehry, leaning on the rail beside him, squinted at the woman, and observed:

"Indo-China standing in the mud and glare."

Absently he asked: "What do you think of our native women?"

Batteur's face, taut in the heat, relaxed into a smile; the reflected shimmer gave his eyes a curious effect of blurred and sleepy green.

"Beautiful savages," he pronounced, still smiling.

Father Mehry chuckled. "After a few months you won't call them savages."

Batteur stretched luxuriously, with a play of lithe tendons over his forearms, rippling the faint sheen of yellow hair. He sank into a canvas chair.

"You speak from the broad vantage of one seeking converts" he accused.

"I speak from the broad vantage of one who has seen many Frenchmen take them for their wives."

The younger man smiled. "Wives?"

Father Mehry smiled back at him, wisely. He was a tall, stout man, with a gray beard that was red- streaked as though some of the silver hairs had tarnished. Dressed in that ill-fitting, rusty-looking cassock that trailed the deck, and with his soiled white sun-helmet, he suggested, Batteur thought, a comic old archangel who had grown moldy in the tropics.

"Why not wives?" demanded the priest. "They fulfill the duties of wives—keep house, amuse, give affection, and sometimes children."

Batteur looked sleepy. He was watching the gradually dwindling figure by the bank.

"I had always thought," he observed, languidly interested, "that the cloth made one intolerant."

"*Mon Dieu!*" exclaimed Father Mehry. "It is the cloth that makes us tolerant! And," he added, a glint of humor in his eyes, "may not a priest be a Frenchman as well as a celibate?"

Batteur laughed. "That sounds paradoxical."

Father Mehry shrugged. "Everything is paradoxical—particularly here. Although French women"— again that glint of humor in his eyes—"do not entirely approve of French men living with *congaies*, the Government does not discourage it; it brings us closer to the people. Is not that paradoxical?" [1]

"Quite.... Make soldiers of the men; marry the women. Long live France, the protectress! ...But what of the Church?"

---

1 *Congai* (plural *congaies*) is simply the Vietnamese word for young girl, however it took on other meanings under colonial rules. See the appendix essay "*Congaies* or Concubines?" for details.

Father Mehry shrugged again. "The Church is wise; what good would it do to draw aside its skirts?"

"And the children of these marriages?"

"They become good Frenchmen."

"Probably," said Batteur. "You should know— although I suspect the girls become good *congaies* for future Frenchmen, and the boys—well, whatever half-castes become—disturbers, no doubt."

The priest was an effigy of wisdom, smiling down on the man in the sagging deck chair. "Perhaps, when you have been here longer, you will come to understand Indo-China."

The woman by the bank had become one with the river and the jungle, and the river and the jungle themselves had become one with the pitiless incandescence that sheathed the earth like hot metal. Batteur, his eyes half closed, felt like a great cat, and he wanted to stretch and purr.

"For the good of my books," he murmured, "I hope so."

Batteur dreamed that he was a candle burning in thick ocherous gloom, and he awoke to find himself limp with sweat in the tawny glare that seemed to spring up from the stream.

While he slept his helmet had fallen forward on his face, and he imagined that he must have looked rather ridiculous. To whom? There were only three other white passengers: the priest, a mining-engineer bound for Khone, and the wife of an official at Pakse. They were all folded away in their berths, sleeping through mid-afternoon. The only ones who might have seen him were natives. Cattle, he thought; and reflected that, being a good Frenchman, that was what he should think. But, he realized, that was not what he thought really.

From the very moment he had landed, nearly two months past, he had felt a silent brown mystery rising about him. This intangible element in the atmosphere disconcerted and troubled him. At times he felt up to his throat in a sensual limpidity that flowed imperceptibly out of the tawny people surrounding him. He had expected to find himself in the midst of gay colonial life as a prelude to his voyage into the interior where he intended to study and write. Gay colonial life he had found. But it was an arabesque imposed upon a viscid and swarthy background. It was true that the Rue de la Paix haunted the Rue Catinat at Saigon, but it was an anemic harlequin that danced to the cadence of throbbing sunlight and the darker measure of native life. Here in the jungle it was the same. All this green seemed subject to the dominant sepia of the people (a color not so much of the skin as of something under the skin) as though the beauty of plants and trees were simply set there to limn [2] a brown silhouette.

It was strange, he reflected, how an illusion of dark moisture seemed to well up out of the earth and bathe his being; it was not an illusion induced by humidity or dampness but by a force even less tangible.

Of course, he realized, sprawled in the deck chair, it was too hot to be greatly disturbed over a matter so entirely subjective. It was simply that he had to readjust his preconceived opinions. And it was too hot to do that very quickly. The manager of the rest-house at Angkor had said he would find it cooler in upper Cambodia.... There was a beautiful savagery about these damned natives, he thought persistently. "Beautiful savage"—that was what he had said to the priest.... But as for having one—Women were a physical necessity that became less urgent when one created— anything. Sublimation. His life in Paris had been singularly free of them; for he belonged to that earnest group of younger Frenchmen who so far forgot their traditions as to go clean shaven and live without mistresses, and in consequence brought down upon themselves the hint of vices less traditional but more eminently sophisticated.

His blood was too thoroughly Latin for his admiration of women to be confined to the esthetic; but he was also too thoroughly provincial immediately to allow himself to do more than regard brown women with technical appreciation. What their natural grace symbolized he felt with disturbing intimacy, but he was too well poised mentally to permit himself more than analytical excursions into the mystery. Often, while in Saigon, he was startled when the searching equatorial sunlight, touching some woman exquisitely *Parisienne,* disclosed a golden shadow haunting her throat.

---

2 To limn is to describe something in painting or words.

Now he had left the coast behind, with all its implications, and in two days he would reach Stung Treng, where colonial life was a somber duty instead of diversion with pay.

Batteur sat up and surveyed the stream. There was something epic in the breath of the Me-Kong. It flowed luminously out of the blue-hot sky, settling down into thick, flat brown. Numerous craft drifted by, manned by natives who stared at the passing river boat. The swells in its wake rocked their tiny pirogues and then sank into the copper calm; just as, Batteur reflected, that rude phenomenon progress must at times rock their thoughts and pass on into the magnificent placidity of minds not involved by the elaborate pretensions of civilization.

In a small space aft, separated by a railing with a gate, were more natives. Their meal had just been served by a deck-boy. The majority squatted as they ate, knees thrust up almost to breast and balancing by some equilibrium unknown to white men, while chopsticks flashed the food from bowls to eager mouths. Some of those mouths sickened Batteur. The lips were stained dark red with betel juice, the teeth black. How could I love a woman with such a mouth? he thought.

Towards dusk the boat stopped at a village. Standing on the upper deck beside Father Mehry, he watched the unloading.

High steps rose from the floating wharf to the embankment that fronted the river. Beyond that were shops built in a long, low arcade. A few lamps smote the crepuscular air. In the soft light Batteur could see that the whitewash was peeling from the plaster arches, and green mold gave them a soiled, haggard look. They seemed, he thought, as old as the shops of Nineveh; and as wise.

In the road were many native soldiers, suave in khaki and spiked helmets, and barefoot. Moving among them were native civilians with classic profiles ; slim men naked to the waist; and tiny women in immense turbans, carrying baskets of food to sell or simply mingling with the crowd. Several Frenchmen stood on the landing, immaculate and red-faced, and all talking at once. Soft words in a strange tongue blurred their harsh syllables. The voice of Father Mehry, speaking from the deck, mingled with the others. Batteur heard himself being introduced, and he spoke automatically while his gaze rested elsewhere.

There was something husky and inarticulate in the night, in the village itself. The Frenchman felt it— like warm groping fingers. The dead arcades and the young soldiers so alive; the coolies with thighs like stags'; the girls in smoldering colors—bright colors that seemed to become fluid, as sweat made them cleave to warm skin and take on a certain naked life. They were the moods of moving bodies, those colors; and the bodies themselves seemed to flow into a greater mood and poignantly enclose Batteur. For a moment he felt like a palette over which amazing color was splashed.

"…See you next week!…" Father Mehry shouted "…*au revoir!*…" The boat's whistle gave a thick cry. It was like something white and strangled that cried out in Batteur. He lifted his helmet to the Frenchmen who receded with the landing like pale distortions. Father Mehry waved…. Batteur felt hot and swarthy.

"Stung Treng is like that," the priest was saying; "and so are most of the towns along the Me-Kong."

Batteur had a crazy idea that the night was a woman's throat, tawny-dark under the powdering dusk. A faintly cool breeze shivered against him; he luxuriated in it, vaguely disturbed, as in a half-unwilling embrace.

"Is that so?" he murmured, surprised at his own banality. All alike, he thought uneasily.

Stung Treng appeared on the bank ahead, a huddle of brown and buff-colored houses peering out of the forest.

Batteur was glad. It had been a sultry, brooding voyage, sweaty with showers that left an illusion of hot flanks in the sensitive air.

A group of natives made a brown sprawl on the shore, and in their midst a white helmet caught the sunlight. As the boat drew nearer, the man wearing the helmet began pushing back the natives. In one hand he held a cane with which he struck the half-naked bodies, shouting in a voice that seemed to melt out in the sunlight and lose its invective by the time it reached the little steamer. Batteur laughed. "It's Malardier," he said aloud; Malardier, his friend.

"Yes, the good Malardier," affirmed Father Mehry, joining him by the rail.

The boat had glided close to the bank now; there was no landing-stage, a plank would be flung between deck and shore. Coolies were plunging into the river, mooring lines between their teeth. Malardier called out, waving his cane. He was much stouter, Batteur observed, but that was to be expected. A flushed, mustached face looked up from under his helmet, dripping perspiration. His white jacket was open, displaying flabby chest muscles under a moss of black hair.

Around his hips was bound a plaid sarong such as many that Batteur had seen natives wearing. Instead of shoes, the fat man on the bank wore dancing-pumps above which his bare ankles gleamed puffily. Batteur could not help laughing. Malardier, immaculate companion of the boulevards, had become as lush as the jungle. Fecund—that was it He looked positively fecund. And those slippers, so derisively civilized, added a ridiculous note.

A thick jet of voices spurted up and filled Batteur's ears: Malardier shouting to him to wait, that he was bringing a coolie for his baggage; Father Mehry calling down to two other Frenchmen who had suddenly appeared; the cries of running brown men mingled with the loud creaks of taut hemp as mooring-lines strained.

When the gangplank was secure, Malardier came hurrying aboard, his red face jovial.

"Batteur, my friend!" he panted, seizing the other's hands. "Ah! and you have come with Father Mehry…. Your baggage…. You are well? …Meet Monsieur Desbouillion—agent of the *Fluviales* [3]—and Monsieur Rival…. But come, they will have dinner with us tonight; and Father Mehry, too—eh, my Father? …Ah, good Batteur—after four years!

My God!…

---

3 Founded in 1881, *Messageries Fluviales de Cochinchine* was the French-run company that operated shipping services on the rivers of Indochina.

Batteur emerged from the grease-hot air of the lower deck, where the stilled engines hissed steam and a gush of excited voices clotted the atmosphere, into the thinner but no less enervating heat that scoured the bank. A muddy path slithered up to a road. Natives stood on either side silent, bare shoulders glistening. Among them were a few women, their slender waists molded firmly beneath tight little jackets and their hips caught by brightly colored sarongs. Some wore flowers in their hair. Batteur, following Malardier up the path, let his gaze blur past them. Nevertheless, he felt something intimate in the humidity. It was like a tryst between himself and an anonymous presence—a tryst half unwilling on his part.

At the top he found himself in a road that looked like white powder in the glare. Beyond were houses smothered in foliage that seemed pinned to the earth with extraordinarily tall palms. A few native soldiers were lounging about. They straightened up as Malardier approached. The latter carelessly returned their salutes with a sweat-moist handkerchief. But for the gleaming emblem on his helmet, Batteur thought, one would never have guessed that he was *Commissaire* of Stung Treng.

The heat was like a tyranny inspired, crucifying the shadows on the soil. Warm clots of languor accumulated in Batteur's body and thickened about his muscles. Along the road were familiar signs, utterly exotic in this atmosphere. "*Douanes et Regies,*" "Service Forestier."

"As you suggested," Malardier was saying, mopping the flooded pores of his face, "I have arranged a house for you on the edge of town where you can be quiet. But for a few days you will stay with me." Then he glanced at the other with sly good nature. "There is one detail I did not attend to in advance.... You'll have to choose your own *congai.*"

Batteur laughed with an effort in the heat; his gaze seemed diffuse.

"Why should I have a woman around the house? She'd be a nuisance when I wanted to work."

Malardier gestured explosively with both hands, waving the wet handkerchief and the cane.

"What? No woman? My God! A man cannot live here without feminine companionship. As to your work …well, if it were a Frenchwoman I would agree with you. But a native woman, no. Ah, they are so delicate, so—so submissive! And I have had my eye on one or two little beauties for you. There's one, a *phusao* [4] from Thakkek, Kamphion is her name, and she's well trained, for Moran had her for more than a year—before he sent for his wife. Then there's little Thi-Linh, part French…. But you must have a *congai*. Otherwise how do you expect to know the country?"

In the road behind them was a stealth of bare feet. Glancing around, Batteur saw two coolies following with his baggage. Pulses of light seemed to throb down their bare muscles. They sweated. But they did not appear hot as he and Malardier were hot. There was a certain glorification of the heat in their rhythmic stride; something persuasive in their lyrical brownness, so fluent with perspiration, and for a moment Batteur felt a swooning submission. Why could not white men flower with such voluptuous bloom in this equatorial region? he wondered. Inevitably must they become like Malardier? Perspiration ran over his mouth, it stung his eyes. There was, he decided suddenly, a certain sensual gratification in being so hot.

It was as if the sunlight, flowing in as the sweat flowed out, unfolded something within.

"Yes, I must know the country," he muttered.

To himself he said: Why should I try to resist? It was, he tried to explain to himself, not a matter of scruples—scruples be damned. For why shouldn't he take a temporary native wife? Other men did it without violating their racial integrity. Was there a fullness of being, earned under this burning sun, that relaxed prejudice and welcomed a blending with darker women? After all, he had no actual prejudices against color; he liked to believe he had no prejudices of any kind. It was part of French tradition to be tolerant; in fact, sometimes Frenchmen carried tolerance to the point of prejudice. No, it was certainly not a matter of scruples, he repeated to himself; rather, of

---

4 Laotian for "woman."

fealty to his work as he saw it. Yet there was a haunting challenge in these natives.

What lay behind the voluptuous calm of these people whom the heat seemed to enrich, even visibly, giving a lacquer-gloss to the sweat that ran down their bodies?

"Who was it," Malardier resumed, "Baudelaire, who said, 'Be always drunken! With wine, with poetry, or with virtue, as you will. But be drunken'? Only I pray you, Batteur, as a good Frenchman, not to be drunken with virtue! If you come to Indochina to know it, then become intoxicated with it—and the surest draught is a woman.... The *congai*, she is our symbol—the symbol of the ability of the Frenchman to mingle with the natives, whereas the Englishman only conquers them. And this climate demands diversion. With the English, it is whisky-sodas, with us, women. Name of God!" he panted jocularly, "will you forsake tradition?"

Batteur only laughed. He had not sufficient energy to do more, for suddenly he had become merely an undulant motion in the hot air. This surrender to the heat seemed to sling his body like a hammock between the two burning poles of his desire to work and his curiosity to penetrate that dark limpidity that had risen steadily about him since he had arrived in the country.

From behind came the caressing sound of naked feet in the dust.

His thoughts seemed to fall in with them, stealing back to the woman who stood on the bank that afternoon when he and Father Mehry discussed *congaies*; and that same sunlight that crucified the shadows upon the soil seemed to crucify the white radiance of his desire upon that tawny figure.

"Thi-Linh," he heard himself murmuring. "You say there is one, half French, called Thi-Linh?"

PART ONE:

Helmet and Sarong

er name was Thi-Linh. But lately she would have preferred Yvonne or Marie. They expressed a certain French elegance she wished to acquire. And why shouldn't she? Pale French blood marched side by side with her dark Annamite blood. Since she was a very small girl she had been studying French—lessons divided between her mother and the Father at the Mission—and now this study was giving flower to a treacherously sweet bloom. She read the French journals from Saigon, and often she purloined the Parisian fashion sheets wrapped about parcels in Vu-Trong-Khai's shop, with the result that her warm, slender little body yearned for the extravagant feel of a French gown, and in fancy she called herself Yvonne or Marie. Although when Kim Khouan made poetry for her she was content with the name her mother had given her.

"Thi-Linh," he would sing, stroking his guitar, "I am a harpstring shivering at your touch, as the forest shivers at the touch of the wind...."

His rich voice gave a vibrant quality to the name that he could never have put into Yvonne or Marie.

She wondered when his father, who was one of the wealthiest merchants of Stung Treng, would make an offer—it was sure to be a

11

liberal offer—and thus seal their betrothal. She was fifteen now, and most of the girls her age were wives already, if not mothers. But Kim Khouan promised it would be soon.

"My father will want me to marry a girl who is pure Annamite," he told her often; "so wait, Thi-Linh, until some time when he is in an excellent humor— you know he has not been well—and then I shall ask. And we shall go to Saigon, and I shall get a position there." For Kim Khouan also nurtured a secret restlessness.

At such times Thi-Linh felt a little annoyed and wondered if she would not do better to become the *congai* of a Frenchman as her mother had done. For fourteen years now her mother had been the second wife of Vu-Trong-Khai. But there were days when little lights swam into her eyes, like twin fireflies, and Thi-Linh had come to understand that on those days she was remembering the white man with whom she had lived in Haiphong, Tourane, and Saigon, those fabulous cities whither Thi-Linh had journeyed only in fancy. She had seen a photograph of this Frenchman; a dark-bearded man with kindly eyes who her mother said was a doctor. "He was a very handsome man," her mother told her, "a scholar. He not only cured the afflicted, but he wrote books on medicine."

Often she wondered why her mother had married Vu-Trong-Khai after her Frenchman had gone back to France. But perhaps, she decided, it was because he was kind and would take care of her and her child. Vu-Trong-Khai had been a good stepfather—although he had tried to arrange a marriage between herself and a middle-aged Chinese trader with a big belly.

Once when she was a little girl she had been sitting on the bank as a river boat passed on its long journey to Vientiane; and she saw on the deck a slender young woman in a tunic of flowered black tissue over yellow, with diamond earrings in her ears. Thi-Linh admired her air of aloofness toward the other natives on the deck, implied in her very posture. Her face, pale with rice-powder against which her lips were scarlet as a grenadine flower, haunted Thi-Linh. One of the women on the bank made a joking remark to another; she heard the name Theou-lan. Later she told her mother about the bewildering creature on the river boat, mentioning her name.

Her mother nodded. "She is the *congai* of Monsieur the Prefect of Police of Vientiane," she said.

"I should like to be the *congai* of a Prefect of Police," Thi-Linh thought involuntarily; and she thought it many times after that, voluntarily.

That day her mother had drawn her swiftly to her in a sudden glow of affection and whispered mysteriously, "You must never lacquer your teeth, little one, nor chew betel."

Her mother was very beautiful in those days; and her teeth were white. When she went to walk late afternoons, holding Vu-Trong-Khai's baby astride her hip with one hand and trailing Thi-Linh with the other, she wore a lilac kerchief about her head, and her *cai-ao*, or coat, was a rich plum color heavy with brocaded designs. Now her mother's cheeks sagged; and her teeth were black and rotten from chewing betel. She rarely went walking; all day she sat on the little platform in the rear of Vu-Trong-Khai's shop, one knee drawn up against her breasts and the other bent and lying motionless. Her coats were dark, and very shabby.

She had given Vu-Trong-Khai two children, both boys, and she also had to take care of the three children that his first wife, now dead, had left.

Sometimes at night her mother would bring out an old guitar and sing in a voice that was a mimicry of her youth. For a reason Thi-Linh could not define she thought her mother looked inexpressibly tragic when she sang. And there was one little song—a French air called "*Clair-de-Lune*"—that stirred a poignant uneasiness in her breast. [5] But this song seemed to please her mother, for she would sit for a long while and croon it, with those drowsy fireflies in her eyes.

Her mother's sister, who was the wife of a Cambodian, lived in Phnom-Penh, a journey of two or three days down the river. Each year

5 French for "moonlight," *Clair de Lune* was a poignant love poem written by Paul Verlaine in 1869. In 1890 it inspired Claude Debussy's musical composition of the same name.

Thi-Linh would go to visit her. She did not like her cousins, for they felt no hesitancy in discussing her white blood in terms impossible to misinterpret, but she was fond of her aunt; and she loved Phnom-Penh.

It was the Great City. Of course it was not as large as Saigon, but it was big enough to fill her mind with trembling wonder. The canal crowded with gay little boats, with eyes painted on their prows, the laughing *sampaniers*! The shops filled with Chinese silks and dresses from France! The streets stealthy with color and life, all flowing about the mysterious flushed walls of the Palace!

The Palace, which she had seen only from the outside, fascinated her. She knew that within were many dancing-women wearing jewels and brocaded *sampots*.[6] And often she used to sit and stare at the spires that flamed above the wall, dreaming that a genie changed her into a beautiful mauve and scarlet butterfly, and she lighted on one of those spires; whereupon the king, beholding her, commanded his mandarins and guards to fetch this lovely creature, and when they drew her down she had returned to her natural shape, and the king, ravished by her beauty, chose her for his chief concubine and dancer. This dream persisted until someone told her that the joints of the dancers were broken to enable them to perform with greater agility. "I shall have to marry a Frenchman after all," she thought, "perhaps a Prefect of Police."

She saw a great number of Frenchmen in Phnom Penh. Many of them were fat and red, with long beards; but there were others very young and brown, and some who looked dazzlingly pale as they rode along in the dusk behind sweating coolies.

Once while making a purchase for her aunt at the *magasin* she had noticed the glinting blond hairs on the wrist of the young Frenchman who handed her the parcel; and that night the memory of them drew little fires in her thoughts.

On the return from one of her visits to Phnom Penh she said to her mother: "Aunt says the French are very naughty. Is that true, Mama Thi-Bao?"

---

6 A long, rectangular piece of fabric worn wrapped around the lower body in Cambodia, as well as Thailand and Laos where it is called a *pha nung*.

"Some Frenchmen are naughty," replied her mother, "but others are very good. It is the same with Annamites."

"But aunt says they have taken our land and our money, and that they make soldiers of our men and bad women of our girls."

"It is true that they have taken much—but the Chinese would have done it if they had not; and I prefer the French. It is true also that they have little reverence for tradition, the French, and their manners are very bad. And yet—" A little glimmer came into her eyes and passed.

Thi-Linh persisted. "Aunt says they marry our women when they have other wives in France."

"The Memorial of Rights grants a man more than one wife—"

"But she says they go away and leave Annamite women," the girl interrupted.

Again that little light passed through her mother's eyes. "It is true," she said wistfully. "But we cannot understand the strange thoughts and reasons that move Frenchmen. Perhaps we should not try, but simply accept the love they give, great or small, and the gifts, and try to think they have not acted cruelly but only naturally."

Thi-Linh did not quite understand all her mother said, but she was sure she meant for her not to hate Frenchmen. And so on those warm afternoons when a brief twilight ached in the streets and the scent of wild lilacs drifted down like an urge to dream, she allowed herself to think of a slender wrist soft with little golden glints; and to fancy that it belonged to a Prefect of Police.

When she was ten years old civilized erudition touched her definitely for the first time. On this particular morning she was sitting in front of Vu-Trong-Khai's shop, making designs in the dirt with her toe, when Father Mehry, the pleasant-looking priest of the Catholic Mission, came along and rumbled at her jovially in his long beard. Her mother, seeing the Father, emerged smiling.

"*Bonjour*, Thi-Bao," said this genial-faced priest to her mother. "Was the little one's father French?"

"Oui, mon Père."

"Ah! And shall we make a good Frenchwoman and a Catholic out of her?"

"Oui, mon Père."

"Good! Send her to me at the Mission tomorrow."

Before that, religion had not troubled Thi-Linh greatly. Of course she prayed and burned incense before the tablets of her ancestors; and she had a profound reverence, impressed by fear, for two supernatural beings, one called Sakya-Muni [7] and the other Huyen-Vu.[8] But she had much more actual respect for my Lord the Tiger, who stalked abroad after nightfall, and the Great Mandarin, the elephant, who could rip immense trees from the earth and pound a man to pulp. And, naturally, she avoided all the Ma, or evil genii, that lurked behind trees, in bushes, in fact everywhere; some of whom hurled the thunder and others bred sickness, while the majority simply frightened one at night.

But now religion became complex and often very annoying. For instance, confessing seemed quite silly, for generally when you did naughty things you weren't sorry for them, and to say that you were was simply adding lies to the original transgressions. Also she had to remember new prayers. This seemed useless and a nuisance, for if the priest's genie was as good as the priest said he was, then he would be just as pleased to hear old prayers. Nevertheless, she thought, the priest's genie was rather beautiful, with his sad, thin pallor and tragic eyes. He was carved out of ivory and hung on a great black, silver-studded cross in the priest's pagoda. On the altar at his feet were many dolls, much lovelier than Chinese or Annamite dolls.

But religion was not as difficult as the lessons in French. Her mother had taught her a little, but that little seemed very small indeed when the priest thrust strange books at her and rumbled words equally barbaric. But gradually she came to like those queer sounds which slipped from

---

7 An honorific for the Buddha, born with the name Siddhartha Gautama

8 One of the Four Symbols of the Chinese constellations called the Black Tortoise, or the Black Warrior of the North as it represents the north and the winter season (also transliterated as *Xuan Wu*). Though the English translation only mentions the tortoise, it is usually represented by a snake coiled around a tortoise, with both reptiles symbolizing longevity.

her tongue so hesitantly and made familiar things seem new and foreign. When she had learned to speak fairly well she boasted of it to the girl whose father had a shop next to Vu-Trong-Khai.

"Hussy," said the girl scornfully, "you only learn this French tongue so that you can more easily trade your virtue when you are older!"

Whereupon Thi-Linh scratched her face and pulled her hair until she screamed; and then at confession she devoutly declared she was sorry.

Girls did not like Thi-Linh, and she reciprocated. Nor did she like her two little stepbrothers and Vu-Trong-Khai's three children. Being older, she was frankly scornful. Her playmates were Kim Khouan and his friend Thao-Nhi. Kim Khouan—Ong Kim Khouan was his full name—was the son of Ong-Binh-Thai, the wealthy merchant. He did not have a flat nose like many Annamite boys; it was a classic nose, like his Lao mother's. He was a slim boy with skin smooth and brown as sandalwood and shiny black hair that fell irregularly over his eyes; curiously dark eyes with something luminous behind them—like the dart of a fish in night waters. When he grew beyond the age of nakedness he wore black silk trousers that flopped loosely about his ankles, and on special days added a long tunic of gauzy material and patent-leather sandals whose heavy heels clicked when he walked. He had a strange, slow smile; and sometimes he stuck a flower behind his ear. Thao-Nhi was a Laotian; a muscular little fellow who was a shadow of Kim Khouan.

Kim Khouan lived in a splendid house with a garden where magenta bougainvillea spilled over the walls and lemon-flowers bruised the warm air. In the house was a shrine that boasted a figure of Sakya-Muni, of Huyen-Thien, and the six good genii, and many sacred tablets to his Ancestors. His father had two wives and seven children, six of whom were boys. The family, like the house, was very splendid; and Thi-Linh came to understand that the genie who controlled friendships had been very generous with her.

Kim Khouan studied French at the Mission; he was a convert. Often they used to read aloud from their books while Thao-Nhi sat in silence, listening. But Thao-Nhi remained serenely a Buddhist. Very soon he would go and study with the bonzes—not French but sacred Pali script—and after six months or a year he would come out of the monastery versed in the knowledge of those who sought the Noble Eightfold Way.

The warm dusks came and went over Stung Treng, while the days kindled tawny fire in the roads; and out of all this mingling of twilight and heat crept something passionate and subtle that entered into Thi-Linh. At times she was aware of an intensity behind her consciousness, glowing as sunlight glows behind a pale-veined petal. She felt this more when she thought of Kim Khouan. There were moments, talking together or strolling through the forest drowsy with coming night, when she experienced a fluid indolence that made her want to stretch — slowly — luxuriously — until she touched his smooth shoulder or the black hair that hung irregularly over his eyes. Then, she felt, all that golden smoldering would be quenched. Thao-Nhi was in the monastery now ; and she was glad. She was fifteen, and her body ripe with a slender maturity.

Often she and Kim Khouan would walk along the mud-red roads beyond the town where bare-hipped women worked in the rice-fields, and water-buffaloes lay nostril-deep in the drench. Or they would sit on the river bank and he would read from the Lac-Van-Tien or the poetry of Nguyen-Du. Being an Annamite of good family, it was part of his inherited culture to know poetry. And for Thi-Linh he translated the beauty of living into words. Behind his soft voice, the warm drowsiness in his eyes, was a restlessness that at times flowed out and touched her electrically. It was at such times, that he talked of Saigon, of the future.

"Kim Khouan," she said one afternoon when they sat together on the bank of the Se-Kong, "when we are married will you give me a tunic of black lace over yellow?"

"Yes."

"And earrings of diamonds?"

"Moonstones would be better—for they are the stones of happiness."

She frowned. "But when will your father ask for me?"

"I shall speak to him soon, Thi-Linh; he is not well, he is irritable, and I must wait until a more propitious time."

"But if you do not hurry, some fat old man will make an excellent offer for me, and Vu-Trong-Khai will force mama to accept. I am not his daughter; he would be glad to be rid of me."

Below their feet, where the Se-Kong mingled with the reeds, purple irises bared their throats; and she ran her fingers over her own throat involuntarily. It was a movement of appraisal, and she was pleased with the softness, the faint throbbing of her pulse beneath her fingers.

"And what do you think your father will offer? He is a wealthy man. Eight *mau* [9] of rice-fields—or perhaps ten—and four hundred piasters; and a long necklace of gold beads; and earrings...."

She dreamed voluptuously. Two pirogues out in midstream seemed to drift with the lazy richness of her thoughts.

"And when you come to offer me betel at our betrothal, you will wear a fine *cai-ao* of black brocade— and leather sandals—and you will bring the betel in a box of red lacquer—and your father will come with the servants bearing gifts.... Oh, Mama Thi-Bao will be very happy!" She paused to wonder if Mama Thi-Bao *would* be very happy, then quickly skirted the thought. "And we shall have a splendid feast at the wedding," she murmured.

"*Banh'u* [10] with millet," he drowsed on; "many syrups, and beans, and roast duck—and of course jars of *choum-choum*.[11] " After a pause he added: "And surely we must have eggs for the Ancestors."

"Oh. it will be very splendid indeed!" she cried. "And shall we go to the pagoda or the Mission? I think we would have a larger wedding if we went to the pagoda."

"We must go to the pagoda," Kim Khouan decided. "My father would demand it. But we can go to Father Mehry afterward."

"Yes," she agreed. "That would make it more secure."

---

9 A *mau* is roughly 5,000 sq. meters or 54,000 sq. ft. so this would have been a generous dowry.
10 Vietnamese dumplings made from sticky rice and a variety of fillings, wrapped in a bamboo leaf.
11 Locally fermented rice wine, averaging about twenty percent alcohol.

Several afternoons later Thi-Linh's mother, sitting on that little platform in the rear of the shop, stirred from her lethargy. "You will go to Phnom-Penh soon, Thi-Linh."

"But why spend so much money this year?" said Thi-Linh very righteously. "It is not necessary."

"You are fifteen now," her mother announced solemnly. Reaching into the box at her side she drew out a slice of areca, dipped it in lime, and then wrapped it in betel-leaf, placing the whole in her mouth. She chewed a moment before she continued. "I have not allowed you to use betel," she said.

For an instant the vision of a splendorous creature in a tunic of smoky yellow spun before Thi-Linh, then she grasped at the slim, tawny image of Kim Khouan and clung with tottering poise. A glow spread over her with the consciousness of her fealty, uncertain though it was.

"Do you think you would be happy with a Frenchman?" her mother continued.

Another vision smote Thi-Linh, that of an old woman with sunken breasts, seated crooning over a guitar. Why must Frenchmen always leave their women? she demanded of herself with savage vehemence. No, she would never be left to sing little *chansons* that were faded ghosts of love! "Thi-Linh, I am a harpstring shivering at your touch…The remembrance of that voice was like a luminous movement in the dusk of her thoughts. She said:

"How can I know if I would be happy with a Frenchman?"

"Some are very pleasant to look upon," murmured her mother. "In Phnom-Penh there is a *congai* who makes arrangements between Frenchmen and girls."

Thi-Linh sank beside her mother and kissed her in Annamite fashion, rubbing her nose against hers and sniffing affectionately.

"But wait a while," her voice caressed. "I do not wish to leave you yet, Mama Thi-Bao. Next month I will go to Phnom-Penh."

The older woman lapsed into silence, now and then spitting a jet
of blood-red betel-juice. Those misty little fireflies swam in her eyes.
Finally she spoke, and very tenderly.

"I have always dreamed that you would be the wife of a Frenchman;
I think you would be far happier."

Thi-Linh trailed her fingers across her mother's gnarled hand.

"Yes, yes," she murmured. "I know—my blood." Again her thoughts
were drunk with the vision of an exquisitely lovely figure on the deck
of a river boat; and again the figure sank into the dark forests of Kim
Khouan's eyes. "Next month I will go to Phnom Penh," she repeated.

2

Kim Khouan went on a visit to Saigon.

He was away three weeks, and toward the end of his absence Thi-
Linh pretended that she was not well so her mother would not bring up
the subject of Phnom-Penh. It did not require much pretense, for since
Kim Khouan had gone she had been conscious of a desperate emptiness,
at times amounting to acute misery, troubling her sleep and excluding
the desire for food.

When he returned she noticed a look of sensitive bewilderment in
his drowsy eyes. The very afternoon he arrived they went to gather red
jasmine in the forest, and when they were alone he suddenly pulled her
to him clumsily, and kissed her upon the lips. It was the first time she
had been kissed in the French manner; she seemed to go limp with an
almost unendurable ecstasy. Kim Khouan looked frightened, and was
silent for the rest of the afternoon.

She did not see him for some days following that. When finally he
appeared he had a confused, melancholy air. It remained with him,
a disturbing shadow that lifted only when he spoke of returning to
Saigon and taking a position in the office of one of his father's friends.
Thi-Linh experienced a pain vaguely nauseating whenever he talked of
going away.

"There are many lamps on the streets, Thi-Linh," he told her, "lighted by strange wires which the French work. And there are theaters—oh, more than in Phnom-Penh! And there are cafes on the sidewalks where the French sit in white clothes and drink wines! And the women! Such clothes, Thi-Linh! And jewels!"

"Are they more beautiful than Annamite women?" she demanded.

"Yes." Then he caught himself. "But you are not all Annamite." And after a pause he added so swiftly that a flame caught at her throat, "Oh, none are so lovely as you!"

The days brooded caressingly on Thi-Linh, and the nights made carnival in her thoughts. Often in the hushed dark she sang *"Clair-de-Lune"* to the trembling chords of a guitar, hoping that the Con-Tinh, those siren genii who dance at night, would carry the echoes to Kim Khouan.

At Stung Treng the Me-Kong thrusts a bronze arm into the forest— the tributary Se-Kong. Between these two streams are many little pools sunk in the jungle. The natives say that toward dusk the Ma-da, or water genii, haunt these pools, lying in wait for those indiscreet enough to bathe there.

But Thi-Linh had studied at the Mission. She had been told that the water genii were a myth, and although she did not believe it entirely, this half-assurance gave her the courage to steal away from the town late afternoons and lie dreaming in a lucent green bath.

It was to this pool that she went one afternoon at sunset when the dust was golden on her body; and it was here that Kim Khouan found her, with her slender limbs caught in the silky stems of waterplants, the fireflies careening above her. She did not hear him until he had stepped into the water beside her. Then she sat up quickly, crossing her arms over her breasts.

"You were not afraid?" he murmured in a voice husky-soft, dropping beside her. For a moment they were silent, her heart trembling its intensity. His fingers slipped into the floating dusk of her hair. "Thi-Linh!" he whispered.

All the life of the forest seemed to close about them like a day-blooming flower, holding them close to its silent heart.

"Thi-Linh!" he whispered over and over, a drunken look in his eyes.

"When will you speak with your father?" she asked breathlessly.

"Soon," he murmured, "soon."

Then he had bent and his lips were moving slowly over the dazzling pallor of her throat and shoulders. Kim Khouan had learned a lot in Saigon.

3

After that there were many trysts at the pool— fragile moments that tangled her thoughts in cobweb.

One afternoon three weeks later she went there just before dusk, the usual hour of meeting. Clouds spumed darkly over the sky, and mosquitoes hummed in the swollen quiet. The water lay motionless except where insects skimmed over the black surface. Thi-Linh felt that vague little creatures were skimming across the surface of her mind. She lay down beside the pool to wait.

When he came he did not drop beside her immediately, but stood looking down at her with a troubled gaze. The mosquitoes twanged viciously.

"Thi-Linh—" he began. Then he sank beside her and kissed her, his lips clinging fiercely. Her fingers browsed over the soft tendons of his throat. The mosquitoes made only a drowsy singing now—as though they had retreated into folds of gauze.

"Thi-Linh," he repeated. "My father—"

"You have spoken?" she whispered.

During the long silence her nerves seemed to vibrate. An insect brushed against her ear with a violent singing.

"My father," she heard him say, "has arranged for my marriage to Keou-Thanh, the daughter of Ly-Binh."

A laugh snapped in her throat. "Kim Khouan!" she cried, raising herself on one elbow. "How can you—"

"It is true," he said quietly.

Suddenly that taut silence seemed to rend and loose those singing insects upon her. Loudly her pulse responded, and she was lost in dusk that hummed and throbbed. The gloomy forests of his eyes dwindled to points that stung her. For a long while she lay there nauseated, her flesh burning. Black rings, yellow-tinged, expanded and contracted before her, each seeming to frame thoughts that pranced into her mind, absurdly inconsequential thoughts. She remembered the greasy cooked fowl hanging in the arches of the Chinese market; the way that certain people walked; how the bar of light thrust out from the doorway of Vu-Trong-Khai's shop at night. Silly, meaningless things. Behind them and over them lurked a dark agony, intensifying their insignificance.

She stirred, still nauseated, and sat up.

Kim Khouan's eyes beseeched from the pale blur of his face staring up at her. Tomorrow, she thought, he will put on leather sandals and a coat of black brocade, and carry betel to Keou-Thanh, daughter of Ly-Binh.... And suddenly she reached down and sunk her slim nails into his cheek and pressed with all her strength. He did not cry out, or even speak, only continued to stare with dumb pain. She could not endure that look: she sprang up, darting into the midst of the trees and shivering as velvety creatures hurtled against her.

4

Ten days later she came into the shop of Vu-Trong-Khai to find Monsieur Malardier, the fat, red-faced *Commissaire* of Stung Treng, talking with her mother. As she entered, the Frenchman looked startled, then smiled and held out his hand. She returned the smile, although the feel of his moist, flabby hand made her want to grimace. He seemed stuffed into his tight-buttoned starched coat.

"Ah, Mademoiselle Thi-Linh! And looking more charming than ever!" Then he added jocularly to her mother, "My God! She is more beautiful every time I see her!"

Thi-Linh experienced an overture of dread. But she continued to smile, and sat down beside her mother, one bare foot stroking the floor with animal flexibility. Although her heart beat swiftly, she knew she looked quite unconcerned.

Monsieur Malardier drew out a package of cigarettes and offered her one. She took it with lazy grace, coolly meeting his eyes as he bent to light it.

"She smokes with the air of a Frenchwoman!" he observed, and Thi-Linh only continued to smile, all the while gazing at her slender fingers. If he asks me to be his *congai*, she thought, what shall I say? He is so fat that his eyes bulge. But he could give me a fine silk *cai-ao*,[12] many of them, and diamond earrings. But sweeter than that was another prospect. Gossip had brought the news that, the moon being propitious, Kim Khouan's marriage-day had been set. If before that time …And so she ceased to smile at her fingers and smiled at Monsieur Malardier.

"How old are you, my dear? Sixteen? Or seventeen?" Without waiting for a reply he went on humorously. "Old enough to think of men, eh? And perhaps"—he winked at her—"to want one?"

Thi-Linh pretended that she was embarrassed; she was wondering if she could suffer this huge man who seemed stuffed into his clothes. And if she could— what sweet revenge!

Monsieur Malardier was in excellent spirits. He chuckled and said: "And how would you like a Frenchman, little one?" Then he laughed and winked at her mother. "Well, *au revoir*, Thi-Bao. I shall see you tomorrow." He lifted his helmet and made a mock bow to Thi-Linh. "Au revoir, mademoiselle. And may you get a nice Frenchman some day!"

Still chuckling, he went out.

Thi-Linh glanced at her mother searchingly; her temples throbbed, half with excitement and half with distaste.

---

12 *Cai-ao* is Vietnamese for "dress." Above, Thi-Linh would have been envisioning the *ao dai*, or "long garment." This graceful outfit consists of a tight-fitting silk tunic worn on the upper body (the *ao*) and loose pantaloons (*dai* means "long"). It originated in the 18th century royal Nguyen court and gradually became the traditional Vietnamese national costume, particularly for women.

"What did he want, Mama Thi-Bao?"

The older woman spat a red stream before she answered. "There is a new Frenchman just come to Stung Treng," she said.

"And he wants me to be his *congai*?" Thi-Linh divined breathlessly.

Her mother nodded.

"Have you seen him? What does he look like? What did you tell Monsieur Malardier?"

"The new Frenchman wishes to see you tomorrow."

"What is his name?"

"Monsieur Batteur."

"You do not know what he looks like? Is he young?"

"I have not seen him. But he has made a very generous offer."

Thi-Linh was dreaming swiftly. She pictured various Frenchmen she had seen and fitted their likenesses to this anonymous person. A fire was smoldering in her, and very soon it would flame up to torture the naked image of Kim Khouan.

"Is it your wish that I marry this Frenchman?" she asked.

"You know I have always desired a French husband for you."

"And what of Vu-Trong-Khai?"

"There will be one less mouth to feed."

A poignant jet filled Thi-Linh's throat. She swallowed it as a tiger-cat would swallow blood.

"And this Frenchman, will he leave me after a while?" she continued.

"Probably," said her mother with a wistful vacancy in her eyes.

Thi-Linh smiled faintly. *Banh'u* with millet, many syrups like thick rainbows, beans and roast duck; and a great procession, swaying under pale lanterns, carrying a jar of *choum-choum* to the pagoda.... The procession vanished in the blur of an anonymous Frenchman. A dream, she thought bitterly, a silly, childish dream. And this Frenchman: surely he would buy her a coat of black lace tissue over yellow.

5

In the morning Thi-Linh awoke with an excited trembling in her
temples.

Very early she went with her mother to the shop of a Chinese
merchant and bought a violet-colored kerchief to wear about her head.
"I have no new tunic," she complained to her mother, who replied that
it was just as well, for it would not be good to have too many clothes.
Thi-Bao removed several gold bracelets from an old chest where she
kept a few treasures and slipped them on Thi-Linh's arms, enjoining her
to return them when Monsieur Batteur gave her others. Thi-Linh had
put on her best *cai-ao*; it had been a rich plum color, now it had faded
to ashy purple. Her little black trousers peeped from under it with a
certain charming impertinence.

She spent some time making her toilet, seated cross-legged before a
cracked, fly-specked mirror. Carefully glossing her hair with a sweet
pomade, she twisted it into a chignon, then stuck a yellow bloom in it
and examined herself critically. That flower made her lips look too pale.
She told her mother, who went to the chest again and brought out a
piece of red Chinese paper. With this she carmined Thi-Linh's lips. The
effect was very pleasing.

Of course, Thi-Linh thought, my kerchief will hide the flower, but he
will see it when I take the kerchief off.

Humming to herself, she smoothed rice-powder over her face. "Thi-
Linh, I am a harpstring shivering at your touch…." As that darted
through her mind she saw a cold little smile in the cracked, fly-specked
mirror. I shall leave a crack in his heart like the crack in this looking-
glass, she told herself.

Her toilet finished, she stood up and appraised herself from the curve
of one lifted foot, arch convex, to the slim erectness of her shoulders.
She was no longer a thin shaft of a girl. A rich bloom had come into her
figure, expressed in the delicate contours of breasts and hips. Satisfied,
she thrust her face close to the mirror and crouched there gazing
into her own eyes; wide eyes, tawny-flecked as an intruding quiver of
sunlight slanted across her forehead and crashed upon the mirror. Her

throat, pale with a golden luster, rose to a face not too sharply oval and a fragile flower of lips. The faintest length of narrowness at the corners of her eyes gave an illusion of sultry brooding together with a quality of exquisite frailty.

When her mother called her, she slipped her feet into wooden sandals and went click-clacking across the hard dirt floor to where Thi-Bao waited in the entrance to the shop.

The house of Monsieur Malardier was near the other end of town, and they followed the long main road which flanked the river. The vertical sunlight made little wasps that stung and left Thi-Linh's body under a film of moisture. She hoped it wouldn't spoil her appearance.

When they reached the gate of the *commissaire's* house she experienced a little flutter of fright. Pausing, she gathered her courage while she re-tied her kerchief under her chin, then she followed her mother toward the steps, heart aquiver.

A pleasant sprawl of a man reclined in a cane chair on the veranda, one hand playing with an empty glass and the other holding a sheaf of papers. As Thi-Linh and her mother clattered up the steps he gazed at them with an expression at first surprised and then vaguely ill at ease. The women paused on the top step, and for a moment the three exchanged stares. Then he smiled, and Thi-Linh observed that it was a smile indolent and kindly.

"You are Thi-Linh?"—gazing upon her.

The wild beating of her heart quieted. She lowered her eyes and murmured, "Yes, *monsieur.*"

Her downcast eyes were filled with the fluid drowsiness of his gaze. She heard her mother speaking to the Frenchman, then Monsieur Malardier's voice rumbling out of the house. She looked up to see him emerge wearing a sarong and that stiff white jacket buttoned tight about his torso.

The other Frenchman also wore a sarong, and one leg, crossed over the other, was thrust out from between its folds, lazily balancing a sandal that hung from the tip of his toes. Thi-Linh felt a hot wave pass up through her as she noticed his bare forearm. A door of memory swung open to reveal another forearm covered identically with a sheen of glinting hairs. Immediately there was something familiar and friendly about this Frenchman; and something of fulfillment.

He smiled at her with a half self-conscious, half satirical lift at one corner of his mouth.

"Do you think you would like to be my wife?" he asked, while Monsieur Malardier talked loudly with her mother.

She smiled back at him. "Monsieur is very pleasant to look at," she pronounced in her best French.

He laughed and spoke to Monsieur Malardier. "Both discreet and flattering," he commented. "An admirable combination."

"Did I not tell you she was intelligent as well as pretty?" boomed out the *commissaire.*

Whereupon Thi-Bao began gravely to recite her daughter's virtues. "And she speaks and reads French," she finished.

Monsieur Batteur had listened with a hint of a smile in his blurred green eyes. "Where did she learn?" he inquired.

"At the Mission, *monsieur.*" Then Thi-Linh's mother added proudly, "I taught her a little when she was very young."

"She is Catholic?"

"Yes, *monsieur.*"

Monsieur Batteur looked neither pleased nor displeased. He merely stirred and stretched, running one hand over his forearm; and Thi-Linh felt something within herself steal out and follow that luxurious gesture.

"Does she know many native legends—and poetry?" the Frenchman interrogated.

"Many," said Thi-Bao, "And she has read the Lac-Van-Tien [13]—also the verses of Thuy-Kien,[14] and others." She showed her black teeth in a smile. "Monsieur likes poetry?"

"Monsieur is a writer," spoke up Monsieur Malardier. "A distinguished man of letters in France."

Batteur seemed not to hear him; he was gazing at Thi-Linh, and she realized that he was suddenly wondering about her teeth. She could have smiled to show him, but a natural perversity kept her lips together. She was thinking: he will write verses for me…. Then a little ghost laughed and murmured: Yes, he will say he is a harpstring shivering at your touch; and then he will leave you. …

"Come here, Thi-Linh," commanded Monsieur Batteur.

She approached him with a certain proud humility in her carriage. He gazed at her so fixedly, with such an intense look of quandary in his eyes, that she laughed. Then he smiled—an expression that suggested relaxing muscles.

"Yes, you will do," he decided. Then he went into the house, returning with a box which he held out to her. "A little gift from your affianced," he said ironically.

Thi-Linh wondered if it would be rude to open it now, deciding quickly that it would not.

In the box was a necklace of moonstones. It made her a little dizzy, for it was more beautiful than any she had ever dreamed of possessing. Then, as she continued to gaze at those softly glowing stones, they seemed to congeal. "They are the stones of happiness…Brown boy lying on the river-bank, talking of love. With a sensation of almost physical agony she seemed to feel his dark eyes close to hers; and then they grew misty as with cataracts, and multiplied; and now they lay in the little box which she held in her hands.

She heard herself murmur, "Thank you, *monsieur*."

13 *The Tale of Luc Van Tien* is a 19th century epic poem by Vietnamese poet Nguyen Đình Chieu.
14 Known as *The Tale of Kieu*, the plot and content of this earlier epic poem by scholar Nguyen Du speaks directly to the story of Thi-Linh and the political symbolism of *Congai*. See the appendix article "Francophilia" for more details about these works.

"And you will come to my house tomorrow," he instructed.

As she walked back to her home, moving in a shimmer of heat, a sudden limpness seized her, and all energy seemed to run out of her into the shadow that swam at her heels. All of her feeling reduced to a shadow, bruise of the sunlight. And when the sun went down, that shadow would evaporate. What would she have left to take Monsieur Batteur tomorrow?

6

For three weeks now Thi-Linh had been in the house of Justin Batteur.

It was not as fine as the *commissaire's* house. But it would do. There were three rooms, all carpeted with mats and furnished in teakwood; and rattan blinds gave the veranda an illusion of dusk throughout the day. In the great living-room a tiger-skin sprawled across one wall between mounted gaur-horns.[15] Mythological pictures painted on Chinese paper hung on the other walls—and a few Laotian scarves. In the doorway between the bedroom and the living-room was a red Annamite banner embroidered with a Tao, the symbol of supreme intelligence, which served as a curtain. To Thi-Linh this seemed a little incongruous, perhaps a bit undignified. But, she realized, there was no accounting for the whims and tastes of Frenchmen. And this Frenchman of hers was extremely eccentric. When she placed the crucifix that Father Mehry had given her on the table in the bedroom, he suggested that she put a Tonkinese incense-burner in front of it because, he explained, he liked the effect.

He was indeed a very strange person, this Justin. (He had told her to call him that.) At first he awed and mystified her; of course she did not let him know that, for instinct warned her it would be unwise. He would lie stretched out on a chaise longue on the veranda for hours, pencil in hand and paper on the table; and then suddenly he would look at her in a queer manner (usually she sat cross-legged on the floor

---

15 Also called the Indian bison, the gaur is the largest bovine animal native to South and Southeast Asia, formerly playing an essential role in farming, transportation and nourishment. Their impressive horns can reach a span of nearly 4 feet.

a few feet away, embroidering or merely thinking) and ask the most absurd questions.

Once he said, "Thi-Linh, what sort of soul have you? Won't you show it to me?" And he went on murmuring, "I wonder if souls have colors… Then he broke into that lazy smile and stretched; she liked to see him stretch, for then the muscles rippled across his sun-flushed jaws and forearms in a way that made her thoughts undulate with them.

She had asked him to tell her what a soul was. She had heard Father Mehry talk of souls, but she did not understand.

"A soul," he said, "is a reason for the body." He laughed at her expression. "You don't understand that? Naturally. Well, a soul—" Suddenly, he pointed to a lamp in the house. "See that? When you touch a match to the wick it makes a flame. The same with a candle. The oil goes out of the lamp; the tallow gathers around the foot of the candle; there is no flame. That is death, Thi-Linh. So we get another wick, or another candle, and we touch a light to them. That is birth. They change, these lamps and these candles—but the flame is the same—always. This flame is soul…." He had become interested in what he was saying, and he bent toward her, pupils contracted thoughtfully. "We may have a thousand bodies, Thi-Linh—grotesque or beautiful— shapes of flesh that dry up like the wicks or burn to tallow like the candles—but invariably someone—call him God, Buddha, or Nature— strikes another match."

Another time he had started out of his silent mood to say, almost irritably:

"I wish you wouldn't sit on the floor, Thi-Linh; it isn't dignified."

"But Mama Thi-Bao and all the girls I know sit on the floor." She was not averse to sitting in a chair but she wished to know why she should.

"To the devil with them!" he replied. For a moment she thought he was going to be angry, then, swiftly, he smiled. "But no—sit on the floor. You are Annamite—do not change. You must not let me try to make you into a Frenchwoman."

Nevertheless, the next day while he was folded in thought she slipped into a chair and waited with a smile of satisfaction. When finally he became aware of her he frowned.

"Did I not tell you to sit on the floor?" he asked; then, seeing her hurt expression, he rose and kissed her on the back of the neck. "Do as you please, Thi-Linh—but do not consciously *try* to be French." With an ironic smile he added: "I am sure your mother is much more charming than your father was."

And so quite soon she learned that one should not pay very much attention to the eccentricities of these Frenchmen but do as one pleased so long as it was not too apparent.

The morning after she arrived in his house she deliberately put on her worst tunic. It was rusty black, frayed and soiled at the cuffs. As she hoped, he noticed it and told her to go to the tailor's that very day. With fear in her heart she asked if she might get a tunic of flowered black tissue over yellow. "You may get whatever you wish," he said. "But of course," he added, "you need not be extravagant."

So she changed to her plum-colored *cai-ao*, tied the lavender kerchief over her head, and set out for the shop of Yuen Lok, the Chinaman.

What ecstasy! She sat in the midst of drifts of color as bolts of cloth were unrolled. Smoke of black tissue and smoldering cerise; dragon-green and stiff purple.... She felt quite economical when she ordered only two tunics, one a simple brown *cai-ao* with black trousers, and the other a rich affair of flowered black grenadine over burnished silk. For the latter she chose trousers of black stamped in gold with a longevity pattern. After that she went to a shoe shop and bought two pairs of sandals. Then she returned home, coolly answering those who spoke and pausing only to tell Mama Thi-Bao of her purchases. It gave her extreme pleasure to observe that, as she told of her new clothes, Vu-Trong-Khai's three brats stood by listening with amazement and not a little awe. I am a person of importance now, she thought.

During the next few days she organized the household. Justin had employed two Annamite boys, one to cook and another to serve and keep house. The former did not meet with her approval, so she dismissed him and arranged for another. She was careful to find out beforehand if this second cook knew how to plan meals for a Frenchman; she knew only vaguely what Frenchmen liked and ate. However, with a splendid flare of authority, she instructed this cook to show her the day's menu each morning, also to draw up an account of the money spent in marketing at the end of every week. She was determined to show skill as a manager, for she knew the servants would talk and eventually Kim Khouan would hear this gossip and realize he had missed an exceptional opportunity.

She did not allow herself to spend much time thinking of Kim Khouan. But now and then when his dark image rose before her she indulged in the luxury of cruelty. Having told herself that she no longer loved him, she could afford to consider his faults. Undoubtedly he would remain always in the shop of his father and grow fat and want many children. Or, if he did go to Saigon, he would never be more than a clerk. While she—ah, she would seize every opportunity! Later she would make this French husband take her down to the coast, perhaps even to Hanoi or to China. And when he left her—well, there were other Frenchmen, and by that time she would have learned much. Oh yes, she would rise! She could see herself in a French gown, with her hair done in the European manner, and answering to the name Yvonne or Marie. Yes, it was much better… much… Those dusks by the pool… frail little cobwebs that were torn… but only cobwebs…. I am a person of importance now, she told herself for the second time.

And this Frenchman was very kind to her. At first she seemed to draw within herself when he touched her or kissed her. It was not revulsion, for he was very handsome; perhaps, she reflected, it was because she had never been caressed by anyone except Kim Khouan. But soon that feeling drifted into obscurity—although she was not yet conscious of a complete yielding. Whenever he came close to her she felt that another and darker presence was approaching; and it was not his touch or mouth that caused a momentary breathless swooning of her senses but the hands and lips of a phantom lover.

The compound was hedged with crimson hibiscus, and through the breach at the gate the river was visible. Here, when the brassy sun smote the foliage, lemon-trees unloaded their fragrance; or, the brief twilight vanished, a ghost of wild lilacs prowled across the air.

Justin liked the compound, particularly at night. Usually he sat on the steps after dinner and listened to Thi-Linh play the guitar. Thi-Linh too found contentment in those evenings. She would sing the few little French songs her mother had taught her and also many Annamite songs. Justin seemed to prefer the latter.

"Indo-China—" he murmured once after she had sung a little Cambodian air, "do you suppose I, a Frenchman, shall ever know it?"

She did not quite understand but after a moment she ventured:

"Indo-China is a very superstitious country." Something apologetic in her tone. "When I was a little girl I was told that the Sacred Dragon held up Annam, with his heart in Hue, and that one must not dig too deeply in the earth or he would be disturbed, perhaps even wounded, and his blood would turn the soil red." She laughed. "Then I went to the Mission and—."

"I suppose they told you it was not true?" he interposed with that half satirical smile of his. Then he leaned toward her and touched her shoulder. "Believe me, Thi-Linh, they lied at the Mission—for a great dragon *does* hold up Annam, and you must always believe it. Do you understand?"

She could not tell whether he was serious or not; he smiled yet there was an earnest look in his eyes. He laughed at her mystified expression.

"Keep your legends, Thi-Linh," he added. "For they will be here when the French myths are gone."

And then he leaned back against the veranda post and was silent. In the dusk his white forearms gleamed. She had an impulse to touch them, to run her fingers over the silken hairs and the muscles that rippled when he moved. In the cool air idled the scent of frangipani.

"Li-on-li-on-sai" she sang huskily, plucking the strings of her guitar. Behind the words another voice sang softly: "Thi-Linh, I am a harpstring shivering at your touch. ..." The chord twanged, and a sudden flight of fireflies reeled upward like sparks from that metallic

singing. Tonight, she thought, for the first time. ... I want him ... but I shall be happy merely to touch those strong, pale wrists....

That was a week ago; and now it had been three weeks since she had come to his house.

7

With her surrender she seemed drawn into a protecting presence. Immediately she found herself taking a pride in his physical being, in the lazy strength of him as he lay about the house or his attitudes of unconscious grace as he sat talking with her or working. This strength was not of muscles but of hard flesh, and it seemed to express a passionate restraint.

He was not, she realized, entirely handsome. But there was something arresting about him. Particularly his hair. A little reddish streak lay like rust on the tip of one deep wave, and she liked to see it take fire in the light and possess a darting nimbus that made her think of the ghostly radiance hovering over the faintly russet hair of the priest's genie. Whenever she saw this her spirit seemed to bend down at his feet as Father Mehry had taught her to genuflex before the image in the chapel. Suddenly, mysteriously, he had become a figure almost symbolical, to whom she gave without understanding.

Most of the time he seemed drawn in behind that sheath of strength, emerging only when they came into actual physical contact, and then this touch translated a feeling impossible for him to speak because of the differences in their racial temperaments. That these differences were great she perceived, and she made an effort, immensely pathetic, to annihilate them.

She had learned to like the food that Justin ate, and she was rapidly cultivating his table manners. There was one habit of the French that she found very easy to enjoy, that was the use of *nuoc-da*,[16] "the stone

16 Scotsman William Cullen is credited with inventing artificial refrigeration in 1748, but it was nearly a century before ice-making machine patents were filed around the world and the industry took off. This Western technology clearly made a strong impression on the peoples of Southeast Asia, most of whom had never seen ice, snow or even frost. Following the Vietnamese example above, the Laos call ice *nam kon* (water chunk), the Thais, *nam kang* (hard water) and the Cambodians *dteuk kak* (water "hardening or stiffening", with *kak* also used for cement, tar or paint).

of water," or, as Justin called it, *glace*. It was extremely pleasant to take drinks chilled with ice. However, she found difficulty in learning to drink without making noises. Those little sucking sounds were part of Annamite etiquette; they expressed approval. But they distressed Justin, therefore, they must not be.

He was very patient. When she used the wrong fork or knife he pretended not to see; this kindness made her ashamed and eager to learn. Only once did he become angry with her, and that was in the dead of noon when the hot air shone as though polished. "In the name of God, don't sit like a monkey!" he exclaimed as she crouched nearby, knees thrust up and body hung between them, like an Annamite. A painful flush spread over her, and she felt miserably grotesque.

How can I be like his people? she cried out within herself.

But when dusk came and they sat together in the compound where the palms rocked softly, the notes of her guitar seemed to weave them closer together.

"Thi-Linh," he said suddenly, "has there ever been another man?"

It came so abruptly that the breath seemed wrenched out of her throat.

"Yes," she half whispered.

"He was not a Frenchman?" he guessed.

"He was an Annamite boy...."

"You loved him?"

Why did he ask her these questions? They hurt her terribly. She could scarcely articulate the words:

"Yes, I loved him...."

Her eyes were lowered and he commanded: "Look at me, Thi-Linh."

In the dusk his blurred pupils seemed filled with a remote trembling—she wanted to grope behind that look and draw out what was hinted there. Did he care? Or was it only egotistical jealousy?

"If I went away," he asked, "would you go back to this Annamite boy?"

Suddenly she felt very calm. "Never," she said; and repeated, "never."

He smiled slowly, and there was something sad in his eyes.

"Faithful Thi-Linh," he murmured. Then he sighed, and another look came over his face, strange, distant, and ironic—an expression he often had and which she had come to regard as a barrier unconsciously flung up between her and the thoughts that lay at the core of him. When he spoke he talked to the dusk.

"How much our women could learn from you; yes, and we men, too—if we only would."

He smiled that half satirical smile to himself.

"Such fools, we Frenchmen! We come here and take you as wives, and we say, 'Ah, we know the Annamite woman!' Stupid! As if a race could be translated by going to bed with its women!"

She let her hand rest lightly on his knee. "You always say things I do not understand."

He looked at her quickly, as though unaware of her until she spoke. The firm softness of his knee was under her hand. She knew that she could reach up and draw him to her, hold him fast. But she knew also that this could not destroy the world that lay between them at that moment.

"How can I explain to you when I cannot explain to myself?" There was a momentary silence. "At times …well, at times I feel like a small, white shadow in the midst of something dark and warm—something friendly—but something I can only feel with my hands, or my body, but never understand. If I could, then I might be great. If I could, then I would be able to tell France a little about this colony of hers." He sighed. "I wonder if France, too, is not a small white shadow in the midst of something dark…." Again he was silent for an interval, then he quoted ironically:

"I am cool water flowing with the night;

I am the sweat of men flowing with the day—"

Thi-Linh experienced a little sensation of pleasure. "It is your own poetry?"

He nodded.

"Why do you never write verses to me?" she asked.

He caught her chin in his hand and looked at her.

"All that I am doing now is about you, about this country—which is you…. I am trying so hard to learn it, this Indo-China of yours; and will it simply result in incoherent feeling? …God! how much emotion we accumulate in living! What capacity to feel! And how many half-ideas, half-dreams—a mass of incomplete erudition! We fill up with it—slowly— like a glass filling with red wine—and then suddenly someone crashes the glass, and the wine spills—to earth, of course, to be absorbed, and then later distilled again by who knows how many such inadequate fools as I." And again he fell into poetry:

"But this I know,

That all things cease when I have ceased to be."

"'Ceased to be.'?" she repeated.

"Dead."

She was puzzled. "But you said …there was something in us that went on—like the light of a candle—didn't you?"

"Yes," he affirmed. "But I mean the I that I am, Justin Batteur—he will be finished." As he talked a cold twilight seemed to sift upon her. "And with him all the beauty, all the ecstasies, all the half-learning that he has picked up. Stupid, isn't it?"

The sudden stridulation of an insect made her shudder, "Talk of something else," she begged. "I do not like to hear you speak of souls."

And so she abandoned her desperate efforts to understand this Frenchman and contented herself with the mysterious but kindly being whom she had acknowledged as protector; the half-man, half-god who lay working on a chaise longue through the day, brooding and repressed, and who for a moment in the twilight took on the semblance of a lover.

Often Monsieur Malardier came to visit, and while he was there she felt herself excluded from the conversation. Or, if she was noticed, it seemed that the *commissaire* smiled upon her as he would upon a prize chattel that he envied his friend—an envy made amicable in view of the fact that at least she belonged to one of his countrymen. She resented it, and in consequence adopted toward him an attitude of tolerant friendliness.

Once three Frenchmen who had arrived on the boat from Phnom-Penh came to the house for *dejeuner*. She sat at the table with them because Justin wished it, and as they talked in quick, staccato French, often smiling in her direction, she heard her name once or twice; and it seemed to her that the sharp tones were spear-points upon which she was tossed about playfully and cruelly. One, a tall, bearded fellow with dark skin, chucked her under the chin and remarked that she was "a pretty little piece." She merely smiled contemptuously, all the while gazing intently at the tawny shadows under his eyes and throat. Afterward, with fine scorn, she told Justin that he was a "dirty half-caste"; and it annoyed her when Justin smiled faintly.

Justin gave her many French books to read, some of them books of poetry. She liked the flowing lines of Lamartine and Baudelaire. Among these volumes were several French novels. They disturbed and excited her.

In fancy she saw cool streets dappled with the shadows of trees where men and women sat at tables and drank wine and ate strange food. Or she tried to construct pictures of great Parisian theaters, with the result that she created a preposterous vision of immense lamp-beaded glooms, in which bodies with French faces and Annamite costumes gesticulated and screamed as the actors did in the theaters at Phnom Penh.

When the day had stretched itself and yawned, and a passionate breath of flowers excited the air, she and Justin would sit with the cool darkness about them, and she would urge him to talk of France. More than once a question trembled in her throat, and she let it die. But to herself she said: Why should not he take me to France? And following that a sickening dread would run through her. What shall I do when he goes away? she asked herself. Then, with poignant hunger, her gaze would fasten upon him, seated a few steps above her, his legs faintly outlined in a sarong, his strong shoulders sagging in a khaki blouse; and that feeling of dread would become so intense that she seemed to contract to a white shaft that, sword-like, forbade him to leave.

A month had passed since her uncelebrated wedding.

8

It was the first night of the full moon.

All day Thi-Linh had tried to convince herself that she was very calm. But whenever she stirred she seemed aware of a shadow that slipped out of her and lagged momentarily, like another figure that moved with her and now and then lost step.

In the late afternoon a vicious purpose, forming nebulously through the day, led her to put on her finest tunic, that dream garment of black tissue over yellow.

Once in Phnom-Penh she had seen a plant the French called agave, a tall bush with thorned leaves cruel as sabers. As she dressed she felt that she was draping silk over an agave. Once or twice her finger-nails caught in the frail stuff and she indulged in the fancy that she had pricked herself.

Justin came in while she was dressing and looked surprised.

"I am going to visit Mama Thi-Bao tonight," she told him. "She has not seen my new *cai-ao.*"

"Charming!" he smiled, surveying her. When he came closer to kiss her she wanted to tell him to keep away or he would be pricked.

At dinner she went through the pretense of eating and afterward sat on the veranda with Justin for a few minutes, restlessly tapping the floor with her new sandals. When darkness groped into the compound she took her leave. "I shall return in an hour," she said.

As she moved along the road a pirogue, stealing by near the bank, filled the quiet with stealthy sound. The boatman was crooning. *"Ho, kouan! Ho, kouan!"* Perhaps, she thought, he is going to the wedding.

The road was white underfoot, powdering away into thick darkness. Often shapeless forms passed with a lisp of bare feet. Suddenly she thought of the evil genie that prowled abroad after nightfall, but her heart was too heavy to admit fear. Nevertheless, she was glad when she reached the shops and pallid rays of dusty light shone athwart the street.

Suddenly her blood leaped excitedly. Did she hear laughing voices above the indefinite murmur that swelled from open doors and passing figures—or was it her imagination? Could it be that they were coming already?

She hurried, reaching Vu-Trong-Khai's shop breathless.

Her mother was seated on the little platform in the rear, and the one lamp seemed to accentuate the hollows of her eyes in which only faint gleams told of life. Vu-Trong-Khai was lying on a mat smoking opium. The acrid smell, mingled with the smoke from the lamp, was sickening. The children were nowhere in sight. She tried to appear calm under her mother's searching look, sinking beside her and beginning a conversation about the incidents of the day.

The moments crawled by, prodded by her rush of inconsequential talk. Suddenly a crowd of chattering little boys ran by the doorway. She started. Did she hear the smothered ring of gongs?

"It is Kim Khouan's wedding procession," her mother announced.

She laughed nervously.

"Oh yes," she said coolly. "I had forgotten this was his wedding-night."

As the clanging sounds came nearer she wanted to creep into her mother's arms and cling. But she kept on smiling and talking; something of hysteria in her voice.

Now a buzz of voices swelled the ringing, spinning toward her like a hot crystal filled with bees. Her mother rose and went outside;

Vu-Trong-Khai looked up startled, then drew himself to his feet and followed. In front of the shop, a group of children had gathered, clapping their hands and shouting.

Thi-Linh felt herself drawn irresistibly toward the approaching music. She was standing beside her mother, gazing down the road. The children were looking at her, and one little girl stroked the edge of her tunic. On a sudden she was aware of her rich dress. A ghostly bride, decked out for a phantom wedding! In a moment the specter who was her bridegroom would appear, and then—

The gongs were beating against her ears now, and in the road not twenty yards away a carnival of torches and lanterns advanced in a luxury of color.

She set her face in a cold, cruel smile.

Several nearly naked little boys scampered by, casting flowers in the road.

I wonder if all these people see the thorns under my tunic, she thought crazily.

At the head of the procession walked two figures, one with a dark, folded turban on his head. As she saw him cymbals seemed to clash against her ears and vibrate down her spine. In a moment, she said to herself, he will be here and I shall throw off these robes and fling myself before him, so that he will fall upon the thorns of me and be crucified.

Deliberately she stepped out in front of her mother; there the gauzy quiver of passing torches and lanterns would wave against her.

He was abreast of her now, and for an instant she thought he would pass without seeing her, then something, perhaps the intensity of her gaze, drew his eyes.

And suddenly all that vicious sharpness within her seemed to go limp and fall into the dust under his feet. In that fraction of a second, his dark eyes looking into hers, she saw an expression that sent a blinding ecstasy through her. For a moment she was lying in the jungle pool, and he was bending over her....

"…Thou wilt share the couch of thy Master; wilt give him sons to perpetuate his race…. And they will maintain the Cult…. Thy hair will whiten; wrinkles will meet in the shrunken skin of thy cheeks; but thou mayest behold with serenity the approach of old age…. Ye newly married, go in peace…."

Yes, newly married! For had not she already celebrated a deathless wedding with him, there at the pool? This ceremony was only a gesture—for the world….

He had passed on, and where he had been were torches and lanterns swaying over slender shapes. And although she did not stir, a body hot and slim stepped out of her and joined the procession…. They were in the pagoda, beneath a canopy embroidered with the phenix and the lotus, and their hands were joined as they prostrated themselves before the great Buddha Huyen-Vu whose gilded face shimmered through a film of incense…. Gongs throbbed again; they were in the street, marching at the head of a gay procession…. She saw the open door of his house, the red banners staring vividly from the walls of the Hall of Honor. Before them was the altar of their Ancestors, the little tablets gleaming like white tombstones….

"It was very splendid," she heard her mother saying. "I suppose they will be happy."

She was still staring at the empty street, but she was no longer hot and nauseated. Her serenity surprised her. She felt as though she had divided magically into two parts, as she knew the tiny creatures of the swamp divided and became separate living entities, and one part had drifted off—forever. Something eternally youthful and shining had gone out of her to keep a tryst, while she herself stood behind and watched it dispassionately. Yes, she echoed to herself, I suppose they will be happy.

<h1 style="text-align:center">9</h1>

Thi-Linh thought a great deal and very seriously in the days following Kim Khouan's marriage. The result of it was that suddenly she realized she had grown into a woman.

Her affection for Justin was quite genuine; and equally genuine was the quiet love for Kim Khouan that had been molded out of all the passionate anguish of her first intense feeling for him. As a girl she could not have maintained this fealty to two loves. But now, as a woman, she could surmount infidelity (which was an extravagance of the undeveloped—she had read that in a French novel) and herself be the faithful mistress of one man while in her heart she was the wife of another. To the boy she had given the voluptuous excess of young love, which made her capable of a more even attachment to the man, and both experiences created an emotional balance that unseated neither one.

Life became less a romance but more dependable; whether more satisfying, she did not pause to analyze.

She did not have to worry with the uncertainties of love as it was sung by the poets; there was the reality of tenderness in Justin's touch, and there was poignant glamour in the image of Kim Khouan that now dwelt unobtrusively but no less enduringly in her mind.

Thi-Linh had learned enough about her Frenchman to understand his needs and desires; if she had known more, such as those intricacies of thought that had troubled her in the beginning, undoubtedly they would have had many arguments. As it was, she understood him enough to know he wanted her to read books and discuss them with him; also to help him in his work without knowing too much about it. That she had a very definite part in the creation of his book she realized. Justin asked her many questions about the customs of her people and their legends. He had begun this book shortly after she came to live with him, and he told her that within another month it would be finished; he was writing swiftly, he said, "under an inspiration." The title was "*Une Fille d'Annam.*"[17]

The rainy season had commenced, and it affected Justin's disposition. He was never deliberately unkind, but often he hurt her unintentionally. Once a friend came to call, accompanied by her mother, her

---

17 For actual titles of this genre that may have inspired Hervey, see Pico Iyer's foreword and the appendix article, "Francophilia."

grandmother, her two aunts, her three little brothers, and her baby sister; and when they departed, after an hour or so of chattering and exchanges of betel among themselves, she found Justin in a rage.

"I won't have all those screaming brats coming here!" he said. "Nor those women, spitting betel juice all over the floor."

"Then must I give up my friends?" she asked.

He was contrite. "No, of course not. But they irritate me when I am working." Then he added tenderly, "I want only you, Thi-Linh."

She herself was not unaffected by the heat. A permanent dampness had entered the house and was soaked into the boards, into the furniture, and even into their clothes. A hot indignation against the elements made her weak every time she found mildew on one of her garments. At times she seemed to swell with an ineffectual fury directed at the humidity and the damp-lipped clouds that browsed sensually over the panting earth. The nights sagged down like saturated black wadding; the days fumed with showers, and in the brief intervals between rains the sky was a streaming cobalt that seemed to include earth and people in a sticky, limpid bath.

Justin went off on a journey with Monsieur Malardier to visit some ruins on the other side of the river, deep in the jungle. He was away ten days, and the lonely house seemed like a shroud that contracted about her. She could have gone to stay with her mother, but she hated the thought of returning to those smelly rooms behind the shop. Moreover, she would have had to sleep on a mat, and she was accustomed to a bed by now. Often she awoke in the mornings feeling nauseated. At midday, when the heat was most intense, the slightest incident irritated her. Twice she thought she had fever, for her temples seemed to expand hotly and generate febrile ripples. She decided to see her mother and get some medicine, but she put it off, and then she felt better.

The empty house became unendurable, so she invited Nanette, the *congai* of Monsieur Malardier, to stay with her until the two Frenchmen returned. She did not like Nanette, but she was company. Nanette, in spite of her name, was a pure Annamite from Quan-Tri, a restless little creature with incendiary thoughts. In turn, she made Thi-Linh restless, and filled her mind with smoldering dreams. Nanette had lived in Hanoi with a French officer, and she told Thi-Linh about the gay life there, and the great number of men who had been her admirers.

She brought with her several French novels, among them one that sent Thi-Linh's thoughts tumbling into dangerous patterns. It was by a man named Pierre Louÿs — *"Aphrodite."*[18] The story of a certain Chrysis, courtesan of ancient Alexandria. She and Nanette discussed the book at length.

"When Monsieur Malardier gets tired of me," said Nanette, "I shall return to Hanoi—or perhaps I shall go to Saigon—and be like this Chrysis."

"Isn't that dreadfully wicked?" asked Thi-Linh, excited.

"Well, if one is going to be wicked then why not be as wicked as possible? Certainly I have no intention of being good—it is stupid. No Annamite would take me for a wife now, and French husbands do not last, so why not have many and get everything I can out of each?"

"But to have so many men," Thi-Linh persisted, "and think only of getting money out of them is no better than being like girls who sell themselves for a night."

Nanette smiled indulgently and wisely.

"No," she contradicted with the air of one who knew. "There are degrees of love. Love has its distinctions—like society. First, there is the woman who is married to a man by a priest or a bonze; then the wife who simply lives with a man because he wants her and can give her the things she desires; and then the woman who is beautiful and clever enough to choose her temporary husbands and change when she wishes; and last, the stupid little creature who sells herself indiscriminately. *Femme, maîtresse,* courtesan, prostitute—what difference except in the degrees of respectability and profit?"

For some reason Nanette made Thi-Linh feel uneasy. Thi-Linh decided that Nanette was very bad; and she felt relieved when she went

---

18 Pierre Louÿs was a poet and writer renowned for lesbian and classical themes that "expressed pagan sensuality with stylistic perfection." See the appendix article "Francophilia" for details on all the French writers Hervey references in this book.

home. But in her drowsy hours the image of the woman Chrysis dwelt fabulously in her thoughts.

The night that Justin returned she was awakened by a jerking sensation under her heart that brought her upright in the bed. She must have uttered a cry, for Justin awoke and asked her what was the matter. "Only a pain," she said, "or perhaps it was a dream." But for a long while she lay in humid blackness, frightened and trembling.

The next morning she set out for the shop of Vu-Trong-Khai. A brutal radiance blistered the river, and the palm fronds quivered against the sky like green gashes. Suddenly, as she neared the shop, the tremulous flanks of sunlight seemed to sweat blood. All those little red drops made her dizzy, and she hurried frenziedly. She saw the familiar doorway ahead, and then all those little drops ran together and streamed across her eyes.

When she became fully conscious again she was breathing winy coolness. Her mother was bending over her, a look of interrogation in her eyes.

"Mama Thi-Bao…."

"That such a disgrace should come upon us!" her mother moaned.

Thi-Linh felt tears in her eyes. She was not crying because of what she had suddenly realized but because of that look of her mother's.

"It is terrible," the older woman wailed. "He will turn you out."

A cold sickness filled Thi-Linh's heart. She closed her eyes.

"If he does," she breathed, "I shall go away."

"To give yourself to other men?" her mother demanded angrily. "To further offend the Ancestors?"

She opened her eyes to a blur of tears. "I am sorry, Mama Thi-Bao…."

"Who is the man?"

A tiny stream of betel-juice made a red thread across her mother's chin; Thi-Linh thought she looked pitifully grotesque.

She choked as she pronounced the name.

"Kim Khouan!" Thi-Bao echoed. "If it had only been a Frenchman, then your husband might… And I had believed you so innocent!"

Her face sank upon Thi-Linh's breast. With each quiver of her mother's body the girl felt a growing despair. She tried to imagine what Justin would say, and the despair increased.

Her mother, now quiet, raised herself. "You must tell him," she said. "I shall go with you."

"No. I will go alone."

"But—"

"No. You must not suffer that interview."

She faced the blackness that was careening upon her. Half-remembered words of Nanette darted maddeningly through her despair. The very dreadfulness of this catastrophe demanded urgent action.

"I will go now," she decided. She dried her eyes and smoothed rice-powder over her face. "Do you forgive me, Mama Thi-Bao?" she asked, pausing at the door.

Her mother had assumed that old pose, that attitude of tired resignation. She was chewing betel listlessly; the red thread had dried on her chin.

"You are my daughter," she said at length. And then she sighed: "But I had thought to be the proud grandmother of Frenchmen*"

10

Justin was reclining on the chaise longue writing when she reached the house. He merely glanced up as she approached.

A damp breath of soggy earth and rain-bruised flowers rose on the heat that throbbed up from the ground and spilled its fluid cadences, diluted, between the rattan blinds. Even the stillness had a radiant quality.

Thi-Linh sank down at his feet.

His sarong had fallen apart and one bare leg hung on the edge of the chaise longue, a sandal dangling from the toes. As she observed this characteristic pose all the breath seemed to stop in her throat. Suddenly he stretched. She knew that his body under the clothing, made a warm cross; and she wanted to throw herself upon it and die nailed to his strength. Instead, her gaze dropped to his ankle, very close and touched with a faint glisten as the sunlight irradiated the tiny hairs, and she bent swiftly and kissed it. She did not look up, but she could feel his surprised gaze.

"Justin," she began, "you have been very good to me...." Still she did not look up. "I am going away, Justin."

He laughed. One hand slipped under her chin and lifted it.

"What is all this?" he demanded, smiling.

Her eyes met his, glazed with unhappiness. He seemed far away and in twilight. Gradually the smile left his face.

"Are you sick?"

Then she took his hands and pressed them under her heart. "Can you feel something stirring there?" she whispered. Then, suddenly, a fierce nausea passed over her. She dropped her hands and clinched them. "I don't want a baby!" she cried piteously.

Her eyes were fixed upon him, and she thought he would never speak. In the compound, insects sang monotonously. His lips were tight, and the muscles of his cheeks stood out. Finally he said:

"The ...Annamite boy?"

She nodded. Again he was silent for a long while. She could scarcely believe it when she saw a faint smile being born in one corner of his mouth.

"What a joke!" he muttered, more to himself than to her. Then he spoke directly to her, that satirical smile still at the corner of his mouth. "I would be a very poor Frenchman," he said, "if I could not accept this—this little joke that your country has played on me."

11

One evening four months later a black-toothed *baya*[19] came to the house, and a few hours afterward a thin, startled wail mingled with the soft cries of the night birds.

Two mornings later Thi-Linh was up and about the house. She decided to call the boy Justin—which brought again a faint ironic smile to the Frenchman's lips. At first he took more notice of the child than she did; indeed, Thi-Linh tried to appear utterly indifferent. Justin did not write that day, and he lay on the chaise longue smoking many cigarettes and drinking brandy-sodas. She sat in a chair beside him and tried to read a novel, but most of the time her gaze stole to the wailing little figure that squirmed on the bed inside. Several times she caught Justin's studied gaze upon her, and finally those looks drove her into the bedroom where she stood looking down quizzically at her baby.

There was no resemblance to Kim Khouan in the shriveled little face, she observed critically. As she stood there, trying to be impersonal, her feeling was half resentment and half an emotion that she tried to force out of her heart. Suddenly it came to her that this child was born of her first love, and as she accepted that realization, those little waving fists seemed to beat against her breasts. She knelt quickly and buried her lips in the warm, palpitating flesh.

She kept little Justin for two weeks. Justin, the man, said the baby might stay in the house, but Thi-Linh knew he was only being kind and that the child would disturb him, and later annoy him. So at the end of a fortnight she took little Justin to her mother. Vu-Trong-Khai objected until Thi-Linh told him she would give her mother part of her monthly allowance to keep the child.

When Thi-Linh returned to the house a thin ghostly wail haunted her. Her hands, for the past fourteen days so busy with a tiny brown body, felt robbed of a tender occupation. Of course she could see her child every day but the fact that he was no longer with her all the

---

19 In Japanese, *baya* means an old housekeeper or midwife, with variations ranging from granny to hag or witch. It means the same in Indochina, but how it entered the local lexicon remains a mystery.

time gave her the feeling that she was permanently severed from a part of herself.

Justin was compiling a book of Indo-Chinese legends. The manuscript of *"Une Fille d'Annam"* had been sent to France. He told her that very soon great machines would make many copies of it.

"And when you see the book" he said with a smile, "you will find your name in the front. " 'To Thi-Linh this story belongs,' it will say."

He was very considerate of her. Not once had he asked her about Kim Khouan. Now that the baby was born, he seemed to regard it as a fact to be accepted without discussion or reproach; a closed incident.

As for herself, she looked upon the child as something inexplicable but, now that she thought about it, inevitable. The straight line of her life had momentarily broken to admit another life, and then continued in the same even course, unaffected except by a memory of exquisite suffering and the realization that a part of herself had become another tangible being. For some reason Kim Khouan and the baby had no connection in her thoughts. Each was a separate and distinct event; one a poignant romance destined to remain that because it was finished, and the other a somewhat puzzling reality whose future was darkly indefinite.

Once or twice she saw Kim Khouan in the village but she turned off quickly before they met. She did not know whether he knew of his child or not. It was possible that he did know, for there had been talk among the villagers, and although they might not be aware that it was his child, he would realize the truth. Often she caught smiling insinuations as she walked along the street, and she returned them with a look of utter indifference or contempt. She was the mistress of her own life, and the innuendoes of others did not affect her imperviousness or trouble her.

The tension of the past few months settled down to an even tempo. When she was not helping Justin she was reading or sewing; and in the late afternoons she would visit her stepfather's shop and smile over a tiny gurgling creature. The baby amused and distracted her; Justin had become a pleasant warmth that satisfied her natural craving for

affection; and the memory of Kim Khouan was the wistful indiscretion
that relieved the stable reality of the man she possessed. What more
could she want? She saw little of Nanette and allowed herself to think
even less of the lurid ideas the girl had planted in her brain.

Stung Treng faced the east, and every late afternoon when all the
light seemed dead except behind the houses and palms where the sky
throbbed a rosy hue, it was Thi-Linh's habit to walk along the main
road and watch the people. At this time of the day their bodies seemed
so soft; and the young men's throats shone with a pallor that disturbed
her. She wondered if she liked to watch those young men because they
reminded her of Kim Khouan, but the reason seemed more subtle than
that. Always there were numbers bathing in the river and still others
lying with their brown flanks against the faun-gray flanks of mud; and
all those wet or drying bodies seemed to twist together deep within her
like the roots of desire.

This emotion was alarming. It was not lust, she knew. Was it the
impersonal expression of an affection for people at large that was in
no way untrue to Justin? It made her think of that Frenchman's book,
"Aphrodite." Chrysis, the exquisite, walking beside the shores of
Alexandria, craving men. But, Thi-Linh reflected, she did not crave
men—at least, not as this ancient Egyptian woman had. It was simply
that her vision seemed to draw them close while she herself yielded an
indefinable warmth to them, as a mother imparts warmth to the buds of
suckling nakedness that later become men. In those moments, walking
there beside the river, she felt old with the age of forgotten years.

One morning Nanette came to call bringing the news that Kim
Khouan and his wife had gone to Saigon. "He is going to work in a
bank," announced the girl, closely watching Thi-Linh, who looked
sufficiently interested not to appear utterly indifferent.

When Thi-Linh was alone she breathed a sigh that was relief. Now
there would never be any danger of an encounter. The reality of Kim
Khouan had completely yielded to a romantic ghost; and ghosts, she
knew, did not track the polished surface of illusions. Thi-Linh felt
secure in her complete possession of him.

12

Six months had passed since Justin sent the manuscript of *"Une Fille d'Annam"* to France; and one morning, after the boat from Phnom-Penh had arrived, Thi-Linh held in her hand a paper-back volume and gazed at an inscription in the front. "To Thi-Linh this story belongs." A fierce pride rose in her. It is my book, she thought; I have given it to him. Justin glowed.

"From my friend Leroux," he said, tapping a letter that had come with the book. "He says the Académie Française has recognized my work. Do you know what that means?"

She felt a little dart, half joy and half dread. "It is a very great honor," she replied slowly. His success filled her with immense pride, and at the same time it made her vaguely uneasy. Praise from France was a bit alarming; in some way France seemed her enemy.

"It means that my books have a chance to live," he went on. "It means I have produced something of permanent value." And he added simply, "I owe it to you, Thi-Linh."

He took her in his arms, and that embrace was reassuring. Often during the past two months she had seen in his face that distant look that always disturbed her; and now she was happy that this news had come to distract him.

"Tomorrow Malardier and I start for Wat Phu," he announced. "We shall be gone about fifteen days."

"And I may go with you?" she asked.

"It is no trip for a woman," he protested. "And think, how glad you will be to see me when I return!"

"You are tired of me?"

That lazy smile that she loved rebuked her.

The next morning she went down to the river to watch the boat leave. Justin, leaning on the aft-rail, waved to her as the craft glided out upon the Me-Kong. That picture would always remain in her mind: the flash of white teeth under the blur of his helmet, the sunlight golden on his khaki shirt, and the little gleams that twinkled on his leather boots; a figure that gradually contracted to a pale pin-point as his topi winked a last time in the heat haze.

That night Thi-Linh, alone in the house, felt transfixed by the black heat. She had decided to go to stay with her mother when a click-clack of wooden sandals in the compound preceded Nanette.

"Well," said the girl, dropping upon the chaise longue and lighting a cigarette, "I am going to Saigon."

Thi-Linh looked at her in surprise. Her attention was distracted by the insolent grace with which Nanette held her cigarette. Her hands, she noticed, were beautifully slim, and there was a certain narrow loveliness in her face, accentuated by a heavy coat of powder. Reclining there in her soft tunic, with the faintest hint of diamonds at her ears, and gazing at Thi-Linh through a drift of smoke, she had something undeniably French about her. It was an air that Thi-Linh admired. At the same time she did not entirely approve of Nanette; she was a little vicious, she thought.

"To Saigon?" she repeated.

Nanette smiled cynically. " 'Love is a form of vanity, and when the beloved ceases to flatter, nothing remains but wounded pride,'" she quoted lightly. "After all, there is much truth in the proverbs.... I am leaving Monsieur Malardier."

"You mean—"

"To be exact," she interrupted, "we quarreled—he has been most odious of late—and as I suspected he was about to suggest that we terminate our little marriage, I was clever enough to make the suggestion first." She exhaled through her nostrils, coolly, adding: "It is always best to forestall a man, for later he respects you the more for preserving your face however much he may hate you at the time. Anyway, I think I have got as much out of Monsieur Malardier as possible," she went on. "And his odor has become most offensive to me lately," she finished with a grimace.

Thi-Linh was dimly troubled. "What will you do?"

Nanette shrugged. "Continue my profession of acquiring husbands." Very deliberately she flicked her cigarette away and smiled at Thi-Linh. "Your Monsieur Batteur is going back to France," she announced.

For a moment Thi-Linh stared at her without emotion. Beyond her, gauzy ephemera hurtled about the lamp in the living-room. Suddenly the mad flight of those insects made her dizzy. She laughed uneasily.

"How do you know that?" she demanded, forcing herself to smile back.

The other made a French gesture with her exquisite hands. "I know what my ears hear. Last night he showed a letter to Monsieur Malardier, a letter from France, from a friend. Monsieur Malardier said, 'Then you will be going home soon?' And your Monsieur Batteur said, 'Perhaps it will be necessary.' Then they talked about France for a long while. It was after he left that we quarreled. I said that Frenchmen were dirty pigs."

Thi-Linh had grown calmer. "Did you hear him say actually that he was going?"

Nanette looked annoyed. "No. But is it not enough that he said it might be necessary?" She drew out a package of black cigarettes and extended them to Thi-Linh. "My advice to you," she said, striking a match, "is to go to Saigon with me."

The smoke flowing through Thi-Linh's nostrils seemed to cool her head. She resolved not to let Nanette see that she was disturbed.

"Why should I go there?" she inquired, successfully at ease.

"Saigon is full of officers who wear gold braid," Nanette responded.

Thi-Linh crushed down the thoughts that came into her mind. "I do not believe Justin would plan to leave without telling me," she announced.

"Little fool!" Nanette's smile seemed to say. "When he has left," she observed, "you will wish you had gone to Saigon with me." Her small, delicate face came closer to Thi-Linh and she looked at her appraisingly before she remarked, "You are very pretty, Thi-Linh—

although a trifle pale—you would look well in a gown from Paris and high-heeled slippers."

There was an uncertain quiver in Thi-Linh's laugh. "I think you have a devil in you," she said with pretended lightness.

Nanette smiled inscrutably. "Someday," she dreamed aloud, "perhaps I shall add the epaulettes of an admiral to my collection." Then her nostrils distended visibly. "I hate Frenchmen!" she said quietly.

Thi-Linh was glad when Nanette had gone. For a long while she sat on the veranda. The trees in the compound seemed part of a restless sea that lapped against her. "You would look well in a gown from Paris...." Nanette was a wicked little fool, she thought. But that did not serve to dismiss Nanette or what she had said.

Thi-Linh had never pried into Justin's affairs, consequently it had never occurred to her to look at his mail. Nor had she had any reason to do it. But now the desk where he kept his letters drew her. The thought of what she might find made her hesitate. But at least, she told herself, I shall know the truth.

Reluctantly she went into the living-room. On top of a pile of recent mail in his desk lay a letter which she recognized as the one that had come with the copy of *"Une Fille d'Annam."* Her fingers were stiff and cold as she drew it out.

In the dead silence she heard the darting whirl of insects circling around the lamp. Tiny shadows flickered across the page.

"... and of course, my dear friend, you will be returning to France now, for although your position is secure, it is always wise to be in the midst of things and to make new contacts.... There is a little apartment overlooking the Rue St. Honoré (Gournot is occupying it now, but it will be vacant in a few months) which I think is just what you desire.... A great book, my friend. How in God's name did you learn so well that scorched country of exile?..."

The paper crackled harshly as she folded it and returned it to the envelope.

"…but it will be vacant in a few months…" And this house, too, will be vacant in a few months, she thought, looking about dazedly. "… A great book…" Great! And I gave it to him, she told herself with fierce exultation. I! For even he said so. "… How in God's name did you learn so well that scorched country of exile? ..,Yes! How in God's name? She wanted to laugh, hysterically. Not in God's name; no; in her name!

A picture of Justin as she had last seen him rose in her mind. He had seemed so warm and certain. But now she wondered if that last glimpse was not significant, his gradual shrinking until he was lost in blinding sunlight. And was there not something of ultimate farewell in that final wave of his hand as he was carried out upon the river? Frenchmen went like that, smiling and with a light gesture. … Of course he would return; all his things were in the house. But that departure was a presagement.

They were cruel—white men. But, she relented, perhaps no more than dark men. For had not her brown lover forsaken her? In that moment, for the first time, Kim Khouan's love seemed pathetic and grotesque. How insufficient he had proved in the one great test! If his love had been strong enough he would have followed it, even at the cost of his father's displeasure and of offending his Ancestors. Thi-Linh had read too many novels still to think that the code of Annamite behavior could not be violated when love was opposed to filial duty.

Men: frail caricatures of what women believe them.

Her pride throbbed with a new wound. Would she always be deserted by her lovers? Her own reflection, contracted to an absurdly thin sheen on the glazed surface of a vase on the desk, seemed to spin before her in mockery. In sudden rage she seized the jar and dashed it to the floor.

A moment later the house-boy appeared with a sleepy, startled look, and she screamed for him to get out.

She wanted to rush out on the veranda and cry to the whole village that her Frenchman was about to leave her, or better still, run through the streets and give voice to her indignation. Instead, she sat down on the floor and beat the matting with her bare feet. After a few minutes this seemed ridiculous; it was reminiscent of the conduct of black-toothed *bayas* giving vent to their rage. She, Thi-Linh, had French blood. Half-caste! she flung at herself the next instant.

Presently she got up and went to the shelf where Justin kept his books. A little wave of tenderness went over her as she opened the copy of *"Une Fille d'Annam."* "To Thi-Linh this story belongs," she read with a pang. Then she turned the pages, skimming the sentences. After a little while she sat down beside the lamp.

As she read, she passed out of the room into the pages of the book. She had become a little girl in Annam, the daughter of a mandarin. She grew quickly through cool scenes that drifted across her like sea winds. Suddenly Justin had entered the print beside her, and they were living together in a little house near the Pass of the Clouds, between Tourane and Hue, and overlooking the ocean. The days were sweet, and they became even sweeter when she carried a fragile shape in her arms: their son. And then, abruptly, the days seemed chilled. Justin's face had a distant, dreamy stare. She looked into his green eyes and saw the meadows of France…. He went. The loneliness of that little house near the Pass of the Clouds became unbearable, and so, with her son at her breast, she went to sleep in the ocean—that great blue ocean stretching between France and Annam.

As she finished reading the book she noticed that the light had burned low. A coolness, as before dawn, filled the room. A few insects lay dead about the base of the lamp, and the smell of kerosene and singed wings floated on the heavy atmosphere.

She drew a deep sigh, sat there for a few minutes breathing the impure air.

Finally she stirred and went into the bedroom. The stark, pale figure of the crucifix caught her gaze. Resolutely she got some joss-sticks and lighted them before it.

"Mary, Mother of Jesus," she prayed. "You were a woman. . .

When she fell asleep she dreamed she saw her own body lying naked before her, magnified a thousand times. Ranks of twinkling boots marched over her; rifles were stacked upon her mouth; and a whole army spread out in bivouac upon the undulations of her bosom.

13

But no miracle occurred before daylight to show her the way; and, impatient, she went to the pagoda and burned incense before the dusty, tarnished figures on the altar.

After that she made her way to the pool where she and Kim Khouan had held their trysts. The black water was branded with sunlight, and the lotuses, no longer in bloom, spread their broad leaves in empty cups. The heat seemed to seal her reflection upon the surface in fantastic denial of her youth; it was a shriveled *baya* looking up at her, teeth black with betel and hands grasping for a guitar on which to strike the notes of bitter *chansons*. She gazed at the caricature with a challenging smile, and then hurried away as though afraid it would follow.

When she reached the shop of Vu-Trong-Khai her limbs ached. Her mother greeted her with a look that anticipated trouble. Little Justin sprawled gleefully on the floor, kicking his feet. She picked him up and kissed him, a dank loneliness chilling her.

"I am going away," she announced abruptly.

The baby squirmed against her. Thi-Bao rolled a betel-leaf in lime and put it into her mouth.

"I am going to Saigon," Thi-Linh amplified.

Her mother chewed for a moment before she spoke. "Does Monsieur Batteur know it?"

Thi-Linh shook her head. "I found a letter.... He is going back to France soon...."

There was another silence. Finally her mother nodded. "Where will you get the money?"

"I have saved a little—and he has not given me this month's allowance. I shall break open the box where he keeps his money and take what belongs to me."

Thi-Bao stirred and spat. There was no expression in her face, but Thi-Linh thought she saw a glimmer in her eyes; perhaps it was only reflected sunlight.

"When does the boat leave?" the older woman asked.

"It is due in four days. … I am going with Nanette." After a pause she added: "I shall send you money each month to take care of little Justin."

A tremor passed over her as she said that. First her lovers, now her baby…. Kim Khouan, weak …Justin, simply the way of Frenchmen. … At least, she thought with pathetic exultation, I am leaving him before he leaves me.

Presently her mother spoke. "Saigon is a large city…."

"Yes," said Thi-Linh, "I shall be lonely at first." Her thoughts momentarily drowsed in the memory of Justin. Simply the way of Frenchmen, she repeated to herself. Then she finished aloud. "But not for long."

Thi-Bao chewed on in silence, her face still expressionless.

"I shall pray that you make a successful marriage," she announced suddenly. After that she did not speak again.

I shall have to go back to the house and get my things, Thi-Linh thought. The baby whimpered, and the little cry drew her down until her lips moved over the tiny hands.

Her mother might have been a statue but for the slow working of her jaws; that same statue that she had been since Thi-Linh was a little girl; gaunt, melancholy, one knee thrust between her breasts and the other bent and lying motionless. Her vacant eyes were upon the doorway. Did she smile, Thi-Linh wondered.

Outside, the road trembled in a bath of white heat, and the few people who were astir seemed to blur past the doorway. Thi-Linh was only faintly aware of their movements.

But after the heat, she thought, they will go down to the river to bathe.

14

It was some months later, in Saigon, that Thi-Linh received a letter from her mother saying: "… It was, perhaps, a great mistake—but how could you know that he did not really intend to return to France, at least for some time? I suppose it was Nanette's fault, but of course she did not do it intentionally.... I saw him often; he always smiled most kindly and asked how the baby was...He had gone to Luang Prabang when the fever came. Nguyen, who was with him, said he lived for three days, very delirious. Nguyen brought all his possessions to Monsieur Malardier. That kind gentleman told me that the last page in his diary might interest you, and asked me to send it...."

Enclosed in the letter was a crumpled piece of paper, evidently jerked carelessly out of a notebook. Written across it in faltering letters was a single line:

"Thi-Linh, ma femme.... *O pitié, mon Dieu....*"

Sabre and Tunic

our months had passed since she came to Saigon; and now she called herself Marie Linh. She worked as a sewing-woman in the shop of some Bombay merchants on the Rue Catinat. For more than a month she had been living alone, Nanette had a house on the Rue Paul Blanchy, and a husband who wore chevrons.

The shop where she worked faced a broad sidewalk blue with the shadows of tamarinds. Through the day the sunlight lay stagnant in the streets, giving sustained throbs as vehicles and people coursed rhythmically by. But toward late afternoon a wind scooped the heat out of the air and left it listless and dying, to be revived almost immediately by a limpid dusk in which the colored tunics of the Annamite women floated like glints in a prismatic drink.

It was then that Thi-Linh felt a sudden flow in her blood. The stupid sewing was finished; she would go home, and after dinner she would call a rickshaw and ride about the city, enjoying the dark vibrance that was Saigon at night. Or she and some friend would go to the theater. But she preferred merely to ride. There was something voluptuous in the life that stirred under these French lamps. And, then, there was the added excitement of looking for that nameless white face....

63

It had happened late at night, during those hours when the air was the embodiment of a quiet rhythm. She and Nanette were riding back from the cinema. A door on the right opened abruptly, and a French officer came out; she knew he was an officer because the sudden release of light glowed about his white uniform. For a bare instant she saw his face as he turned to speak to someone inside—a quick bloom of pallor in the darkness, flower-like in its uncertainty; a gleaming edge on the contour of cheek and forehead, losing itself in shiny black hair. A moment he lingered there, then a slam shut him in darkness, and a shadow of him seemed blown down the street on the hot gush of opium fumes that followed him out.…

Thereafter when she rode about at night and a door opened she experienced a startled expectancy.

The room where she worked was in the rear of the shop, opening upon a court that in the morning was filled to the brim with shade, which ebbed as the sun thrust straws of light into it. By noon it shone with the motionless luster of a dry glass. And, like a glass, it responded musically to sound-touch. Chirp of scissors and ring of sandaled feet; voices and the droning tear of silk; all set to the concerted rhythm of life beyond the walls. These noises from outside were the yearning tongues of the world; Thi-Linh was a nun in this cloister of pattern and design, patiently waiting , . . only now and then a little restless.…

Three other women worked there besides herself. She did not like them. She felt that they said things behind her back—things about her French blood. They all were under a fat French dressmaker, who wore shoes too tight and then complained that the equatorial climate made her feet swell. This woman, Madame Dessard, had lived in Tientsin. But also she had lived in a town on the Bosporus. Her mother was a Georgian, she said, her father a Breton.

"I met my husband in Constantinople," she recited for the sewing-women regularly every few days. "Oh, he was very rich! Then we went to Tientsin, and he became director in a bank. Oh, I had an automobile then, and ten servants! And I was going to send my little boy to school in France. But, my God, the fire came! …I stood in the street and watched my house burn with my little boy inside and my husband trying to save him.... Everything went, everything—for my husband died of burns afterward. Now here I am, Madame Adrienne Dessard, working for Bombay men!"

Thi-Linh could never understand why, but when Madame Dessard was telling that story she always had an insane desire to laugh. It was a story utterly tragic, but this powdered, sweating woman, her feet cramped into shoes too small, made it seem ludicrous.

Invariably, a few minutes after she had told of her misfortune, Madame Dessard would become very angry and scold the women. Or she would thump one of them on the head with a thimble. "Look at that seam!" she would scream. "Name of a black bitch! You Annamite women are cows!"

For hours she would be very confidential, recounting her history for the benefit of the four women who went on sewing without listening; then, suddenly, she would remember that she belonged to a superior race, and go into a fit of temper over some trivial incident.... Every night she rode about in a rickshaw—alone. Often Thi-Linh saw her seated by herself in some café, her face flushed with drink, and her feet, half hidden under the table, discreetly crossed above shining high-heeled slippers. She wondered why Madame Dessard was never with Frenchmen....

The Indians who owned the shop moved about with dark scowls that, when doing business with French customers, metamorphosed magically into a fluid willingness to please. Thi-Linh had a great contempt for them. In spite of pomades and perfumes, they had an odor that made her think of greasy bodies soaked with food-smells and lying in the sun. They worshiped at a walled temple on the Rue Ohier. She had to pass there on her way to and from work, and its portal always yawned at her with a half rancid, half musky breath. One of the priests, a young black fellow with a red mark on his forehead, smiled at her frequently.

Many Frenchwomen came to the shop, and they interested her extremely. Suave and cool-looking in their imported clothes, or very fat and fanning themselves breathlessly, they hovered about, stroking metal cloths from Benares or running their white fingers over furs from Yunnan, all the while talking swiftly among themselves or arguing over prices. Generally the Bombay merchants swore after they had gone—but they always smiled when they returned. Whether fat or ugly, or sallow-skinned and flabby from the climate, they had an air, these women. They were, to Thi-Linh, Paris.

But they had something else, and it was that she envied them most. Prestige. Thi-Linh knew she was better looking than most of them, and that in time she also would possess clothes like theirs, but she would never ride along the Rue Catinat and be pointed out as the wife of Monsieur This or Captain That, And simply because her skin was not entirely white.

There must be some recompense, she decided; at least, revenge. But conscious revenge seemed a tedious and ineffectual effort. After all, were not they women dependent like herself upon their ability to hold men? Competition. A rivalry in which vengeance had no part except where personalities challenged it.

Nanette was right; there were distinctions in love as well as in society. Fastidiousness was an asset. In her instance, it was a score that brought her nearer the average of these Frenchwomen with all their prestige. Not that they were fastidious; she had heard that white women in the tropics spoiled swiftly. But discrimination in a native woman, or a woman with native blood, gave her more power as an adversary.

And so, although four months had passed, still she rode about the city at night without answering the smiles of Frenchmen. Virtue, she realized, belied its original implications; for, instead of chastity, it meant the period of waiting before fulfillment.

And then there was that white face that had bloomed suddenly in the night and passed.... Chirp of scissors ...droning tear of silk ...and the yearning tongues of the world.... Nun in a cloister—waiting.

2

It was curious that upon her arrival in Saigon she had no feeling of strangeness. Of a certainty she saw unfamiliar things, but the city itself might have been a well-remembered place that had simply been remodeled and re-peopled.

She and Nanette had first rented a room in the house of a Tonkinese family that Nanette had known in Hanoi. This house was identical with all the other houses in the same row: tawny plaster, red tile roof, and green fingers of mold groping up from the lush soil.

In the daytime, naked or half-naked children played on the doorsteps. Women squatted within, gossiping, and chewing betel or smoking. In the road a low fog of dust was raised under the cumbersome wheels of ox-drawn carts and rickshaws; coolies went soundlessly by, pale-flanked with that same dust, and bent tinder great bales or with bamboo carrying-poles swinging to the polished rhythm of their bare shoulders.

The barracks of the *Tirailleurs Annamites* was nearby, and at night soldiers drifted past, slim in their dark tunics and spiked straw helmets, their soft tread augmented by the muffled rattle of occasional vehicles.

To the west a short distance a canal made an oily track for sampans and barges gliding down from Cholon, the Chinese city, to Saigon River. To Thi-Linh that river was a source of mystery and delight.

With high tide it came sucking in from the sea, drawing men and ships. From the docks of the *Messageries Maritimes* to the Botanical Gardens, masts made crucifixes upon the sky, seeming hung with the blunt black smudges of smokestacks. Clustered about these foreign ships were junks from Malaya, Tonkin, and China, with eyes painted on their prows.

Frequently dead-gray battleships were moored by the Marine Barracks, to release a brood of laughing, curly-haired sailors upon Saigon; noisy young men who rode two and three in a rickshaw, the little red pompoms on their caps darting in all quarters of the city like a holiday of fireflies.

From the Quay Frances Garnier the long Rue Catinat slanted coolly between French and native shops to the square under the great twin spires of the cathedral.

In this street the air was always aromatic with the smells of perfumes and powders and imported wines. Gilt signs peered between the tamarinds, bearing incongruous words: Huyen-Tran, *Charcutier*.... Ly Binh, *Tailleur*.... Behind plate-glass windows that blazed under the tropical sun were the latest modes in clothing and millinery. Crowded between *bijouteries* and *magasins* were tiny shops that sold Tonkinese embroidery and brass gods, or bazaars rich with silks from China and India.

On the Rue Catinat also were the main cafés.... These cafés! Whenever Thi-Linh passed them they started a little throbbing in her throat. Officers and women sat at marble-topped tables in an atmosphere electric with voices. In the later afternoon, orchestras made French music; and sometimes the people danced.

Around the cathedral spread a great open space that frayed into the streets which were the blue-blooded veins of Saigon. Here in the houses set back from these shady thoroughfares people moved in an orbit that Thi-Linh would never be permitted to enter. Here majors and colonels, civil officials and wealthy business men lived with their wives or mistresses in pale yellow plaster houses smothered in tropical luxuriance. Here the heart of France beat with almost hysterical gaiety to the surrounding measured rhythm of darker blood.

Thi-Linh found something ancient and inevitable about Saigon; an oldness that had nothing to do with actual years but with an accumulation of experience that seemed distilled into the streets, like the smell of wine soaked into the boards of an old table.

For that reason she was glad she had seen that white face a few days after she arrived.

It was strange how his pallor persisted in making a glow behind her thoughts. She tried to quench it, but it remained—imploring her. Imploring her to do what? To find him.

There were many officers in Saigon, a number of whom had dark hair and who smoked opium. So how could she expect to find this man who had stood poised momentarily in the doorway that night, and thereafter stood silhouetted in her mind? And if she did find him, what then?

Suppose he had a wife or a *congai*? But he did not; she knew that. A man who was not terrifically alone could not have leaned out of the night so tragically and charged her to find him.

"I know a woman," Nanette announced one day before she had met her officer, "who can introduce us to some French army men. She procures girls for many lieutenants and captains, and I think her commission is not too high."

"Let us see her,'" Thi-Linh decided.

It proved a most unsuccessful experience. They went to see the woman, a highly perfumed, haughty creature who lived near the market, and the next day she came to their house with two non-commissioned officers. One of them was very red-faced, and a blot of sweat darkened the back of his khaki tunic. He pinched Thi-Linh's cheeks and said she would do; she could move her things to his house the following day. She merely smiled and informed him that she desired a younger husband. Nanette laughed insolently. … The two Frenchmen could have struck them with pleasure, but instead they kicked their rickshaw coolies and rode off in a rage. The procuress was even angrier; she departed refusing to bring any more gentlemen to be insulted by two such strumpets.

It was then that a woman next door told Thi-Linh about the work in the store of the Bombay men. Immediately she went to see Madame Dessard, and the following day started in as a seamstress. Nanette told her she was a fool. Why should she work with her hands when she could live by her wits? A bumboat woman called Mary, who trafficked down on the river, knew all the captains and officers of the foreign ships. Often these men desired to be entertained…. But Thi-Linh was determined.

"I must send Mama Thi-Bao money for little Justin; sewing is easier—until I can get a suitable husband."

She thought of her baby a great deal these days. To have kissed the gurgling brownness of him would have dissolved all the inertia of these weeks of search and waiting. Her thoughts lingered tenderly upon Thi-Bao, too. And Justin; that was before she heard of his death. He could not, she realized, be blamed for the faults of his race, of his sex. The love of men was such a pitiful splendor; it came with great pomp and ebbed so inauspiciously. Perhaps it was not the love that passed, but the resolution that made love permanent.

It was strange, this knowledge she had of men. She seemed born with an awareness of their capacities and faults.

As she cut and sewed daily under Madame Dessard it seemed as if she were taking apart her past and making it into a new model. Although the fat Frenchwoman, fussing about in her tight slippers and yielding to fits of temper, was ludicrous and sometimes irritating, Thi-Linh felt a curious sympathy for her. Son and husband consumed in one fire; and now, pathetically arrogant in her memory of them, she rode restlessly about the city at night or sat in one of the cafés, flushed and alone, until she swayed into a rickshaw and was taken to her empty little house in a lane off the Rue Paul Blanchy.

Since the first day in Saigon Thi-Linh had expected to encounter Kim Khouan. Nanette had told her that once she had passed him coming out of the bank where he worked. "He was dressed in European clothes" she said.

It was inevitable that a meeting should occur sooner or later. When it did it was so brief and unexpected that she did not have time to lose her poise.

She was riding along the Rue Taberd when another rickshaw swooped around the corner. The two coolies cursed, and hers swerved, whirling her into the intersecting street, and leaving flashed upon her mind the photograph of a startled face in which the eyes seemed bruised with poignant recognition. She did not look around, although her temples felt caught in a revolving vise. A brief impression of his clothing pulsed in the heat-waves that rose about her: white suit and black tie, and a large felt hat such as Frenchmen wore. It was like seeing a familiar ghost in strange attire. She had a vague idea that he looked absurd. For an instant she seemed to drown in his dark gaze, as of old, then the sensation passed, leaving with her the feeling that she had been baptized with the blood of an old wound.

She hoped she would not see Kim Khouan again. Long ago (was it a hundred years?) she had celebrated a phantom wedding with him, and she wanted no touch of reality to draw it out of spectral security.

Sometimes in the shop she had to rip a seam and sew it again; seeing Kim Khouan was like that, a new tear in an old seam. And she had so many things to mend these days. She seemed continually basting her life and Frenchwomen's dresses. Needles and thread; cloth and scissors; and Madame Dessard fuming about with a mouthful of pins. Dull days, opaque.

Her only pleasure was at night. There were so many people astir then. People searching. Like herself. She loved to watch their forms mold patterns against the night. Not only the men's, but the women's as well. Was it wrong to love bodies? she wondered.

The priests said it was…. ("Blessed are the pure in heart; for they shall see God!" intoned the voice behind the curtain whenever she went to confession. "Bless me, Father, for I have sinned!" "The Lord be with you. And with thy spirit!" "I confess to Almighty God, to Blessed Mary, ever Virgin …that I have looked on men and wanted them, not in an evil way, but wanted them close…." "Be calm and pray for strength, my child….") But that was the trouble with holy men, they seemed unconscious of the beautiful importance of bodies…. Sweet smoke of censers, sweet musk of bodies…. Bodies so pliant and eager, yearning to one another. Bodies of sailors. Bodies of soldiers. Bodies of young girls calling to sailors and soldiers. Shimmering music that flowed between flesh. Like the poetry that Kim Khouan used to make. Like Justin's poetry. Like the poetry of their bodies, one flushed with gold and the other a rippling pallor. At times she felt like undulant music set to the poetry of moving forms. What was life but an immense desire, an immense yearning interpreted through bodies?

And these girls who nightly walked the Rue Catinat or rode in rickshaws …Yes, she understood…. A certain adventure in meeting strange men, seeing what they would do, what they would say. Undoubtedly these girls felt that, and it made their motives appear less evil and less a matter of necessity.

What was the difference between herself and them, if any? Yes, there was a difference, a very subtle difference. "… a woman who is beautiful and clever enough to choose her temporary husbands …and last, the stupid little creature who sells herself indiscriminately.…" Clever Nanette—devilishly clever. But she, Thi-Linh, was not hunting for this man with the white face for any definite reason; he had simply hurtled against her, like a frightened bird, his very air of helplessness mysteriously commanding her to find him.

Long ago at Stung Treng Father Mehry had told her a story of a woman who washed a man's feet in ointment and wiped them with her hair. Women, she thought, were always waiting to minister to men in just such a manner, a certain joy in the humility. Perhaps she was hunting for this man simply to wash his feet in pity.…

Often she hovered about the street where she had seen him. She had learned that the house was kept by a Chinaman, and Frenchmen came there sometimes for a pipe.

She knew it was useless to inquire of the proprietor, for he would disclaim any knowledge.

One night her quest led her to the gardens behind the Governor's palace. An Annamite youth slouched on the other end of the bench where she sat. Through the park, scattered lamps drowsed in the warm, sweet air, with a vortex of insects circling under each. A few women circled under them, too; women suddenly attentive when the sound of rickshaw wheels ground the silence.

She felt the young Annamite looking at her from under his broad French hat. Presently he said:

"You do not live in Saigon."

She regarded him suspiciously. "Why?"

A dim impression of a shrug. "If you were an old one," he told her insolently, "you would know that too many come here." Then he added: "I don't often—most of the time along the quays. …"

Previous to that the bruised earth-smell that rose from the damp grass had made her want to stretch and exult in her young body. Now, in an instant, she had grown old and wise, with something sick in the pit of her. She understood....

She studied the boy with contempt; the instinct of rivalry disguised.

He was a slim-loined fellow, clad in loose white trousers and only a coat, with his sandaled feet drawn up under him and clasped in encircling arms.

A pity for his youth crept through her resentment.

He drew out cigarettes and offered her one. She refused; he lighted his with lithe, swift movements, tossing the match deliberately into the sweet-smelling grass.

Thi-Linh considered him gravely now, caught in a curiosity that was half fear. "Do you know many of the French officers?" she forced herself to ask.

He nodded in a drift of smoke. "Many."

Suddenly she was angry; the curiosity had become all fear. "Do you know one—I don't know his name—with black hair and a very white face—who sometimes smokes opium at the little house on the Rue Ormay?"

He looked at her intently for a moment. "No," he said. Then: "Why do you want to know?"

Something forced her to go on although she felt vaguely ashamed. "I want to know—his name."

"Why?"

Thi-Linh did not answer. The boy was still studying her.

"You have seen him—you like him?" he guessed.

Finally she answered, "Yes."

He laughed. "Perhaps I might find him for you." She did not speak and he fell silent. "He is handsome, you say?" he interrogated after a moment. He moved closer. In the dimness his face looked extremely pale; she realized it was powder. "Describe him again," he said.

She told him reluctantly of the figure in the doorway, wondering why she did. The boy nodded.

"Come back tomorrow night about this time," he enjoined. "Maybe...."

Thi-Linh rose. Suddenly she wanted to hurry away, for she felt that she had profaned a secret.

"Don't forget—tomorrow night," he called after her.

She returned the next night and waited for more than an hour. Of course he did not come; she was a fool to have believed he would come.

The experience left her feeling soiled. What was the use of waiting? All this searching in the night through streets and parks was becoming sordid. In some inexplicable way it seemed as though she were prostituting herself. Before, she had moved through the days and nights with destination, in the midst of life, but remote, untouched. Now her immunity seemed perforated. To her, virtue was not in loin but in purity of purpose. If that purpose was threatened, then what? ...("Blessed are the pure in heart...." droned the voice in the box every time she went to confession. "Bless me, Father, for I have sinned—or have I sinned? ... Can a woman be a prostitute without giving herself actually, but simply moving in the midst of people and feeling their desires? And wanting someone terrifically—not his body—but him—and searching through evil for it?" "Be calm and pray for strength, my child...." Words that explained nothing....) And each evening the girls on the Rue Catinat; the painted boys. The cool smells of wine; the lights; and the flutter of bodies against them. Hearts beating, eyelids beating; people themselves beating; beating softly with the rhythmic darkness....

And then that night on the Rue Paul Blanchy. She was wandering aimlessly and she had dropped down upon the curbing, tired and hot. A rickshaw stopped by a lane; in it a fat woman who stooped and put on her shoes, and then got out. In the light from a distant street-lamp the coolie's shoulders gleamed with thick strength. A white hand hovered for a moment on those gleams.... After Madame Dessard had hurried into the lane and the coolie went springing off down the street, all muscle and shimmer, Thi-Linh felt nauseated.... Son and husband in a single blaze; now the lonely nights of riding, sitting at a table over empty bottles. Madame Dessard who never had a Frenchman.... White hand hovering on a gleam of shoulders.... Thi-Linh seemed filled with an accumulation of lust.

Perhaps Nanette's way was the best. Nanette had lost no time. Through a friend she had heard of a lieutenant who desired companionship. For three weeks now she had been living with him in a house on the Rue Paul Blanchy; happily, Nanette said. She came often to see Thi-Linh.

Staying with the Tonkinese family was getting on Thi-Linh's nerves. She did not like to see the stains of betel-juice all over the floor; and living with Justin had spoiled her for native food and sleeping on a mat. And the crying children! The insects in the unscreened house! The smells from the street!

Then came the letter from her mother telling of Justin's death. In her little trunk was a copy of *"Une Fille d'Annam,"* wrapped in an old khaki shirt that she had taken when she left. She did not cry, but she got out the book and her fingers caressed the pages, and then she held the old shirt close, breathing deep the faint smell of his sweat that still clung to it....

Wedded to a phantom of Kim Khouan, loving the memory of Justin, seeking a nameless white face. Fealty to each. Could it be, she wondered, that there were some women who temperamentally were the perpetual brides of many?

So why wait? If she waited too long she would be soiled.

At the docks were ships, and in them swarthy beautiful men from Europe or great blond men from a colder hemisphere.

Indeed, why wait?

Scissors cutting cloth, and the flash of needles. Bombay men unfurling silks. Madame Dessard thumping women with a thimble, and complaining that her feet swelled; Madame Dessard who never had a Frenchman. And then night. Roads cutting the dusk, and the flash of lamps. Girls unfurling bodies. Darkness thumping the city with its rhythm, and white men complaining that the heat made their desires swell; white men who wanted wives. Rip and sew; rip and sew. Tedious garments of day and night.

Thi-Linh felt that she was being sewn into a bag that was suffocating her.

And then one night, riding past the hot brilliance of one of the hotels, she saw a familiar white profile against the blur of lamps and faces.

For a moment a hand seemed to hold back her heart-beat.

She stopped the rickshaw at the corner, and standing on the opposite side of the street by a stall where a Chetti sold cigarettes, she gazed at the white face which alone seemed stationary in all that quiver of lights and people.

An inclosing-rail shut in the café proper; below it, on the sidewalk, were other tables, all filled. At one of them he sat in company with two other officers. She could make out the insignia of captain. There was a frail slimness about him that hurt her; and when he smiled, as he did often, the insolence of that expression seemed to mock his own physical weakness. Slender legs crossed and uncrossed under the table. He smoked incessantly, clouding his sharp profile and sheening black hair. When he was not smoking he was drinking. He seemed afraid—afraid to relax.

Thi-Linh understood. He had been ill. For a moment she suffered acutely at the thought of that white body hot with fever.

Back and forth she walked. The Indian in the cigarette stall smiled impudently. This waiting wrenched her dignity. But it would be over soon, she told herself triumphantly.

It was late when the two officers at his table rose to go, and she was limp from standing so long. All three shook hands, then he moved indecisively toward the corner. Instantly a group of rickshaw men, squatting in the shafts in the broad plaza, rushed at him.

Quickly Thi-Linh signaled a coolie.

He had got into a rickshaw and was turning into the narrow street that ran between the hotel and the opera-house.

As she jolted along after him, cold at her fingertips, a lurking form parted from the gloom of the theater and broke into a swift run in front of her, following the other rickshaw. There was something reminiscent in the lithe frailty of that runner. Suddenly she knew.

She kicked the coolie in the back, urging him faster.

The officer's rickshaw had turned into the Rue Paul Blanchy, and the running figure took refuge in the darkness of the sidewalk, following almost parallel with the Frenchman. How could she stop him without attracting the man in the rickshaw? He must not meet her on the streets, this captain.

The runner turned a pale oval over his shoulder. Evidently he saw her, perhaps recognized her, for he faltered.

Quickly Thi-Linh directed her coolie to the curb; instructed him to wait. Springing out, she ran toward the boy who, after a momentary pause, darttd across the street and into an intersecting thoroughfare.

The Frenchman's rickshaw rattled on up the Rue Paul Blanchy.

Thi-Linh followed the boy. He slackened his pace, and then he halted and turned to face her defiantly. She stopped, breathless. He was dressed the same as that night in the park.

"Well?" he demanded, but there was fear in his bravado.

Thi-Linh forced herself to be cool. "What is his name?"

The boy hesitated. "I was going to find you and tell you," he muttered, his voice jerking for want of breath. "But he has been sick, and—"

"A lie," she interposed quietly. "What is his name?"

Again the boy hesitated. "Lehrisson—Captain Paul Lehrisson."

For a moment she wondered whether she should strike him or not; then she drew a few coins from the pocket of her tunic, flung them at him, and walked back toward the Rue Paul Blanchy.

Once more, she felt, the events of her life marched with destination.

3

It had all come about so simply since that night of waiting outside the hotel. In retrospect, only one incident seemed offensive to her; that was when she went to the haughty creature who had brought the two non-commissioned officers, and bribed her heavily to approach Captain Lehrisson. Captain Lehrisson came. "What is your name?" he had asked; and when she replied he murmured, "Marie Linh—mmm—I like it." And his smile seemed to add, "You are the one I have been looking for." How frail he looked, standing there that afternoon in the sunlight, with a terrific glow of restlessness seeming visible under his almost transparent skin!

Two days later she went to live in his house.

This house was tawny-yellow and tiled like most of the houses in Saigon, with the same irregular scallops of green mold spreading upward from its base. The garden was wildly overgrown. Traveler-palms leaned on the warm air above turbulent growths torn by bristling agaves and other thorny-leaved plants. This same neglect was visible within, as though the house as well as the garden shared the luxuriant disorder of its master.

Unlike Justin, there was nothing enigmatic about Paul. Very soon she learned that he liked to believe himself master of all that surrounded him. But in this he did not differ from most men, except that in him the trait was peculiarly apparent.

He had an air of experience that pleased her. Life had used him, and in using him had traded a sophisticated grace for the freshness of youth. Used. That was it. Paul looked used. But he did not have an appearance of dissipation. "Asceticism," he remarked to her once with that charming smile of his, "is profligacy of restraint." Men like Paul rarely looked dissipated; they believed too thoroughly in their philosophy of voluptuousness ever to admit that doubt which' reflects excess in the physiognomy.

He could not give her the allowance that Justin had given her, and often he complained about the small pay of a captain. Whenever he talked of money he was extremely irritable. Thi-Linh wanted to buy

French clothes, but he said she looked better in Annamite dress; which she suspected was his way of telling her he could not afford it. She was disappointed. Yet it did not affect her feeling toward Paul. He was, she realized, the type to which women give instinctively, expecting little in return.

Very quickly she learned the routine of his habits. She had his uniform ready every morning when he rose. Most Frenchmen, she had heard, took their baths cold; Paul liked his water tepid. He drank a cocktail before *dejeuner* and brandy-soda afterward. He was very nervous in the heat of the day, and when his house-boy did not obey quickly or made some mistake, he kicked him. With nightfall a certain calm seemed to stroke his tortured restlessness. Immediately after dinner (he ate very little) she prepared his opium-pipe. Usually he took four, sometimes six. He smoked on a great pile of pillows in the living room, his eyes heavy with a drowsy sweetness. He looked like a little boy lying there, so white against the black pillows. Almost every night he went out with his friends. What they did she did not know, nor did she ask.

Poor Paul! His body was an instrument attuned to emotions at times too violent for him to sustain. Moods traveled over him with the swiftness of electricity, fusing him with brief exultation or despair, and leaving him blasted, like a dead circuit. Generally he was so careless and laughing—and uncertain. Then, suddenly, a dazed introspection would cloud his eyes, as though he saw things that puzzled and depressed him. Frenchmen, she had learned, liked to think about what they called "Life." Usually this was not an entirely pleasant occupation. Evidently that was what Paul was thinking about when that introspective look came into his eyes.

He was very jealous. When she told him about Justin he looked extremely angry and sulked until the next day. She asked him nothing about himself; it was not wise to ask men about themselves. Not that it would have mattered what he told her. Women would always call Paul's sins indiscretions, and even the greatest offense to the vanity, infidelity, would be forgiven him because of his boyish laugh. Men who laughed like Paul, she realized, would always be the sons of their wives and mistresses.

There was a piano in the house. He swore at it and the climate every time he touched it. But Thi-Linh, who enjoyed the metallic vibrance of Annamite orchestras, thought its music beautiful. Weeks would pass when he did not play; then he would sit down, browse over the discolored keys and break into music that pounded the air into fury. When Paul played, all that sultry discontent seemed to rush out of his fingers into the piano and leave him exhausted but happy.

At times, particularly after he had been smoking opium, he would drop down beside her and press his face close to her, holding her tight in a shuddering ecstasy of helplessness. Often when he came in late he would wake her, as though there was something reassuring in the sight of her eyes upon him.

There were many books in the house, but Paul rarely took them off their shelves. Thi-Linh, however, read most of the day. Once she was indiscreet enough to show Paul her copy of *"Une Fille d'Annam,"* and he threw it out of the window. Thereafter she locked it in her trunk.

She decided that her position as *congai* of a captain merited a change in her appearance. She had always worn her hair parted and pulled straight over her ears, with a knot at the back. But now she arranged it *"a la Tonkinoise,"* twisted into a single strand and drawn through a black silk sheath wrapped about her head turban-wise.

"You look like the women on the piaster notes," said Nanette when she saw this change of coiffure.

She saw Nanette often. Frequently in the late afternoon they would hire a carriage and ride along the Rue Catinat to the quays and return by the Botanical Gardens. This was the usual route taken by social Saigon after a hot day. Those rides seemed to bring Thi-Linh closer to that uniformed, gaily dressed world which, after nightfall, danced and sat in the open-air cafés.

The passing carriages were occupied by Frenchwomen who stared contemptuously; native nurses pulling at the clothes of sallow little boys and girls who climbed all over the cushioned seats; and officials, resplendent in white twill and gold braid, seated beside their wives.

The sight of all those Frenchwomen, fashionably dressed and riding along with conscious superiority, made Thi-Linh resentful and dissatisfied. Beneath that surface envy was a calm conviction of equality—perhaps more than that—together with a spiteful exultation in the knowledge that many Frenchmen admitted, of course only among themselves, the ascendant virtues of native women.

But her delight in those rides was not in the fact that she mingled superficially with Frenchwomen, returning disdain for disdain, but in-the streets, rinsed in shade and thick with the treacle of voices. At that hour people, no longer contracted with heat, seemed to release an almost perceptible fragrance, like flowers that unseal at dusk. It was then, in the midst of people, that the warm hands of life slipped into her and stroked her softly. She, too, seemed to give out an attar. At times it was almost terrifying, this sense of giving out. With a feeling of physical anguish she seemed to yearn toward those figures eddying away in the dusk.

One afternoon Nanette appeared in a soft pink frock; high-heeled French slippers glimmered on her restless feet; and her large hat had roses on it. Thi-Linh thought she looked like a Frenchwoman drowned in sunburn and then powdered white.

"Why doesn't Paul buy you clothes like this?" Nanette asked.

"He thinks I look better in Annamite dress," Thi-Linh lied.

Nanette surveyed her critically, then said, a shade too sweetly, "Perhaps you do, my infant."

That night Thi-Linh asked Paul again if he would not get her a European dress. For an instant he looked annoyed, then smiled and said he was in debt that month, but next month she could buy whatever she wanted. She knew next month he would still be in debt. But she said nothing. In a little box in her room were a few piasters she had saved; she would add to them, and in a few months, perhaps, she could get a dress like Nanette's.

The rainy season had come, and Paul spent most of his evenings at home. Or, after dark, they would get a carriage and ride. But she preferred the nights in the house: rain sounding light hoofs upon the roof; through the windows, lightning throbbing down a dark pulse of the sky; and the faint smell of opium and pomade that hung about Paul. He seemed less discontented those nights. Sometimes he played for her, not the savage music of his black moods, but little French songs that bantered with the silence and left haunting smiles in their wake. In turn, she played the guitar for him.

One night after she had sung a Cambodian chanson he lay on the pile of cushions gazing at her thoughtfully for a long while.

"Forget this affair, oh, my friend," *the words ran;* "it is but a little flutter of my heart…"

Finally he said: "Wise counsel."

And a dart of dread stung her as, when living with Justin, she had seen that distant, dreaming look in his eyes.

"How do your people learn so much wisdom, Marie?" he asked. Then as an afterthought he added inconsiderately, "But I forget you have French blood."

His thoughtful mood continued. *"It is but a little flutter of my heart'"* he quoted. "But isn't all love that?"

"The love of Frenchmen?" she could not help saying.

He paid no attention to the question. "You native women are so sensible about the whole thing," he went on. "French women haven't learned to believe in inevitability. We men come and go, marry and leave, and you women continue as though nothing had happened."

How little he knew! So arrogantly blind. But one thing he had said was true. Belief in inevitability.

His eyes focused directly upon her.

"You, Marie, you have a secret that I doubt if you recognize." He smiled, a little bitterly. "I envy you it. I don't believe there is a thing you do that you think is wrong. Is there?"

"But what do I do that *is* wrong?" she asked.

He shrugged. "The Church requires a wedding...." Then he smiled again. "But don't try to understand. You have it, this secret; don't spoil it. Listen, Marie,"—he bent forward—"when you hear people say that a certain individual has no conscience don't believe them; what they really mean is that that individual doesn't believe in evil."

She had never heard him talk in this manner before; it surprised and puzzled her.

He became silent, staring into distance beyond her. Then he said:

"You people of the East have something ...something that makes living easier. What is it?"

"Years," she answered involuntarily, wondering why she said it and what it meant.

Suddenly she had a feeling of mysterious expansion and dilution into air. The poignant swell of her seemed to mount the night, circling in widening ripples, until she felt that she enclosed the entire world in the womb of her.

Paul got up and went to the piano, and a violent shattering of chords splintered against the silence, as though he were flinging something impotent and furious out of himself into the mystery of this country that to him was alien and a land of exile.

Poor Paul! A dweller in three worlds.... The brooding world of his discontent; the world in which he lived with her; and that world in which he mingled with official and social Saigon.

It was the last sphere that troubled her. She was mistress in the world where he and she dwelt together, and she could even penetrate that lower darkness into which his inflammable temperament plunged him at intervals. But the other was forbidden. She saw it as though looking at some exotic form of life enacted noiselessly behind a glass pane; a life in which Paul participated, returning to her with rumors of what those soundlessly moving figures said and did. Often, stifled with helplessness, something seemed to cry out down in the silence of her. Just to wear French clothes and sit with Paul at one of those tables in the sidewalk cafés! And then she would grow calm, reassured by the feeling of destination that traveled with her. I shall do it, she thought, perhaps not with him but with another.

After the rains Paul spent much of his time in that world. Duties at the barracks. Tea at the home of some official's wife. Evenings in the cafés. Weekend parties at Cap St. Jacques. When he returned to her (like a man returning from a long journey, she thought) she would have to cool his restlessness. He complained about money. Yet he did not try to save. He took ten, often fifteen pipes of opium a day. There was something stark about him; his vitality crackled from day to day, like a bare live wire snapping with high tension.

Finally he came down with fever. For two weeks she nursed him while he swore at the climate, the country, and at her. But always after he was irritable he would moisten her hands with tears; those cool hands that seemed to lift the burn from his forehead. When he clung like that, so tragically, so repentant, she had a feeling reminiscent of those days just before little Justin was born.

The fever passed. During his convalescence he was very gentle. It was as though the sickness had softened his disposition. How white and used he looked, lying there against the white pillows, with his black hair and eyes seeming the only features that lifted one pallor from the other! He laughed much during his convalescence; that laugh which would always make him the son of his women.

4

Saigon moved to a military cadence that vaguely excited Thi-Linh.

Many barracks faced the shaded streets. At certain hours sentinels marched in front of them, and at all times brown troops lounged and chattered within, visible through open doors and windows. In front of the Marine Barracks, on the Quay Francis Gamier, sailors slouched or drilled until at night a bugle sent them to their bunks.

Through the day officers could be seen moving languidly about the Government buildings; very official-looking men in khaki uniforms, with black braid and gold on their collars, and white helmets. At night they did not look so official. Many of them wore white then, and rode through the streets in rickshaws or sat in the cafés, smoking and drinking.

Sometimes they were very ribald, these officers. Usually that was when a number gathered about a table in the Hotel de la Rotonde, and shouted mad songs over glasses that were filled and refilled. The French were very noisy about their singing, Thi-Linh thought.

Whenever a battleship was in, the quays were alive with the sensual stirrings of sailors ashore. At night, the port-holes were gongs that sounded the throbbing of bands playing for officers and Frenchwomen. Thi-Linh often passed these ships while soirees were pulsing against their steel flanks, and it always made her unhappy. It would be pleasant to know how to dance, and to swirl about in the arms of a young naval officer. Something forbidden and sweet about those gray-dark battleships.

Frequently, after sunset, the lamp-hung streets rippled with the cries of bugles.

On certain days files of rifles flashed a challenge to the sun in the great square behind the cathedral. Generally that was to celebrate the visit of some general or official. Long lines of helmeted shadows lay slanting on the ground, to jerk in unison as barrels resounded with the thud of brown hands and butts crashed to earth.

But the gayest day of all came in July when the French celebrated the fall of an old prison in Paris. On this day flags unfurled in the Rue Catinat, and the burning pavements echoed the rhythmic steps of sweaty columns. That review surpassed any other. *Monsieur le Gouverneur* was there, with his staff; and crowds of civilians. A serried panorama of khaki, creased with the glint of rifles, formed a background for sabers that suddenly became whirring flames; and white-mustached generals pinned decorations upon officers and kissed them. Always the brazen flood of "La Marseillaise" drenched those scenes.

Thi-Linh came to know quite a few officers. Paul had many friends, and sometimes he invited several to dine at the house. She always sat at the table with them, and she enjoyed it; for the conversation was very gay, and there was much wine. These officers seemed pleased, and a bit surprised, when she could discuss recent novels from France and affairs of the day. She observed, after a while, a certain tolerant respect in their attitudes. When she passed one of them in the street he would touch his helmet smilingly and say, *"Bon jour, Madame Marie!"*

When these officers came to dine she put on her best tunic, and Paul seemed quite proud of her. It was an advance, she told herself, to have these men acknowledge her intelligence; and it was something that Nanette, with all her French dresses, could not boast of.

Several times Paul's colonel dined with them. Whenever he came he was the only guest. He was such a fatherly-looking man, with soft silver hair and the sheen of powder on his reddish face, as though he had shaved only a few minutes before. She did not object when he tilted her chin and told her she was a lovely little creature. So fatherly.... He seemed very fond of Paul. He had, she learned, known his mother.

Once he talked to her quite seriously about Paul while he was out of the room. He asked her if Paul was kind to her and if she did not think "the climate was getting him," as he put it. So kind, this colonel! A guardian air over Paul. Even over her. There were Frenchmen like that. Usually they were old.

"Perhaps," he said one night jocularly, "someday Paul may be a major. How would you like that, Marie?"

She did not know how she would like that. But she smiled at the colonel. With higher rank came higher aspirations. Perhaps a French wife. But these thoughts did not make her painfully uneasy, as they would have done while she was living with Justin. She was surer of herself now. A greater belief in—in inevitability.

The colonel's wife was in France. But she was coming out to join him when the cooler season started. There would be no guardian air about her. She was probably very fat and powdered, and dressed in silk that rustled too much. Thi-Linh knew the type. Always perspiring under their powder, which made them look a little untidy. They invariably talked very loudly, these women; and they called Indo-China "exile." Although they wore no insignia, they always commanded the regiment. Sometimes they had affairs with younger officers.... Perhaps the colonel would be sorry when the cooler weather began.

Nanette came to call often, and her visits left Thi-Linh vaguely dissatisfied. She never lost an opportunity to tell what her lieutenant had given her. Thi-Linh no longer envied Nanette her French manner, for she knew she had that air herself. Moreover, she was aware that she had a dignity that Nanette could never acquire. But she did envy her the clothes she wore. It was very strange, Thi-Linh reflected, that women whose intelligence commanded the respect of men were never indulged as much as women who were very superficial.

She supposed it was because men thought they were too sensible to want much.

One day Nanette brought the news that Kim Khouan had a daughter. "I met his wife's sister on the street," she announced, "you know that stupid creature, and she told me."

Thi-Linh's heart always felt rimmed with a little chill when she heard of Kim Khouan. Every week or so after that first encounter she had passed him on the street, and each time a dark gush seemed to well up and leave her trembling inside for several hours. He never spoke, but the anguished recognition in his eyes smote harder than words. She always affected a distant smile. Lately she had perfected that smile.

"Moreover," Nanette went on, "Kim Khouan does not work in the bank any longer."

Thi-Linh knew that she was trying to make her unhappy. She had never told Nanette that Justin was Kim Khouan's son, but she was convinced that she knew. Women like Nanette had a way of knowing things.

"He was very inefficient," Nanette continued deliberately. "So he was dismissed. Now he is in the *Tirailleurs Annamites*."

Kim Khouan in a uniform! Something in that picture caused a warmth to rush over Thi-Linh. Brown body molding into brown cloth; the flex and sway of him as he carried a rifle. Kim Khouan moving to the sound of bugle and drum; pacing up and down in front of the barracks; or lounging inside with other soldiers.

"His father knew some official," Nanette amplified, "so he was made a *doi* in the army. And he doesn't have to drill very much because he does clerical work at headquarters." She laughed. "He always did get out of things easily," she said.

Suddenly Thi-Linh was possessed of a fierce desire to see her son. And Mama Thi-Bao. She would ask Paul if she could visit them. Of course he would complain about the money.

But to her surprise Paul did not complain about the money when she asked if she could go to Stung Treng.

"Next month," he said, "you may go."

Paul had changed lately. It was not often now that he struck the piano into the mad crescendos of his restlessness. All the hot chaos of him seemed submerged in a hazy contentment. He was like a man dreaming behind a fog, satisfied to view the world thus obscurely because life was robbed of its jagged corners.

In trying to understand this change, it occurred to her that it might be the result of his increasing habit of opium smoking. If it was, then she could see no wrong in it. Opium did not hurt men—unless they took too much. Many Annamites used it as Frenchmen smoked cigarettes; the King of Cambodia, she had heard, took forty pipes a day, and he had attained a venerable age.

One evening Paul came in very disturbed. In Europe, he told her, an Austrian archduke had been assassinated.

And now Saigon moved to a military cadence that mounted like savage drums.

France at war—France at war. Words spun like knives in the hands of experts. So much talk about France, the Mother, and Indo-China, her adopted child. It was as if the engraving on the piaster notes had come to life: France, the Protectress, embodied in a big-jointed woman wearing a cap, with her arms affectionately about an Annamite girl and boy.

Now when the files of rifles flashed a challenge in the great square behind the cathedral a. blue intensity seemed to leap from barrel to barrel.

*"Allons, enfants de la patrie….*Brazen flood of "La Marseillaise" [20] drenching the Rue Catinat.

Drums laughed frenziedly in the tamarind-lined streets. Streets that were like white veins flung out by the sun to plunge its fury deeper into earth. Streets striped with marching figures. Figures that sang lustily.

"Le jour de gloire est arrivé …contre nous de la tyrannie…."

Steel flanks quivered against the Quay Francis Garnier, like the flanks of runners before a signal. And within those flanks, down in the groin of them, men talked, talked, talked, until at night the lighted portholes beat like gongs.

"L'étendard sanglant est levé…."

Tin soldiers were electrified into life in the midst of glare and green-lacquer trees, drilling at toy warfare over ground that raised a film of dust like gunpowder. Dry, parched ground that had felt the pigmy excitement of so many men preparing to fight. Ancient ground that made all this hysteria seem futile and childish.

Now those officers with black braid and gold on their collars hurried about the government buildings. At night when they rode in rickshaws they had a tired, nervous air; and when they gathered around the tables in the hotels their songs clashed like sabers.

"Entendez-vous dans ces campagnes…."

A group of young Annamites, gathered in a back room where words whirled and crashed, were surprised by the gendarmes. All were thrust into prison, and two were shot.

The tricolor waved frantically.

"Mugir ces féroces soldats?…."

In the cathedral priests intoned. "Take this the Body and Blood of Christ…." France recited an echo: "Take this the Body and Blood of France, Annamites, …the sweet sacrament whereby you become Civilized, body and soul…."

---

20 "La Marseillaise" is the French national anthem. Hervey features it several times to illustrate the way French patriotism was promoted in Indochina. See the appendices for the complete lyrics in French and English.

Precious communion of blood. Baptism by fire. The glorious oneness of Republic. The deathless trinity of Liberty, Equality, Fraternity. Brothers white and brown. Comrades in arms. Come and die, Annamites! Wrist to wrist you shall bleed with Frenchmen, until the darkness is purged out of you, and in death your pallor shall be chaste as the fleur-de-lis! Sweet burial that is the birth of brotherhood! Death that is the marriage of races!

Civilization is spinning on a flame. Forget those jests of white men who called you niggers. Forget their bastards who ferment your purity! It is the way of them, to joke like that. This Civilization is yours! It has given you Government and God! So up, Annamites! Tremble with hate for the enemies of France! Fill your bellies with the wine of it! Let your thighs run limp with the venom of it! They will rape your women, they will make armies of your men, they will rob you of your lands! The tablets of your Ancestors and the crests of France are one! Listen to the drums! Beating—beating. Let them fill your veins! Let them swell to the rupture of drums! Let them burst in the splendor of death for freedom! Sing, Annamites, sing! "Madelon!" [21] Red music of marching men. Sing, brothers, sing! All together now, in one voice:

"Aux armes, citoyens! Formes vos bataillons! Marchons, marchons!"

Words like knives in the hands of experts. Thi-Linh felt them thud and quiver about her.

---

21 Composed by Camille Robert in 1914, with lyrics by Louis Bousquet, *La Madelon* or *Quand Madelon* was a well-known French song. In his 1997 book, *The French in Love and War: Popular Culture in the Era of the Two World Wars, 1914-1945*, historian Charles Rearick provides this intriguing background:

"One of the most popular songs of the war was "Quand Madelon," about soldiers flirting with a lovely young waitress in a country tavern. What was distinctive was the song's lack of bawdiness (Madelon does not give her body to any of these men) at a time when many soldier-created songs were full of explicit sexual references and when brothels just behind the front lines were staffed by prostitutes "doing" fifty to sixty men a day. "Quand Madelon" appealed to another side of these men, to their desire to return after the war to a housewife not a harlot, to an old-fashioned "girl" who was virtuous, comforting, and subordinate. Madelon also represented an alternative to the "new women" in Paris who were moving into jobs previously reserved for men and who worried soldiers at the front with their more independent ways. Unlike these women, the super-traditionalist Madelon knew her place. The song also reassured civilians with its image of the *poilu* as a clean-minded *bonhomme* and a ready-to-die patriot rather than a client of prostitutes and a war-sick mutineer."

5

She lived in a tense present. Paul would go now. She had seen it in the haggard expectation that filled his eyes. All that snapping and crackling had gone out of him; he sagged.

One morning when she thought he was at the barracks she found him lying limply on the mound of black pillows in the living-room. As she entered he sat up and smiled in an attempt at casual good humor.

"I am going on a mission to Phnom-Penh," he announced. She breathed a sigh of relief. He noticed it and added: "But I may get orders to leave for France any day."

It was wrenching and cruel to think of Paul in the midst of fighting, the pathetic whiteness of him, the marble smoothness of him blurred by gunpowder, and bayonets and shells darting at the soft moths of his hands, at his eyes and lips. Paul, who laughed like a boy. Whose groping toward her was like the groping of little Justin. Paul, who was so used by life, so sophisticated and helpless.

In that moment she could have opened her veins for him.

"I will be in Phnom-Penh only a few days," he said.

There followed a silence. Suddenly he caught her wrist and drew her down beside him. He had a way of moving one persuasively, and very deftly.

"Marie," he began, "do you want me to go away—to France?"

"Of course not, Paul," she answered solemnly.

"You're a pretty thing, Marie," he said irrelevantly, running his fingers lightly over the bandeau of her hair. "You should go far—farther than I can take you."

"I am contented," she told him. Then she added: "The colonel said you might be a major—some day."

He looked at her sharply as she said that. Then he smiled. "It's the colonel I want to talk to you about."

She waited, but he lay there against her in silence. Presently he disengaged himself and went to the window, Standing, back to her, with the sunlight glowing about him, the whiteness of him thickened into a sharp silhouette.

"Marie," he commenced, turning, "it is possible that I may not be sent to France."

"Yes, Paul?"

"It all depends on the colonel," he announced.

Her mind was whirling like a disk, and her intuition wrote swift sentences upon it. "You think if you speak to him," she said, "or if—"

His expression of surprise relaxed into a smile. "You're a sharp little creature, Marie."

"You want me to ask him?"

He dropped beside her and took her hands. "He likes you," Paul began tentatively. "He might...."

His words seemed to slant against her like cold rain. They made something wrinkle under her flesh. Paul, too, feared for the pathetic whiteness of himself.... Those moths of hands were beating against the thought of battle.... Why, she wondered suddenly, had Paul ever become a soldier? But, looking at the grace of him in that tight uniform, the answer was evident.

"He might be inclined to—well, to do something about it," he finished.

"There will have to be some officers here," he took up quickly. "I could be transferred. I've always managed my men well—they like me—I speak the language. ... Of course I myself couldn't say anything. It would be taken for—cowardice."

Cowardice. She repeated the word to herself. Paul wasn't afraid as most men would be afraid; it wasn't fear of death, it was concern over the pathetic whiteness of himself, the marble smoothness—horror of the destruction of it. Paul exulting in his flesh. Paul desiring to be used by life until he was exhausted. She understood, and it was because she did that his words slanted against her like cold rain.

"You could see him—tomorrow—after I have gone," he suggested. "Then, if he agreed, I could stay here —with you—always—and you would be taken care of—"

It was a little thoughtless of him to put it that way, she reflected. But Paul was thoughtless. Always.

"Will you go, Marie?" he asked.

Something seemed to flicker out of his eyes and cling to her. That look made her forgive him for his tactlessness.

She was always forgiving Paul.

"Will you?" he repeated.

He had told her she would go far—farther than he could take her. Perhaps it was part of that rise to do this for him. Poor Paul! She must preserve the white beauty of him.

The next day she sent a note to the colonel asking when she could see him. He replied immediately by one of his men that she could come to his house just after *dejeuner.*

He received her in a large white hall that glowed with the reflection of sunlight filtering through fiber shades. How fatherly he looked, with that silver hair and the sheen of powder on his reddish face! With that guardian air he motioned her into a chair and sat down behind a polished desk that swam with his reflection.

She began with a little beating in the veins of her neck: of course he knew how she loved Paul—.

He nodded in that fatherly manner.

"Where is Paul?" he demanded suddenly. "Oh, I remember...."

It was dreadful that he might have to go to France, she resumed. Her eyelids were lowered and the little throbs in her throat seemed to run up and melt white against them. With so many officers, she asked, was it necessary for him to go? There would be work to be done in

Indo-China. She knew that often officers were transferred; could not this be done in Paul's case? Perhaps he would be angry with her for asking, but she could not help it.

"You are fond of Paul," she finished. "And Paul is very happy with me. If he goes away...."

The colonel listened attentively, gently tapping the polished table—staring at his own reflection. So kindly. As though he were listening to his own daughter.

"Mmmm," he murmured when she had finished.

Of course Paul did not know she had come, she said.

Of course, he repeated.

In the long silence before he spoke again all the clotted hush seemed to press about her and spread upon her eyelids like those white throbs.

"Mmmm," he murmured again. "This is a serious matter. It could be done, yes ...but ...Well, I shall have to think." He paused. "Perhaps," he began, and cleared his throat; "perhaps we might talk this over more fully—I am very busy now—we might talk it over tonight—if you will come?"

As he looked at her questioningly, with that fatherly air, all those white throbs seemed to merge into one great pulsation that smote her eyes. When the blindness cleared she saw his face—so fatherly. A guardian air. Just as if he were talking to his own daughter.

How absurd to have thought that! Those kindly eyes. Eyes of a father.

She was on her feet.

Yes, she would come.

6

"Bless me, Father, for I have sinned. . .

"The Lord be with you...."

"I confess to Almighty God, and to you, Father, that I have committed a grave offense...."

"The Lord listens to those who sincerely are penitent. . .

"While belonging to one, Father, I have given myself to another. . . ."

"Willingly, my child?"

"Willingly, Father."

"Tell me all, He will hear and condone. . . ."

". . .That is all, Father."

"The Lord is lenient with those heartily sorry for their transgressions. . . . For this sin make this act of contrition. . . ."

"Almighty God, it is most grievous to me that I have offended against Thee. . . ."

"O Lord, have mercy upon this child. . . ."

7

Looking back, it seemed to Thi-Linh there were many things she had always known. The surface incidents of life were surprising, unexpected, but never life itself.

She had known beforehand how it would be when Paul was transferred. Now everything that happened had an air of familiarity; a tiring little air that made her feel very old.

Among those books which filled the shelves of Paul's house and which he never read was one called "Katharsis." She had to reread parts before she understood them. Katharsis—the purging of the heart. It was not like the Nibbana of the Buddhists. Nibbana was the ultimate Nothingness, wherein lay everything, to which the individual contracted as the impurities of pride, jealousy, earthly love—in short, all emotion ebbed from his being. Nibbana was the needle's eye through which the thread of life passed in order to enter permanently into the universal design. But Katharsis was the purifying of the body to live. It was part of this Greek philosophy that one could be cleansed by excess. Experience the purgative of evil. It seemed most logical. To her, there was something pernicious in the ascetic cult that sought Nibbana, that washed the flesh of desire and left it, spiced and in shining death-cloths, to become ashes in an enveloping oneness. To Thi-Linh, Katharsis meant living; Nibbana, dying.

Through her Paul accomplished his Katharsis. Purging his own excesses by strength of another.

From the tempestuous experiences of living, bruised by the impact of their pain and sordidness, he turned to her with perfect assurance. The pole on which he gravitated. She wondered if he knew it; it would hurt his race pride if he did. Yet all his weaknesses, his doubts and vanities dissolved in her. It was her ability to give instinctively, and without words or analysis, that made it possible. He seemed to flow into her and say: "I am cleansed, I am strong." Katharsis in the depthless reservoir of her capacity to enfold.

She did not love Paul as she had loved Kim Khouan, nor as she had loved Justin. Yet she opened her veins for him—which she had not done for either of the others.

Forgiving Paul was a habit—like religion. For a number of years she had gone to confession in the cathedral. It was a ritual behind which lay the Mystery that was God. She knew it was only a ritual, but continued practice had surrounded it with a certain superstition. And to overlook Paul's thoughtlessness and weakness was a ritual that she repeated automatically. Back of it was the Mystery of why she did it, hidden like the priest in the confessional-box.

It was nearly a year since he had gone on the mission to Phnom-Penh. Every day now he sat in a little room that was the antechamber of the Governor's office and interviewed those seeking audience with his Excellency. Or he read and wrote official documents. Or moved quickly at the summons of a bell. He had any number of clerks and orderlies under him. Often he dined with his Excellency. Captain Lehrisson, aide-de-camp of *Monsieur le Gouverneur* de Cochin-Chine. It was a very flattering post. Thi-Linh was proud that he had it; proud with a little tired feeling under her heart.

Saigon only sounded an echo of the hoofs of war now.

Nanette's lieutenant had gone to France. She was living with the Tonkinese family again, restless and dissatisfied. Desirable husbands were scarce. Soon after her lieutenant left she went to Hai Phong with a sea-captain, but in a few weeks she returned, smiling in that sophisticated manner and explaining nothing.

And Kim Khouan had gone. Gone to France. Kim Khouan so brown in his brown uniform. Marching in brown mud now. When Thi-Linh thought of it she too seemed to be marching in mud. Mud that clung and pulled her naked feet back into the softness of it. She had seen pictures of the battlefields ; stretches of mud that oozed even in the photographs. Mud with columns of smoke sliding over it, men and guns sliding over it. Or bare flats of mud in which smoke, men, and guns had been absorbed. The ooze of that mud slunk along her limbs when she looked at those pictures. The mud in which Kim Khouan marched, so brown, and spangled with sweat.

She did not go down to the quay when the *Tirailleurs Annamites* sailed. Once she had seen him marching in the Rue Catinat. That was enough. The slimness of him in all that quiver of brown! Brownness of so many men flowing down the street, flowing across the sea, flowing into the mud. That one time she had seen him, something old and wounded had jumped out of hiding. It had frightened her. She wanted to run and throw herself into the quiver of brown.

So she did not go to the quay, when they sailed. It was enough to sit in the house and think of it. She thought of it all that day. And the next day. And for a week. And then she began to think of it less. Events even the most poignant, she realized, had a way of slinking into the back of the mind and sleeping there until awakened by some familiar association. Now she thought of it only at intervals; when she saw those photographs, photographs that Paul showed her; or when she saw a blur of brown troops.

Only an echo of the hoofs now....

Of course, most of the Frenchmen and certain groups of natives were always ready to shout "Madelon" or "La Marseillaise" upon the slightest excuse. Frequently a few officers would sit around a table in one of the cafés, late at night, and sing patriotic airs to the clink of glasses.

Whenever there was a great French victory Saigon whirled like the disk of a gramophone; and, like a gramophone, it soon unwound, to await another turn of the handle.

Two or three times the tune was frenzy when a rumor stole about that a hostile gunboat had been sighted off the coast.

Once a bored half-caste, coming in from a long voyage in a junk, told a Madrassee money-changer that he had seen the entire German fleet near Poulo Condor[22]; and as a consequence two staff officers forgot a dinner engagement with the Governor and were promptly scheduled to be sent to France at the first opportunity.

Only an echo now.…

After all, one cannot live on the other side of the world from a conflict and sustain continuous enthusiasm for it. Certainly not when that place happens to be so near the equator. Too much sun. Sun that makes the body uncurl like a tea-leaf and float in a limp sprawl. The slaughter of ten thousand men becomes simply the name of a town. Unless one happened to know someone who was killed or wounded. Or unless one had lived in that town or visited it. Of course, if most of those ten thousand were enemy men then it made the blood run with pride. Pride in the strength and skill of a nation that could kill so many of the enemy. At least, that was how Thi-Linh understood it from Paul.

Naturally, there was much talk about "the natives." Talk in offices where punkahs swayed; over aperitifs in the hotels. Wondering what they would do. If they would do anything. Surely, spoke the Government through several thousand Frenchmen—who if without mistresses at least had servants—surely the Annamites, the Cochin-Chinese, the Cambodians, the Laotians, and the Tonkinese remembered those tortured centuries before France came to put an end

---

22 Côn Son Island — known by its Malay name of Poulo Condor in French colonial times—is the largest island of the Côn Đảo archipelago, directly south of Saigon off the coast of southern Vietnam.

to internal trouble and bring Civilization. And, remembering them, they would ignore the treacherous ripples generated by the enemy. France, the Protectress, was at war; already some of her tawny wards were fighting, but to be victorious she also had to have the support of those in the colony. She had faith in them, indeed such faith that an increased gendarmerie and *Service Sûreté* continually watched over them to protect the loyal and punish those insolent rogues who forgot their debt to France.

All this talk vaguely amused Thi-Linh. France worrying about her colony. It seemed a bit ridiculous, a bit undignified. She knew that Paul used her to feel the pulse of the natives, just as other Frenchmen used their women. He encouraged her to go among "her people," as he put it, and listen for incendiary talk. She did not deliberately listen, but now and then she heard a little—trickles that came through Nanette or some other gossiping tongue. Of course, the brooding of the older people, they who remembered when rifles were stacked in the temples, smoldered and sometimes broke into inflamed words. But they were too old to be active; and the younger ones, whom their talk might have affected, were too lazy, and they wore French clothes. Nanette, whatever she thought, was too discreet to say much.

Thi-Linh had formed very definite ideas. She had read and talked with enough people to know that colonization was not peculiar to the French alone, and if France did not have a protectorate over Indo-China, some other nation would. The French as masters were as good as most, she supposed, and better than many. Of course some of their pretensions were absurd. But so were the pretensions of all white men.

She did not hate white men, or even dislike them—except in individual cases. Perhaps it was her French blood. But she felt that it was something subtler than that. She was sorry for them; sorry for their absurd pretensions; sorry for the dark people who were the butt of these pretensions. Pity—pity with a certain irony. And desire, almost excruciating at times, to draw them all to her, white and dark alike, and give something out of herself. They would use her and leave her, both white and dark, but that realization in no wise lessened her desire to give. Understanding all this was part of the ancient wisdom with which she seemed to have been born.

She continued to read a great deal. Books that made her think much of what Justin had said about souls. Books that wistfully brought back the poetry of her early love for Kim Khouan. Books that were like Paul, hot and restless, and left her pitying the men who wrote them. And she learned much through talk. Talk with Paul; with friends of Paul. All these friends were men; she had no contact with French women. These women dwelt on the remote outskirts of her life. Only rumors of them came to her. One curious trait she had observed was that they never talked to native women without raising their voices. And they always wore a look of contempt or condescension which she had begun to suspect was fear disguised.

Paul spent considerable time with these French women. "Stupid little sparrows," he called them. Yet once when she ventured an uncomplimentary opinion he became very angry. Thi-Linh knew that most of them were aware he was living with her. "Keeping a half-caste," was how they spoke of it. They hated and envied her, undoubtedly; and she was sure they quarreled with Paul about her in that tolerant half playful manner women had when annoyed with men they desired. These women who never shared his black moods and his weakness! Who never took his tears to their bosoms! Who never opened their veins for him! Often the thought of them made her furious, but just as often she pitied them. Stupid little sparrows. Trying to rob her nest.

The Paul who went to tea with them, or dinner, and who sat through the day in the antechamber of the Governor's office was a different Paul when he was in his house. Then he was the Paul who had called to her soundlessly from that dark street; whose feet she washed in ointment and wiped with her hair; who was in turn thoughtless and tender, brutal and helpless. He was the Paul who purged himself through her.

"What do birth and death matter?" he often said. "It is what lies between that counts."

And so the white current of him flashed through the days and nights, drawing vitality from the very tension at which he lived. It frightened her to think what would happen if he were suddenly denied the stimulation of opium. The curious thing about him was the cleverness with which he used narcotics. Rarely too much; just enough to keep him fusing. Too much would make him dead to the contact of life; and living was too precious for that. It was as though each experience was a fine wine that he held under his tongue for a moment before surrendering it to his fierce craving.

After he had been transferred he was very considerate of her, very thoughtful. He promised that soon she could buy European clothes, and he spent many evenings lounging about the house, playing those bantering little songs or smoking opium. There was something in his attentiveness which gave her the tired feeling under her heart. She felt he was forcing himself to be considerate out of gratitude. He knew what had happened of course. Probably he had known it would happen, even before he went to Phnom-Penh.

The fact that he never asked the colonel to dinner any more proved he knew now, if not then. Considerate. He was deliberately being considerate; and his attitude made her conscious that she had committed a sin for him.

One afternoon he came in very happy.

"Tomorrow," he announced, drawing a crumple of tissue-like piaster notes from his pocket, "you may buy yourself some French clothes."

Her heart jumped, then grew heavy with that tired weight under it.

The feeling was still there when, accompanied by Nanette, she went to a *magasin* on the Rue Catinat and outfitted herself. She also bought some silk at the Bombay store where she had worked, and had Madame Dessard take her measurements for a dress. It rather pleased her vanity to see the Frenchwoman fussing about her, tape-measure in hand and mouth full of pins. Several times Madame Dessard pricked her with a pin—intentionally she was sure.

"You have come up in the world, eh, Marie?" she said with a curious little smile Thi-Linh knew was envy.

Poor Madame Dessard....

I no longer look like the women on the piaster notes, she thought that evening when she put on one of her new dresses.

She remembered what she had thought the first time she had seen Nanette in European clothes: a Frenchwoman drowned in sunburn and powdered white. But her own skin was lighter, the effect different. The image looking back from the mirror had the warmth and glow of old ivory. As she gazed at herself she felt a quick pride in her pallid smoothness, in the straight slimness of a body that wore so well a dress foreign to it.

The smolder of her hair was about her shoulders, black as a night wind in which there were no stars. That was what it needed, a star.

She ran out into the garden, plunging into a blur of flowers, which stroked her like soft hands. She broke off one and stuck it in her hair. Those soft flower-hands held and crushed against her, warm on her throat, on her breasts. For an instant she swayed against them, suffering a sweet torture as she drew their fragrance deep into her. Heavy and sweet; velvet in the night. That was how she felt. Cool plush wrapped around the night, drawing the night into her, letting it swell and whirl within her. Black night in which she glowed like, the flower in her hair.

By the time Paul had come, her mood had passed; that tugging heaviness was under her heart. When he saw her there was a passionate catch in his gaze, as though her loveliness was too much to devour at once. But the persistent heaviness stayed under her heart, even when the sudden impact of his embrace made her senses whir.

That night he took her to the cinema. It was the first time he had gone with her to any public gathering—and he did not look ashamed when the lights flashed on.

It was a night of triumph—cold triumph. A gesture, that was all; a gesture to her pride, to Saigon. She could not feel the emotion her dreams had told her would fuse this moment. Paul was showing off her loveliness. But she could not cast out the suspicion that he also was paying a debt.

Afterward, thinking about it, it did not seem strange that her triumph was lifeless, for there was something familiar about it, as though she had known all along it would be this way when it happened. Why did the events of life seem like simply the substantial confirmation of what she had sensed previously?

Everything familiar, so familiar…. For had not she known before it occurred how Paul's thoughtfulness, his pride in her beauty would fray? She was not surprised when he grew irritable and quarreled with her over such insignificant things as spots of mildew on his uniforms. Nor when he spent fewer evenings with her. Not even when she passed him one night riding with a Frenchwoman whom she could not recognize because they sat so close in the hooded carriage. No; she had known all this would happen. And also that in his moments of weakness he would continue to cling to her. Pouring his weakness into her. Dissolving it in her. Flowing into her and saying: "I am cleansed, I am strong."

Katharsis. Through her for him, and in the excess of her giving, for herself.

8

It seemed to Thi-Linh that there had always been war in Europe, that there always would be. It had entered permanently into the background of her consciousness, brought forth at intervals by talk and reports in the news-journals.

Life seemed filled with desperate repetitions. Food and sleep. Books and the cinema. Household duties. Paul sitting all day in the antechamber of the Governor's office, and prowling about at night. Letters from Mama Thi-Bao telling how her baby was growing. The hot season had come, and each day was a glaring replica of the previous one, the nights woven in a changeless pattern of starry heat.

There was only one change in her immediate sphere. Nanette had a new husband. And he was not French. She was very emphatic about this detail when she brought the news to Thi-Linh. He came from Belgium. "But that is almost France," she added naively. He was very tall and blond, she said, and two fingers of his right hand were missing.

This was why he was not fighting. They had been shot off in Africa. He was quite wealthy. Moreover, he was extremely jealous. When he saw her looking at another man his great blue eyes became little flickering pinpoints. "I call him my white panther," she said in those suave tones in which she sheathed all feeling.

Nanette wore very expensive clothes now. And she had a carriage all her own.

But life continued dull for Thi-Linh. She planned a visit to Stung Treng, but Paul had an attack of malaria and she had to stay with him.

He never complained about money any more. He told her, with a very significant smile, that being on his Excellency's staff had its advantages. He increased her allowance; often he bought her new clothes. But the world seemed motionless and chiseled. She was moving in a corridor lined with bas-reliefs. The dreadful changelessness of things was hardening her, she felt; very soon she herself would become motionless and chiseled.

At times she wished it were possible for her to plunge into that mud of Europe; feel the pull of it, the squirm of it; mud all about her. At least then she would be surrounded by life that moved. Terrible, shattering life, splintering men's bones, feeding their flesh to the earth, making white cups of their empty skulls, filling them with blood. To be in the midst of life again, in the sweat and muscle of life! Anywhere but here where all those familiar faces, limbs, torsos, bodies, everything had the pallor of petrified members glaring under the sun.

9

The *Service Sûreté* had one method of apprehending suspicious characters that had caused Thi-Linh annoyance several times. On certain nights the gendarmerie would fling a net of men about some quarter, and then draw it tight, soundlessly and swiftly. If you happened to be in that net it was most inconvenient, that is if you were unfortunate enough not to be French and without a card of identification.

The Government required this card of identification of all natives or people with native blood, who, officially, were the same as natives. This card stated your name, occupation, age, and other information necessary. The number of this card was registered with the Government; consequently the Government had its finger on those several millions of dark people or half-dark people under its protection. Very thorough.

If it happened, one of these nights when the *Service Sûreté* flung out a net, that you did not possess a card of identification, you were put in jail. If you had simply left it home, then you were released when the card was produced. But if it turned out that you had failed to pay your piasters for an identification card that year, then you contributed a certain sum toward the maintenance of Civilization in Indo-China. In the event that you were unable to pay it, your incarceration was prolonged.

Two or three times Thi-Linh had been caught in this net. The first time she was released when an officer came up and recognized her. After that, when she was better known, she had no difficulty. Nevertheless, it was always a very annoying experience.

One night when she was riding about after the cinema a sudden tension in the quiet, emphasized by the sound of running feet, warned her that again she had blundered into one of these nets. Nothing would happen of course. But she did not enjoy the feeling of hot nausea that traveled over her when anything like this occurred.

A dart of white flickered around the corner ahead. Almost immediately it vanished in a hedge across the street. Following it came a native policeman who also plunged into the foliage. A moment later, as she approached, the uniformed man emerged dragging a figure that jerked and swayed.

The dim greenish lamplight flowing from the opposite side of the street gave those two forms a fluid insubstantiality, like bodies wavering under the sea. Suddenly the dragging figure lurched and broke away.

As Thi-Linh came abreast of them, the figure that had wrenched free lunged out into the street. She had a brief impression of a slim young body and a pale face that rushed at her in the darkness like a blur of phosphorus. But brief as that impression was it sufficed to fling her memory back to a bench in the park, with the same face beside her; only then it had been blenched with powder instead of terror.

The boy was almost at her side, evidently blind to the rickshaw, when she cried out. There was a rattling impact that almost threw her to the pavement, an abrupt sensation of swerving accompanied by a heavy thudding slap. The white face vanished. Only the quick tautening of the coolie's muscles prevented the rickshaw from turning over; with a glance behind, he broke into a run, reaching the corner at breathless speed and whirling her into another street.

Stamped upon her mind was a picture of the policeman bending over the boy with something that he worked like the handle of a pump and that made squashing sounds. It made her weak and ill....

The next day she read in the newspaper that on the previous night a young native who had been bold enough to resist the police and run had died as the result of injuries received when he collided with a rickshaw. As she read it a vision of the scene flared momentarily, seeming to career with the motion of the policeman's arm as he worked that thing up and down upon the prostrate form....

"There is a great deal of dissatisfaction among the natives," Paul remarked when he read it.

10

Often now Thi-Linh saw Nanette riding with her husband, and once they had stopped and talked with her.

He was tall and red with sunburn. All his vitality seemed centered in his sharp blue eyes. Eyes that were steel rivets holding up the immense muscular bulk of his body. He moved with a slowness that those eyes belied; and when he smiled he seemed more blond than ever, as though the expression reflected that brassy alertness hinted in his gaze. He spoke French with a husky heaviness which made it sound foreign. Heavy. That was it, Thi-Linh decided. Something heavy about him. She wondered if those blue rivets of eyes did not grow tired holding up the weight of him. The hand with two fingers missing was vaguely uncanny.

"He thinks you are very pretty," Nanette told her a shade too casually the next time she saw her. "He has asked me to have you over to dinner some night." But she was very indefinite about the latter. Nor was Thi-Linh sorry. She did not think she would like to be near this Belgian, even for a few hours. She remembered too vividly his big fists, on which the large veins stood out with a suggestion of sluggish brutality. The sort of hands that fumbled over one.

Several times after that she saw him with Nanette in the cathedral. When he knelt to pray the blunt strength of him sagged to the floor, with those huge fists, vein-corded, crumpled motionless on the floor at his side. He made her think of a great blond ape. During mass, when long prayers for the soldiers dissolved in swoons of incense, his blue eyes flickered to pinpoints—as Nanette said they did when he saw her looking at other men. Jealous. Jealous of those prayers for soldiers. Thi-Linh could picture the great hulk of him in the mud of Europe, his heaviness smothering men. At such times he seemed grotesque and pathetic. Two missing fingers kept him out of that mud; this blond ape who was jealous of those prayers for soldiers.

One night Thi-Linh passed Madame Dessard in a dim street near the Botanical Gardens. She recognized her by the fact that her feet were crossed above empty slippers. Sitting beside her in the carriage was a man—a white man. The indistinguishable blot of his face startled Thi-Linh. Madame Dessard with a Frenchman! As Thi-Linh stared, Madame Dessard leaned out of the carriage; a moment later a distant laugh sounded down the street. It was a laugh of triumph that seemed to say: "At last I have a Frenchman!"

Some days later Thi-Linh encountered her in front of the Bombay store, and her smile was a reflection of that laugh.

When Nanette visited Thi-Linh next she had an air of suppressed excitement. That Nanette should show even a hint of emotion was extraordinary.

"I am going away, my infant" she announced, trying to be casual. "He is taking me to Europe with him when he goes."

Thi-Linh asked when that would be, and Nanette shrugged. "Sometime soon. Is it not splendid? To Europe, my infant! What do you think of that?"

Thi-Linh thought of it much during the next few days. Nanette going into the midst of life, while she remained in that corridor of bas-reliefs. Perhaps her Belgian, that great blond ape of a man, would go into the mud of Europe to smother men. The brown mud in which Kim Khouan marched. Well, Nanette would always have more than she. But she did not envy her—not with that Belgian.

She told Paul that Nanette was going away. He laughed.

"I doubt it," he said tersely.

A tender night. The stars were soft ashes floating away from the fire of the moon. Paul looked very pliant and boyish reclining in a great chair on the veranda. In the darkness, the scent of flowers was heavy with a damp coolness. She asked him if he would take her riding. For a moment he did not stir, then he shrugged.

They rode along the quays, then back by the Botanical Gardens. Paul leaned against her in silence.

The night was very quiet except for the occasional cry of "Kao!" as some Frenchman called a rickshaw. So silent. The houses, deep in shadow, seemed carved on stone; endless friezes that dripped night. And on the other side of the earth hoofs were beating in the mud.... Thi-Linh let her memory wander among those photographs of the battle-fields. Brown ranks creeping across the mud, and Kim Khouan in the midst of them. Brown ranks which drew her irresistibly, and into which she flung herself, as she had wanted to do that day in the Rue Catinat. Ranks that rippled across the mud in a glide of smoke and reddish flecks which exploded in bursts of blood. It was so real that for a moment she imagined she heard the crackle of gunfire. Suddenly she started.

"Did you hear that?" she asked Paul.

He sat up quickly; he had been asleep. "What?"

"It sounded like guns."

He glanced drowsily at the luminous face of his wrist watch.

"It's over now," he said. "Orders not to say anything about it until afterward. Your friend Nanette and her German lover were arrested this afternoon—and were to be shot tonight. The house was searched the other day. I had my suspicions from the very first …but we had to have evidence.…

11

A year had passed.

Thi-Linh, approaching Stung Treng on the river boat, thought of the night in Saigon when she heard those shots, and it seemed far off, on the other side of a widening gap.

So much had happened since then. So many things that were like spades digging a great trench between her and that night. A trench in which numbers of people were buried.

The war was over now.

The news had come to her with a feeling like the loosening of chains. She would never forget that day in Saigon. Blood-music that streamed out upon the sunlight, upon people; people who drank it greedily. Red wine in white skulls. A great parade bristling in the Rue Catinat. Mass in the cathedral. The glare seemed drunk with a mad tumble of flags and faces. Saigon shuddering in a bath of hysteria, drinking blood from an empty skull.

Nor would she ever forget Paul's face as he came to tell her about it.… White with excitement. Holding out a glass of red wine for her to drink with him.… She dropped the glass and it crashed like chains falling about her feet.…

So long ago—on the other side of a great trench.

Now the green banks of the Me-Kong—Mother Me-Kong at whose breast Indo-China suckled—and Stung Treng ahead. Mama Thi-

Bao, the baby; the house where she had lived with Justin, the pool in the jungle. It was like going back into youth and taking with her the accumulation of wisdom and experience that had come since.

The pattern of Stung Treng on the shore ahead brought a tremble into her throat. She thought she could see the dark pigmy of Mama Thi-Bao at the landing. But there were so many pigmies there she couldn't be sure.

Coming home, coming home. Bringing the gifts of wisdom and experience to her youth.

As the boat jarred against the bank she saw Mama Thi-Bao's face in a crowd of other faces, and a slim little brown body lifted in her arms above all those moving heads and shoulders. Her son. Suddenly she felt dreadfully tired, and her knees seemed empty spools.

12

They had reached the shop—the shop with its streaks of smoke and dust, its border of mold—and Vu-Trong-Khai was grinning at her, and his children, grown almost beyond recognition, were staring wide-eyed. A little crowd had followed them from the landing, discussing her French clothes quite audibly. But all her thoughts were crowded into the brown body held close to her. Little Justin—so big! And wearing black silk trousers, and looking at her in that inquisitive, puzzled way. The luminous darkness of his eyes hurt her. They were like …like Kim Khouan's. Little Justin—six years old! And so awed by this woman in French clothes.

Mama Thi-Bao dropped upon the platform in the rear of the shop in the old, familiar attitude. There was no change in her—except a few glinting streaks in her black hair. Thi-Linh sat beside her, holding little Justin in her lap. Vu-Trong-Khai and the children gathered about; and in the doorway a few curious forms hovered.

Mama Thi-Bao rolled a betel-leaf, dipped it in lime, and then as she chewed asked Thi-Linh how long she was going to stay.

Thi-Linh wished that her stepfather were not there.

"I don't know" she said. Then, after a moment, she added: "I have left Paul, Mama Thi-Bao."

Her mother showed no surprise nor any other emotion. She merely nodded and went on chewing. Vu-Trong-Khai grinned. Little Justin squirmed about and looked at her with dazed questioning in his eyes.

I have left Paul.

How those words brought it all back! That night in the Rue Taberd, the sweating darkness and the crunch of wheels as a hooded carriage drove by.…

"There was a French woman," she said aloud.

A French woman. A French woman who rode in the carriage with her feet crossed above empty shoes; who sat so close to a man in white that the darkness of her dress blended imperceptibly into the pallor of him. A man whose voice drifted to her above the crunch of wheels. She would never forget the sickness of that moment.

"She was old—much older than I," Thi-Linh told Mama Thi-Bao.

For a long while, that night, she had stood there in the Rue Taberd shivering. When finally she moved it was to walk slowly around the cathedral, around and around, until the twin spires seemed to topple against each other. Then she had forced herself to go to the Rue Paul Blanchy and wait near the lane leading to Madame Dessard's house. Finally they came.… After that she went home and waited in the living-room.

It was late when Paul returned. The sight of his white face, so guileless, made her feel as she had felt long ago when Kim Khouan had told her of his betrothal. Blindly she had sunk her nails into Paul's cheek, and then nearly fainted when she saw the blood.

"So—*Madame la Panthère!*" he had said. And she had gone into her room and locked the door.

The recollection of that night was brutally vivid even now. Little Justin slipped out of her lap and stood staring at her.

She went on with her story: "But this woman had a little money.…"

Money. Paul had dared to speak of that the next morning. "Did you think I was able to buy all those clothes for you on a captain's salary?" It was like Paul to say that. So helpless that he seized any weapon. She wondered, thinking about it afterward, how she had restrained herself from walking out of the house then. It was his face that held her. Even as he hurt her cruelly he besought her not to leave him; not in words but in his look. Paul, who was afraid for the soft whiteness of himself.

"I stayed with him for a while after I found out" she said to Mama Thi-Bao, "but when the war was over, I left him.... I—I knew more officers would be coming to Indo-China" she lied.

What humiliation, after that night when she saw Paul with Madame Dessard! Forgiving him, yet feeling contempt for him, and hating herself for the strength that made it possible for her to continue ministering to his weakness. But she stayed. And all because his eyes besought her to help him preserve the soft whiteness of himself.... And then the day when he came with the news that the war was ended; sound of chains falling about her feet. Drinking the blood of freedom while Saigon drank the blood of victory.

"I am going home now," she had told Paul.

He had pretended he thought she meant only for a visit, smiling and telling her, yes, she could go; until the look in her eyes stopped him.

"I suppose you've got all you can out of me," he had flung at her. But as he flung it he knew it was futile and cowardly.

"I am going," she had repeated. He only laughed—laughed to cover his pain.

Oh, the excruciating whiteness of him as he stood there! Something wavered within her. But she had decided. That night in the Rue Taberd she had been freed from Paul, and since then only waiting because his tortured look pleaded with her. Now the war was over, he no longer needed her.

He pretended to read a book in the living-room while she packed all her possessions. She took everything he had given her. Then she sent for coolies to come for her baggage. As she told Paul good-by he smiled. It must have taken all his courage.

"I told you you would go farther than I could ever take you," he had said, still smiling.

And she had hurried out, the whiteness of him like white blood in her eyes.

As Thi-Linh finished her story Mama Thi-Bao merely nodded that meaningless nod of hers. Little Justin had sidled over to her now. Vu-Trong-Khai lighted a cigarette; as he rose he gestured his children aside and clattered into the front of the shop. The children hung about, staring.

Outside the sunlight seemed to catch and intensify the heat in savage waves. Thi-Linh felt it penetrating into the gloom-cool room. Thick smells entered with it. Somewhere in the glaring silence voices sang like beetles. Stung Treng was throbbing in the noon-day with familiar monotony.

With a little sigh Thi-Linh abandoned herself to its inertia.

13

She had expected to slip back into the life of the village and find rest—for a time at least. But the Thi-Linh who as a little girl dreamed in the silence of Stung Treng was not the woman in French clothes who for several years had slept in beds and eaten European food. Stung Treng was lifeless and empty now, and even her memories could not awaken it.

She tried desperately to resurrect the habits of her girlhood. In the late afternoons she walked along the bank of the Me-Kong, but instead of watching the bathers who lay flank to flank with the brown mud, she found herself thinking of the quays of Saigon and the soft rose-bloom that touched them at this hour. And at her approach those bathers slipped into the water, thinking her a Frenchwoman, and then laughed when they saw she was not.

The house where she had lived with Justin was occupied by a Cambodian family. The one time she had seen it, drawn there by memories, two brown women with discolored teeth were talking stridently on the veranda, and pigs wandered in and out of the rooms.

After that, she feared to go to the pool in the jungle. But she did. A tangle of lotuses bled over it in fragrant pain, almost hiding the water. In a tree, a parakeet twittered softly. The silence was unbearable.

Everything had changed, the people included. Once she saw Kim Khouan's father; he looked very old and feeble, walking along with the help of a young Annamite. Monsieur Malardier had been transferred to some town in Laos; in his place was a much younger man, a slender, angular Frenchman with a reddish beard and horn-rimmed spectacles, who always squinted at her through the thick lenses of his glasses and then belatedly touched his helmet with an uncertain air. Father Mehry lay under a cross in the Mission compound. He had been succeeded by a sallow priest with a watery blue gaze who had a distracting habit of wiping the moisture from his eyes during confession.

Only Mama Thi-Bao was the same—and Vu-Trong-Khai. When he smoked opium the air seemed warm with the presence of Paul.

Little Justin had overcome his shyness. But often she saw those luminous-dark eyes upon her with a look half of wonder and half of awe. That gaze was so like Kim Khouan's it always startled her.

There was no one to write her news of Saigon. Nanette, who might have done it, Nanette, her only friend, was buried in the trench that separated her from the past.

Whenever she thought of Nanette a great pity filled her. Poor little creature! A wasp who had stung herself to death. Poor Nanette … and, yes, poor blond ape of a man lying under the soil …poor Justin, likewise in the ground …poor Paul …and Madame Dessard with her swollen feet …painted boy crashing into the wheels of her rickshaw …poor everybody. Herself she did not pity; her acceptance of the inevitable was complete. That, and the richness of experience, seemed all she had gained from those years of contact with the world. But was not that enough?

She read through every newspaper that came with the weekly mails. The familiar names gave her a sensation of pleasure. Madame the wife of the Governor was giving a reception. Major So-and-so transferred. Monsieur Such-and-such going to France. Precious little echoes of Saigon.

The last journal brought the announcement that the *Tirailleurs Annamites* were coming back from France. This news startled and vaguely frightened her. Of course she had known they would be returning soon, but seeing it in print made it so definite. Why was she frightened? At Stung Treng she would not see those brown ranks; and Kim Khouan would stay in Saigon—unless he came to visit his father, who was too old to make the trip down to the coast. For some reason the thought of the *Tirailleurs Annamites* returning made her cold in the pit of her.

Several days after she saw the notice in the paper she passed a white-clad woman in the street. Not until the woman had gone by did she recognize her; and then the fact that she wore mourning thrust Thi-Linh's nerves into dark carnival. She hurried to the shop.

"Mama Thi-Bao," she said, "I passed the sister of Kim Khouan's wife a moment ago, and she was wearing white."

Mama Thi-Bao nodded. "Kim Khouan's wife died last month," she said.

It was several minutes before Thi-Linh was calm again. Then a heavy lethargy settled upon her.

All that day little Justin's eyes disturbed her more than before.

That night she did not sleep well. She wandered between the feverish jungle of dreams and the heat of a black room. Early in the morning she went to the pool in the jungle.

The sun had not yet reached the tops of the trees, and the little clearing was a cup of shade, sweet-scented with the breaths of drowsing lotus-buds. For a long while she lay there in the cool water, the stems of the plants soft against her; and as the sun rose higher, a stream of gold crept over the tree tops and lay beside her.

In the afternoon she passed the *commissaire* in the main road. He stared through his thick lenses, then stopped abruptly, awkwardly.

"Good day," he said, smiling.

"Good day, *monsieur*."

He was studying her through those horn-rimmed glasses.

"Mademoiselle Thi-Linh, is it not? I have heard of you." He hesitated; and she smiled inwardly. She knew what he was going to say. And how stupid it was, how banal! She was impatient; she wished he would hurry and get through with it.

"I should be glad to see more of you," he announced finally. "I am living alone, and . . ."

"*Monsieur* flatters me," she interrupted quietly. "But I am going back to Saigon on the next boat—to meet someone."

His eyes had a puzzled look that seemed magnified by those thick lenses. Then he smiled.

"Ah! To meet someone!" he repeated. "An old lover, I suppose."

She smiled.

"Yes, *monsieur*, an old lover."

14

When Thi-Linh arrived in Saigon she went immediately to the house of the Tonkinese family with whom she and Nanette had stayed. They told her the ship bringing the *Tirailleurs Annamites* had come three days before.

She was disappointed but it did not upset her greatly. Now she would go to the barracks and find him. She was sure he would not have started for Stung Treng to see his father so soon.

As she dressed, an ecstatic singing filled her body.

She tried to suppress it, for experience had taught her that too much happiness in advance was an invitation to disaster, but it would not be hushed. And, after all, did she know how he would receive her? Or how his appearance would affect her? France might have made great changes in him.

She drew the long coil of her hair into a black sheath and wrapped it about her head. It was fitting that she should go to him dressed as an Annamite. That dream tunic of black tissue over yellow had frayed with the years, but in its place she had another equally fine.

As she click-clacked out and called a rickshaw, the Tonkinese family gathered to stare, their number augmented by curious neighbors.

It was a bright morning, and the heat seemed to beat on the pavement with a silent clanging. Overhead, the clouds drifted like pure thoughts in an azure brain. All this warmth and light, seeming friendlier because of the presence of so many people, made her pleasurably conscious of the curve and dreamy pallor of herself under the tunic. A tremendous joy of living filled her to the very throat. It was like cool, fragrant water; water poured into a vase; gleaming vase of white porcelain in which she was carrying the flowers of her love to him.

As the coolie set down the shafts in front of the barracks she felt a muted, vibrant fear that was the uncertain overture to rhapsody.

The sentry, leaning on his rifle, gave her a casual glance; other soldiers, gathered about the windows, stared. From inside came the sibilant clicking of a typewriter, and the hollow sounds of people moving in uncarpeted halls.

She did not deign to question the sentry but demanded to see one of his officers.

Another soldier led her through the hall.

She was taken into the room where the typewriter was clicking. A half-caste was seated before the machine, and he gave her a long look, continuing to write until the keys caught, whereupon he muttered something and jerked the paper out.

That purring rip of the typewriter-roll seemed to release a shiver in Thi-Linh. Anxiously she watched the faces of the orderlies who came and went.

The soldier who had brought her appeared from behind a screen set before the doorway to another room, motioning her inside.

An officer, bent over some papers on his desk, looked up with a frown as she entered. Slowly the frown vanished.

"Mademoiselle?"—waving toward a chair.

As she sat down she became suddenly ill at ease. She must hurry this interview through, she told herself.

"I am looking for a man named Kim Khouan," she began, "who is a *doi* in the *Tirailleurs Annamites.*"

He was staring at her with a wrinkle between his eyes; but suddenly he smiled. "Ah, Madame Marie!" he exclaimed. "My God? I hardly knew you in those clothes. What is this masquerade?"

She had recognized him also—some officer whose name she could not remember. His familiarity annoyed her.

"Where is Paul?" he asked.

"I do not know," she said, her annoyance growing.

"Mmmm! You do not know, eh?" He laughed. "Well, well..."

"I came...." she began again.

"Yes, yes! About some native.... But tell me what is the trouble between you and Paul?"

Her face suddenly went hot with anger. She could scarcely control herself. "I have left him," she said sharply.

"Ah! So you have left him, eh! *Madame la Panthère*, clawing at hearts, eh? Well, well...."

Madame la Panthère! Those words seemed flung toward her from taut, quivering haunches, like an actual furry body. How did he know what Paul had tailed her? Had Paul talked? A final insult from him, thrown at her out of the past. *Madame la Panthère, Madame la Panthère.* The name throbbed with the blood in her temples. She looked at the officer through a film of rage. For a moment she thought she would spring upon him. A panther, yes—protecting herself—all those years—preserving herself—for Kim Khouan. She clung to the arms of the chair.

"I came...." she articulated.

"And who will be your next one, eh?" bantered the officer.

All that thrumming in her brain threatened to burst in dizzy carousal.

"I want to find...."

"Yes, yes, I haven't forgotten. A fellow named Kim Khouan."

He tapped a bell. An orderly stepped from behind the screen, and a few words passed between them. The Frenchman shrugged. He looked at her with an apologetic smile.

"I regret it," he said, "but they left him in France—for good." He smiled again, shrugged. "It is war!"

She stared at him, uncomprehending. It seemed that a tremendous vibration had started in her head and it shook her eyes until the officer's head danced absurdly on his shoulders. Several seconds passed before her vision became stationary, and she saw the ghostly confirmation of his words in his face.... Brown mud and a brown figure drawn down beneath it, earth feeding earth from an empty skull.... In that instant she slid down ages, into the beginning of anguish. Something crashed. A vase. She had come bringing the flowers of her love in a white porcelain vase. And now someone had dropped that vase down ages. Shattered it against an empty skull, so that the flowers fell into vacant sockets and made mockery of their hollowness.

"Planton!" she heard the officer shout.

How silly! Calling an orderly to help him gather up the pieces of a shattered vase.

15

When she fell asleep that night she had a strange dream:

She was in the cathedral praying before a figure on a cross, a young Annamite whose pathetic slimness was like yearning done into bronze. Suddenly there came a crash of rickshaw wheels. Stained-glass windows fell into sharp little rainbows all over the floor, and Nanette was lying in the midst of them, a lighted candle in one hand and a sheaf of yellow hair in the other. Whirling through the air was a delirium of faces, white faces, sick with over-desire. They dissolved into a wan vapor that lay swimming over the incense-burners. Banners and drums filled the cathedral, arousing shadowy thunder. She buried her ears under her palms. Then all that ghostly clamor melted into a ringing that made the silence well in great ripples and eddy away from her, leaving her spirit free to ascend like mist sighing up from a pool; a dark pool that breathed into space. "Blessed Mary, Holy Virgin …I will share the couch of my Master; will give him sons to perpetuate his race …and they will maintain the Cult …It was her own voice, flung down from the immense etherous space whither she had aspired. There, high above earth, the naked pallor of her spun like a white pole controlling the body of her kneeling in the cathedral. About her, crushing music of silence. She whirled in an ecstasy of light, carried higher and higher. Far off she saw a cloud. It unrolled to greet her. Then she saw that it had human form. It was a man, dark and shining, who came toward her with the eager step of a lover. He was neither Kim Khouan nor Justin nor Paul, and yet he was all of them. Spinning white pole of her balancing that body centuries below; spinning magnet of her lover balancing the pole of herself. Looking down through sea upon sea of silence she could see the twin spires of the cathedral, like the upthrust thumbs of a primitive altar. On that altar the body of her knelt, making vain prayers, while the pole of her yielded to that dark lover, passed through his lips into a swoon of pallor. Far below a thin voice was intoning: "May God receive this, the soul of thine unworthy servant.…

Her dream contracted to a frail body taking its last communion from an empty skull.

Piaster and Phenix

It was that mauve-dark hour when social Saigon, having perspired through the the-dansant at the Hotel Continental and imbibed an alarming number of cocktails, emerges into the streets, laughing and talking very loudly, to return home in rickshaws, carriages, and automobiles, there to continue to perspire and drink more cocktails in preparation for the interminable courses of a French dinner.

The café was almost deserted, but the orchestra was still playing, and one couple—a Jugo-Slavonian dancer who had drifted down from Shanghai and his partner—swayed and undulated to a tango while the few remaining people watched over aperitifs. Soft-shod "boys" came and went with a rattle of glasses that made castanets click to the Andalusian rhythm. Webs of smoke stretched on the heated air and frayed, leaving a thick haze in which the smells of liquors, perfumes, and hot breaths curdled and clotted.

In the street, rickshaw-coolies hovered, leaning on uplifted shafts; little Annamite boys waved news-sheets; older natives drifted about with inlaid trays, incense-burners, and Buddhas to sell.

Across the way, in front of the opera house, stood rows of taxicabs.

A gentle cadence measured off the flowing sounds in the Rue Catinat.

Among the lingering groups at the sidewalk tables around the Continental were three men flushed with drink and all talking at once. That was no particular distinction, except that two of them happened to be British. The third was very fat and very French. The incredible fact that these Englishmen were talking as much as their Gallic companion could be traced to the empty bottles before them.

"…yes," the fat Frenchman was saying, "just like the Queen of Sheba! But you saw her—sweeping out of the café, with not so much as a look at anyone, and into her motorcar. *Her* motorcar! Of course, that old imbecile gave it to her…. *Mon Dieu!* I shall never forget it! Like the Queen of Sheba!"

And he laughed until his red cheeks looked raw with tears.

"Incomparable!" he went on. "I wish I had a picture of it. Not a word, not a bow, not even to me, *me*…. Oh, *mon Dieu!*" He wiped his eyes. "And did you hear what Ledou said as she got into the car? Ledou is the gentleman I introduced you to, who sat at the next table. Did you hear what he said? 'Well, I wonder how long that will last…' She heard it, too. But not a look; she simply dropped into the back seat of the car and rode off …just like the Queen of Sheba….[23]

He drew a deep breath and swallowed the remaining grenadine in his glass.

"I knew her when she was a little girl," he continued; "I was *commissaire* of the town where she lived."

---

23 Hervey describes the real-life inspiration for this scene in *King Cobra*, the non-fiction account of his travels in Indochina:

> A little later, when dusk had thickened and the *thé-dansant* threatened to end, I observed a very opulent limousine that glided alongside the curb and stopped. Immediately a woman came out of the café. Even had I not seen her face, I should have noticed her because of her bearing as she descended the steps and got into the waiting car. If the limousine had suddenly turned into a golden palanquin I should not have been surprised, for surely Balkis of Sheba on her way to conquer the young Solomon could not have moved with more proud assurance.
>
> Several Frenchmen at the next table laughed as she drove off. "I wonder how long that will last!" said one…. *King Cobra*, (Holmes Beach, FL: DatAsia Press, 2013), 35.]

"Was she as flashy then?" one of the Englishmen asked.

"Too bad she's a half-caste," said the other. "You know, you really couldn't tell it—unless you looked closely, of course."

"Flashy?" repeated Monsieur Malardier. "You mean—Ah, yes, I understand…. No—she was a pretty little thing, prettier than most—and very wise. A golden little creature. … I knew her first husband."

"Husband?"

"By Jove, you Frenchmen are broad! We wouldn't for a minute…."

"Why not husband? He took care of her, loved her…. Poor Batteur! He died of *fièvre-de-bois* [24]—up in Laos, where I have been for eight years. But since then there have been many others, I hear. I had not seen her for years—not since she was at Stung Treng. I would not have recognized her today if she had not been pointed out. It was Ledou—you heard him. He said, 'Look, there she is. She is making her papa give her a big dinner tonight.' And I looked.

My God! Those clothes! Her present husband is quite rich—he is one of the directors in the *Banque de Indochine*. And quite old, I understand. But what does that matter? She has had young ones—it is the piasters now. They say she got him in Hanoi, And now she has him wrapped around her little finger. But, as Ledou said, I wonder how long that will last?"

"What do your Frenchwomen think of her?"

"Yes, what do they think?"

Monsieur Malardier laughed loudly. "They do not think about her often—it makes them too angry! *Métisse! Catin!* [25] But, after all, what difference does a marriage ceremony make? It only makes it more difficult to get out of! But women—they do not understand….

"*Allez, allez!*" he shouted suddenly as an Annamite peddler, insinuating himself in front of him, held out an inlaid teakwood plaque.

---

24 "Jungle fever" generally meant malaria. Harry drew from his own experience, as described in *King Cobra*, when he contracted malaria in Laos, became delirious with fever and almost died.
25 French terms meaning, respectively, "half-breed or mixed-blood" and "harlot, slut or trollop."

Then, on second thought, and with a wink at the Englishmen, he called the fellow back.

"*Combien?*"—tapping the plaque.

The Annamite smiled importunately. "*Dix piasters, m'sieur.*"

Monsieur Malardier flung up his hands.

"*Qui est-ce qui?*" he shrieked, winking at his companions again.

"*Neuf piasters,*" said the Annamite, looking frightened but still smiling.

"*Mon Dieu! Neuf piasters? Ridicule!*"

"*Huit piasters, m'sieur.*"

"*Non! Voleur! Allez, allez!*"

"*Sept, m'sieur,*" the Annamite persisted.

Laughing again until his red cheeks looked raw, Monsieur Malardier gestured him away.

"You see?" he said to the Englishmen. "If I had wanted it, I could have gotten him down to five piasters, perhaps four. Robbers, these natives!"

"Same in India," said one of the Englishmen.

"Or in F.M.S.," added the other.[26]

"Pigs," concluded Monsieur Malardier.

Then, after a pause, he remarked: "Incredible, is it not, that she has the blood of such people in her, eh? She danced around in there, doing the new steps and dressed like a Frenchwoman, yet really she was dancing naked to a *khene*—a *khene* is the native instrument of the country where I live, Laos. There is no such thing as half-caste; they are all natives. Selling plaques and asking twice what they are worth. And she, well, some day she will have to come down in *her* price. Half-caste! Pouf! They are brown underneath."

---

26 From 1895 until 1946, FMS stood for the "Federated Malay States", a federation of four states protected under the British government in the Malay Peninsula: Selangor, Perak, Negeri Sembilan and Pahang.

"I can't bear the blighters," remarked one of the Englishmen.

"Yet she was jolly good-looking," ventured the other.

"They are beautiful, some of these *métisses*,[27] and even some of the brown ones; and they are very gentle. But one must not forget that they are half white or brown.... Boi-ee!"

A "boy," sandaled feet darting under flopping trousers, came running.

"*Trois* Martel-Perrier !" ordered Monsieur Malardier.

"Oh, I say!" objected one of the Englishmen faintly.

"Really, old fellow...," began the other.

"One must drink more in the East" laughed Monsieur Malardier. "It is the tradition."

"To keep your liver afloat, as they say," proposed one of his guests.

"Right-o!" verified the other.

"To drink freely and still be gentlemen," expounded the Frenchman, "is the proof of our ability to remain civilized among barbarians. A-a-a-ah!"—as the drinks arrived. Then he chuckled. "*Mon Dieu!* I shall never forget her sweeping out of the hotel and into that car! *La grande maitresse!* Just like the Queen of Sheba! And, you know, she has a son— by a native—he must be fourteen now.... Well, *salut!*"

"Cheerio!"

"Ditto!"

Slowly the people ebbed out of the café. "*I want to be happy . . .*"[28] wailed the orchestra. Clash of glasses and droning voices, all caught like flies in the webby smoke. The little Annamite boys in the street stood listening with puzzled gazes. In the Rue Catinat, the tamarinds sighed faintly as a breeze roved up from the river.

---

27 A woman of mixed race ancestry (feminine form of *métis*).

28 The play *No, No, Nanette* became a hit after opening in New York, London and Chicago in 1925. Two songs helped to increase its popularity: "I Want to Be Happy" and "Tea For Two."

2

Thi-Linh, riding home in her motorcar, was extremely annoyed.

One gray-slippered toe tapped the foot-rest, and the other, crossed over an ankle suave in chiffon hose, moved restlessly. She tried to light a cigarette but the wind was too strong; impatiently she ordered the chauffeur to slow down. Her narrowed, intense gaze, in a swathe of smoke, saw the cathedral advancing toward the wind-shield. In a moment she would be home; and suddenly she realized she did not wish to be home. She might be late for dinner, but—well, let them wait.

"Go out the Govap road a little way and back," she told the driver.

Her gaze strayed down to the illusory sheen of her dress. Gray silk crepe—from Paris. She remembered how cool and svelte she had looked before going to the hotel; now all the poise that her appearance had given her seemed destroyed. And merely because she had heard a Frenchman question her ability to hold Monsieur Chauvet.

"Well, I wonder how long that will last!"

She had blazed as she heard it. Now she seemed turned to velvet, cut-velvet in which there was a definite pattern of cold anger. She was not irritated by what he had said so much as by the realization that she was not above words. The very fact that she was disturbed made her wonder if, subconsciously, she did doubt her own ability. It was a challenge to her faith in herself.

Long ago all the terrific emotional surfeit that was the quick-flesh of youth had run out of her—like fertile soil suddenly become sand, and leaving in its place a hard luster. It was not that she had grown callous; it was simply that she had learned a greater imperviousness. Words seemed to have lost their power to hurt her. Words. What were they, she asked herself, but the false symbols by which people accomplished a beautiful and studied deception or achieved some imaginary venom or nobility that satisfied their fears?

Yet, in spite of this knowledge, the Frenchman's words did trouble her. Had he heard something that caused his remark?

For two years now she had been living with Urbain Chauvet, and often he had stroked her hair (with those hands so immaculate and bloodless) and said: "It is a pity more do not know how clever you are—and yet I might be jealous if they did." The remembrance of this was reassuring. She knew that she had a lithe intelligence, that she helped him in many ways, but it always pleased her to hear he also was aware of it.

An ironic smile touched her lips. He was a man of influence, one of the guardians of much of the wealth that flowed in and out of Indo-China; and how amusing it would be, she thought, if Indo-China were suddenly told that often his decisions were her own made public!

She, a half-caste, with her finger in Indo-China's finances!

Once Monsieur Chauvet had said to her: "I used to wonder why the Annamite women always sit in the front of the shops and the men idle in the rear; now I think I understand."

The recollection of those little incidents was dissipating her uneasiness, leaving her concerned chiefly with the fact that she had allowed herself to be disturbed. She was valuable to Urbain Chauvet; moreover, he loved her, passionately, jealously, with the desperate affection of a man who realized he had reached the age when it was difficult to hold women.

And this dinner tonight, was not that proof enough? *Monsieur le Gouverneur* would be there, and other important officials. No women, of course. But she had long since dismissed the idea of ever associating with French women, and now regarded them with the contemptuousness that is jealousy suppressed. A few days before, Monsieur Chauvet had remarked that there were certain matters he wished to discuss with the Governor; and very casually she had suggested that he invite him to dinner.... She did not know whether *Monsieur le Gouverneur* and the others were aware she would be present. Nevertheless, they had accepted, and whatever happened, she was sufficiently mistress of herself, or any situation, to keep this triumph from turning into anything else. Furthermore, Frenchmen were very liberal where their wives were not concerned, and even where they were concerned it was not a matter of intolerance but a greater liberalism that included also the peculiarities of the women to whom they were married.

How inconspicuously this triumph had come! For eight years she had been working for it, not the actual dinner but what it symbolized; and suddenly, with no trumpetry to forecast it, it had come. But that was the way significant events happened—easily, simply. For a moment she reflected bitterly on those two words—easily, simply. Consciously striving for eight years—and blindly for how many before that? Many; since she had been a child; since she had first looked at illustrated journals and learned there was a world beyond Stung Treng—a world whose blood she shared. Easily, simply?

Not those years of striving …those years at Stung Treng, unfolding to the magic of Kim Khouan, then disillusion …taking refuge in Justin …the coming to Saigon …Paul, the war …and then that morning in the barracks. Ages ago. And as she had fainted, stunned by the news of Kim Khouan's death, she had thought of a vase crashing to the floor. Fragments of glowing white porcelain. She had picked them up afterward, and put them together; and they had gleamed with the same shining beauty, only something had spilled. Fertile soil turned to sand…. in its place a polished luster.

But tonight, she thought, I dine with *Monsieur le Gouverneur*…. All those years …simply part of the price of becoming civilized…. Civilized; she repeated the word vehemently. I am civilized, am I not?

Yes …but long ago …in a native tunic …to find a brown man … dirty brown fellow, the French would say …whom another governor had flung into the mud of Europe …and when she had learned …had shattered like a vase …long ago …so painfully long ago….

And after that? …Utterly alone…. No Kim Khouan to fold warmly and darkly about her thoughts…. No Justin to offer refuge…. No Paul in whom she could submerge herself…. After all …Kim Khouan …her only love…. An Annamite—and he was dead…. White was the color of mourning…. And so, in remembrance of him who was an Annamite, she had worn white in her heart….

Thoughts pitting the surface of her mind like rain.

And with that mourning in her heart she had gone to work.... Sitting behind the *caisse* in the Hotel de la Rotonde ... a high *caisse* from which she could look down on those who occupied the tables.... Civilians in stiff whites ...soldiers in khaki ...women complaining of the heat.... She had felt very wise, sitting there above them ...so wise that she had allowed only a few actual beings to emerge from that pattern of faces that shifted about her daily....

Only a few.... That young lieutenant who was going to marry a girl in France ...who was so pathetically young and lonely.... And the American who had an office over on the Boulevard Charner.... And Jeannerat ...Jeannerat—hardly more than a boy ...little Breton sailor.... Looking up from the *caisse* one evening, she had seen him laughing at her from the street ...and later when she came out he was still there, laughing.... "I am never going away," he had declared.... How prophetic! ...Curly hair of him tangled in the roots of the cemetery.... Out of that earth the fever had crept, stealing back with him.... Jeannerat ...who had left her that little bag filled with soiled, wrinkled francs ...who had wanted to marry her but instead had celebrated a more permanent and ironic marriage....

And then the shop she had opened on the Rue Catinat ...very little in it at first ...but soon *sampots*, embroidered hangings from Hanoi ...Annamite needlework ...Laotian scarfs and *sinhs* that Mama Thi-Bao sent down from Stung Treng ...carvings, bronzes, Buddhas ... things for tourists to buy.... And Hoa to help her, faithful Hoa, who reminded her of Mama Thi-Bao as she sat chewing betel in the rear of the shop....

Business had flourished.... Many people came ...travelers ...officers from foreign ships ...among them that young Scandinavian who had taken her to the *dansant* at the Continental.... Her first *dansant* ... music pouring over her, the warm drench of lights.... Ah! how she had wished that Paul might see her that afternoon.... But Paul was in France....

Other *dansants* had followed.… What did it matter that women stared and made nasty remarks? …Men took her there …danced with her.…

And then that eventful trip to Hanoi …trip to buy things for the shop. … A room in the best hotel …evenings in the open-air café, smoking and drinking aperitifs …watching the cinema that flickered across the street.… It was sitting there one night that she first saw Monsieur Chauvet.…

She sighed deeply, checking those staccato thoughts that rained upon her mind.

The two years following that meeting at Hanoi had been calm, a steady rise upward bringing her to this night when the Governor would dine at her house. She could regard those years coolly. They had seemed to rinse her of the hot film left by emotional tumult. And that meeting—it had come so easily. Sitting there in the café at Hanoi, she was suddenly aware of Monsieur Chauvet's intense, nervous gaze. But she did not speak, or even give evidence that she saw him. He wore glasses fastened to a thin black ribbon; his white beard was close-cropped, his clothing immaculate.

A stomach a bit too large, but that was to be expected in a man his age.

The next evening the manager of the hotel approached her table with tolerant good nature, and behind him walked the gentleman with the close-cropped white beard whom he introduced as Monsieur Urbain Chauvet of the *Banque de l'Indochine*.

Thinking about it now, it seemed to Thi-Linh that he had an air of destiny as he sat down at her table that night in Hanoi. They dined together. The next evening he came with a scarlet flower in his lapel. His wife had died several years past, he told her; he had been living alone since then.… It seemed that she was hearing ancient words that had lain under her consciousness and were only then emerging. When he had finished, her only answer was a smile, a tired little smile. Later, when he kissed her, a quiver traveled down her backbone. But she would get over that, she had assured herself.

And so she had sent a telegram to Hoa, following the message herself and selling out the shop; and then, accompanied by Hoa, she had returned to Hanoi.

She had not abandoned her ideal of the physical male, and during the first few months with Monsieur Chauvet she had invariably felt depressed when she regarded his stomach. But as his little habits and eccentricities became more familiar to her, this defect in his figure became less obvious, and she became aware of the growing warmth that comes with continued association no matter how unromantic. He was exceedingly shrewd and generally good-natured. But he was also very jealous. She admired his intelligence, and the fact that he was rarely out of humor made it easier for her to forget that he was nearly twice her age. But it was most distressing when he indulged in a fit of jealousy.

Unfortunately those spells usually came in public. Suddenly he would accuse her of watching some man too closely, and no matter where they happened to be, he would loudly call for a carriage or a motorcar, announcing with equal loudness that he was going to take her home. For an hour or more he would be very insulting, questioning her fidelity and charging her with preposterous indiscretions, and then he would go storming to his room and shut himself up for the rest of the day. Always on the following morning he would suggest casually that she needed a new dress.

Often he would invite friends to dinner—men of course—and beforehand he would tell her, "You must talk tonight—you must show them how clever you are." But if her conversation led her to be too gracious he was very irritable afterward. "You talked to him too much," he would complain. "What was it, the uniform or the handsome face? My God, why must I be so old?"

When he was pleased with her he would stroke his beard and call her "his wise little peacock." It sounded stupid and senile, and it grew to annoy her.

And then they moved to Saigon. She was glad to be back, for there was a charm about the city stronger than the bitter suggestions of the past that lurked in certain parts of it. He had a large house beyond the

Place de la Cathedrale, and many servants; and in addition to the car which he had shipped down from Hanoi, he bought another which he said was her very own. He also allowed her a personal chauffeur.

Her days were very full. From the *imprimerie* on the Rue Catinat she was able to get the latest books, and she read most of the new novels; novels by André Gide, Claude Farrère, Paul Morand, Pierre Benoit and many others. But she was not satisfied with reading only novels; she read much about the history of her country and of other countries as well.

And when the opera came to Saigon she had a box. Most of the Frenchmen said the troupe sang very badly, but she observed that in spite of that they never missed a performance. One did not go to the opera to hear music, she learned, at least not in Saigon; one went because the socially eligible would be there. Nevertheless, she enjoyed the singing. One performance, particularly, aroused her tremendously. It was about a Spanish dancer. Castanets shrilled through it, and the music welled up like blood, making hot revelry in her brain.

This opera disturbed her. Afterward, while she and Monsieur Chauvet were riding along the quays for a breath of air, she was painfully aware of his lack of physical grace. The dark silence over the river, tongued with lights, the pale roads, where people moved in a stealthy pattern, challenged her to dismiss the car, Monsieur Chauvet included, and walk, walk, walk until she was exhausted. That, she felt, would have sublimated all her restlessness.

It was her habit to go to the cinema twice a week. Often those films, like that Spanish opera, left her passionately dissatisfied. Was it, she wondered, because in most of them the men were young and handsome? Romance—was it that she wanted? She did not think so. Long ago she had had romance; and because of it all the fertile soil of her had turned to sand and run out, leaving that cold luster. No, it was not romance. But it was something …something even more intangible and which at times she craved with insuperable and exquisite anguish.

Monsieur Chauvet (she never called him Urbain) was very generous. He allowed her to go to the weekly *thé-dansants* at the Continental. But even they sometimes left her with that excruciating discontent. Her car would take her to the hotel, and she would go to the table reserved for her. But she never had to sit alone. Always some young Frenchman, one or more, would join her, and her dances were filled. Then, the *dansant* over, she would go out to her waiting car, followed by insolent glances from the women, and return home, there to be questioned in detail by Monsieur Chauvet.

Pleasant days.... And her gratitude to Monsieur Chauvet developed into a warm affection—an affection, in a lesser degree, such as she had for Mama Thi-Bao and little Justin. Which, she realized, would not entirely please him if he knew it.

But there were moments, riding along the docks at dusk or in some thickly peopled street, when a passing face would seem to rise up and touch her poignantly. Flashes of yearning, reminiscent of those nights when she first came to Saigon. But her fidelity was complete.

Eight years since that morning at the barracks, she reflected again. And had they been easy and simple? ...Eight crowded years, each circumstance a step that she had mounted with the sureness of one following a design.

Now, sitting in her car and thinking of those years, the remark of that Frenchman seemed ridiculous. And equally absurd was the fact that she had permitted it to upset her. She could see no reason why everything should not continue as it had been for the past two years.

Monsieur Chauvet seemed extravagantly proud of her, and in return she held nothing from him. Nothing ...except those sharp, scattered moments; and they were her own; precious moments, close to life, when a hint of that old prodigality of emotion stemmed a swift, fragile bloom.

3

When she entered the hall she found Monsieur Chauvet waiting, dressed in evening clothes and nervously adjusting his nose-glasses as he paced the floor.

"And who was the handsome young man who made you late?" he demanded with forced joviality.

She kissed him automatically. "I took a drive afterward to clear my mind of all those silly faces."

He laughed—still uncertain. "Whom did you dance with?"

"The usual ones...."

"Was Lieutenant de Brissac there?"

She smiled tolerantly. "Yes, he was there—and he danced with me twice. I suggest that you meet him tomorrow morning in the Botanical Gardens, swords preferably."

His laugh was genuine now; he kissed her. "Hurry, it is late."

She stopped to look into the dining-room. Candles burned on the table, and their light defined dark hangings and spaciousness. Between them was a savage splash of hibiscus, reflecting a winey shimmer in the empty glasses. One of the serving-boys moved about soundlessly, hovering over silverware and heavily embroidered linen.

Hoa was waiting in her room. Immediately she began to denounce Thi-Linh for being late. "Have you forgotten that *Monsieur le Gouverneur* is to be here?" she demanded.

Hoa was a privileged person. She had been with Thi-Linh since the days of the shop in the Rue Catinat. Thi-Linh submitted to the tyranny of her guardianship because a shadow of Mama Thi-Bao lurked in her face and dress. But aside from her appearance she was quite unlike Mama Thi-Bao. She was a common peasant woman from Mytho, and at times her manners were very inelegant. If, for instance, she became angry, she would promptly sit down, no matter where she was, and loudly recite her grievances for the benefit of whoever happened to be passing and for the world at large. Although Hoa did not talk outside the house, very little of interest happened in Saigon that did not ultimately reach Thi-Linh through her.

"Have you forgotten that *Monsieur le Gouverneur* is coming?" she repeated with rising inflection when Thi-Linh did not answer.

Thi-Linh gazed at a smear on the floor, then at Hoa. "You have been chewing betel again," she accused.

Hoa looked guilty. "It must have been the house-boy," she said.

"The house-boy does not defile himself with such a filthy habit; and if you do it again I shall send you back to your village…. Unhook me," she ordered sharply.

As she slipped out of her dress she thought of what Hoa had said about forgetting that the Governor was to be there. Forget! For his benefit she had bought a new gown at the *magasin* on the Boulevard Charner, and because of him she deliberately planned to be late. That gown would show off to excellent effect as she descended the long stair, with the guests assembled below.

It was an exquisite gown; and it emphasized a certain glowing fragility in her beauty. Sunk in the misty whiteness of it, and gazing at herself in the mirror, she experienced a sensation of acute pleasure. That dress made her pallor seem as if golden smoke had been breathed over it. "Get me a hibiscus," she said to Hoa. When the old woman brought the flower, she crushed it into her hair, against the temple. It was a barbaric touch, and she liked it blazing there in the rippling blue-black of her short-trimmed hair.

When she moved, the dress floated out about her. It made her think of the soft wash of spume over coral rock. Several times she strode back and forth in front of the glass, smiling at her reflection with lips heavy with carmine.

"Am I not beautiful?" she demanded of Hoa.

"Beautiful as a mimosa flower," crooned the old woman.

"Bring me my bracelets." She slipped them over one wrist. Silver, made bluish by sapphires. An Annamite would never wear silver unless in mourning, she reflected; the fact that she did was proof of the dominance of her French blood. "Do I not look like a Frenchwoman?"

"You are lovelier than Frenchwomen," Hoa replied tactfully.

A sudden passionate charge made Thi-Linh's supple body rigid. Eight years; and all the concerted discord of them crashing up to this attenuated moment. For an instant she felt dizzy. Her image blurred in the mirror, then blossomed in all its smooth perfection.

"I wish they could see me tonight, those Frenchwomen," she said. "Is it not a triumph, Hoa? Dining with *Monsieur le Gouverneur*—Marie Linh, whose father was French, whose mother is Annamite. Hoa," she commanded abruptly, "it seems—tonight—as though something dark is here—here in me—perhaps it is Indo-China—laughing behind this French manner. Not sultry and brooding, Hoa, because Indo-China is too wise, but laughing. Do you understand what I am saying?"

"You are hating the French," said the old woman quietly.

A sense of futility caught back the laugh that rose in Thi-Linh's throat,

"Hating! You are a stupid *baya*, Hoa. Not hating, no, but pitying, pitying as I laugh—pitying Indochina—pitying France—pitying the ineffectualness of this—this triumph."

For a moment a terrific dissatisfaction shook her. To herself she said: What will it mean tomorrow, this dinner tonight? Simply that all those French strumpets will hear of it, and their tongues will leap like snakes; and what they say will come to me, and their jealousy will delight me for a while. And I shall go on dining with their men, and dancing with them; and—and then?

"Give me a cigarette," she demanded.

She could hear voices rising from below, muffled; in a moment she would join them.

Annoyed with herself, she paced up and down the room, spheres of smoke drifting up from her lips. Hoa watched her with a puzzled, dull look that added to her irritation.

"Get out," she said tersely; then, "Wait—am I all right?"

"Lovely as—"

"Get out!"

As the woman went, Thi-Linh studied herself in the glass. A mimosa? Hardly. More like that flower crushed against her temple. Its petals seemed to beat there like throbs of blood. It was a blossom of insuperable brutality. With that against her temple, she thought, she could be equally savage. But how white and chaste she looked in the clinging gossamer of that dress! A virgin with one flare of lust against her temple. What a paradox, a virgin! And yet, centuries ago, in the temples of her Ancestors, there were vestals who attained the gods through priestly intercessors ; courtesans in body but in spirit perpetually wedded to heaven. Was it possible, she wondered, to give freely, not promiscuously, and keep deep in the heart a more vital chastity? For an instant she had the feeling that all the shimmering whiteness of her gathered momentum and spun ahead, bearing on its crest an incredible bloom that was her gift to ironic destiny.

A gong sounded faintly. That would be Monsieur Chauvet ringing for the cocktails. She would go now.

Stamping the cigarette on the tiled floor, she moved to the stairway.

As she swept down, the tumultuous beating of her heart seemed to race through her entire body. She could see faces lifted toward her. A little shiver of exultation responded. She could picture her descent. How old am I? she thought irrelevantly. Twenty-nine? Ten years ago I could not have done this.

On the bottom step she paused, and with a soft clash of bracelets, she pressed her hand tentatively against that flower in her hair, all the while smiling serenely at those faces that swiftly were becoming more definite.

Monsieur Chauvet advanced with a look of anxious benevolence.

"Ah!" he said, and she thought his voice sounded agitated. Was he afraid of how she would be received? She experienced an instant of dread.

"Ah!" he repeated, clearing his throat. "Gentlemen, I think all of you know my wise little peacock—all except *Monsieur le Gouverneur.*"

She saw a swarthy, kind-looking little man with a gray mustache. Doctor Martel, the Governor; she had seen him often at public functions.

He inclined his head forward. "Madame," he said in gracious acknowledgment.

Later, at the table, it all seemed so natural; *Monsieur le Gouverneur* on her right and *Monsieur le Préfet de Police* on her left. Monsieur Chauvet's white beard flickered at the other end of the table, above the piled hibiscus. Their lustful color reduced him to ashy remoteness. She had never before realized how old he looked. Not even the vitality of his eyes could atone for the life those flowers drained from him. Dead ivory holding together a bronze chain of faces. Her casual gaze moved about the table as she talked. Most of the men were middle-aged, one or two young, but all had the luster of living. All except Monsieur Chauvet. Suddenly he had become pitifully grotesque, and so very old.

One of the serving-boys entered soundlessly with an elaborate dish: a great pinkish-silver fish congealed in transparent amber with rinds of lemon and pimento. From outside came warm fragrances that mingled with the smell of burning tapers. Another boy made the wine-glasses seem burnished. The voices mounted to a staccato dissonance that almost drowned the occasional shrilling of a lizard on the ceiling. Thi-Linh's senses blurred with pleasure.

"These Chinese are amusing devils" an elderly man near the other end of the table was saying. "My comprador …he was describing the executions in Yunnan…. He said the condemned men simply knelt down and the executioner walked along the line chopping off their heads; and I said, 'But I don't see why some of them don't move their heads out of the way'; and he looked immensely serious and said, 'Ah, no, *monsieur* …lose face if they do that!' …Incomparable, eh?"

Monsieur Chauvet began telling an anecdote, laughing in anticipation of the point.

Red wine suffused the glasses now; following the fish-gelatin had come a great silver platter of cock's-combs imported from France.

"… perambulating journalists are a nuisance," remarked a dark-bearded man next to *Monsieur le Gouverneur*. "They come with letters and expect the Government to prostrate itself! There is a joke—" He glanced slyly at the Governor. The latter laughed.

"Go ahead, my dear Armand," he shrugged.

"There is a joke on *Monsieur le Gouverneur*," resumed the dark-bearded man who was a cabinet official.

"It happened about a year ago," volunteered the Governor; "no, longer than that—"

"Some journalist came with a letter from the Minister at Peking," continued the cabinet official. "His Excellency was very busy—"

"Busy!" exploded the Governor. "I was more than busy! It was at the time of General Fournereau's visit! Could I neglect official duty for a journalist?"

"Consequently," went on the cabinet official, "this journalist visited the sights in a car that cost twenty piasters a day instead of having a Government motor at his disposal. When he reached Paris—he knew someone in the cabinet—he stamped like an angry bull. And so—"

"And so I received a letter," interposed *Monsieur le Gouverneur*, "politely requesting me to be more considerate of journalists in the future because, the letter said, Indo-China needed publicity!"

"Then," the other pressed on, "an American writer appeared about eight months ago, immediately after the letter from Paris. Naturally—"

"Naturally," broke in the Governor, "I exerted every power to make sure that, as Paris had requested, Indo-China should receive more publicity!"

"His Excellency gave this gentleman a car to use here and at Phnom-Penh," the cabinet official persisted, "and when he went to Hanoi—"

"I telegraphed the Governor," His Excellency continued excitedly, "and he arranged for this writer to have his private boat for a visit to the Baie d'Along."

"Every courtesy!" emphasized the cabinet official, seizing the pause. "And when he returned to America—"

"Yes, when he returned to America" the Governor interjected, his face flushed, "what did he do?"

He paused to take a swallow of wine, and the cabinet official plunged on desperately.

"He wrote an article attacking the Colonial Government of Indo-China!"

"Yes!" inserted the Governor, having swallowed the wine. "And he called it '*The Exquisite Jest*'!"

"Very bitter, very caustic!" said the cabinet official in a last valiant effort to finish his own story. "I remember the concluding line—"

"Indeed, so do I!" shouted the Governor. "Listen, this was it—" He paused, but the cabinet official only opened his mouth and then shut it with a snap.

"He said," quoted the Governor, "'If the natives of Indo-China had a sense of humor, they would appreciate the elaborate pretensions of Frenchmen, and their convulsive laughter would completely unseat their masters, who, contrary to popular belief, are not at their best when the joke is of a personal nature!'"

The air had grown heavier, as though the mingling of fragrances from the garden, the heat of candles and all those human breaths sagged upon it. Sparkling golden chill of Perrier-Jouët [29] frosted the glasses; a boy moved quietly from elbow to elbow with a dish of fowl drenched in sherry.

Thi-Linh's mind was abnormally alert, and the quenching warmth of champagne seemed to multiply glittering words that ran from her tongue easily. Most of her conversation was with the Governor, but now and then she addressed the Prefect of Police, who had an annoying way of listening with smiling vacuity. Yet when she turned away she was conscious of his close scrutiny.

She had seen him about town often; several months before, Monsieur Chauvet had introduced them. He had a thin face burned the color of dried cowhide, with a small mustache, and sinewy wrists that moved with arresting flexibility. His impassiveness, amounting almost to austerity, gave her the feeling that the man himself was carefully

---

29 Founded in 1811, Perrier-Jouët is a Champagne producer in the Épernay region of France.

encased in leather. Even when he smiled vacantly his eyes had a penetrating directness. He alone, of all those men at the table, seemed hostile to her; and his hostility took the form of an unspoken skepticism that questioned her intelligence. Evidently, she thought, the women he had known outside French circles were all like Nanette.

A young officer new to Indo-China was talking about Algeria. Silently she accepted the challenge of the Prefect of Police.

"You were long in Algeria?" she inserted deftly.

Monsieur Chauvet was telling a joke about a hare-lipped nun, chuckling as he talked.

"Two years, madame," replied the young officer.

"I only know the country through *Le Roman d'un Spahi*[30]" she said tentatively.

"Which is, perhaps, inadequately," he returned. "For Monsieur Loti saw flowers where flowers were not." After a pause he added laughingly, "And I assure you, madame, that all officers do not consort with black Fatou-gayes!"

An abrupt silence descended upon his speech. Monsieur Chauvet, in the midst of his story, paused with an injured look. Thi-Linh was conscious that the attention of the entire table was upon her; a subtle tension tightened the air. It suggested to her what was going on behind all those faces. They were associating her with those African women, black creatures and mulatto wenches who were the mistresses of Spahis and other soldiers. Involuntarily her hand went to the flower in her hair. The touch seemed to impart a velvety coolness to her fingers. A well-poised cruelty balanced her emotions, and she assorted her words with the care of one choosing stones for a catapult.

"But in spite of seeing flowers where flowers were not," she pronounced evenly, "Monsieur Loti made savage music out of Africa—

---

30 Pierre Loti was among the earliest and most influential authors to promote Orientalism and French colonial literature. See the appendix article "Francophilia" for a biographical profile of Loti, his relationship to Hervey, and details on other French writers mentioned in Hervey's books.

sometimes ironic music, with a little tremulous obbligato"—she smiled—"that, perhaps, is the loneliness of Frenchmen in exile."

After a brief silence an elderly man at the other end of the table snorted:

"Loti! *Pouf!* A young naval officer observing the world from the quarter-deck! A sailor with a penchant for exaggeration!"

Monsieur Chauvet gave Thi-Linh an apologetic look. "I prefer the style of Anatole France—" he began.

She ignored him. "Perhaps Loti exaggerated details," she said, "but not moods. In spite of being French, he was able to catch the nostalgic beauty of Asia. Indeed, in his habits he was extremely French—Fatou-gaye, Suleima, Aziyadé [31]; how many were there?—but his reactions, when he put them on paper, were undeniably Eastern. Now of course"—she paused, running her fingers over the stem of her wine-glass—"he seems a bit archaic. For in these days Fatou-gaye doesn't kill herself, she gets another Frenchman." And she smiled deliberately and distractingly.

Several of the men laughed—hollowly. The Prefect of Police sat so rigid in his brown casing that she expected to hear a leathery creak when he moved. Monsieur Chauvet looked a bit distressed—as though she had said something very personal.

Suddenly the Prefect of Police spoke; indeed, so suddenly that Thi-Linh almost jumped.

"Quite so." His black interrogative gaze smiled at her—or was it laughter? "Has madame, by any chance, read a book called *Une Fille d'Annam?*"

His question clashed against her, like steel suddenly thrust out of that leather casing. She met the direct focus of his black pupils with a smile.

"A beautiful book" she said.

"But the psychology?"

---

31 Thi-Linh cites three of Pierre Loti's female protagonists, all described in "Francophilia," to expand the discussion of interracial relationships between French men and colonial women.

"It cannot be questioned up to the point where the girl throws herself into the sea." Then she added. "But, you see, I am prejudiced in its favor—it was dedicated to me."

After she spoke she felt Monsieur Chauvet's jealous gaze. She did not look at him, but continued to smile at the Prefect of Police. He also was smiling, with that polite attention that so annoyed her.

Talk commenced at the other end of the table. She transferred her attention to the young officer from Algeria.

"Speaking of Africa," she began, "there was a book—by René Maran—called *Batouala*."

"*Batouala!*" burst out one of the Frenchmen near her. "Hot words written by a Negro! It is stupid—it is too bitter—it is merely ridiculous!"

She was pleased, for she had thought that mention of *Batouala* would bring a heated reaction.

"Its violence made it ineffectual," she said. "If Monsieur Maran had been a European instead of a Negro, his bitterness would have taken the form of satire. Or if he had had some French blood instead of merely a French education—" She paused, aware that she was spinning over fire, yet sure of herself. "Then," she finished, "he would have written with more artistic despair and less obvious purpose...."

"Exactly," came Monsieur Chauvet's voice from the other end of the table. His eyes were still asking her about *Une Fille d'Annam.*

"Consider the other extreme," she continued, not satisfied; "that novel of Pierre Benoit's, *L'Atlantide.*"

"Merely a romancer, Benoit," pronounced the Frenchman who had been so vehement about "Batouala."

"But he is also very French," replied Thi-Linh. "For him, Africa is—well, grist for his literary mill. He is fantastic, his story impossible. Monsieur Maran is bitter, his story not impossible but improbable. There we have the two, native and Frenchman, both writing about a continent—and neither a great artist."

The Prefect of Police spoke again. "You are suggesting?"

"Simply that Monsieur Loti, compared with the other two, is more artistic. And more truthful, paradoxical as that seems. He interpreted the moods of the East—of Indo-China as well as Africa—with passionate felicity—perhaps because, in spite of being born a Frenchman, he was, emotionally, a strange blending of both Oriental and Occidental."

The conversation at the other end of the table had grown into a rapid discussion. In the midst of this dissonance of talk she heard Monsieur Chauvet resume his story of the hare-lipped nun.

Coffee and brandy were served in the living-room. It gave upon an enclosed veranda beyond which the dark contours of the garden were visible, made misty by the wire screen. The concerted humming of insects drifted in, carried on a breath of flowers. Monsieur Chauvet, the Governor, and several others were gathered into an earnest group, their faces enveloped in bluish smoke. Thi-Linh was talking with the officer from Algeria.

The Prefect of Police had wandered out on the veranda and was gazing into the garden. But presently he turned, deliberately crossing the room to where she sat.

She looked up at him with veiled insolence; whatever his attitude now, his challenge at the table could not easily be forgotten.

"A charming garden, madame," he announced conventionally.

"Some of the flowers came from Japan—and one camellia plant was brought from Peking."

"Ah, Peking," he murmured reflectively. His smile was like sunlight on leather. "Roses, mimosa, agaves, acacias, palms—an exquisite ensemble, with just enough thorny growth to make it interesting. Such a garden is the perfection of desire."

Thi-Linh lighted a cigarette. Poor dead Nanette, she thought irrelevantly, if she could see me tonight! For a moment she studied the ascending smoke.

"I doubt if anyone ever attains the perfection of desire," she began slowly. "Desire is too transient, perfection too much a matter of mood. Do you not think so?"

The young officer, feeling himself excluded, strolled across the room and pretended to examine a picture.

"Perhaps," said the Prefect of Police.

He was studying her openly—and there was something relaxed and languid behind his gaze now. He was, she decided, a very rude Frenchman.

"May I be brutally candid, madame?" he commenced suddenly.

"Is not that the privilege of *Monsieur le Préfet de Police*?"

He shrugged. "You remind me of someone." There was a long pause before he went on. "Many years ago, in Peking, I saw a woman.... She rode in a sedan-chair, I think it was yellow, and as she passed down the street, all the Chinese prostrated themselves."

"In a yellow chair?" she repeated.

"A yellow chair."

Thi-Linh expelled the smoke from her nostrils before she said: "The imperial color.... Her name was Yehonala?"[32]

"Madame is very erudite." She could not tell whether he was mocking her or not. "It was not because she was an empress that I spoke of her, but because that morning when she passed down the street, I remembered that she virtually ruled the empire when she was twenty-two, and to have done that, she must necessarily have known a great deal about men." He bowed satirically, but she caught a gleam of sincerity in his direct gaze. "It is the pretense of my department to deal out justice; now and then justice is actual. I assure you, madame, Monsieur Chauvet is to be envied...."

---

32 Empress Dowager Cixi (Nov. 29, 1835–Nov. 15, 1908) was a powerful, charismatic woman who became the de facto ruler of China's Manchu Qing Dynasty from 1861 until her death. As *Monsieur le Préfet de Police* implies, she was especially skilled in the court intrigues—including murder—required to maintain her position. The empress's final words on her deathbed were: "Never again allow a woman to hold the supreme power in the State...."

4

Afterward when she thought of that speech it seemed the symbol of her triumph. The entire dinner was a gesture of vanity thrown back to her youth. Actually, now that it was over, it meant little more than this: in the future the Governor, passing her in the street, would speak; she had forced a compliment from the Prefect of Police, who in the beginning had seemed inaccessible; and (the thought came with a certain irony) she had given Monsieur Chauvet the opportunity to be proud of her publicly.

Of course, he had acted ridiculously about *Une Fille d'Annam* after the guests had gone. But it was not a violent scene, for he was too pleased otherwise, and it ended with his stroking her hair and calling her his "wise little peacock."

"You were clever," he had said, "very clever. And, *mon Dieu!* the way you replied to Chagny's remark about Africa! Even his Excellency was impressed; and *Monsieur le Préfet*, too. He is a strong man politically, that Prefect; some day he may be Governor of Cochin-China. I am glad you exerted yourself to entertain him." Then he added, "But I trust you were not too engaging."

Triumph, yes; to make those men acknowledge her. Yet it had not given her the exultation she had anticipated. "I doubt if anyone ever attains the perfection of desire." Her own words came back to her with somber conviction. If this had only happened with—with Justin—or Paul—anyone younger—younger than Monsieur Chauvet.

She wondered if her sudden antipathy toward age was the result of her own increasing years. Studying herself in the mirror, she saw no hint of age but a ripe maturity. Yet she had no illusions about her ability to remain young in appearance. She would not fade as quickly as Annamite women, but in a few years that soft gold-flushed skin would begin to sag, and her eyes would lose their intensity of color. She was nearly thirty, and her son (how strange that word seemed!) was— fourteen or fifteen?

Thirty. Suddenly she felt incredibly old, with a multiplicity of experiences that mounted beyond her years. How intolerable that the throbbing beauty of body should become insensible flesh before the ultimate decay! Perhaps it was for this period wise men had created the word "soul."

She was, she realized, at the height of her charm now. Yet she was denied the dignity of a mature passion. But after all, she told herself, she was through with emotional tumult—that had ended long ago.

Monsieur Chauvet had gone to Hanoi on business.

He was making the trip in his car because he could not wait for the next boat; and he would be away about a month. He had told her apologetically that if he had gone by water he would have taken her.

"It will be a quick, rough journey, my dear," he had said. "You would not enjoy it—and I shall be extremely busy in Hanoi." He took her face between his hands and kissed her on the forehead; it shamed her that she was glad he had not kissed her on the lips. "I hate to leave you alone," she added.

"You do not trust me?"

"I trust you—but—well, there are too many charming young men about, always ready to distract." Then he chuckled in an attempt to cover his jealousy. "But you are too wise to be indiscreet—aren't you, little peacock?"

And she said, then, what she had so often thought lately: "I am through with all that."

At first she was annoyed because Monsieur Chauvet did not take her with him; now he had gone, she contented herself with the prospect of several weeks alone, interrupted pleasantly by *dansants* at the Continental and other amusements.

It was the first time since she had been living with Monsieur Chauvet that she had been by herself in the large house, and she was surprised at her feeling of buoyancy and freedom. It was, on the other hand, a little disconcerting to realize his absence could give her this sense of utter holiday.

Her days were spent idly. As usual, Hoa brought *petit-dejeuner* to her bedside, and through the morning she lay in the cool shade of rattan blinds, reading or otherwise indolently amusing herself. The crushing forenoon over, she rode among the shops, buying indiscriminately because of her mood; and then, in the late afternoon, she motored to Thu Dau Mot or Bien Hoa. In the evenings she dined alone, with two candles burning on the table; and afterward she went to the cinema, or rode about the city lying back in the open car with the night wind weaving soft silk on her throat.

In one of the exclusive shops she saw a vivid gown from Paris—a warmth of fuchsia kindling in depths of orange barely visible under metal tissue—and she bought it. Naturally it called for an occasion. Therefore, seeing Lieutenant de Brissac sitting in the café of the Continental, it occurred to her to invite him to dinner. But this would be indiscreet. So she decided to invite several others as well, making it a party. Surely Monsieur Chauvet could not object to that.

She told her plan to Hoa. The old woman talked for an hour, trying to persuade her that Monsieur Chauvet would be anything but pleased, but she gave in when Thi-Linh found betel-stains on the floor of her room.

Lieutenant de Brissac would be delighted to come, said his charmingly informal reply. And so would the three other gentlemen whom she asked.

It was an entirely successful dinner party. Lieutenant de Brissac looked pleasantly bronzed in his immaculate uniform, and the other three were most acceptable. She wore the new gown—it seemed to sift a radiant pollen over her. The same glow fused her conversation.

After dinner they played the gramophone and danced; and later they rode out to Cholon in her car, and Lieutenant de Brissac held her hand persuasively. A wistful anguish filled her. It was not the man's touch that stirred her, but something more tenuous—it was the feeling of being close to people. All the lights of the Chinese city swam together, and the surge of bodies in the streets—Cholon never slept—seemed to flow endlessly as if mingling in a precious tryst.

Lieutenant de Brissac made it a point to linger after the other three had told her good night. An uncomfortable silence followed each speech. As he left, the rheumy languor in his eyes made something bend through her like wind-driven flame.

She went into the garden; she was too disturbed to go to bed. A dark plow had turned up the moon—a young moon that seemed tossed into the upper branches of tall cycad-trees and traveler-palms. The foliage made a cask that held hot scent. Unsubstantial noises drifted in from the surrounding city, melting into the vibrations of insects. She had a feeling of shadowy unfolding, as though a flower within her opened and gave up a prayer of fragrance. All the warm musk that she had drawn from those crowded streets of Cholon, from de Brissac, from the other men, now seemed distilled into the singing quiet. In that moment life rose up to meet her like a swarthy lover, and the moon was his mouth.

In the morning she awakened with a sense of incompleteness. Monsieur Chauvet had been away nearly a week now; could it be that she missed him? It did seem strange with him not about, particularly in the evenings, but she suspected that his absence was not the cause of her vague discontent.

She decided to motor to Cap St. Jacques and spend the night. The hotel there looked out to sea, and one could fall asleep listening to the waves.

It was the middle of the week, and she knew she would find few guests at the hotel. She arrived just before sunset when the vivid cerulean of the China Sea, reflecting the last glare, was burning to ashes of mauve. The wind was sultry and briny. To the east, the dark blue mountains of Annam rode the coast-line, stirring in her a transient curiosity to see the country where her mother had been born.

Sitting alone at dinner—there were only three other tables occupied—she wished, for a moment, that Lieutenant de Brissac were with her. Then she was glad he was not. He was, she decided, infinitely more interesting in her thoughts. If he were there, undoubtedly he would seek to translate the look she had seen in his eyes the previous night; and this, she reflected, would spoil the illusion. What illusion?

she asked herself immediately. Certainly she had none concerning him or his motives where she was concerned. But the night before, as he left, he had imparted to her a sense of husky emotional intensity that she did not want destroyed. It could never occur again. Men, when they desired, often were capable of an exquisite and intangible beauty which rarely survived constant association or consummation.

After dinner she walked down to the shore. The soft incoming rush of the water made an organ pulse under the sand. When she closed her eyes it sounded even louder. It was the music of ships far out and invisible in the darkness, some of which glided by the mouth of the river without their crews and passengers knowing that a few miles up the stream was the beginning of a country which made up the entire world for millions of people, herself included.

She felt a sudden desperate futility. Would she ever escape this small world? Never before had she consciously wanted to; of course she had dreamed of going to France, but always behind this dream was the knowledge that if she went she would return. Now the thought of those invisible ships aroused an aching desire to get away—anywhere. To live fully, swiftly, was not that better than slowly drifting into old age?

For an instant her longing was so transcendent that she became, in fancy, a spirit enclosing all those ships that stole by, far off in the night; men were in her, their bare torsos dripping and blood-flushed with the light of incredible furnaces; and all their groping desires, their torments and joys were hers; emotions that lived an eternity of fulfillment in the hope, born of whatever circumstances, that had thrust them into those ships which, in this moment, she seemed to draw into herself.

She was glad to get back to town the next morning. Yet she was lonely. It occurred to her that she might go to see Mama Thi-Bao and little Justin, but Stung Treng, she knew, would only increase her depression. Suddenly she wanted passionately to see her son. It was a wish she had learned through habit to suppress, but now and then it sprung up fiercely. If she sent for him, he could come and leave before Monsieur Chauvet returned. Monsieur Chauvet did not know he existed. If she had told him, it would only have resulted in unnecessary unpleasantness.

That very day she wrote to Mama Thi-Bao and enclosed money for Justin's passage.

Justin—her son—no longer little. How would he look? Brown and slim, like Kim Khouan? Or, as he had grown, had he become pale, like herself? She had a picture of him, hidden in an old trunk—it was taken when he was eleven. A thin, dark little boy with shy eyes and the hint of a melancholy smile in his sober gaze. Thinking about him frightened her a little. When he came, how would she act? How would he act? What would they talk about?

Mama Thi-Bao had written that for a while he had helped Vu-Trong-Khai in the shop, but the father at the Mission had interested him in studying for the *Service Télégraphique*, so that when he grew older he could have a position with the Government. In her last letter she had said that the *commissaire* had taken an interest in Justin, and a position was assured.

Poor Mama Thi-Bao …still sitting on that platform in the rear of the shop, chewing betel and dreaming of the past? Perhaps a little sifting of white in her hair, …Justin would tell her all about Mama Thi-Bao. And he would come within two weeks.

5

Several days later Lieutenant de Brissac asked to take Thi-Linh to a Rugby match between the army and navy teams.

She went. It had rained that morning, and the game was played amidst sprays of mud squashed up from seemingly innocent stretches of grass. Several Algerian Negroes were on one team, and the features of the Frenchmen, sweat-drenched and muddy, were scarcely distinguishable from those of the black men. Swarthy faces swooped and tumbled above a writhe of muscle, as if impelled by the shouting from the stadium.

When the game was over one Frenchman—or was he an Algerian?—was borne off the field above a rush of arms and heads, his sweater torn and hanging from one bare, soiled shoulder, his face darkly grotesque; an ooze-spattered effigy that the sun painted red and pressed into Thi-Linh's mind.

There had been, she thought, something intentionally violent about the game, reaching a climax in the dirty, tattered hero carried on the shoulders of shouting men; a figure that, no matter how muddy or ridiculous actually, was the idol of the cheering crowd.

That exaltation of physical skill awakened her to something she had not fully realized before. She perceived a menace in that absurdly battered figure reflecting the ruddy west. It was like seeing France in a new light.

She could not help contrasting this game with the mild, almost effeminate sports enjoyed by the better class Annamites. This Rugby match had been so consciously virile and competitive. And there was a presagement in the coating of mud that made white men the color of brown men. The fact that those brown men were Algerians instead of Annamites, or any other people of Indo-China, did not rob the illusion of its significance. Algeria, as well as Indo-China, was a French colony. Were these vigorous Frenchmen, with their instinct of active competition and ideas of physical perfection without the impulse of beauty, slowly forcing their virile culture upon the people they governed?

She had enjoyed watching the game. But that was a symptom to increase her fears. She did not belong to the Indo-China that the Imperial Court at Hue represented, an Indo-China slowly expiring; she belonged to this period of infusion, when French blood, ideas, and culture were mingling with the blood, ideas, and culture of the country.

She knew that some of the ancient sports of Annam were deliberately cruel, but it was studied brutality and not the spontaneous expression of national vitality such as European sports were. There seemed something imminently threatening in the idea. France awakening the muscles of Indo-China; injecting new ideas into the nerves that controlled them;

even giving them blood. The old Indo-China, exemplified by her mother! and the passing of which was coincident with herself, would be gone in another fifty years. Then, perhaps, it might not be Indo-China at all, but New France. Justin, her son, would be in the first generation of that country.

In the past, intelligence and literary skill were the virtues most respected; muscular development belonged to the people who served and entertained the higher caste, or those who made a living by labor or trade. India ink and brush were the symbols of power. But in this new Indo-China virtue would be in thews [33] and biceps, in quick wit that triumphed over commercial adversaries; and the symbols, whatever visible forms they took on, would be vital and progressive.

Suddenly she realized the tremendous physical resources of Indo-China. "It is one of the richest spots in Asia," Monsieur Chauvet had often remarked. Because of these resources, exploited by Frenchmen, he was here, one of the directors of a great bank; and because of them she possessed her clothes—all that she had.

The slow, uncoiling strength of Indo-China! Rich life in the arteries of her, substance in her drowsy muscles!

Why had she never thought of it before? A muddy, torn figure carried from a field above cheering men; and suddenly it had come to her.

Coolies in the mines, like figures of running jet; peasants in the rice-fields, transplanting green shoots or harvesting; fleets of junks swooping along the coast like flocks of gulls; naked brown savages tapping the rubber groves; women in the factories; fierce-looking men drifting down the rivers on floes of teakwood; bare, dripping bodies drawing in trapped silver in nets that writhed with life; and in the cities, thousands of shops where deft hands worked the looms and shaped bronze and precious metals. Swarthy muscles of Indo-China, those men and women; France the brain. Soldiers of commerce deployed from coast to coast, and through the jungles. White men on rubber plantations; directing copra mills; rice plants; tin and coal mines; a hundred other

---

33 I.e. muscles, good bodily proportion.

industries; all grinding out material that fell into the mold of piasters. In that process Indo-China also was being transformed. Would it eventually absorb the French? Or would Annamites, Cambodians, Tonkinese, Cochin-Chinese, and Laotians ultimately become European bodies with Asiatic hearts?

Frenchmen. How they had fought for this colony of theirs! Blood and guns; piracy; dysentery; fever; disease of all kinds. Bodies fertilizing the soil from which future French dreams would grow. Thousands of sun-burned white men—and from them, sunburned souls. Colonial children. Some born of native women, but all touched by the dark influence of an alien continent.

New France? Or new Indo-China?

She could see her country entering into an entirely different phase, as vigorously competitive as that Rugby match, with the battered victor borne high above a demonstrative multitude and carried into the face of the setting sun.

6

She received a telegram from Justin saying that Mama Thi-Bao was ill and she did not want him to leave until she was better; he would come later.

It was a bitter disappointment. It meant that she would not see him for a long while, for she could not have him when Monsieur Chauvet returned, unless he stayed elsewhere in the city and they met outside the house. The fact that he was unable to come, together with Mama Thi-Bao's illness, brewed a melancholy over her thoughts.

It was Wednesday afternoon when she received the telegram—the afternoon of the *dansant* at the Continental. She had no desire to go, but the quiet of the house was unendurable. Perhaps the music, and the tense, hot air shot with smoke, smells, and talk would drown her mood.

Lieutenant de Brissac was there, seated with several other Frenchmen, and he joined her, followed by the jealous, half-contemptuous smiles of women. She scarcely heard his conversation.

His flushed, handsome face was an effigy made dimmer by the smoke from the cigarettes he smoked constantly when not dancing.

When it was over, he rode home with her, lingering in the hope she would ask him to stay to dinner. She did not want him—nor did she want to be alone. She chose the loneliness. His breath was heavy with liquor, and the languor in his eyes had deepened.

She would, she told herself as she dined alone, be glad when Monsieur Chauvet returned; at least there would be someone in the house.

After the meal she sat in the pale spaciousness of the living-room smoking. Lizards pursued insects over the ceiling; from the screened veranda came a faint, scented breeze. The moon would be up, she thought. Perhaps it would be better to ride: the people, the wind along the river....

She rode past the cathedral, down the Rue Catinat. The soft whir of rickshaw wheels; now and then the hollow blatancy of a motor horn. On the sidewalks, sauntering shapes—the glow of a white suit, a passing naked back as oily as though anointed. The Indian shops were open, splashing the pavements with light. Black Chettis [34] sat imperturbably in the money-changers' shops, watching the people who passed. But the languid activity of the streets did not arouse her from her mood. She wanted spaces, winds.

A complete immobility masked the river, intensified by the quiver of lamps along the shore and in midstream. Sampans skulled close to the bank; at intervals shrill voices raveled the quiet.

The Marine Barracks glided past; the Botanical Gardens swept by a little faster. The chauffeur, as though sensing her mood, had pressed down the accelerator. She called directions to him, the wind rushing between her lips.

The town was fraying out into a suburb where the only lights were from scattered huts. Natives walking along the road, bewildered by the headlights, barely had time to leap out of the way. A bridge shot the car

---

34 A title used by certain merchant castes in South India (variants include Chettiar or Chetty).

into open country, where the black, flat ground merged imperceptibly with the scarcely lighter sky. The moon was just rising, touching the countryside with haunting effulgence. In its light objects flowed together. She could smell the paddy-fields ; they seemed to ferment the wind into sour wine. A ghostly blur of light lay on the drenched stretches, suffused with the shadows of rice-shoots. The breathless speed stripped her mind of thought. It was what she wanted. To ride this way for hours—wind-cleansed—racing the stars!

Suddenly, with a scream of brakes, the car swerved. She gripped the side, finding herself abruptly at a standstill, with silence pressing against her ears. The quick cessation of motion left her bewildered. She was acutely conscious of the still darkness of the ricefields, with nowhere a light.

"What is it?" she demanded.

"Somebody …" she heard the chauffeur articulate.

She stood up and leaned forward. The car had stopped diagonally across the road, its hood pointed toward a ditch. At one side lay what looked like a large white clot.

"What is it?" she repeated.

The chauffeur did not stir out of the seat. "Frenchman—maybe drunk—maybe dead."

The intense quiet, the body, the remoteness of the road, all ran together in her mind with a feeling of dread. She looked behind. In the distance a few lights—native huts. She had an instant of helplessness, then she ordered:

"Get out and see."

The Annamite slipped from the seat, and a moment later she saw him bend over the white clot. His short laugh sounded grotesque in that desolate spot.

"Drunk."

She felt relieved but still disturbed. After a pause she got out.

The man lay with his head in the grass at the side of the road. A shudder traveled over her at thought of him lying there where things could creep over him. The rest of him sprawled in the dust, one arm bent under him, the other flung out, palm down. His profile was blurred by the grass; soft hair caught the diluted radiance from the automobile's lights.

"He is not hurt?" she asked.

The chauffeur laughed again. "Smell," he said laconically.

But she had already caught a hint of alcohol. It disgusted her.

"Are you sure he is a Frenchman?"

For answer the chauffeur gripped the man under the arms and dragged him into the glare of the headlights, letting him fall with brutal carelessness.

It was a young face, white against the reddish dust. At first she thought some of that dust was sprinkled in his hair, then she saw that those glimmers were little russet auras in its wavy dark, created by the lights. At sight of this a memory shimmered and ran like quicksilver. The recollection nauseated her with its intensity. For an incredible instant Justin Batteur lay there in the road, as if the earth had yielded his spirit in ironic jest. Although the resemblance was transitory, it sufficed to lend a certain familiarity to that white young face.

"He can't be left here," she said tentatively.

Then she noticed that his pockets had been turned inside out. Apprehensive, she bent and pressed her hand over his heart. His skin felt warm through the thin shirt. At her touch the tendons of his sunburned throat moved, and he uttered a low groan. The sound startled her.

"Lift his head," she directed the chauffeur. "See if he has been struck."

The callousness with which the Annamite raised the head and then let it drop made her angry.

"No," he reported tersely. It annoyed her that he did not add, "Madame."

The white face seemed to stare up at her pathetically. After a moment of indecision, she ordered the chauffeur to put him into the car. The Annamite stared. "Did you hear me?" she said sharply. "And be careful."

The native dragged the inert man to the side of the car and pushed him into the rear, head first. Another groan followed. Thi-Linh struck the Annamite across the head. "Did you not hear me say to be careful? Put him in the seat."

When the man lay in one corner, head thrown back against the lowered top, legs sprawled across the floor, she got in.

"Police station?" asked the chauffeur.

She did not reply but went through the man's pockets. In his coat she found several letters.

"Give me the electric torch."

By the flashlight she read the name and address on the envelopes. "Richard Garstin, White Funnel Steamship Line, Singapore, F.M.S." An Englishman or an American. The letters bore the postmarks of Manila and Hongkong. She shifted the light to the man.

His white suit was very soiled, and his black cravat twisted awry. The face, in spite of its pallor, was sunburned. There were little lines at the corners of the mouth and eyes; a hint of a frown traced on his forehead. His skin was granular and rough, as though coarsened by exposure. One wrist, hanging motionless against the edge of the seat, caught her attention. It had a mark over the thick veins. As she saw that it was an anchor delicately stenciled in blue, she understood.

There was a dry clot on one cheek, and smears of dirt—evidently he had fallen or was thrown upon his face. His mouth, in contrast to his general appearance of ruggedness, was thin and sensitive. There was nothing about him suggestive of Justin Batteur except that rusty sheen which tipped the waves of his dark hair.

"Police station?" the chauffeur repeated; and she thought she heard a malicious eagerness in his tone. It added to her irritation.

"No," she said coldly. "No—drive home."

After she spoke she was startled and a little frightened. Her first impulse was to countermand the order, but she saw how ridiculous that would make her. Something in the way he lay there, head fallen back, body inert, made it impossible for her to turn him over to the police. Of course she could leave him at a hotel, but that would be too conspicuous. The only thing she could do was to take him home or leave him here.

The chauffeur had started the motor, was backing around.

What will the servants think? she wondered. She knew they would carry no tales to Monsieur Chauvet, for even though they disliked her, all except Hoa, they were also afraid of her. But they would talk among themselves and others, and their imaginations would be unrestricted. Yet she could not wash her hands of this man simply to avoid gossip among the servants, no matter what circumstances had brought him to this isolated spot and in this condition.

Perhaps he would become conscious before they reached the city— that would relieve the situation—then she could take him to his ship or wherever he wished to go. If not, she would have to let the houseboy and the chauffeur put him in one of the guestrooms for the night. After all, she could depend upon Hoa to mute the servants' talk.

Now and then the man stirred and made some faint sound. The moon rode high, and its light lay on his face; his cravat flapped noisily. In the night, that face had a strange innocence, although she could smell the alcohol on his mouth.

Her mind was slashed with conjectures.... For some reason it depressed her to realize she would never know all she wanted to know about him, for if she had to take him home for the night, he would leave in the morning with only the perfunctory remarks that such a situation required. She had known few Englishmen and Americans, and it was a natural curiosity. Undoubtedly, she decided, he would be the traditional coarse and untutored seaman—in spite of the delicate hint of his lips.

She remembered that recent night at Cap St. Jacques when, standing on the beach, she had felt the nearness of ships on the black sea; perhaps his ship had been out there then. Curious. And she had seemed to surround those ships with the intensity of her desire, drawing all their terrific power of men and machinery into her own heart-beat.

The lights of Saigon were multiplying ahead; flares from open doors slipped by, silhouettes of people, and odors of cooking.

The man lay there as though drugged. He had been so quiet the last few minutes that she felt for his pulse. With that touch the thought flashed into her that she would be glad if he did not wake up before they reached the house. Is that wrong? she wondered. But why should it be? It was simply—adventure; a brief encounter without significance, except that, in spite of the sordid circumstances of his predicament, it had the illusive flavor of romance.

A momentary apprehension seized her as they drew near the house. It would be awkward …but it was too late to regret now. Nor did she regret, she told herself emphatically.

She glanced at the man anxiously as the car crunched loudly over the graveled driveway. He still lay in a stupor, although his breathing had become audible.

When the car drew up under the porte-cochere and the chauffeur opened the door, she jumped out, ordering him to wait. In the hallway she called for Hoa. After a moment the woman responded sleepily from upstairs.

"Come here."

Hoa came, with a dragging clack of sandals.

Thi-Linh told her there was a man, an Englishman or an American, out in the car, whom she had picked up unconscious on the Hoe-man Road, and she wanted her to call the house-boy and put him in the east bedroom. "I think he has been hurt," she added, despising herself for lying.

Hoa stared stupidly. "A man?" she repeated. An Englishman, or an American—in the east bedroom? A stranger? Her look became a warning. "But Monsieur Chauvet—"

"Don't ask questions," Thi-Linh interrupted; "do as I say."

She waited in the hall, her nerves tense. Presently they came, Hoa holding open the door while the two Annamites entered carrying the unconscious man between them like a hammock. There was something pathetic in the way his limp hands dragged the floor. She wanted to tell them to lift him or those hands would be knocked and bruised, but she merely watched, fascinated, as they mounted the stairs, his wrists and fingers now and then thudding against the steps.

She followed, reaching the top as they disappeared in a doorway at the end of the hall. Hoa reappeared almost immediately with an accusing look. "Hurt!" she sniffed.

Thi-Linh ignored her. "Get some water and wash his face," she directed.

Hoa smoldered. "Am I the servant of drunken Englishmen?"

"If you do not," Thi-Linh threatened, "then I shall." Hoa went mumbling toward the bathroom. When the old woman returned, carrying basin and towel, she said:

"What will Monsieur Chauvet think?"

"He will think nothing," replied Thi-Linh, "if you

make certain that he does not hear about it."

Hoa moved on without answering, still muttering to herself. ,

As Thi-Linh undressed she heard the muted music of leaves in the garden—branches whispering and brushing, broad-leaved fronds clashing shadowy cymbals. A phantom appassionato to which her thoughts moved.

…White face in the red dust of the road, red dust sprinkled on the crests of dark hair. And those hands swinging against the stairs. A sense of wistful and ineffable beauty permeated her. Adventurous encounter! Brief, fragile as lines of poetry. In the morning he would go. Always the picture of that white face in the road, from which time would exclude the memory of alcoholic smell and soiled clothing. No matter what he might say before he left (perhaps he could not even speak French!) his departure would come so quickly that any crudity would be easily dissolved in the aspect of adventure.

When she had put on a dressing-gown, she went into the hall. Hoa met her in the doorway of the east bedroom.

"He is still asleep?"

The old woman nodded sulkily.

For an instant Thi-Linh hovered on the threshold, gazing at the fog of mosquito-netting that made mystery of the form in the bed, then she returned to her room and lay listening to the breeze in the garden.

7

She sat in the cool blue shadow behind the blinds of the veranda waiting for him to come down.

A few minutes before, Hoa had made a reluctant but full report.

The house-boy, she said, had found him awake, staring about the room quite bewildered. He tried to speak some language—perhaps it was English—and the house-boy had called her. When she went in, he spoke French—it was very bad French but it was French. He asked a thousand questions. "I told him," said Hoa, "he would have to ask madame; that *she* knew all about last night, and not *I!*" The boy had carried *petit-dejeuner* to him, and now he was shaving.

Thi-Linh instructed Hoa to take Monsieur Chauvet's old dressing-gown to him, and tell him she would be waiting on the veranda.

Beyond the blinds, a glittering silence submerged the garden; it was like a radiant pool into which the noises from the street fell and were dissolved.

She was wondering what she would say, her mind drowsily resisting the heat, when he came—so silently in his straw sandals that she was not aware of him until he appeared in the doorway. It was a little disconcerting, to see him standing there like that.

He looked compactly slender, but not thin, in the dressing-gown, and a bit fantastic with Monsieur Chauvet's ridiculously lilac pajamas bagging about his ankles. A blur of powder was on his newly shaven cheeks. As their eyes met, a deep red suffused his face.

"I am—" he began in French. Then he said something in English which she supposed was an inquiry as to whether or not she understood his native tongue.

She shook her head. "I do not speak English."

He hesitated. In the daylight he seemed very tawny with a sunburn which the dissipation of the night before had drained to a pale coffee-color. Immediately she was conscious of the dense brownness of his eyes—eyes that haunted with their very luxury of color.

"I—I speak French very badly," he commenced. It was a voice that made her think of thick dust—something heavy and husky about it, a hint of inarticulateness in it. Perhaps that was because he did not know French very well. "I want to apologize," he said.

"Won't you sit down?"

When he moved there was an inconspicuous flexibility about his body that suggested lithe strength.

"It's all very—unfortunate," he began again; then, "May I smoke?"—gesturing toward the cigarettes on the table nearby.

She noticed that his hand trembled as he struck the match and held it to the cigarette. Observing her eyes upon him, he laughed in an uncertain manner.

"You are English?" she asked.

"American."

He looked a little dissolute, she thought—the shadows under his eyes, the cut on his cheek where he had struck the ground—but that was because of last night. As she studied him, she had a recurrence of the feeling she had experienced briefly when looking at his dim face in the motorcar—a curious illusion of innocence. It was, she understood intuitively, an innocence that could not be affected by experience. Men of his type went to sea, or entered into any adventure or reality, without formulated reason. They did not lack intelligence ; it was simply that their thoughts moved with the languid cadence of their blood. Because they believed in emotion instead of analysis they remained untouched and guileless.

"You are from a ship?" she questioned.

He glanced guiltily at the tattoo on his wrist. "Infallible, isn't it?" His smile, stirring remotely in those densely brown eyes, seemed to diffuse without any objective and yet to regard something disturbingly imminent.

"It's all very unfortunate," he repeated. "My ship—"

"Tell me what happened last night," she interrupted.

The lines in his forehead creased into a deliberate frown. In the following silence she imagined he was constructing French phrases. At last he said:

"I remember now—I saw you at the hotel—dancing with a French officer. I was there—sitting at a table on the sidewalk—with the mate. He had to get back to the ship early—some matters. I wandered around—pretty lonely, I guess. You know—or do you know?—what a sailor does when he's lonely? …What's the name of that other café—not the one where you were dancing—the Rotonde? From there I drifted to another—Café des Nations, I think. The last I remember was getting into a rickshaw and telling the coolie 'Waterside, steamship *Nassau*.' I guess I was awfully drunk." After a pause he asked: "Where did you find me?"

Briefly she told him. That flush stole over his face again. Then, when the color had receded, he looked at her and she felt as if something actually physical had passed through her body.

"You were—very considerate," he said simply.

"It is nothing."

The glittering silence of the garden seemed to creep between them. He pressed his cigarette into a tray on the arm of his chair; waited as though expecting her to speak.

Finally she remarked:

"I suppose the other officers on the ship will be concerned about your absence." She designated him an officer because she was certain he was not a common seaman.

He smiled—that smile that regarded something disturbingly imminent.

"The *Nassau* was to sail some time after midnight—last night."

For some reason the words came to her with a shock. She managed to say calmly: "You mean—"

"I mean I got just what I deserved."

She offered him a cigarette and took one herself. His hand was a little steadier now.

He did not seem in the least concerned about having been left behind. The next moment she understood why.

"The *Nassau* is due in Hai Phong in eight days," he announced; "she stops for cargo at—what's the name of the place, Quinhon?—and Tourane. I suppose I can make it up there by then."

"The railway does not go beyond Nhatrang," she said; "that is not a fourth of the distance."

He accepted the news with no evident emotion; but for a while he smoked in silence.

"Did you lose many valuables last night?" she inquired.

"I don't know how much I had when I got in the rickshaw—but not much."

"Do you remember the number of the rickshaw?"

He only laughed at that. "I do remember riding for a long while; and then I seemed to fall on my face." Again he looked at her. "I suppose—well, I don't know what would have happened if you hadn't—" He stopped, incoherent. More and more his voice made her think of thick dusks—an inarticulate groping.

He rose tentatively, obviously ill at ease.

"If you—you will tell the servant to bring my clothes," he began.

"I told Hoa to have your suit washed; but she will bring you one of Monsieur Chauvet's—I think it will fit. We have *dejeuner* at eleven-thirty."

His embarrassment grew. "I—I shan't trouble you any longer—as soon as my clothes are ready—I'll go and see the Consul—perhaps he—"

"You mean—you wish to go?"

The look in his eyes hurt her—he seemed so at a loss what to do or say.

He tried to laugh. "I don't want to, of course, but—"

"Suppose we talk of that at dejeuner?"

"You are very kind ...mademoiselle?"

That glittering silence drew in until she could feel

it trying to quench her breath.

"Madame—Madame Marie Linh," she said.

8

He appeared at dejeuner fresh in one of Monsieur Chauvet's suits. It fitted him a little loosely—but he was not the type to wear tight clothes. Instead of making him look slouchy, it gave an effect of careless relaxation to his supple firmness.

During the meal his manner was still constrained. This reticence, almost awkwardness at times, was due partly, she thought, to the fact that he could not fathom her. He did not understand her position in the houses—of course he knew she was the mistress—nor what she was. To relieve the situation she announced casually that her husband was in Tonking at present—in Hanoi. He, Monsieur Chauvet, she added, was a director in the *Banque de l'Indochine.*

She watched him closely, but his face reflected nothing. Yet when he addressed her, a moment later, he called her "Madame Chauvet." It made her uncomfortably conscious of herself; had he done it deliberately or did he fail to understand?

After luncheon he announced that he was going to the consulate. She suggested that one did not go out in the terrific midday heat in Saigon, but when he showed no sign of changing his intention, she did not add that undoubtedly he would find the Consul resting, there was a hint of stubbornness about him that did not invite persuasion. It was not a defiant quality, but a simple resoluteness that came inevitably with any decision. Before he left she said that in the cool of the afternoon they would motor to Bien Hoa.

As she lay in the artificial dusk of her room, trying to rest, the persistent image of his limp hands thudding against the staircase swung in her thoughts. In spite of that air of resolution, there was something helpless about him. Now that he had not left that morning, as she had expected, she resented his presence, for it had the power to make her restless. "I am through with all that," she had said to Monsieur Chauvet. I am, she repeated to herself. She wanted him to go, knew that he should, yet, perversely, she sought, in her thoughts, and even in her actions, to delay him. He had, she admitted, a decidedly distracting quality. A few years before, that complication in his character would have challenged her. It challenged now, but she had sufficient emotional poise to regard it from a distance.

She was, indeed, "through with all that."

When she went below she found him sitting in the frail gloom of the living-room, the air about him thick with smoke. He wore his own suit now, stiff with starch and too tight—he looked uncomfortable. He had been to the consulate twice, he said; the first time the Consul was resting.

"He told me a way I could get to Hai Phong." He took a sheet of note-paper from his pocket and read: "Train to Nha Trang, bus to

Tourane; then train to Dong Ha, and bus again to Vinh; after that, rail all the way to Hai Phong, via Hanoi." As he spoke he looked very depressed. "He said it could be made in about five days."

"When will you go?"

"In the morning." Then he added hastily: "But tonight—I—I can stay at a hotel."

"That is unnecessary," she said simply.

Now the motorcar was purring toward Bien Hoa, over a road that plunged through groves of areca-palms relieved by stretches of rice-fields where peasants stood' thigh-deep in succulent green. As it was late, he wore no hat, and she found his dark, sunburnt hair very disturbing. He talked little. But the quiet was eased by an emotional content they both shared and which, in him, was slowly absorbing the faint depression that had settled on him at the house. She was aware, suddenly, that he had a protective strength reminiscent of Justin—yet the fact that he abandoned himself to impulses, a fact she sensed, made that solidity physical rather than a mental attitude. Affection, in men like him, was permanent without changing their habits.

The sun had almost set when they reached Bien Hoa. The yellow, moldy houses had an air of soft anguish in the ruddy afterlight, and the river took on the dignity of dusk. They stopped at a little café facing the stream. The association of ancient, drowsy decadence clung about its mildewed walls.

They took a table on the sidewalk, facing the glimmering air of the west.

Out on the stream, the shadows of clouds drifted in a lazy herd; the sound of a bugle, ringing tremulously from the barracks, momentarily turned the air to silver.

"It—it's beautiful here, isn't it?" he said as though surprised at the discovery.

For an instant a sleeping sense of beauty was aroused in his eyes, bringing a quick flush to her emotions. All his incoherent, inarticulate being had seemed to draw a swift breath. Her sensitiveness to his feeling startled her.

"I—I like this hour," he said. "At this time I—I imagine all sorts of things—and sometimes"—he laughed nervously—"I repeat idiotic words aloud—words that seem like they've been—well, dipped in color—" He stopped abruptly, as though he had betrayed something.

"You haven't finished—you were going to say—"

"I was going to say, you should be in the bow of a ship at this time of day—it—it's magnificent. Sometimes there are birds flying around the cargo-booms—gulls. I—love gulls."

There was a swooping suggestion in his words—they dipped into her blood and started it roving. She had seen gulls at Cap St. Jacques; they always made her think of pain.

"Have you ever heard a gull cry?" he asked.

She thought she heard a gull cry then—shuddery and dark. For a moment the wistful luxury of feeling in his eyes seemed to become articulate in a desperate sound.

"I remember . . ." He stopped, painfully embarrassed.

"Won't you tell me?"

The gathering dusk was a soft cocoon weaving them closer together. He had clasped his hands on the table, and in his nervousness, he pressed his fingers together so tightly that they darkened under the nails and the tattoo over his thick veins moved like a shadow. He smiled to cover his awkwardness.

"It's something—one shouldn't tell a woman. I forgot for a minute."

"It was something about—gulls—and dusk?" she urged.

"Really. . . ."

"Really I should like to hear it. What is it that makes you afraid, the traditional Anglo-Saxon restraint?"

His laugh was uncertain. "It's rather—sordid." As he spoke he looked at her with that curious innocence in his brown irises.

She regarded him quizzically. "You don't really think that."

He smiled—that expression that sought after something remote. "No," he said at length. "No, I don't. …It happened in a little town where I lived for a while. I was quite young—about seventeen—I hadn't gone to sea then. There are lots of cliffs along the beach there—fine and gray—sort of tumbling up out of the sand."

He paused, and she had the feeling that his appreciation of beauty was seeking frantically to make itself audible. It would have been easier in his own tongue. Yet the fact that he had to struggle to find the words, gave a deeper intensity to what he said, as though all his senses had become attenuated.

"I used to go there late afternoons—the air was full of gulls. One afternoon I stayed there until dark—all the gulls were gone except one that kept circling over the water and crying. I didn't see the girl on the beach until I'd climbed down—I can't remember at all what she looked like, except that she was pale and—and something about her white look was like the crying of that gull. …I didn't want her—it seemed as if I were trying to find something that was in the cry of that bird…. Afterward, I was disgusted, I—" He stopped, the knuckles of his tightly clasped hands white. There was something taut and pinched in his face, too. He tried to laugh. "You see how—how sordid it was—that story? I told you…." The fierce emotion behind that face struck her with blanching force.

He was trying desperately to tell her a thing that had troubled him for years. She could see that young boy on the cliff—the gull planing over the sea. His hair was darker then, without those little ripples of sunburn; his eyes less intense but more authentically innocent. There had been other experiences in the following years at sea, but never under cliffs, with a bird crying in the dusk. Mere physical gestures— behind them an almost savage bewilderment.

Bien Hoa—the river, the trees, and the ancient decadence of the café—all lay sensually quiet under the powder of early evening. She felt it with a sensation as of suspended breathing.

"I think I understand," she managed to say.

How grotesquely inadequate! But how could she tell him that so often in the twilight region of her mind she had heard the dark music of gulls?

The hush drew about them; she was aware that his poise had raveled, and she could think only of conventional things to say. She began to talk. Empty words poured forth inconsequentials. He seemed grateful, responding almost eagerly with banalities. She wanted to hurry away, to return quickly to the familiar atmosphere of Saigon.

When they left, soiled lamps had been lighted in the café, and a black silence flowed with the river.

That ride back to town was painful. She was no longer conscious of an emotional ease—their silences were strained, nerve-racking. Her thoughts blurred and raced by like the palms beside the road, seeming to become audible in the whirring of the motor.

Some of her assurance returned when the car drew up at the house. In the hallway he paused uncomfortably.

"I think," he said, "I had better go now."

She did not know whether she was relieved or not; her surprise was carefully concealed behind a cool tone when she spoke.

"But the train does not leave until tomorrow."

"It leaves early in the morning—and I don't want to disturb you."

She knew he was lying, but she knew also that he was determined to go, if not immediately, before the evening was over.

"Surely you will stay until after dinner?"

He hesitated, then murmured, "Thank you."

She was sorry she had asked him to remain; through the meal her nerves danced with each clash of glass and silverware. His self-consciousness was visible in a positive agony that darkened his eyes. Afterward, over liqueur and coffee in the living-room, he stepped close to her to take a cigarette, and an enervating warmth almost made her sway nearer. Thereafter when she spoke, the silence following her words seemed to jangle about her like broken glass.

Finally he said he must go.

With that announcement the tension relaxed a little—but it left her vaguely frightened. He had no hat, and she offered him one of Monsieur Chauvet's old ones, but he refused it with quiet decision. His effort to put his gratitude into words was pathetic. How many hundred years had passed, she thought, since she had found him lying in the red dust? His hand was moist and heavy as he told her good-by; he stood on the top step, and over his shoulder she could see the dart and glide of two rickshaws beyond the low iron fence. She said something else— afterward she could not remember what it was—then he had descended the steps, heavily, quickly, and had become a silhouette receding in the graveled driveway.

Inert hands, brown and thick-veined, thumping against the stairs. When she went into the house she could imagine them swinging there, limply, as they had done the night before.

Her thoughts were weaving painfully through a dark texture. He had gone. Adventurous encounter! Brief, fragile.... More like the white flare of gunpowder.... Love him? No, it was not love—not as she understood love.... Something else—something strange.... Gone. And there was no way she could have prevented it without making herself absurd. None. Unless—She endured a sensation that was an ecstasy of regret. Why had not she thought of it before? She could have taken him in the car—to Vinh—six days, maybe seven, for the entire trip. Monsieur Chauvet would never have known—or she might have gone on to Hanoi—surprised Monsieur Chauvet. Outwardly he would have been annoyed, inwardly pleased. And then she could have stolen those few days out of life—not to touch him—only to ride beside him—see that luxury of brown in his eyes—the little ripples of rust in his hair—a gull swooping over the sea—a boy seeking the mystery of pain in its cry—herself seeking the pain and joy the man expressed.

But how fantastic. Impossible. She was glad she had not thought of it. Through with all that. Respectability—the paradoxical respectability of being Monsieur Chauvet's mistress.

Limp hands thudding against the steps—following her upstairs.

She undressed and tried to read. Insects blundered about the light, cicatrizing the quiet. They seemed to enter the printing and buzz before her eyes. She closed the book and turned out the light.

Sleep! To imagine she could sleep! Smells from the garden stole up and haunted the darkness; a wan diffusion of moonlight made fluid rectangles of the windows.

Rising, she thrust her feet into bedroom sandals, slipped on a peignoir and went downstairs.

The boy had not put out the lights in the living-room. Taking a cigarette from the table, she lighted it and moved out on the veranda.

She sat down; it was the chair he had occupied that morning.

The shrubbery in the deep yard made formless contours on either side of the driveway; fence and gate were starkly silhouetted against the lighted street. Even the street was deserted. Gradually she made out a pale figure against one of the gate-posts—the house-boy. That was the only bit of life in the dreadfully inert night. Even that was motionless.

What is he doing there? she wondered. Waiting for some girl, perhaps. The thought annoyed her. A tryst at the gate. She would stop that.

"Nham!" she called. "Nham!"

The figure started away from the post; she caught the flash of a white suit. Something in that movement brought her to her feet, her heart-beat trebling.

"Wait!" she cried involuntarily.

The figure was hurrying along outside the fence. She rushed down into the yard, lost a sandal but went on. When she reached the gate the man had paused a few yards away, a white shadow under the trees. Slowly he turned, walked back toward her, reluctance in his stride.

"I—I shouldn't have come," he began, his voice thick with embarrassment. "I was restless, so I walked, and suddenly I found myself here—and I—I just stood by the gate—for a moment—"

"I should not have let you go," she said, composing herself. "I am sure you have no money—nor do you know where to get any."

There was a long silence. Her blood seemed to thicken and stand still. She wondered if, in the darkness, his eyes were filled with that liquid intensity. Finally he articulated:

"No, it's true—I can't make it to—to my ship. I'll have to wait here until something comes up. The Consul said—"

"But you have no place to stay," she interposed. He had gone, without money, without anything, rather than accept charity. The realization stirred an overwhelming pity.

"You—you had done so much—already."

He was going—going. How could she keep him? That quiet stubbornness, that stubbornness without defiance; what weapon was adequate to penetrate it?

"But you must come in," she commenced. "The same room—" She caught her breath; something winged and perilous had risen out of her despair. Its quick rush made her dizzy. But when she spoke her voice sounded calm.

"My husband—Monsieur Chauvet—telegraphed for me to join him in Hanoi—I am leaving in the morning at sunrise—in my car." She laughed—a cool, decisive laugh. "After all, you see, you can make your ship.... No, you must not protest—my"—again she laughed—"my reputation can sustain the shock of traveling up the coast of Annam— alone with a man."

9

In a few hours they would reach Hue.

Richard Garstin sat in silence beside her, his gaze on the passing countryside. Now and then, when their glances met, he looked a little dazed and smiled faintly; he did not attempt to talk. He wore one of Monsieur Chauvet's helmets, and, in the face of the wind, the strap was lowered and molded tightly in the crease under his lower lip. That brown strap gave him the appearance of heightened virility. It also seemed, curiously, to offer an excuse for his silence.

The chauffeur slouched in the front seat, plunging the car ruthlessly ahead with deliberate menace to the natives or animals in the road.

Her thoughts slipped back to that night at Saigon—to the hours between. Now that they had been on the way for almost three days, the incredible folly of the thing had lost its fantastic aspect. Nor was she frightened any more. The vital present excluded the future, even the past, temporarily. There was little danger; few men that she knew traveled along this coast; and at Vinh she would leave him, returning to Saigon and—she had to admit it—a life that was a sterile gesture. This indiscretion—Monsieur Chauvet would never know of it. And it was not wrong—simply to ride beside him, to talk with him, to watch the velour softness of his eyes. On the surface he was simple, simple as the soil, an ordinary man who lived instead of analyzed—yet deep within was a delicate complexity of character that had disclosed its presence that afternoon at Bien Hoa.

Although he had lived—never extravagantly, she realized, but to his own satisfaction—there was something withdrawn about him. It suggested an unconscious reserve that guarded a spiritual purity more essential than physical chastity. This ability to withdraw was a quality they had in common. She, too, had lived—yet there were no flaws in her conscience; a few regrets, perhaps, and immeasurable pity. She could not believe that she had done any great wrong. Her life had been the antithesis of convention, but, after all, morality was tradition. In the beginning—before human beings became so complex—there were no laws regulating emotions; laws were necessary when men came to recognize their own instability. Humanity had been forced legally to confess its weakness. How tragic that proud blood and body should become so humble!

It was impossible now, as a result of ages of increasing sophistication, to realize any desire not entirely conventional without bringing ingenuity and deceit into play. Simple as this journey was, it involved a certain amount of subterfuge and intrigue which Thi-Linh detested. It had been necessary to leave several letters with Hoa, one to be mailed to Monsieur Chauvet every other day. She had also given Hoa instructions to telegraph her along the way if she had any news of importance.

Poor Hoa! Thi-Linh would never forget her expression when she announced her intention of taking Richard Garstin up the coast to Vinh. At first, she had been too surprised to say anything, and when she fully grasped what Thi-Linh planned to do, the enormity of the indiscretion smote her dumb. Her silent, accusing gaze followed every movement of preparation; and it was the last thing Thi-Linh saw as the car glided away from the house.

Perhaps that look was responsible for the strange thudding emotion that struck her after they had passed Bien Hoa. The sun had been up an hour, and the golden mist of early morning was just clearing. It seemed to evaporate from her own mind, and the tangible nearness of the man, coupled with the reason for his presence, was a distinct shock. She was terrified for a moment. Daylight was a cruel fluid that brought out the secret and invisible writing of nocturnal impulses; and she perceived actually, for the first time, what she was doing.

But with the passing of a few hours, that fear dissolved. She felt contented—contented as she had not been for years. But he was a difficult companion in spite of the sense of physical and mental warmth that he gave her. He seemed still bewildered by this sudden development. His words were few, and without significance.

The first night they stopped at Phanrang, a little town on the coast. Behind it were the blue mountains that rose to Dalat. After dinner in the tiny hotel, she suggested a walk.

Sea-wind and star-swoon; the moon still loitering below the sky-line. All the bewilderment seemed to lift from his brain. He laughed—hesitantly, for that was his manner—and hummed little songs as they wandered through the streets. Once he quoted poetry in English—he could not translate all of it, he said, but it was by a young Englishman who died in the war. It was called "The Great Lover."[35]

---

35 Rupert Chawner Brooke (Aug. 3, 1887–Apr. 23, 1915) was an English poet known for idealistic war sonnets written during the First World War.

" 'Wet roofs,' " he murmured; " 'live hair that is shining and free…the comfortable smell of friendly fingers…' " After a pause, given courage by the darkness, he blurted out awkwardly: "It's funny—but I love little things, too …white roads—and ships' ropes—the smells of resin and canvas—the feel of water and sand—hair in the wind—the look in some people's eyes…. And of course," he added, "gulls…."

To her his words were like the beat of wings—a flutter of something beautiful and wild, half-seen in the blurred core of his crystal simplicity. Her thoughts swung back to that evening at Bien Hoa; a baffling insecurity filled her.

The next morning they started early. The superb shoulders of that mountainous coast were bathed in an orient drench of sunlight. This setting imparted a singular beauty to the coolies passing in the road. These common people walking with bare feet seemed to possess an enviable intimacy with the mountains. Assignation of skin and soil. Life surging into them from the green veins of the earth, from the coral veins of the sea; chameleon blood that linked them into a rhythmic whole.

Annam—her mother's country. The sudden realization of her inheritance seemed, in some mysterious way, to allow her to share this intimacy. Was there, she wondered, anything so beautiful in France? She felt a quick pride in Annam. She had never discussed her blood with Richard Garstin—undoubtedly he knew she was a half-caste—but suddenly she said:

"This is my mother's country."

There was nothing apologetic in her tone. He responded with a curious little smile that seemed to say: "And did you think I didn't know your heritage was as ancient and authentic as these mountains?"

It was the first direct compliment he had given her, even with his eyes, and it was reassuring. Prejudice had been dissolved in the warm tolerance that experience had given him. It would have been almost tragic to find him like …like the others. She was happy, for she felt that she could have told him about Kim Khouan, Justin, Paul, all, and he would have understood. Nevertheless, she had no idea of doing it. No matter what he sensed, the truth in words would destroy a certain chivalry that existed between them.

At sunset they reached Quinhon where they dined. The town was a huddle of pale houses riveted together with lights, and pigmy-small under the somber mass of the rocky coast; a coast that here thrust a tongue of sand into the sea.

"It makes me think of the place where I used to live—the mountains and the beach," he said. "Shall we walk by the shore? I used to, there…."

The white sand underfoot was like a strip of accumulated dust from the stars that swarmed over the mountains and down into the bay. Far out in the harbor, an off-shore breeze slipped its hands into the charging manes that rode against the promontory. The surf was visible to her in pale scars that writhed and vanished.

His presence—a white form swinging along easily and in silence—seemed to rinse her thoughts in aromatic coolness. Although he had become an indistinct shape, she was aware of his suavely muscular body. And the breeze twisted strands of his hair into a dark blur between his eyes—the hair that always disturbed her.

How full he made the darkness seem! The realization was vaguely alarming. How would she react when he was gone? Would the days quickly fill in the rift he had made, like sand in the wake of a wheel? Or would his passage leave an indelible mark, a bruise to bathe and swathe for many months? "Through with all that." Yes, she had said this. But how stupid!—how stupid to say one was through with anything until death!

Death. That word, with all its implications, slipping into her mind so vibrantly alive, seemed utterly incongruous. Yet it brought a significant aversion that was not fear but distaste. Beautiful flesh woven through with a tapestry of worms, and soil softening the decay, cleansing the bones, until sockets and skull became the acceptable refuge of seeds; hungry seeds that drained the last marrow from the bones and uncurled to the sunlight in incredible colors; each to emulate the sacrifice of flesh that had given it life, perpetuating a cruel and bitter principle of succession. How dreadful, to lose all this consciousness of living! Suddenly even pain seemed precious. And yet, she reflected, there was sardonic beauty, even satisfaction, in the law of rot and bloom. In some other night, far removed, would she spring from earth, with singing in her veins, and open an extravagant flower to the morning? Or would all the golden sap of her flourish again in limbs that stretched with ecstatic rigidity to the sun, expressing in fiber and tendril the awareness of living that filled her now?

"Oh, live swiftly, swiftly!" the night whispered.

Ah, yes! Live! What did tradition matter? Or creed? Or laws? On one side of the earth, men cried out their fears to gods of wood and stone; on the other, just as many prayed to a deity without figure or image. In another hundred years or so these gods would be cast aside for new ones. And what would be accomplished? Only a little more knowledge, contradictory and ironic, to be distributed among the wise. But no greater security, no deeper convictions.

What had religion given her? Certainly no conception of life; what she knew of life she had learned from living. It had only filled her youth with superstitious fears and her maturity with doubt.

For a moment she was startled by the realization of her utter escape from dogma.

Had nothing of the faith of her Ancestors survived in her? As she looked at that faith now, dispassionately, it seemed a lifeless cult built on the vainglory of past generations. Worms were crawling in the rotten wood of the pagodas; mold on the tablets; bats, careening among the spiders' webs woven between the carved and lacquered beams, powdered the altars with dung.

And the faith that France had brought? What deposit had it left on her? Pontifical words. The incense lifting in the churches was the smoke of burning years; and with the ashes the faithful were baptized, while chant and song drowned their whimperings of fear. The cross was not the symbol of hope but of the final ecstasy of pain before death.

And God—what was God? The agonized cry of the body facing the fecundity and decay of nature? A chorus in which she, too, sang frenziedly? But her voice, suddenly, had grown weak.

In the heart of Cambodia were the remnants of a religion.... She had heard whispers at Stung Treng, when she was a child. ...In those stone altars was there a simple truth which men, burdened with years of servitude to a false ideal of intellect, called obscene?

But what did it matter? Nothing mattered at that moment except that she had grown weary of complicated conjectures. The man walking in silence beside her seemed the key to a dimension of simplicity that promised rest. Abruptly she said:

"Tell me about your country; what is it like?"

He laughed. "That's queer. I was thinking about it then.... America." He mused over the word. "America is sort of—well, you may smile, but—but sometimes I think of America as a blond giant—why blond, I don't know—but a blond giant—lying in the sun—and wearing a mask—a stupid, grinning mask—with a fine face underneath. I—I suppose that's absurd, but...." The sentence ended in silence.

It was one of those moments when, having surprised his reticence, she was rewarded with an expression of that sensitiveness hidden at the center of his nature.

"Go on," she said.

"America...."

He talked of the marvel of tall buildings. But she saw a mammoth body—a giant taking life from the bosom of ripe hills. His chest was hairy with fields of grain; steel and iron were his muscles; mills ground in his brain, whirling strange laughter; and in that magnificent torso the spurt and scream of industry jetted rich blood into arteries eager for life. Nude body stretching in the sun, its mask turned toward Europe and its feet thrust Eastward.

She had seen pictures of men working in iron-foundries in America. In the heat and activity of such surroundings he had been produced.

She understood a little now: foundries pulsing in his veins, the chant of mills—and a savage wistfulness in his heart.

Yet, although he was significant of his nation, she could not associate him entirely with one country. Perhaps, she reflected, that was proof of his being American. There was a stamp upon all the Frenchmen she knew. It was Europe—Europe, a vain and tired woman, burdened with vices and art, but imperious, cruel; not cruel as Asia was cruel, with an inherited and refined barbarity, but with the attenuated maliciousness of a pampered woman.

Suddenly any contact with France—which, to her, was Europe— seemed fatal. It was corrupting Indochina. In her own experience she had seen abundant evidence of it. Her mother, Nanette, Kim Khouan—yes, herself; and thousands of others unknown to her but of which these instances were symbolical.

As she reflected upon herself and her country she was aware of a new element in the dark water that expired quietly upon the beach. Currents flowing in it touched America, his country. How splendid it would be, to plunge into that sea and swim, on and on, to the shores of that new continent, washing herself clean of Indo-China, of all its implications and entanglements!

"I should like to go to America," she found herself saying.

A moment of silence before he said, "Would you?" Something abrupt, startled in his voice. "But you—you belong here."

"You mean—on this beach—tonight?"

He laughed uneasily. "No, I mean in Indo-China. In another setting; in America, for instance, you would be—well, different."

His words seemed the crystallization of what she knew already; they had the curious effect of weaving her, in her thoughts, more inextricably into the country. It was depressing. In a way she felt as though he had pronounced judgment.

"Why, I wonder?" she asked aloud.

"You are Indo-China," he said simply.

"As definite as that? But you—you are America—yet you seem to fit into this setting."

He laughed again, diffidently; the reference to himself seemed to make him a little shy.

"I'm—fluid, I guess. Sea-spawned, they call it. I like the sea—going to new places—not knowing what will happen—drifting everywhere. I'll never amount to anything—but I'll enjoy living."

He seemed to pass sentence upon himself, too. Fluid. Running into strange corners of the world, leaving no track—like quicksilver. There were men of that type. Something withdrawn inside them. How widely separated the two of them were! Her depression grew, intensified by the continued silence to which he succumbed.

That night, after she had gone to bed, she tried to picture the circumstances from which he had emerged, those forces, so foreign to her, that made him what he was. She could see him as a little boy in some town where mills ground the days into monotony. Close by was the sea; canvas beating against his fancy. He would have gone to school, for he had an air of quiet education. Then he would have left school to go to sea. Years of sailing, of valiant living—and little niches into which he crawled, reading poetry and dreaming shyly.

As she lay there thinking of him, he seemed to contract to a white gull, crying far off across a limitless sea. Even when she fell asleep that wistful note echoed through her slumber.

The next night they stopped at Tourane. As usual, they walked after dinner, but he talked very little; he was heavy, moody. Once, when her hand brushed his, he jumped and she knew his face grew swarthy with blood in the darkness. That brief contact suffused her senses with a blurred radiance.

"Tomorrow," she said hopefully, when they returned to the hotel and he had told her good night, "we shall pass through Hue, the old capital. Suppose we spend the day there? We have time, and . . ."

"You think it won't make us late? I must get the ship." Doesn't he want to prolong the journey? she wondered. Then, before she could reply, he added: "But of course you know how much time we have—and I—I'd like to see the old capital."

They started at dawn. A road, climbing the mountains to the beginning of that mighty gorge called the Pass of the Clouds, carried them to an immaculate height where, looking back, they could see the Bay of Tourane lying like a tiny pool surrounded by toy hills.

The motor seemed to sing over that high road. Turning sharp curves and purring along the edges of dizzy precipices, it plunged higher into the sky, until the herds of lazy clouds seemed to fly before it. Now and then the crystal shattering of a brook drenched the stones on the side where the mountain continued its ascent; or, on the other, the wall of rock and foliage suddenly dropped, to reveal, far below, the shock and glitter of sunlight on water. Where the white beach merged with the mountainsides the sea flung up silent clouds of surf.

Thi-Linh's veins seemed to run with the cool wind.

This, she knew, was an ancient highway—the old Mandarin Road. Dreams slept under the macadam. Emperors had traveled here, with swinging corteges of hot orange and staring purple; and armies had marched through this pass—the chased-silver blades of Annam, and the blue-bright bayonets of France. In the past, palanquins; now, motors. Very soon, fleets in the air; and the grind and roar of a great railway that the French planned, linking Saigon with Hanoi. And yet would all this vitally change Annam? Only in certain physical and political details. Still the peasants would work the soil with buffaloes yoked to wooden plows; would sow and harvest the rice-fields, half-naked and thigh-deep in the ooze. That peasant, she realized, was the symbol of a changeless Annam; a spirit that moved on impervious to the alterations in style and government.

She felt a growing pride in her mother's country, in *her* country. Was it not part of Indo-China, and did not she belong, inextricably? Even the man beside her had realized that.

As he sat there, one brown hand gripping the side of the car, face thrust forward eagerly, he made personal the epic vitality of those mountains. Fluid. That was it. Flowing quietly into every corner where circumstance took him—molding without losing his individuality—

then moving on, leaving no track—like quicksilver. But when he slipped out of her sphere he would leave a track.

In a few hours now they would reach Hue.

The mountains had dwindled into flat green country that seemed to swim in heat. The villages that whirled by were blurred by vertical rays; a wind, hot and dusty, rushed against the car. The man wore a dazed, tired expression, as though forced suddenly to contemplate the strange circumstances that had brought him there; an exertion that, in the heat, was exhausting. Once their eyes met and he smiled fugitively.

"A week ago," he murmured, "I never thought...." The words yielded to a burning swirl of wind. He removed his helmet and mopped his forehead. Sweat moistened his brown face.

"And in another week . . ." she breathed.

"God, but it's hot!" he muttered.

10

The hotel at Hue faced the river; the River of Perfumes, the natives called it.

From the windows of her room Thi-Linh could see the stream and the drowsy green of the old town and Citadel on the opposite bank, reached by a modern French bridge. Immediately, and for no apparent reason, that bridge seemed to link her with something imminent and significant.

After the noon heat had passed, they took rickshaws for a ride about the city.

Garstin still looked tired. The dense brown of his eyes had thickened to a sluggish dark; his back was streaked with sweat, and there was a soiled rim about his shirt collar. All his vitality seemed to sag in a body temporarily flaccid; he was pathetic, an astonishing caricature of himself. She could not understand the change. Nor did his diffuse glances betray even a hint. He seemed, she thought, to cower before her.

When they rattled across the bridge and into the native town, the restful, almost foreign atmosphere aroused him a little; once or twice he spoke, calling her attention to some figure or object.

The irregular roof-lines topping the narrow streets slanted down to awnings above doorways thick with gloom and smells, and between these shops moved men and women in oiled silk garments and folded black turbans, the mingled clattering of their sandals sounding a sharp obbligato to the cadenced thud of bare feet as coolies raced by, drawing rickshaws. The blanched face of France was not in evidence here, and only infrequently did the ivory skin of mixed blood show itself in that tawny motley. Annam undiluted, Thi-Linh thought; whispering in the sleazy black tunics, in the little dragons of light and shadow that wove stealthily in tissue robes.

On the canals, sampans with patched sails drowsed in a midst of warm, offensive odors or moved lazily impelled by flexing women who sang as they poled. Nipa-palms inclined on the banks, staring at their tremulous likenesses.

Beyond the shops, across fragile bridges, was a quarter where the hot air was filled with the sweetness of lime-trees and other fragrant growths. Within the houses, seen through open doors and windows, were embroidered silk panels whose gilt characters quoted the precepts of ancient sages. In little courts and gardens, hidden by walls, old men with a straggly floss of beard on their chins sat and read yellowed scripts, while in the scum-green bowls of fountains fish with transparent red and azure fins turned the water into rainbows.

Thi-Linh thought Hue was like an immense garden; a hothouse of scented green that blurred together under the glazed panes of sunlight. Little bungalows peered out from hedges; the walls of pagodas; the aged battlements of the Citadel with its Chinese-looking gates; the tongue-like eaves of the Palace and its throbbing pink wall; darts of color appearing and reappearing in the inundation of foliage.

"Chinese," said Richard Garstin, with a gesture that took in the entire city. "It reminds me of some of the towns in the interior of Szechuan and Yunnan."

Thi-Linh herself had observed the peculiarly Chinese character of the place. It was like pictures she had seen in books about China. The roofs of the pagodas, the gongs hanging in red lacquer frames, the walls, the gates—all were Chinese. That was not so in Cambodia, or even in Cochin-China. Chinese influence was there of a certainty, and very strong, but it was not so forcibly apparent

She found this a little disturbing. Here in a green pocket of Annam where the old blood still pulsed sluggishly the physical aspect was Chinese. It was only the exterior, she knew, for the heart was Annamite. But it suggested a peculiar analogy with Saigon, that city so obviously French in its pretensions yet native in its impulses. More than two thousand years had passed since the first Chinese invasion of Annam—and still Hue reflected those conquerors.

The past, a past in which the influences that had produced her were woven very definitely, was colored with Chinese influence. Off and on, since the earliest times, Annam had been the vassal of China, and slowly the architecture, the dress, the manners and the learning of that empire had filtered in; with the result that at the end of China's suzerainty Annam, physically, was a replica of it. Even some of its blood was Chinese. But the soul? Thi-Linh had the feeling that it had remained Annamite. Yet how could a country change on the exterior and retain its native spirit?

Suddenly it seemed to her that Annam possessed a great secret— the power to assimilate, even simulate, without losing its national individuality.

Now, since France had come, the landscape was rapidly metamorphosing again. The fleur-de-lis had taken root deep in the soil—yet it had a curiously exotic and Asian appearance. It resembled the lotus-flower of Annam.

She remembered the significance of the Rugby game she had seen in Saigon.

Here in Hue it had another significance. The French had come with bayonets stinging in the equatorial sunlight, with the roll of sharp-tongued drums, sowing the legend of Civilization in soil too fecund to resist any new growth. Civilization became an orchid, springing up lush and brutal from the morass of colonization. It smelled savagely of Asia. Motorcars, railways, mills, factories, all took on the aspect of the country, flourishing quickly—and suggesting that just as quickly they would rot.

It was a few miles from Hue, she remembered, that a French admiral had swung in his gunboats, landed his marines to the red hysteria of "La Marseillaise," and made the waters of the lagoon stagnant with the blood of peasant soldiery, afterward marching on the city and forcing a protectorate upon Annam. With the signing of that treaty, China, politically, expired upon the polished tiles of the Palace. The sign of the bayonet swiftly changed to the sign of the piaster; the orchid spread its roots and exhaled a treacherous sweetness upon the air. The fleur-de-lis had spawned a harlot.

Now, behind the walls of the Palace, an Emperor was dying, an Emperor who, like his predecessors under the French regime, had been merely a gesture. Around him still was the splendor of a Chinese court—mandarins, concubines, and eunuchs. To be sure, white French uniforms gleamed sharply in the midst of these brocaded robes. But, esthetically, China dominated. It colored even the names of the quarters of the Palace: the Imperial Purple Gate, the Court of Supreme Peace…. In France, the heir to the throne was being educated: a little boy with smooth yellow skin, narrow eyes, and a tongue that suavely recited French…. When the present Emperor died, would the lingering shadow of China pass, dissipated in this new phase? The fountains of Versailles where once lotus-pools had been; trains crashing through the silence of Hue; mills wounding the quiet above the graves of powdered emperors…?

Perhaps. But for some reason Thi-Linh could not be alarmed by the possibility. Hue seemed to assure her. France, it whispered, was not destroying Annam; it was destroying the face of old Annam and giving it, very scientifically and neatly, a new one. And she, Thi-Linh, daughter of Thi-Bao and a Frenchman, belonged to the period of transition when France was working with plastic surgery upon a corner of Asia.

It was late afternoon when they reached the tomb of Tu Duc, one of the ancient rulers.

In the dusk, the pools scattered through the gardens were tarnished with silver lily-pads, over which pink clouds of lotus-flowers drifted low. The air was nostalgic with the scent of frangipani.

Thi-Linh, pausing below the terraces, thought she had never seen a place so still and lovely.

Stone mandarins stood guard in the court, and beyond them the sheen of red and gold lacquer, of tiled roofs with grotesque finials, all subdued by the lilac half-light, seemed to breathe a fantastic dream through the thickening air.

The buildings were three: an enclosure for the mortal remains, a pavilion for the memory, and a temple for the soul.

A look of drowsy wonder blurred the pupils of Richard Garstin's eyes. He carried his helmet in his hand, as though humbled by the melancholy loveliness. In the swiftly descending dusk his suit was spotlessly white. It shed an actual radiance. Was he real, she wondered.

Involuntarily she touched him. His skin was warm, moist. A quiver of muscles ran across his cheek; his eyes swerved to her, dense and luminous. As she withdrew her hand, startled, she realized she had touched his wrist—that strong wrist with the heavy veins. The tattooed anchor seemed to have needled its pattern in fire upon her finger-tips.

He had stopped, rigid, motionless.

"I—" she began.

Quickly he caught her, drew her so close that she seemed to mold into his fluid strength. His lips were upon hers, a whiteness over her eyes. For a moment all the vital force of him surged into her throat like hot wine. Then he had released her, and stepped back, a pallor spreading under his tan.

"I was afraid—" he articulated.

She forced herself to speak. "I think—we had better go back—to the hotel."

In silence they returned to the rickshaws. The air seemed bruised and quivering about her. She did not speak during the entire ride, and when they reached the hotel, she hurried to her room without a word or a glance.

11

When the hour for dinner arrived it found her undecided. She did not know what she would say when she saw him, yet she knew she must see him, and soon. The very thought of being in his presence brought a fear that was ecstasy.

She realized, now he had kissed her, that she had cheated herself with a dream. In playing truant from life, she had become tangled in a reality that made all those years in Saigon fall away like the cinders of a dead planet. An impulse had swept her out of the circumstances of her former life, and now she had to return—without the delusion of happiness which in the past had made that life seem full. Before, she had been able to believe that in rising above blood and environment she had attained contentment. Now, she knew, she could never be satisfied with Monsieur Chauvet and all that he signified.

She had blundered—tragically.

But she had been so sure of herself! All genuine feeling, together with her susceptibility to deep attachments, seemed to have died with Kim Khouan, and the following years, unmoved by any great disturbance, had given her an emotional poise that was like a rapier ready to fend off complications. She had arrived at her triumph so coolly—the mistress of Monsieur Chauvet dining with the Governor! And then, within a fortnight, the integrity of her defenses was violated. Trembling before a man who had come in utter simplicity, flung into her life by an incident sordid and commonplace. The very image of him, floating before her now, put salt and fire into her blood. And how would it all end?

It was, she recognized, an impossible situation for which there was but one solution. When she was younger, before the details of material existence had become so involved, she could have gone with him—

anywhere. But not now. Nor was it left for her to choose. The mode of living that she had created held her with a thousand little impulses and habits, trivial necessities that, no matter how inconsequential, were strong as linked iron. To break them meant breaking something within herself.

Why, she demanded of herself savagely, had not this thing happened years ago? Life, the jealous lover, was taking revenge upon her for having lived without fear.

Trying to analyze her feeling toward Richard Garstin, it resolved into a metaphor: a needle swinging to a pole. It was not the physical being that drew her but a force of which the physical was a tangible expression.

A number of facets made up that physical aspect; his easy strength, the little reddish tinge in his hair, the clouded, half-wistful intensity of his eyes.... Beyond these, deep within, was a power; a power that did not necessarily have to do with will or character but that nevertheless turned her heart to quicksilver.

It was the forces that had evolved him, reflected now in the circumstances of his life, which galvanized her decision not to go away with him. He was born to the sea and the sun, filled with echoes of those dynamos of power that rumbled in the groin of his country; and out of that simplicity sprang an unquenchable yearning, desperate but not strong enough to lift him above the elemental qualities to which he was bound temperamentally.

He would always be what he was now.

From across a wide space she touched him, clung momentarily. But almost immediately she would have to relinquish him. She would continue to Vinh, and there turn back. His gift to her would be equally unsatisfactory: a restless passion that would haunt the ashes of her years, never able to rise, phenix-like.

She would not see him tonight, she decided.

Summoning the chauffeur, she instructed him to go to Monsieur Garstin's room and say that, as she was not well, she would dine alone, but they would start early in-the morning, as planned.

The room-boy brought her dinner but she did not touch it. Beyond the windows, Hue pulsed softly under the sifting of night, a dark, colorless gleam on the river, and the lights of the native town swarming among the trees like luminous insects.

A knock on the door quickened her breathing. She knew before she answered who it would be.

A gaze hooded and furtive met hers. His suit clung moistly to his frame, and there was dust about the bottom of his trousers.

"I got your message a moment ago when I came in," he said in a thick voice.

She stepped aside and he moved past her to the window. For a moment he stood there, staring out, fatigue in the droop of his shoulders. When he turned, he seemed pitifully perplexed.

"You know, of course," he faltered, "that I love you."

Those words struck her with almost physical force. No one had ever said that to her in just that way. "Love," as he pronounced it, had no implications.

She remained standing by the door. "You forget my blood." A ridiculous, futile thing to say.

He smiled wearily. "What does that matter?"

"And Monsieur Chauvet…."

"He—he doesn't exist—except as a name."

Standing there by the window, in the dim light, he seemed ringed with a dark radiance. His dusty trousers, the perspiration that sagged in his clothing, all these proofs of his soiled and tired being, were absorbed in something authentic and immaculate behind his gaze.

"But what about my—my life?" she continued. "You know nothing…."

"I know enough," he said. "That afternoon I saw you at the hotel in Saigon, I heard some Frenchmen talking…." After a moment he added: "I think you are a drum beating down men's resistance."

He said it so simply that it did not sound astonishing. It was one of those unexpected, fugitive things that now and then darted out of the wistful depths of him.

"I don't think it would matter what you did," he went on. He drew a deep breath. "Will you go away with me—to America?"

She met his eyes evenly, while all her being trembled.

"No."

He did not seem surprised. "Why?"

"Because it—it is impossible."

He did not repeat that he loved her; it seemed as if he thought it unnecessary. He merely turned and looked out of the window again. She wanted to move swiftly to his side and burn her lips in the soft rim of fire on his hair.

Presently he said :

"We will get to Vinh tomorrow night." It was not a question. "From there I'll take the train to Hanoi and Hai Phong." Then he turned. "Perhaps you will change."

She smiled—she felt that it was a remarkably calm smile.

"No, I shan't change."

He hesitated. "Would you rather—turn back here?"

"I am going to Vinh"—quietly.

He ran his fingers through his hair; a gesture of indecision. He looked a little dazed, and utterly exhausted. His smile was heavy.

"We start at five o'clock?"

"Yes."

She opened the door.

"Good night," he said, moving out awkwardly.

After he had gone the room swam dizzily. Was the light growing dimmer? When she understood, it seemed very strange; she had not cried since she was a little girl.

12

The darkness was being ground to powder when they left in the morning. Hue seemed to lie under gray dust that made it haggard and colorless. A wind, drifting across the river, brought the smells of viscid mud flats and sickly-sweet flowers.

The early morning grayness did not subdue Thi-Linh's emotions; they were sharp, and italicized with a cold verity. Garstin's eyes were blood-veined; his suit was faintly odorous of sweaty skin. Life at that moment, to her, was attenuated and ugly.

With the rising of the sun the world became more normal. It seemed incredible that the man beside her was the one who had come to her room the night before with such amazing humility. He sat there like a tired, travel-stained stranger. The night seemed only to have added to his weariness; he had become leaden, and entirely withdrawn.

At noon they stopped at Dong-hoi. It was a fairly large town, umber-walled and facing a flare of blue sea. It bristled with a military air.

As they rode into the main street she saw a familiar face, red and bearded, that she dimly identified with Saigon. The man was in a motorcar, and he leaned out and stared as her automobile shot by. Undoubtedly he had recognized her. But it did not matter. Nothing was of much consequence now—except these last few hours. Let the following days take care of themselves.

Leaving Dong-hoi, they crossed a stream on a ferry poled by natives. Beyond there, the coast rose into blue undulations mightier than the mountains between Tourane and Hue. Azure islands, far off in the sunlight, drifted like hazy exhalations of the water. The valleys were sprinkled with infinitesimal figures working the fields. As she watched, Thi-Linh was oppressed by the inexorable necessity of toil. It seemed to rob emotion of every sublime quality, and make it simply the reflex of tired minds and muscles, the animal-like escape from the burden of living.

Purple shadows ripened on the flanks of the mountains, dripping into the valleys and clotting them. A little vein of fire outlined the crests.

Twice that afternoon they had stopped because of motor trouble. The last time the chauffeur made no progress, and Garstin, drawing off his coat, bent under the lifted hood, his hands working expertly with plugs and coils. Perspiration streamed from his flushed face; his shirt molded to his torso. As she watched him, her thoughts seemed to become limpid with his every movement, and she shut her eyes, only to feel a golden burn upon her eyelids that spread and shaped until his vigorous form filled her vision.

Those stops delayed them considerably; now it would be near midnight before they reached Vinh.

Dusk ran quick fingers over the mountains, blending them into the darkness that rushed out of the sea. The road was a Milky Way stretching endlessly before the headlights. Now and then they passed villages, the open doors hot with dusty light. A swarm of hot stars sprawled over the sky.

Garstin had not spoken since the last stop. He was a white shape in the corner of the seat, his ruffled hair waving against the blue night. But the warmth of his presence spread to her and excited her. A few hours—then Vinh. The realization that their time together was so brief relaxed her strength. She wanted to draw close, to whisper that she Would go with him—anywhere—anywhere! Frightened, she sat there watching the road slide under the wind-shield.

Lights sprang out of the darkness ahead. Another town. Her mind groped—Ha Tinh. The gleaming mile-stone beside the road announced the nearness of Vinh.

The car tore into the lighted streets of Ha Tinh, scattering people and vehicles before it. A rush of yellow doorways, street-lamps, dark houses and figures that ran together in an animated panorama drawn rapidly past. Sounds, smells dwindled; and lights. Again darkness over the white road and spinning mile-stones.

The lights of another car dilated in the gloom ahead. Suddenly a spotlight shot out from its side, waving frantically. Thi-Linh called to the chauffeur to slow down. A moment later the other automobile drew alongside, stopping with a shriek of brakes. From the dimness behind the wind-shield a French voice spoke.

"Are you going to Vinh?"

"Yes," Thi-Linh replied.

"It's absolutely impossible," said the voice. "The road is entirely under water. The floods. Raining for two weeks. Absolutely impossible," the man reiterated.

There was a moment of silence. Finally Thi-Linh asked:

"How did you get through?"

"By boat from Ben-Thuy. You can make it in the morning. Telegraph to the *commissaire* at Ben-Thuy, and he will send a barge to the village a few kilometers from here. But tonight—absolutely impossible!"

The man accelerated his motor; a roar filled the quiet.

"Thank you," Thi-Linh called.

The car slid forward with a flash of its mud-spattered sides, the sound of its motor rapidly sinking into a purr.

Thi-Linh felt Richard Garstin's gaze upon her. She did not yet know how to accept this unexpected check.

"What are we to do?" the man asked.

"Go back to Ha Tinh—there is nothing else to do. We can send a telegram from there. I suppose there will be a hotel."

She ordered the chauffeur to turn around. "No French hotel at Ha Tinh," announced the Annamite briefly. "Only Chinese hotel."

Thi-Linh shrugged. "I am sorry we must turn back," she said to Garstin. But she was not.

"It can't be helped," he returned quietly. "But will this Chinese hotel be fit for you to stay in?"

She smiled.

"You forget I lived in the jungle for years."

13

The Chinese hotel was a hotel in name only. It was on the main street, facing a flare of hot light from the wide doorway of a grocery store owned by the same Chinaman. It was low and whitewashed. The entrance led through a dirty storeroom piled with bits of iron, furniture, and other objects lost in gloom. In one corner stood a broken rickshaw; opposite, was a narrow stair that turned sharply into a square of pale light. Below the stair was a table, obviously where meals were served, with a torn punkah hanging motionless above it. All this faintly outlined in the light of an oil lamp swung in a ring from the soiled ceiling.

There was an air of age about the place that was like a treacherous essence spilled long ago and soaked into the walls.

Out in the street, the glare from the open shops was harsh and lustful. Sandals clicked the dust from the ground, and a wavering film enclosed the moving figures, some in black Tonkinese dress and others half naked, their bare skins shining.

The air was crowded with heat and smells.

A group of natives collected about the door of the grocery store while Thi-Linh and Garstin made arrangements for rooms and food. Coming out into the street, into the dust and hot sprays of light, Thi-Linh felt that the air was curdled by the presence of so many people.

Garstin smiled wanly as they entered the storeroom that occupied the ground floor of the hotel.

"Do you mind?" he asked.

"It doesn't matter."

A Chinese boy in dirty, flopping trousers, bare of chest and feet, led them up the stair, out upon a veranda that ran past several doors and above a courtyard. The stars were incongruously pure above that courtyard gloom-soaked and heavy with the effluvium of a latrine.

Thi-Linh's room was small, its white walls, taking on the color of the lamplight, seeming coated with yellow dust. The only furniture was a chair and a single bed clouded by a torn, rust-streaked mosquito-net. The one window looked down upon an unlighted road, invisibly astir, that crossed the main street. In the distance she heard Chinese music—ribald and sharp as scraping metal.

Garstin's room was at the end of the veranda.

The place seemed to contract about her; she felt pressed into a lambent shaft of heat, suffocated.

Stepping out upon the veranda, she met Garstin coming from his room. He looked haggard, spent.

"It's dreadful," he breathed with difficulty, "this heat...."

"Like the jungle...."

For a moment she had the illusion that, out in the street where all those people crowded through the dust-ridden light, sinewy flanks were stretching.

"Do you think you can stand it?"

She laughed—the sound seemed quenched in the. odorous black heat of the courtyard.

"I think dinner will be ready—if we go down."

She saw him shudder.

The food, although prepared in the French manner and apparently clean, seemed to absorb the sordid atmosphere of that storeroom. A little boy, the punkah cord wrapped around one toe, worked the flapping fan above their heads. Thi-Linh's thoughts rasped back and forth as on rusty hinges; she felt that her brain, corroded by the humidity, had gone to mold and in **a** moment would disintegrate in her skull. She could not swallow the food.

"Let us go outside," she articulated, her lungs laboring with the heat.

Beggars whined about the doorway. On the sidewalks and in the street, figures drifted languidly through the spills of superheated light; forms pale and dark, mingling, shifting, until the dimness reeled like a drunken harlequin. The clacking sandals smote the drone of heavy voices. In the distance, that Chinese music introduced a note of madness. Again she had the feeling that all these people clabbered the air, to which the lights added melting clots, thick with dust and odors.

"It's little better...." he murmured.

Curious faces peered at them.

"It seems unreal," she heard herself saying. "It's like being able to step back ...behind the mind ...into cells hot and quivering ...a spillway where all the evil accumulates...." She laughed; it startled her. "Do you think there is such a place ... at the back of the brain?"

He, too, laughed....

She became obsessed with the thought: Ha Tinh, a calorific dimension behind the intelligence where desire sprawled and flexed like a tawny cat.

"We're near the sea, aren't we?" he asked.

"Yes...

"God! Where's the wind?"

The wind, she repeated in her mind. It was somewhere. Involuntarily she looked up at the black sky, sweating with stars, as though expecting to find it there. If the moon was up she could beat on it ... a gong to summon the wind. But when will the moon be up? she wondered impatiently. Later. An old moon, tawny as Ha Tinh. A yellow cat of a moon. Perhaps it would come creeping on the wind.... But that is silly, she reflected. How could the moon come creeping on the wind?

"Let us go back...." she said. "Perhaps the rest, the sleep...."

He mopped his forehead.

"Funny," he muttered. "What made you think of that? A spillway behind the mind…."

14

How long had she been in her room? How many hours? Or was it years? That white room turned ocher by the lamp—how she hated it! But she did not dare to go outside.

Several times she had heard Garstin moving about on the veranda, and his footsteps had seemed to walk over her heart. He was in his room now; she had heard him enter and close the door. He was not sleeping. But sitting; walking down centuries as he sat.

Like herself. Why didn't she go to him? Why didn't she go and simply sit there beside him; walk down the centuries with him? But she was afraid—afraid she might not be able to climb back into the present; back to Saigon, to Monsieur Chauvet, and herself.

The street that ran below the window was quiet now. The night was quiet. Yet it gave her a sense of suppressed drums.

Black heat panted over Ha Tinh, swelling the flanks of silence. She could feel those flanks rubbing against her. Black flanks of silence that moved to a stealthy purring.

Why was she waiting? You know you want to go to him, she told herself. So why wait? Or, if you must wait, at least lie down. But she continued to sit there, fatigue heavy in her. Perhaps I am waiting for the moon, she thought. She still clung to that absurd illusion that the moon would bring a wind; wind to clear her mind; make it possible for her to go to him and talk calmly. But she could not go now, with those flanks of heat rubbing against her.

What did that heat mean; and the silence, and Ha Tinh? Although the town was comparatively still, and most of the people sleeping, she had the feeling that the streets were darkly astir. Indo-China prowling in the streets of Ha Tinh. Asia prowling in the streets of Ha Tinh. They will be prowling here, she thought dully, when France is gone.

Asia… an hermaphrodite …half an ancient sage …half a sloe-eyed woman …creeping through the streets of Ha Tinh. Asia …a spillway behind the mind of the world …where all the evil accumulated, surviving time. But what was evil? Stagnated wisdom—an imaginary sirocco blown through the minds of men? Was evil simply a chain wound around the world's throat by its own frightened fingers? A hallucination?

Half an ancient sage, half a sloe-eyed woman. Because of these mingled traits, masculine and feminine, Asia could go on producing and suckling. Limbs of a man, brain of a man; torso of a woman, drowsy gaze of a woman. Asia: a phallus crowned with wisdom. White blood grown dark upon it. Asia: the death-continent of the races; brown, yellow, white, all celebrating their marriage about the lingam.

Asia. Ha Tinh. Richard Garstin. Herself. What did they all mean, thrust together, congealed in this night?

Richard Garstin. America—panting with mills, singing its songs of iron, but desperately stirred by an illusion of beauty. America—the death-house of Europe. And Asia—the dark reservoir into which both filtered.

She, Thi-Linh, was the dark reservoir into which men filtered.

All the dusky glory of her seemed to enfold Richard Garstin.

If I have ever lived before, she thought, I have lived a thousand times, I have been a thousand courtesans, a thousand nuns; giving body, giving soul. Tonight I can feel men within me. Bodies—aching—tired—hot—rigid—cool—relaxed—bodies in starlight—bodies pressed close to earth. I can remember something forgotten, something without lust. I see it for a moment—flickering—far off—can I hold it? Will I understand tomorrow? Something terrifying—yet something that I knew—long ago. Sound—all sound—dew—rain—sand—green things—earth-touch—ether rushing in men's veins—blood rushing in men's veins—muscle—biceps—sinew—tendon—spirit—soul—life—death.

What am I?

A woman sitting in a soiled room in Ha Tinh. Indo-China sitting in a soiled room in Ha Tinh.

And how did I come here?

Through long darkness. Justin: an enclosure for the mortal remains. Paul: a pavilion for the memory. And Richard Garstin: a temple for the soul? Behind all three, Kim Khouan, the dark impulse.

I wish the moon would rise. Then I could put out this lamp and take it for my lamp, and go to him…. Perhaps it is up now.

Thi-Linh rose and blew out the light. A thin pale gauze seemed to float in through the window. She looked out.

The sky was dark blue; under it the road seemed asleep in an unnatural twilight. Somewhere in that great cluster of houses someone was singing—the broken notes limped down the silence. A muted click-clack from the main street.

But where was the moon?

She opened the door and emerged upon the veranda.

A pale flush purified the courtyard; it mounted the walls, running past black shadows, and shone dimly on glazed roofs. The moon. And did she feel a wind?

I am a tide, she thought, rising with the moon. It has drawn me up through centuries; and I am cool and limpid. I will lift him with me—up—up—to the moon. He is my sacrifice to the moon. I am a sacrifice to the moon.

She heard a door open at the end of the veranda.

He was beside her. "So hot…" she heard him murmur. His face looked swarthy, darkened by the moonlight. But the veins of his wrists stood out in silver.

"I wanted to come to you," he was saying, "but I was afraid…."

Those silver veins were against her now. He had slipped his arm about her, and his face, hovering close, had blotted out the moon.

"The last night…."

As he kissed her, all life seemed to flow into him, through him to that moon.

I give all, she said to herself, all.

"I've been waiting," she sighed, "hoping you would come." "And I've been waiting to come."

A sharp breath escaped her; he was trembling.

"It's like—like passing through you—to something I can't understand," she said.

"I know—that time I heard a gull cry—and wanted something—something I couldn't touch—"

Suddenly, as he spoke, she felt ancient, and very tired; hidden years seemed to lunge out of her heart, stilling the blood in her veins, and sagging in her body.

"How old did I tell you I was?" she breathed, frightened.

"It doesn't matter...."

A gull crying—its notes piercing her ears, piercing her heart. Strange that a gull can come between us, she thought dully. But it had. With a dark swoop. A thin tremor of anguish wrenched a moan from her.

"Oh, I wish you hadn't said that!"

"Why?"

He was asking why! Couldn't he understand? But men never did. A flash had illuminated that complex fissure in his nature. The same flash had blasted her emotions. It was useless to explain, to try to tell him that he had heard a gull crying beyond her, and if she yielded, that cry would become a lethal blade plunged into the precious thing which had grown between them.... Oh, why couldn't men understand? ...A girl on a beach, below cliffs.... She would be like that ...like all the women he had known.... And he would be gone ...still haunted by that plaintive wail....

She thrust him away, almost abruptly. But how cool were those silver veins on his wrists! They seemed invisibly joined to hers, and drawing away was like tearing them apart, pouring their lives out upon the floor.

"Early in the morning," she said quickly, "we start. The chauffeur telegraphed—"

He caught her hands but she slipped free again.

"Don't!" she whispered. "Do you want me to be like—like that girl on the beach?"

"But—"

"No, of course you don't understand—"

"—I love—"

"Yes, I know—and that is why—that is why—"

"If you go—"

"I must!"

"I will kill myself—"

She laughed—desperately. "Very well—kill yourself—kill me—but don't kill *that*."

Swiftly she stepped into the room and closed the door. But she had scarcely closed it before it opened and he came in.

15

She was awakened by a persistent knocking.

Her first impression was of a burst of shrill sunlight on the floor, and, through the window, the sky savagely blue. A cold remembrance brimmed her mind.

Her body dragged with inertia as she rose. Opening the door a crack, she saw the chauffeur standing outside.

"Car is ready," he announced.

Other remembrances lurched into her awakening brain now. She felt a little sick, dizzy.

"Have you called Monsieur Garstin?"

"He is not in his room. Chinese man said he went out early this morning, asking the way to Vinh."

This announcement did not shock or startle her. Subconsciously, she had known that he would be gone. A feeling almost of relief came into her. But she was impressed with the necessity to get away quickly.

"We will not go to Vinh," she said, "but back to Hue—to Saigon."

She sat down on the side of the bed. She was tired physically, but curiously, her mind was at ease.

It was over now.

She realized it without regret.

It was, she reflected, immensely satisfying to know that in the future Richard Garstin could not hurt her; he had passed. And she would never allow anyone to come so close to her again. Never. But how could she say that with any degree of certainty? She had said it before, and meant it sincerely. Yet surely life was through with her. She did not need anyone now…ever. From so much giving she had learned to sustain herself. Yes, she understood so much; and the knowledge was enormously cruel.

It was the end of all to know too much.

I suppose I should feel soiled, she thought, but I am too tired now.…

Yes, surely life was through with her. Peace. That was what she wanted. And she thought of Monsieur Chauvet.

16

It was late afternoon, and raining, when the automobile whirred into Saigon. A nostalgic smell rose from the wet pavements, like an aura of old pain yielded up by something dead and wrapped in musky cloths. It made the city seem over-familiar to Thi-Linh. Yet she was glad to be back. It was reassuring to be in the midst of old surroundings again, even though they breathed an air of faded anguish.

The house was dark and deserted looking. But as the automobile stopped under the porte-cochere, a light appeared in the hall. She recognized Hoa's form in the doorway.

"It is fortunate for you that you got here tonight," snapped the old woman; but her eyes held an affectionate light. "Your telegram said it might be morning—and in the morning Monsieur Chauvet arrives from Hanoi—by boat."

Questions rose into Thi-Linh's mind, but she put them aside and said, "Have some tea brought to my room, Hoa; I am very fatigued."

Her room felt cold, and had a musty smell. Unconsciously her gaze searched the floor to see if there were any betel-stains. How familiar to be doing that again!

She put on a dressing-gown. Presently Hoa came with a tray. Cinnamon toast and tea! Something comforting about them.

"Now tell me all about it, Hoa," she directed.

"Five days ago," said Hoa, "Monsieur Chauvet telegraphed that he was returning by boat because of the floods. I sent you a message; you did not get it? When your telegram came yesterday, I did not know where to reach you or I would have told you that you must get here before tomorrow morning." Then she added: "However, it might have taught you a lesson if you had not arrived in time."

Thi-Linh smiled faintly. "It would have been unfortunate for you as well as for me, dear Hoa," she said, and patted the old woman's cheek.

How simple everything would be, she thought, if she were like Hoa!

"The American?" asked the old woman.

A little dull sensation thudded against Thi-Linh's heart; it was not regret, she knew that, it was bitterness.

"He made his boat—I suppose," she replied.

"You left him at Vinh?"

"Yes." …Then she smiled at Hoa again. "It's pleasant to be back—not to have to think—or to plan—but just to live—and drift."

Hoa's eyes were upon her questioningly. Thi-Linh considered her for a moment, divining that look, then spoke, her words unconsciously falling into a mold:

"I am through with all that, Hoa—for always."

Habit led her to dress for dinner. The same smell of mildew that haunted the air upstairs lingered in the dining-room, mingling with a trailing, subtle fragrance from the garden. Moldy—the house was moldy. So was Saigon, she thought. A city old and yellow, with moist rot about the bases of its houses, making maps of decay upon their walls, dripping under their eaves like stagnant water. Gangrene at the heart of Saigon, its effluvium mating with the treacherous sweetness of tropical plants and producing an atmosphere of beautiful decay.

Suddenly the thought frightened her.

She went to the mirror in the hall. The light was dim and a gray shadow lay over her features. She wondered if it were a sifting of age. How old was she, twenty-nine? She had not considered her age seriously since that night the Governor came to dinner. She was twenty-nine then. But surely she was years older now. Had only a few weeks passed? That seemed incredible.

Her face looked out from that gray shadow with a fragile luster emphasized by rouged lips. It was the same face which had gazed at her from the mirror that night a few weeks ago, except that the eyes seemed a little heavier, the lips drawn down at the corners with fatigue. That grayness was only an illusion of the shadow. Or, perhaps, a reflection from her heart. Gray heart, filled with dust; and over it, as over Saigon, an aura of old pain. But her body—there was no visible change—no mold creeping up from her limbs, making maps of age upon her thighs and breasts, streaming from under her hair in horrible greenish ooze. No, she was still beautiful. Beauty sifted with gray dust; dust of old pain.

She did not return to the table, but sat in the living-room and smoked.

A thought which had come to her that morning in the hotel at Ha Tinh returned. "I suppose I should feel soiled...." At the time, she remembered, she had been too tired to analyze. She was still tired. But she could think clearly now.

I suppose I should feel soiled, she repeated mentally, but instead I feel…purified.

Katharsis. That old word, learned while she was living with Paul, slipped into her mind as a simple explanation. Immorality was a legend, pernicious to those who believe it.… This did not seem a dangerous creed. But it was not a creed; it was herself. She had simply heard the constant crying of a gull beyond life—Richard Garstin had given her that figure of speech if nothing else!—and repeatedly she had given herself to life, seeking in that way to translate an intangible beauty. And the men who were the symbols; each had received something from her. To one she had given a son; to another, a book; to a third, a temporary strength; to a fourth, a certain happiness in his old age; and to the last—ah, a vital thing!

Evil? No, she was not evil; she did not believe in evil. "You have a secret.…" Paul had told her. Was that it? But what did that knowledge gain her? A little assurance, perhaps—but this would flicker out with her. Suddenly she was oppressed by the thought of death. A grave: beauty mending a gash in the earth? Merely that? Surely something went on—what was it? The essence of anguish and wisdom distilled into the air by bodies that had suffered, a haunting legacy to future generations whose suffering and knowledge added to it century after century, producing a vapor of ancient awareness that permeated each new consciousness?

Not soiled, purified.

On an impulse, she rose and put out the light. There was a curious intimacy in the darkness. Pale night outlined the windows, and from the dining-room, across the hall, came a diffusion of yellowish light. A tall vase, almost as high as a man, stood in one corner. It seemed to catch all the seepage of light and glow spectrally, outlining a dark phenix upon its rondured body. A phenix. It seemed to explain her calm. She had risen out of the ashes of her heart.

She smoked on, lighting one cigarette from the other.

That vase held her thoughts.

She did not know how long she had been sitting there, immersed in quiet and darkness—the light in the dining-room was out now—when she heard footsteps in the front. Shortly afterward the door-bell rang.

She waited, but the house-boy did not come. "Nham!" she called; then, after a moment, "Hoa!"

The door-bell rang again, followed by a click-clacking on the stairs. Thi-Linh heard Hoa cross the hall. Followed a murmur of voices, then the old woman passed the doorway.

"Here I am, Hoa," she called. "Put on the light."

"It is a boy who wants to see you," said Hoa, pressing the switch. "I forgot to tell you when you came—he was here yesterday, asking for you. I told him you might be back today."

Thi-Linh frowned.

"I don't want to see anyone. Who is he? What is he—Annamite?"

"Yes. He wouldn't say what he wanted, simply that he had a message for you."

For no comprehensible reason, her temples began beating quickly.

"Send him in."

17

The boy who entered was slender, and pale for a native. But that pallor, she saw, was due more to a scarcely discernible coating of powder than actual color. Thi-Linh took in his clothing: a gray Norfolk jacket, full white trousers, and a tie of bright blue. His eyes were dark with an intensity that was disconcerting; black oily hair was plastered down upon his head, a head classically poised and beautiful. Thi-Linh had seen many young boys of his type in the Rue Catinat, but few with such an air of authentic breeding and reserved assurance. He did not seem in the least disturbed, facing a stranger; indeed, he smiled, his large felt hat held easily in one hand.

"I am Justin," he said simply.

But in the fraction of a second before he spoke she knew. The confirmation left her staring at him with a sudden lack of poise, amounting almost to embarrassment, which she hoped he would not see. He took a step forward, then paused. His uncertain movement impressed upon her the necessity to stir, to say something. Quickly she rose, and he crossed the room to meet her, his smile a little shy now.

She kissed him. "Justin," she said.

They stood looking at each other, both smiling reticently. Thi-Linh was not at ease yet. Her son. That thought bewildered her. What should she do? What should she say?

She gestured toward a chair. "Sit down."

This seemed to relieve the tension a little. She stared at him intently. For some reason that sheen of powder on his face and his clothes so utterly French vaguely alarmed her. Her son—Kim Khouan's son. She tried to grasp the fact. But she was deflected by insignificant details, such as the powder, the Norfolk jacket.

"I am glad you have come," she articulated finally. "When did you arrive?"

"Yesterday morning." Then his gaze darkened, as though reflecting a bruising thought. "I—"

"Why didn't you tell Hoa who you were when you came yesterday?" she interrupted. "You could have stayed here."

He seemed abashed. "I didn't know whether—I—"

"I am sorry," she said. Where *could* he stay? Monsieur Chauvet would be back in the morning, and he could not remain in the house then. But Hoa could keep him with her, in the servants' quarters. Her son in the servants' quarters! Yet, if he was to be near her, that was the only place he could stay.

"How is Mama Thi-Bao?" she asked.

That bruised look came into his eyes again. Suddenly she understood.

"She—"

"She is dead," he said, his eyes filling with tears. "That is why I came. You wrote, you know, sending me the money—so after she died—"

He was apologizing for having come! This wove back and forth across her mind, tangled in the thought that Mama Thi-Bao was dead. An old woman sitting in the rear of a shop, vacant-eyed and chewing betel. The picture seemed to inject a bitter fluid into her veins. The ache that followed was dim, faded, but none the less poignant. It was as if a shadow had suddenly dissipated out of her past, leaving a vague emptiness. She tried vainly to impress upon herself the fact that Mama Thi-Bao no longer existed except as a pathetic memory. It was a relief when she felt her eyes grow moist; at first she was afraid she would not be able to cry.

"So after she died," Justin repeated, "I came to tell you."

"Of course," she murmured.

Again she found herself gazing critically at his powdered face, his French clothes.

"Where did you get that suit?" After she had asked the question, it seemed utterly trivial. Yet she had to say something—she could not sit there thinking about Mama Thi-Bao.

He smiled with a faint hint of pride.

"*Monsieur le Commissaire* gave it to me—after Ninh-Binh washed it, it was too small for him."

Fear darted at her with his words. France was touching her son, reaching out for him. And he was an Annamite. Annamite, she repeated in her mind. Only a little French blood …from her. But the fact of that blood, no matter how negligible the quantity, caused her a sudden alarm. It was like being forced to regard, for the first time, a weakness he had inherited from her.

"*Monsieur le Commissaire*," she repeated, trying to remember something. "Ah, yes! He is helping you—you are studying for the *Service Télégraphique.*"

"Yes, Mama Thi-Linh."

It was as though a flicker of light had sprung across her eyes; her vision went white. She wondered, for a moment, if she were blind. But she knew she had only closed her eyes—closed them so he would not see the look in them. Mama Thi-Linh! Had Mama Thi-Bao taught him to call her that?—poor Mama Thi-Bao who was dead! She suffered an excruciating pride of possession, the first she had felt since she held him in her arms years ago. She wanted to draw him to her, to let her hands move hungrily over his face, and to kiss him again and again. But she only stared, her fingers tightening rigidly about the arms of the chair.

Forcing herself to speak, she repeated: "Yes—you are studying for the *Service Télégraphique*—of course. And you must study hard."

He smiled; and it was Kim Khouan smiling at her.

"I do. Already I am nearly as clever as a Frenchman."

His words clashed a warning. Clever as a Frenchman! Desperation seized her. She had been right: any contact with France was fatal. In a little while, perhaps within a year or two, he would be like those smart young men who paraded up and down the Rue Catinat at night; young men powdered and pomaded, disgustingly proud of their French manners and French clothes. Caricatures of her country! French bodies with Annamite hearts. Native simplicity corrupted by European vices. And he must not become like that, he must not! But what could she do to prevent it? She had a little money—no, more than a little. She had not been stupid during those years with Monsieur Chauvet. And she could get more. France was drawing her son into an involved net. How could she outwit it? Not by telling him he must remain Annamite—not by sending him back to Stung Treng. But how?

"You like studying for the telegraph?" she asked tentatively.

He hesitated. "Yes.... But—"

She felt a surge of hope. "But what?"

"But I would rather go to school. I like books, poetry."

Books, poetry! Kim Khouan talking now. "Thi-Linh, I am a harpstring shivering at your touch...." An echo vibrating out of her youth; it made a ghost of sweet singing in her ears.

"Perhaps," she began, groping vainly; "perhaps—" She paused. Suddenly it had come to her.

Send him to school in France! Send him into the very heart of France! Let him absorb the authentic technique of these white men; their manners, even their thoughts! Was not that her best weapon against France? Knowledge against knowledge. But suppose—Her plan sagged under a ponderous fear.

Still she would have to take that hazard. An experiment. Not the cheap imitation of French civilization picked up in Indo-China from tropic-tired colonials, but the genuine erudition of a scholarly nation. A sound French education—and an Annamite heart. What would the result be? It was worth it—it was worth it. And it was less dangerous, for if he remained in Indo-China undoubtedly he would take on the veneer of sophistication that was moral death to a native.

A great joy rose in her. She looked at her son through tears.

"It may be possible," she began, her voice tremulous, "for you to go to school in France."

Slow wonder transfigured his face. He tried to suppress his feeling, but it brimmed over.

"France! Oh, Mama Thi-Linh!"

He sprang up and kissed her—on the mouth. The pounding in her temples mounted fiercely. As the blood subsided she heard a muffled crunching outside. It resolved into the sound of wheels rolling over the graveled driveway. For an instant she sat there, vaguely apprehensive, then she moved to the window and looked out.

A flare of light was spreading under the porte-cochere, flung by advancing headlights. She saw the machine draw up. A strange car. A taxicab. Monsieur Chauvet. But how had he come ahead of time?

Swiftly she turned to Justin.

"Go in the dining-room—at once—and wait," she directed. "No! Go outside—in the rear—through the dining-room! Wait there. I will send Hoa out as soon as I can. Quickly!"

Without a word he went, crossing the hall and vanishing in the darkness of the dining-room.

She drew a deep breath and composed herself to meet Monsieur Chauvet.

18

She met him in the hallway. Instead of hurrying to him and kissing him, she stood just inside the door and waited for him to approach her.

"I'm sorry," she began. "I would have met you with the car, but the telegram said—"

"We caught the tide," he broke in.

His voice was abrupt, tired. He bent and kissed her stiffly. For an instant she thought he was angry, then she decided it was fatigue. He was very pale, his eyes blood-suffused, and when she tried to look at him directly, he evaded her gaze. She sensed something furtive and repressed in his manner. Perhaps he had been ill. Fever. He looked feverish; those red veins in his eyes, his blanched, haggard face.

"Haven't you been well?" she asked.

He laughed; it seemed to clot in his throat. He appeared incredibly old, so old that it frightened her. Then a suspicion increased her fear.

"Well enough," he responded.

He dropped his hat on the table—usually he hung it up with meticulous care—and moved into the living-room. The air was thick with the stale odor of smoke. He sniffed.

"Cigarettes? Who has been smoking?"

As she followed him in, he turned with an accusing look.

"I have, of course," she said easily.

"No one has been here?"

She forced a smile. "No one."

As he sat down, she had the illusion that he collapsed in the chair—he seemed to droop and fill it pathetically. Linking his white fingers together, he gazed at her with a deliberate smile that was mask-like in its utter insincerity.

"Where's the man who went up the coast with you?"

After he spoke she realized that he had calculated to startle her. He had startled her, but she knew her expression did not change. The only change was within. Her face had become like parchment; behind it the blood spurted hotly. She waited a moment before she spoke, and he seized the pause. He was trembling now.

"I thought you were wise," he said in a thick voice, "but you are not. My God! Right under the noses of everybody! Didn't you know you would be seen? That I would be told sooner or later?" He raised his thin-veined, transparent hands violently and dropped them, a flushed spot glowing on either cheek, like absurd smears of rouge. "Mullanax saw you at Dong Hoi—he got on the boat at Tourane. He also saw the man in the car…. Well?"

His gesture and his words seemed cut into her consciousness with the precision of an etching. She felt that she should be extremely emotional, at least palpably disturbed. Instead she was faintly sick. She detested scenes.

"Well?" he demanded, rising. "I suppose you deny it?"

Suddenly the room became enormously overcrowded with furniture; she wanted to push pieces aside, relieve the feeling of cluttered surroundings that pressed upon her. She was acutely aware of too many objects …the draperies in the windows, the chairs, the table, the bookcase, the gleaming vase with the phenix on it…. Phenix. Could she rise above the nauseating melodrama of this scene?

"No—I do not deny it."

Her disciplined voice surprised her. But evidently it was more surprising to Monsieur Chauvet. Those two red spots vanished. For an instant she thought he would crumble before her eyes, drop into a pile of disintegrated bones and dry flesh. Then the pallor withdrew from his face, yielding to a creeping flush that rose as if red wine were being poured behind that thin skin; hot wine that was swelling, swelling. She saw him gasp. He looked positively ridiculous.

She had seen a caricature in *La Vie Parisienne* that resembled him, and she remembered it now: idiotically red face behind a white beard that looked false. The man in the cartoon was slightly bent, holding his paunch, and staring in senile rage at a delicately stockinged leg that had kicked him.

Monsieur Chauvet had fallen into that same attitude. How preposterous! She had kicked him in the paunch, and now his face, inflamed behind a false beard, was almost bursting with blood. The absurdity of the thought made her laugh hysterically.

Suddenly something leaped stinging across her eyes.

"Whore!"

The room lurched, drunk with the pain that stunned her. As it became steady, she slowly grasped the fact that he had struck her.... That red-faced, false-whiskered man of the cartoon ...struck her across the eyes ...called her a whore ...simply because she had kicked him in the paunch.

The room was suffocating, and spotted with vanishing throbs of vertigo. She had to have air.... Now she was at the window, clinging to the draperies and drawing in the cool night. She smelled flowers; the garden ...camellias, hyacinth, jasmine.... And behind her an old man nursing his paunch.... Again an hysterical laugh broke from her. But she mustn't laugh, she mustn't. He would go from anger into fury. And he might strike her across the eyes again ...with that pathetic, thin-veined hand.

She heard a choking sound. He was strangling ...strangling from all that blood in his face. She must go to him ...he was so old ...he might burst ...clot the floor with his blood.... But it was too thin to clot....

Suddenly there came a shattering thud; as though someone outside had thrown a huge stone through one of the windows, a stone wrapped in cloth, that struck the floor with a muted impact and then split into little pieces.

She swung about, still gripping the drapery.

Stone …where was the stone? …No stone …only Monsieur Chauvet …lying in the corner …the corner where that phenix-vase had stood …gleaming pieces of porcelain scattered about him …porcelain that caught the light and glittered cruelly.

Something in her vision seemed to snap, like the released shutter of a camera, and for one staring second her gaze focused a livid clarity upon the entire room. Foremost in the picture was Justin…. Justin standing near the doorway…. Justin, hatless and disheveled, staring down at the huddle of Monsieur Chauvet…. Then the brutal lucidity of that scene blinded her.

"Mama Thi-Linh," she heard his voice saying, "I didn't mean …I heard you quarreling…. He called you …and when I came in …caught my collar …and I pushed …pushed…."

She saw, thrown upon her eyelids, a pigmy reflex of what had happened. Again the room lurched. When she opened her eyes, it had settled down.

Unsteadily, she crossed the floor and bent over Monsieur Chauvet, lying in the glitter of the broken vase. Where was the phenix, she wondered dizzily. Under Monsieur Chauvet? Or soaring above him and the shattered vase …mounting swiftly out of the ashes of Monsieur Chauvet …the cold deadness of Monsieur Chauvet?

She got up, meeting Justin's dark eyes. Their pupils were luminous with fear. In their depths she saw the flash of something else. For a moment it seemed to sever her reason. France was defeating her…. France who punishes murder with the guillotine.

"I must be calm," she whispered to herself; "I must be calm!"

"Mama Thi-Linh…."

She put her hand over his lips. The warm touch gave her strength. It also impressed upon her the urgency of quick action. Evidently none of the servants had heard or they would have appeared. Perhaps they had all gone to their quarters.

She caught Justin's shoulders.

"Where have you been staying?"

"At a hotel on the Rue Pellerin."

"Go there immediately," she directed, "and wait until you hear from me."

The boy hesitated, his frightened eyes questioning her. She pushed him toward the hall.

"Go—the front door—I will attend to everything."

His look lingered upon the body lying in the midst of broken pottery.

"Is he…?"

"Yes…."

As he started off she drew him back and kissed him fiercely; then she held him a moment, looking into his eyes. Those eyes reassured her. In the little flecks of light deep in the pupils she read a message of hope…. Her dark blood pouring back into Indo-China through Justin, the son of Kim Khouan …pouring back, filtered through French ideas…. The dark blood of other women pouring back into Indo-China through the same sieve …torrents of blood swelling the anemic veins of Indo-China …taking life in the veins of millions of unborn…. All this tumult of blood rising in mighty fountains, turned gold by the sunlight …the tawny triumph of Asia…. She was, suddenly, no longer afraid.

"Hurry," she said briefly.

Quietly he slipped out of the room.

Portrait of Another Frenchman

 onsieur the prefect of police sat in his office and regarded the pile of papers on his desk with visible annoyance.

Outside, the Rue Catinat lay stunned under the morning sun, breathing up shimmers of heat that drifted into the Commissariat of Police. From where he sat in humid shadow, Monsieur the Prefect could look into the street, seen between the leaves hanging motionless against the half-lowered blinds. No one was afoot at this hour, and only a few rickshaws moved over the hot pavement. Monsieur the Prefect decided that, at that moment, the Rue Catinat was profoundly depressing.

Nor did the pile of papers on his desk offer a more engaging prospect. Routine work. As if he did not have enough to do this morning! Well, at least, he reflected, the matter first on the docket was of a nature sufficiently extraordinary to make up for the dullness of those reports.

The heat gathered about him with oppressive, moist intimacy. He glanced at the motionless electric fan.

Damn that fan! he thought. Who had broken it? One of the natives undoubtedly. They tampered with everything—exactly like monkeys.

In fact, they were monkeys. He glanced up as an orderly entered, half expecting to see him dragging a tail across the floor.

"Planton!" he called sharply.

"*Oui, monsieur!*"

"Who broke this fan?"

"I do not know, *monsieur.*"

Monsieur the Prefect fixed an accusing gaze upon him, then said:

"Tell Monsieur Marceau to come here."

In a moment Monsieur Marceau appeared, looking at his superior with polite interrogation.

"Marceau," said Monsieur the Prefect, "who has been meddling with this fan?"

Monsieur Marceau smiled charmingly. "I do not know, *monsieur.*" After a pause he added: "However, I tried to turn it on this morning before you came, and it started, then, *pluff!* with a little purple light, it stopped." Monsieur Marceau illustrated his explanation with a gesture.

This news provoked Monsieur the Prefect. "You will see that it is fixed immediately," he commanded.

"Yes, *Monsieur le Préfet.*"

As Monsieur Marceau went out, Monsieur the Prefect again contemplated the pile of papers on his desk, and with the same distaste as before. Damn these papers! Also damn the heat and the fan! Then a thought wandered across his mind, and he paused to study it.

It was something of a dream, this thought. A dream that he had nursed for a number of years, indeed, since he had come out to this accursed land of exile. This dream was a secret dimension of the future into which he peeped now and then and saw himself, suavely dressed, with a flower in his lapel, descending the steps of the Governor's palace. No longer Monsieur the Prefect, he thought, immensely pleased, but Monsieur the Governor.

In that moment he forgot the heat and the fan and the pile of papers on his desk.

But to his enormous disgust he was abruptly brought back to contemplating them as a door opened and one of the clerks, an Annamite solemn and spectacled, insinuated himself into the office.

"Are you ready for me, *Monsieur le Préfet*?" he asked.

"I am," said Monsieur the Prefect vehemently.

Quickly he scrawled his name across the bottom of the first of the pile of papers, then the clerk, standing deferentially at one side, stamped it with a seal. Monsieur the Prefect sighed audibly. My God! he thought.

The pile of papers had been divided into two almost equal parts when a knock sounded on the door from the outer office.

"Enter!" called Monsieur the Prefect.

An orderly stepped from behind the opened door.

"Monsieur Gaulard is here, *monsieur*," he announced.

"Ah! Bring him in. But wait! Is the prisoner with him?"

"Yes, *monsieur*."

"Good."

Monsieur the Prefect waved the clerk out and sat waiting, impatiently thumping the desk.

Presently the door swung wide. First came a woman, then Monsieur Gaulard. As Monsieur the Prefect met Thi-Linh's eyes he smiled. He did not speak.

"Good morning," said Monsieur Gaulard.

"Good morning," said Monsieur the Prefect. He motioned Thi-Linh to a chair. "Sit down."

He observed that she was remarkably composed; also he realized that he found it immensely gratifying to look at her. She had not, he noticed with a mental smile, forgotten to rouge her lips. Her dress was soft and gray, accentuating the golden tint of her skin. How old was she? Twenty-five—twenty-six? But he could not judge. She had enough French blood to keep her from aging quickly, like native women. My God! he mused, but she is calm! Not a flicker of the eye— and dressed as though she were merely going for a morning drive! He discovered he was admiring her. But, he reflected, she would be like this; he had remarked her poise that night at Monsieur Chauvet's house. Poor Chauvet! Senile fool! But this was a serious matter. I must be very official, he charged himself.

"This is most unfortunate," he began.

Monsieur Gaulard looked very excited.

"She has made it most difficult!" he burst out. "She has refused to talk with anyone but you! My God—"

Monsieur the Prefect interrupted him with an admonishing lift of the hand.

"Let us be calm, my dear Gaulard," he said.

He thought Thi-Linh smiled, and he regarded her severely.

"Is it so," he commenced, "that you have refused to say anything until you talked with me?"

"Yes, *Monsieur le Préfet.*"

"Why?"

She smiled—distantly. "A whim, perhaps."

A whim! It was profoundly disconcerting. He returned her smile ironically; when he spoke his voice was delicately caustic.

"My dear madame, do you realize you are under arrest?"

"Absolutely."

She pronounced the word with a placidity that would have been exceedingly annoying if he had not been, at that moment, appraising the little flecks of gold the intruding sunlight found in her eyes.

"Hmm," he mused.

"May I talk with you alone? I will tell you everything—then."

He entertained the suspicion that there was something like a demand in her tone; then he thrust it aside and decided:

"Very well—if you wish. Monsieur Gaulard? . . ."

"Well, madame?"—when they were alone.

She met his eyes without flinching.

"I killed Monsieur Chauvet," she announced quietly.

That confession struck Monsieur the Prefect as being a bit brutal. Of course he had suspected she had killed him, but—well, he did not expect her to admit it without pressure. It was somewhat upsetting. Now he could bring none of his ingenuity into play.

"Hmm," he mused again. Then: "Do you know the penalty—if convicted?"

"Yes." No fear in her tone.

For a moment he could think of nothing else to utter but "Hmm," which, he realized, sounded quite idiotic.

"The circumstances?" he demanded, after a pause.

Calmly she recited her story. Monsieur Chauvet had returned from Hanoi the previous night, and immediately upon entering the house, accused her of being unfaithful to him in his absence.

"You know how jealous he was; or do you?" she interpolated.

Monsieur the Prefect nodded.

They had quarreled, she continued. He called her a most insulting name; he struck her; and …she pushed him into a huge vase in the corner; when he fell, he must have fractured his skull. In addition to that, the broken pieces of the vase cut the back of his neck very badly.

"That is all," she finished. "I did not mean to kill him—it is most—distressing."

Tears in her eyes? he wondered; or a blur of horror reflected by the memory of that scene?

"Distressing, indeed," he echoed.

He settled back in the chair, arms crossed over his chest, and gazed at her intently. It was one of his favorite poses; it made him look impassive and severe, he thought. Her story corroborated the evidence. Fractured skull. Cuts on the neck. These thoughts swam in the hot cylinder of his brain. Damn this heat! It made the mind run like fluid. A sudden languor possessed him. Her ivory pallor floated before him, magically cool.

"Most distressing," he repeated.

The sound of his voice awakened him to the urgency of some action on his part. He jerked himself up. Hands clasped behind him, he paced the floor. Name of God! Why had this—this mess happened? Of course the court might be lenient with her, but—her reputation was none too good. How many men? A journalist, an officer, and Monsieur Chauvet. Others that he did not know of? And where did she come from? Stung Treng? Sambor? He would have to look it up. A wench. But she did have amazing poise and dignity. And brains. Altogether an extraordinary hussy. Yet, he faltered, was she a hussy? No, not entirely. She was difficult to classify. Women of her temperament were strumpets only when they had no brains; but, if intelligent, they were the consorts of men of power. He remembered a yellow sedan-chair he had once seen swinging along the streets of Peking.

He resumed his seat behind the desk. Once more that languor came over him, and the hot cylinder of his mind seemed to revolve around her pallor. Consorts of men of power.... For a moment Monsieur the Prefect was bewildered by the thought that had spread stealthily in his brain. But Monsieur the Prefect was not a man to remain bewildered long. The decision with which he folded his hands on the desk seemed to put that thought into action.

"As I said before," he began, "you, of course, realize the consequences."

She nodded.

"You are not frightened?" he pursued.

"No." And she smiled faintly. In that smile was a brief glimpse of weariness, hitherto concealed.

He drew a deep breath.

"Of course," he said, "there is a possibility" — and now he smiled — "there is a possibility it might be proved that — well, that he slipped and fell."

A long silence followed, then:

"Yes," she repeated quietly, "it might be proved that he slipped and fell."

For some time she sat there, her dark gaze unwavering. Then she rose and went to the window. As she stood there in the sunlight, her frail chiffon seemed to go misty and radiant. Her eyes were veiled, contemplative. What does that expression mean? he wondered. Triumph? Defeat? Exultation? Despair? He could not read the answer in her face when she turned and moved back to the desk; she merely looked tired, and a little dazed.

"You know," she said, "that I have a son?"

He was surprised. But he did not show it. "Yes," he lied; for he believed in keeping up the tradition that a Prefect of Police knows everything.

"And that his father was an Annamite?"

This additional news was a bit distressing, but he nodded impassively. She sighed almost inaudibly.

"I am going to send him to school in France," she announced.

He became quite jovial. "Excellent! He will become French, like his mother, eh?"

She, too, smiled—wearily.

"Yes, he will become French," she said.,

Monsieur the Prefect tapped a bell. "Monsieur Gaulard," he told the orderly it summoned.

Monsieur Gaulard came, gazing inquisitively at Monsieur the Prefect. Monsieur the Prefect appeared in extraordinary good spirits.

"It will not be necessary to detain madame," he said. "She has explained satisfactorily."

The End

Appendices

Through a Woman's Eyes:
Congaies, Heroines & Harry Hervey
Harlan Greene

Youth in Search of High Adventure
The Hartford Courant—April 7, 1929
Albert J. Duffy

Francophilia:
Harry Hervey's Homage to French Authors
Kent Davis

Congaies or Concubines?
Literary Views of Asian Women under Colonial Rule
Walter Jones

La Marseillaise vs. La Petite Tonkinoise
The Sound of Music in Hervey's Indochina
Kent Davis

Two Quiet Americans:
Alden Pyle & Harry Hervey
Kent Davis

Hervey Bibliography
Kent Davis & Harlan Green

Harry Hervey
November 5, 1900—August 12, 1951

Through a Woman's Eyes:
Congaies, Heroines and Harry Hervey

By Harlan Green

From the very moment he had landed.... he had felt a silent brown mystery rising about him. This intangible element in the atmosphere disconcerted and troubled him. At times he felt up to his throat in a sensual limpidity that flowed imperceptibly out of the tawny people surrounding him. He had expected to find himself in the midst of gay colonial life as a prelude to his voyage into the interior where he intended to study and write. Gay colonial life he had found. But it was an arabesque imposed upon a viscid and swarthy background.[1]

With one look around, Harry Hervey knew something as marvelous as his destiny was about to unfold for him. The search had started years before that steaming hot day in the summer of 1925 when he set foot in Saigon, after years of trying.

He had been born half a world away on November 5, 1900 in Beaumont, Texas into a family that managed hotels. Though he yearned for adventure, he had grown up, stymied, in a series of Gulf coast hostelries, enviously watching guests coming and going from places he longed to visit. Every departure left him sighing as he turned to his only escape – "piles of books" and "yellowed geographic journals containing pictures of far-off places and people".[2]

1 Harry Hervey, *Congai* (Holmes Beach, FL: DatAsia Press, 2014), 3.

2 Harry Hervey, *Ethan Quest: His Saga.* (New York: Cosmopolitan Book Corporation, 1925), 16-17.

As he learned to read, "He struggled with the names. Tangier. Nairobi; Cambodia. He rather liked the sound of Cambodia. 'Cam-bo-d-uh,' he pronounced, wistfully...."[3]

One particular image captivated him—the massive Hindu temple of Angkor Wat with its "great causeway...flung across a marshy stretch, tapering to the foot of ...tremendous stairways and monstrous cone-shaped towers, above the black jungle...." As part of its seductive allure were "dark, naked men moving among the galleries...beneath the picture was a line that he read slowly. 'The Ancient Ruins of Angkor...' *Angkor.* What a splendorous word...! When he became a man he would go there. He knew he would... be among jungles and strange, dark men...."[4]

He was right. Eventually, Harry Clay Hervey, Jr. would gain fame for the stories he'd tell of the dark men—and women—met wandering distant lands. But even before he commenced traveling, his stories began. With a gift for making things up, the young boy started embellishing the prosaic facts of his life with glamorous details, convincing others that his globe-trotting began at the age of ten.[5] In reality, that was about the time his parents separated, and Harry's mother, Jane or Jennie, enrolled him in a series of military schools in an attempt to teach the boy some discipline.[6]

He was an erratic student, getting high grades in some courses while failing others, always giving his dream life precedence.[7] Harry pictured himself in the works of Joseph Conrad,[8] and was even more drawn to the adventures of French sailor Pierre Loti, whose book *Pilgrimage to Angkor*[9]

---

3 Harry, Hervey, *Ethan Quest*,16–17.

4 Harry Hervey, *Ethan Quest*, 17.

5 In a 1930 interview he said he went abroad with both his parents when he was twelve. ("Making the Grade in Gotham," *Dallas Morning News*, August 19, 1930.) A few years later, he said he went to the Orient first with his father when he was about nine. "Harry Hervey in Demand for China Stories," Robin Coons, undated (ca. 1932) clipping from unknown newspaper, Carleton Hildreth/ Harry Hervey Papers, Georgia Historical Society (hereinafter cited as CH/HH Papers/GHS.) Jennie Hervey would not apply for a passport until 1923 and there is no record of one for Harry Hervey, Sr.

6 He briefly attended boarding school at Sewanee Military Academy, in Sewanee Tennessee before his mother moved him to the Georgia Military Academy in Atlanta.

7 A report card shows 90 in Composition, (good for a future writer) but 58 in Math (he'd always be in debt and end up harassed by the IRS), but in English, another 90. (A copy of Hervey's Sophomore Georgia Military Academy report card is on file Woodward Academy, Atlanta Georgia. Copy, author's files.

8 Joseph Conrad (1857-1924), born in Poland, wrote his critically acclaimed novels and stories, mostly about seafaring and adventures in the east, in English. Many of his famous works have been adapted to film including *Lord Jim* and *Heart of Darkness*, which was Francis Ford Coppola's inspiration for *Apocalypse Now.*

9 Pierre Loti (1850-1923) is widely regarded as one of the world's most prolific, romantic and exotic

he read again and again. At an early age Harry realized he was sexually attracted to the "dark, naked" men in the tales. Unlike many others of the era, however, he felt guiltless and comfortable with his desires. Just as he longed for exotic travel, so he craved erotic adventures, love and companionship with another man.

By the age of sixteen, Harry, plump and affecting a monocle, graduated with honors from Atlanta's Georgia Military Academy. By then, he had achieved a literary triumph he could—and would—brag about for the rest of his life.

No longer content to merely read exotic tales, he had begun putting his dreamed fantasies down on paper, concocting stories fueled with color, action and hyperbole. His friends and family were amazed to hear that one of his stories caught the attention of the leading critic, editor and culture arbiter of the day, Henry Louis Mencken. Publication in Mencken's *The Smart Set* was tantamount to announcing your arrival in the world of letters. That Mencken could have selected a first submission from a young school boy was unheard of...for good reason. It never happened, at least not exactly as Harry described it. True, Menken *had* bought one of his stories, but it was not for the high-brow *The Smart Set*. No, it was for one of the low-brow magazines Mencken secretly published, pulp fiction that no one—except adolescent boys—would admit to reading.[10]

Fueled by this hint of success, Harry continued fabricating fantastic adventures about heroes and heroines—and about himself. Toward the end of World War I he tried to enlist in the armed forces by lying about his age and education.[11] Despite his effort, the war ended too soon for his liking

---

travel writers and novelists. In 1912 he published his original French edition titled, *Un Pèlerin d'Angkor*, in Paris.

10 The same thing had happened to playwright S. N. Behrman, who was contacted by Mencken who called the pulp a "sister" publication. "I had never heard of this sister," he recalled more truthfully, "but I was happy to be admitted to the family." Marion Elizabeth Rodgers, *Mencken: The American Iconoclast*. (Cary, NC: Oxford University Press, Inc., 2005), 149. On the back of the dust jacket of *The Veiled Fountain*, published in 1947, there is this author note, "My first sale of a story was when I was sixteen – to H.L. Mencken. Fortunately for me, I didn't sell another for three years. Then I wrote steadily for pulp-paper magazines." A survey of *The Smart Set* shows no stories by Harry Hervey. For his claiming that his first story was in the Smart Set see Nell Flynn Gilland's article "Memories of City Pleasant," Charleston *News and Courier*, September 28, 1941.

11 When it was time to register for the draft, Hervey was working in Greenville, South Carolina, at the Imperial Hotel. There was just the matter of his age to lie about. Born in 1900, he first wrote "1899" on the line asking for his birth year. In doing the math, however, he saw that did not make him the desired age. Hervey then crossed that out and changed it to 1897 to make himself twenty-one. (For good reason he had only scored a 58 in Math on his first term at the Georgia Military Academy.) Across the top of the card, he noted that he was a student at Sewanee. (Harry Hervey, Jr.

**"True, Menken *had* bought one of his stories,
but it was not for the high-brow *The Smart Set*."**

and he found himself back in Texas with his mother, facing a mundane job in an office. He lived a secret life in the sensational stories he wrote.

His *dramatis personae* frequently featured *femmes fatales*—sirens literally trying to lure men to their doom. They appeared on his pages as dangerously wanton creatures who had about as much depth as the paper they were printed on. [12] While he was sexually attracted to men, he was drawn to women; their wiles and ways of seduction fascinated—and even frightened—him. Eventually he'd mature, as would his writing, but he'd

---

World War I Draft Registration Card, 1917 -1918, AncestryPlus data base.) Even that was not totally true. He had enrolled instead as a special student in 1918 to join the Student Army Training Corps. (Email communication from Elizabeth Duncan, St. Andrew's-Sewanee School, to author December 12, 2006.).

12 In one story, "Devil's Business," the hero, looking for his lost friend, is drugged and kidnapped by a tawny beautiful woman, who overpowers him with her castrating femininity. In a country like Cambodia, in a temple like Angkor Wat, Eric witnesses a devil dance where women sway like cobras while attended by white apes, who are really emaciated men, enslaved and virtually emasculated by their seductress. The evil female sets her eyes on the hero, but he kills her, freeing his enslaved male friend from the devastating clutches of a woman. (Published in a magazine called *The Follies*. Undated clipping (ca. 1921), CH/HH Papers, GHS.)

never outgrow his attraction to dramatic women in fiction and real life.[13] In *Congai's* half-caste heroine Thi Linh, he'd create not only his first true-to-life human female character, but also one of his most compelling.

His first two books—*Caravans by Night* and *The Black Parrot*[14]—both featured strong female characters emotionally and physically drawn to handsome men. The literary mask Harry put on gave him the opportunity to write passionately of, and desire for, masculine beauty in a socially acceptable way: through the eyes of a woman. It was his heroines, not he, he could claim, who ached for those beautiful men. (In *Congai,* his heroine "cruises" as a gay man might, picking up lovers as she restlessly roams Saigon by night.)

Despite this literary charade, Harry was actually much more "out" than many other gay men and authors of the time. In his first novel, *Caravans by Night,* for instance, he slyly named one of his characters Dickie Manlove, describing him as "a delicious boy", the only one ever to "penetrate… beyond the outer ramparts" of another male character's "seeming seclusiveness."[15] So much for the subtlety of Harry Hervey's early fiction.

The two novels, published in consecutive years, established Harry Hervey as a rising star in the eyes of the public. They believed—with the help from some exaggerated biographical "facts" from the author himself—that he had already travelled the globe, garnering background from first-hand experience, rather than from magazines and books read in hotel lobbies. Ironically, people's belief in his fabrications turned them true; for with the income from his writing, he began his travels at last.

Harry got a passport, and in February 1923 embarked from San Francisco for a trip that took him to Hawaii, Japan and the Malay Peninsula. When he ran out of money, he took a job as social director on ocean liners plying the Atlantic. [16] Still broke, with nowhere else to go,

---

13 His first attraction on record to larger than life woman comes from his days at the Georgia Military Academy in Atlanta when he saw the diva Geraldine Farrar star in the opera Carmen. . "The more conservative members of the Atlanta audience were scandalized by her accurate impersonation of a Spanish gipsy with few reticences. But Cadet Harry Hervey from the Georgia Military Academy was entranced. Miss Farrar's vivid beauty, her brilliant singing, and her world renown were, Cadet Hervey knew, straight from the high-powered, high-lighted scenes" of romance. (Frank Daniel, "He Wrote His Way to India," *Atlanta Journal Magazine,* February 3, 1950.)

14 *Caravans by Night: A Romance of India,* (New York: The Century Company, 1922). *The Black Parrot: A Tale of the Golden Chersonese,* (New York: The Century Company, 1923).

15 Hervey, *Caravans by Night,* 56.

16 He had left San Francisco in February 1923 and was in New York by the end of April of that year,

he landed in Savannah, GA, where his mother was working in the city's landmark DeSoto Hotel.[17] Harry delivered some public lectures about his travels there and then took off again, this time *with* his mother, who, discretely shaved two years off her age in her travel documents.[18] Together they were quite a pair; he looked older than he was; she looked younger; it was hard to believe they were mother and son.

> I learned a hula in Hawaii and… revisited the homes of …several old friends of Japan…; in China I spent a while with Dr. Sun Yat Sen.…I went down from Darjeeling into Tibet as far as Gyangtse and visited a monastery where the monks bury themselves alive; I went on a caravan trip into the Sahara; I happened to be in Jerusalem on the Greek Easter Sunday, and I saw the service of the Holy Fire in the Church of the Sepulcher; I was almost shot in a May-Day riot in Athens."[19]

…all of which, Harry neglected to mention to the press, occurred in the company of his mother. What he did *not* neglect to tell reporters, however, was what he had done in Egypt when he had been denied entry into the harem of a wealthy Cairo businessman because of his sex. If being male prohibited him from one experience he wanted, he blithely abandoned it, masquerading in women's clothes, skillfully enough to fool the guards, and thereby gaining access. As he later said, "I crept inside my characters and looked out through their eyes, trying to see the world as they saw it."[20] If it

---

as passenger lists attest. He left again almost immediately on another ocean liner, this time going eastward, arriving in England on the 16th. On the very same day, according to immigration records, he got on another ship and went back across the Atlantic, landing in Quebec on May the 25th. One imagines him waltzing with lonely women, signing copies of his books, which he happened to have on him, catering, as the Herveys had, to others who were traveling, and who were probably wealthier than they. The reference to having been a social director of some sort on an ocean liner is in William B. Richardson, Jr., "Harry Hervey: A Bio-Bibliography," thesis Florida State University, 1958, 5.

17 The original hotel, nearly destroyed in a fire in which Harry nearly lost his manuscript for *Ethan Quest*, was rebuilt but later torn down. The site is now occupied by the Hilton Savannah Desoto [www.desotohilton.com].

18 His somewhat trite subjects were "Kipling and India", "Conrad and the South Seas", and "Pierre Loti and Franco-Indo China". But on lecturing on the Fall of the Manchus, he spoke of Yehonala "empress of China" who, according to Hervey, was "as Despotic as Catherine the Great, as amorous as Elizabeth and as cruel as the Borgias." She and she alone "took the reins of state in her twenty-two year old hands and plunged her country in the fire of despotic magnificence whose flames finally destroyed the suzerainty which lighted it." (*Savannah Morning News*, December 1, 1923.) Jane Hervey's birthday is listed as May 6, 1881 (instead of 1879) on both her passport application and in the paperwork returning to the United States. (New York Passenger Lists, 1820 – 1957, AncestryLibrary.com.)

19 "Somewhere East of Suez," *Los Angeles Times,* October 12, 1924 "Books and Authors," *The New York Times*, September 30, 1923.

20 "Books and Authors," *The New York Times*, September 30, 1923. "Georgia Novelist Explores

"Despite this literary charade, Harry was actually much more "out" than many other gay men and authors of the time."

took a change of costume to help complete his female outlook, so be it.

Returning to Savannah, Harry took up residence in a room up under the eaves of the DeSoto Hotel. There he entertained guests, burned incense in front of idols and wore fabulous robes while churning out rhapsodic prose, conflating his two round-the-world trips for the basis for his non-fiction travelogue, *Where Strange Gods Call* (albeit with no mention of his matriarchal traveling companion). The book, published in 1924, sold well, and with his autobiographical novel *Ethan Quest* going to press in

Heart of Woman with a Whip" *Atlanta Journal Magazine*, May 7, 1950.

Harry the explorer as featured in McCall's Magazine, replete with pith helmet.

the spring of 1925, he headed for Southeast Asia to satisfy his childhood longing to see Angkor Wat.

If he had planned to be the first to bring knowledge of those magnificent ruins to the American reading public, however, he was suddenly out of luck. For, in 1924, author and *Titanic* survivor Helen Churchill Candee published *Angkor the Magnificent, Wonder City of Ancient Cambodia,* the first popular English language book on the topic.[21] Perhaps it was this being "scooped" that prompted Harry to come up with an inspired way to outdistance Candee and invent an even *more* flamboyant adventure. In his 1923 novel, *The Black Parrot,* he had created a character

---

21 An expanded and annotated edition of Helen Churchill Candee's 1924 book *Angkor the Magnificent - Wonder City of Ancient Cambodia* was published in 2010 by DatASIA Press.

who spoke of seeing ruins lost in the jungle, similar to those at Angkor Wat.[22] What if Harry himself *became* that protagonist, traveling to a lost temple to seek answers to the mystery of why the Khmer civilization, builders of the spectacular city of Angkor, vanished? In an era still excited over Harold Carter's dazzling discovery of Tutankhamen's tomb, Harry could just steal his own plot, live out his character's life and not just have an adventure like one in books, but actually *write* another book about it. Soon he was telling the press of a fabulous tale of a lost temple heard from a wanderer, and how he was heading to the jungle alone to seek those fabulous ruins to see if the story was true.

Whether the editors believed him or not is unknown, but Harry sold his idea to the Hearst publishing conglomerate, which owned *McCalls Magazine* and Cosmopolitan Book Corporation. With an advance to help underwrite his adventure, Harry set off for Asia, knowing Cosmopolitan would publish his travel book (eventually called *King Cobra*) following *McCalls* promoting first with advance excerpts.[23] Making the trip more wonderful was the fact that he no longer had to travel solo.

Harry's path had crossed high school student Carleton Hildreth's in a Savannah little theatre production. [24] Lithe, attractive and eager to please, Carleton must have found Harry—world traveler, author of four books, and eight years his senior—a glamorous figure. The two men fell in love and Harry soon proposed that the 17 year old join him on the trip. To cloak it all under a guise of legitimacy, Harry engaged Carleton as his secretary. Though he'd take dictation, do research, and help out as an amanuensis for years, Carleton, would, in parlance of today, really be Harry's partner and "inseparable companion" for the rest of his— Harry's—life. [25]

---

22 "'[W]hat I saw was worth all the agony of the journey[',]" the character says. "'Of course, it wasn't as large as Angkor Thom, but there were the same conical towers, the same exterior cloisters; the huge stairways, the carved Nagas and lotus-buds, the daring relief work. And such decay! I can't describe it! The ruins were being devoured by the jungle, a cruel bestial jungle....'" Harry Hervey, *The Black Parrot*, 151–153

23 Three excerpts would appear in the January, February and April 1927 issues of *McCalls*. The January issue has an introduction by Carleton Hildreth, who unequivocally states that he accompanied Harry on the whole trip, but he is not mentioned at all in the book.

24 "Youth in search of high adventure" *The Hartford Courant*, April 7, 1929.

25 Savannah city directories cite Carleton as his secretary; after Harry's death, he referred to himself that way, apparently not daring to mention their real relationship in a conservative era. (An interview with Carleton Hildreth appeared in "The Whitaker Bay Bugle," the newsletter (?) of the *Savannah News-Press*, Inc., undated copy in CH/HH Papers, GHS.) He is called his inseparable companion in Gilland, "Memories of City Pleasant", Charleston *News and Courier*, September 28, 1941.

Saying their farewells to Savannah, Harry and Carleton set off ostensibly in search of the Khmer temple of Wat Phu, "lost" in the jungles of Laos. In reality, they were on a lark to satisfy Harry's life-long quest to lay eyes on Angkor Wat. Traveling to the west coast by train, the couple stopped in Beaumont, Texas, "the place of my birth," Harry noted, where "the natives all but brought a brass band to the station." Alluding to a silent screen actress known for appearing nearly naked in her films, he continued, "Picture this…Betty Blythe[26] on the back platform of her private car, receiving with modest bows the plaudits of the multitude!"[27] Apparently, Harry was already in the practice of personifying himself as a woman, a crucial step in his development in crafting his heroine in *Congai*.

After landing in Saigon, Carleton and Harry dallied a bit to soak up local color before setting off to the jungle ruins of Angkor and Wat Phu beyond. But as soon as Harry looked around the sultry streets of the French colonial outpost, another story, the story of *Congai*, found *him*. He saw sex everywhere—from painted boys to prostitutes -- all parading for eager French men, unmoored from the moralities of their European homes. "Miscegenation," he realized, "is not peculiar to the French, although they have shown themselves… singularly adept at it."[28]

One night he was sitting in a café with a Frenchman. (In the published version of his travels, he'd erase Carleton completely, perhaps finding it hard to explain exactly why he had a teenage boy with him; yet *King Cobra* would be dedicated to Carleton.) All talk in the café stopped when "a very opulent limousine …glided alongside the curb and stopped. Immediately a woman come out of the café." She was stunningly beautiful, prompting Harry to ask, "'Who is that lady?'" to which his companion replied, "She is not a lady. At present she is making life happy—or at least interesting—for a certain elderly gentleman who is both rich and indulgent…."'

The glamorous woman impressed Harry as the embodiment of *haute couture*, but his French confidant continued, "she is just a *congai*, [pronounced *con guy*, the name given to native women in marriages of convenience with Frenchmen] not the sort you see standing belly-deep in the rice fields, but the powdered, smiling little devil who insinuates herself into the graces of her masters. Undoubtedly her mother lived with a Frenchman…She must have been a good business woman, that mother…

---

26 Betty Blythe (1893-1972) caught the public's eye in the 1921 film, *The Queen of Sheba*.

27 Harry Hervey to Pauline Corson, "Tues,, May 26 [1925]", Eugene Rollin Corson Collection, GHS.

28 Harry Hervey, *King Cobra: Mekong Adventures in French Indo-China*, (Holmes Beach, FL: DatAsia Press, 2013), 16.

she taught her French—and men."[29]

The idea of a woman using her sexual wiles to entice, entrap and enslave men was an old trope for Harry, but here, *now*, was a living, flesh and blood woman, a native who appeared triumphant, defying all the force of imperialistic France occupying her country, as well, of the French men occupying her bed. What had she sacrificed to get there, this woman they called *Madame la Panthère*?

Harry's French companion sensed that "Madame" galvanized him, so he turned to him and mused, "'what does it matter now whether you find your dead city or not? You can write a book about *Madame la Panthère*. Doesn't she tell the story of Indo-China eloquently?'"[30]

The seed was planted, just needing time to germinate. Harry left on schedule to go find his "lost city" (although it was not really lost, having been receiving scholarly attention, if not tourists, for years) and he did publish his book *King Cobra* detailing his "discovery." But even while he was dedicated to that, another story was seducing him.

The real epiphany came towards the end of his trip, in a prison camp where men were incarcerated at the mercy of the French colonial government. In that totally male environment, the sexual tension Harry felt translated into a larger paradigm. France, he had come to realize, was the dominant conqueror of Indo-China, with the natives playing the submissively vanquished.

> If I were to personify these elements in a story I should… chose for the first [the conqueror] a French soldier and for the latter [the conquered] a native *congai*. Obviously the odds were against the *congai*. Yet she had certain insidious weapons. This girl…might…be a half-caste. Indeed, the more I thought it the more I was convinced she would better symbolize the country if she had mixed blood.
>
> The opposing force, my French soldier…became several soldiers. Then these miraculously begotten Frenchmen began to change…Only one remained a soldier; another was a writer; another a man with his finger in the colony's finances; another a government official, a resident superior or a governor…. By virtue of their diverse trades they represented France more authentically.[31]

---

29 Ibid., 37.

30 Ibid., 37.

31 Ibid., 268-269.

The idea was so stimulating that it "required no great perception to see immediately that it would not be a short story but a novel...." He saw it "would commence in a jungle town.... Along the Me-Kong, and from there it would shift into the midst of French colonial life in some city like Saigon."[32]

Like Venus, his heroine appeared full born:

> As for my *congai*, she would have all the primitive instincts of her Annamite mother and all the civilized intelligence of her French father. Such a girl necessarily would be destined to become a mistress. She would pass from one man to another—in body a courtezan [sic], in spirit a nun. There would have been a native lover in the beginning, a boy by whom she had a child. It was fitting this child should be sired by one of her mother's people, for then that blood would pass through the girl herself back into Indo-China. Her love for this native boy would make it possible for her to retain a spiritual chastity more vital than actual virginity. To each of the white men she would give something, but within herself would remain a spirit untouched to the very end. And that end..?

> Suddenly I knew. For had I not seen the end one late afternoon in Saigon when a magnificent tawny creature, suave in French clothes, swept out of the Café Continental and into her waiting motorcar?[33]

And so Harry had the heroine, and the story...and a title: *Congai.*

Returning to North America, Harry and Carleton moved to Charleston, SC, where Carleton could still pretend to be his secretary and not have to move back in with his parents. In a quaint setting called "The Pirate's House", he wrote at fever pitch. *Congai* was published in 1927 (just before *King Cobra*) with stunning cover art by his friend, Savannah artist Christopher Murphy, who had illustrated his earlier *Where Strange Gods Call*.[34]

Harry knew it was his best book so far, and many critics concurred, including the *Philadelphia Inquirer's*, who decreed, "Thi Linh is a living woman from the moment of her love-idyll with Kim Khouan to the last sardonic page...."The *New York Times* hailed it as "A poignant and vivid narrative full of observations and understanding."[35] No one noticed that this

---

32 Ibid., 269.

33 Ibid., 269.

34 The dust jacket art is not credited, but Charleston writer and friend of Harry Hervey, John Bennett, noted Murphy as the designer in *The Year Book of the Poetry Society of South Carolina* (Columbia: The State Company, 1926), 49-50.

35 *Philadelphia Inquirer, Philadelphia Record, New York Times,* and *Boston Globe* reviews are quoted in a

***Congai*–Original 1927 Cover:**

Against a field of romantic red roses and iconic French *fleurs de lis*, Hervey's heroine Thi-Linh wears a Tonkinese-style hat and traditional *ao dai*, the Vietnamese national costume. To her lower right, the artist has subtly included bayonets, implying the military oppression behind French colonial rule. To her left is the mythical phoenix—symbolic of both Thi-Linh and her country—that Hervey wove into his plot. Nearly three decades later, author Graham Greene reprised many of the plot elements found in *Congai* in his book *The Quiet American*. For details see Pico Iyer's foreword and the appendix article, *Two Quiet Americans: Harry Hervey & Alden Pyle* by Kent Davis.

The original rear jacket copy reads:

> "*Congai* means literally "woman"—but in French Indo-China the word has another inference. In this new novel Harry Hervey recounts dramatically the character of Thi-Linh, a *congai* who, plunged into the midst of French civilization, rises triumphantly above ever circumstance. There is something of "the woman of all ages" in Thi-Linh; and she stands silhouetted against the background of French gaiety and Asiatic somberness like a symbol of the country itself."

was the first novel by an American in a tradition that had first begun with the French and would be taken up by the English, including the master Graham Greene. And unlike the majority, if not all of them, Harry was the only one to take up the story from the native woman's point of view.

It was breakthrough for Harry. For the first time in his literary career he had created a true, flesh and blood woman, not a caricature of a villainess, as in his short stories, nor a one dimensional, virginal heroine as in his novels. Thi Linh is multi-dimensioned, uninhibited, pure and tragic, more sinned against than sinning. She combines the woman Harry had seen in Saigon and elements he saw in himself. As Gustave Flaubert summed up his character Emma Bovary, so Harry could say of Thi Linh: "*c'est moi!*"

The way Thi Linh eyed men to size them up was how Harry himself did it as a gay man, but there was much more. One can imagine him delivering her lines, assuming the role of a wanton woman to drive handsome men crazy. Harry also shared his inner life with Thi Linh, as well as some of his history. Her comments and analysis of the writer Pierre Loti is pure Harry, a perfect example of him crawling into his character's psyche and looking out through her eyes.

He could not control his sly sense of humor, however, and went a little further, giving his authorial self a cameo appearance in the pages of *Congai,* in a scene at a dinner party hosted by his heroine. The colonial officials sitting at her table complain of "an American writer," who despite being shown "every courtesy" through his travels in the area, nevertheless returned to America to write an incendiary critique about the moral corruption of colonialism.[36] In bringing up this unnamed adventurer, Harry was winking at his readers, and advertising *King Cobra*, while inserting himself in the mix.

Harry came of age during his summer in Saigon, and his Asian experiences marked a turning point in his life. From then on, most of his books would revolve around women, many poignantly similar to the archetype he forged with Thi Linh. Their names (Magda, Zelda, Daphne, etc.) would change, along with their nationalities, but Thi Linh—his most powerful *femme fatale*—always would maintain a strong hold over them, and him. Perhaps it was her half-caste status, half French, half Cambodian, that gave her special resonance in his heart. As a gay man in

---

display ad for *Congai, New York Times Book Review,* May 1, 1927.
36 Harry Hervey, *Congai* ,139-140

a prejudiced world, Harry also lived his life outside the strict gender roles accepted by society. Thi Linh was therefore more than a symbol; she was a mask he wore.

Thi Linh put Hervey on the literary map in a very real way. Her story brought him his first critical acclaim as a novelist, and soon Hollywood was beckoning him, not just for his knowledge of the "mysterious east" but because of his skill creating compelling, sexually-charged characters. But before moving to Los Angeles, he continued his "love affair" with Thi Linh. Too passionate to abandon between the boards of a book, he and Carleton began breathing life into her as character in a stage play. They sold production rights to producer Stan Harris, who chose Rouben Mamoulian[37]—soon to be a famous in his own right for theatrical and movie successes—to direct.

To fulfill Thi Linh's role, Mamoulian chose Helen Menken, Humphrey Bogart's first wife (but no relation to publisher Henry Louis Mencken). Harry and Carleton kept their script close to the original story, tightening it a bit, making it more nuanced, and adding emphasis to the ironies of French imperialism. In the book, Thi Linh gives her illegitimate son by her native lover a French name; in the play he is called Quen, a native name emphasizing the tension between cultures more dramatically. Unlike the novel, her native lover returns at the end of third act, rendering the choices she is forced to make more tragic.

The play's Philadelphia tryouts went well. On the night of November 27, 1928, the opening night audience at the Belasco Theatre in New York was stunned when the curtain rose. Thanks to the production design of Cleon Throckmorton, they saw a jungle before their eyes—mists rising off the water, French men in skirts, smudge pots burning and natives dancing in the heat. And then there was Helen Menken, in her body suit, seemingly nude in her love scene idyll with her young native lover.[38]

The *Washington Post* thought the play perfect; others vacillated, saying it was not a great piece, but not a bad one either. Menken was lauded for her acting, as was Felix Krebs, who played the lascivious Frenchman Monsieur Chauvet. Some critics praised Menken's speech against the crimes of the

---

37 Tiflis (now Tbilisi, Georgia) born Rouben Mamoulian (1897-1987) began directing plays in London in the early 1920s before moving to the US where he established himself as a Broadway director of such classics as *Porgy and Bess* and *Oklahoma!* His Hollywood career stretched into the 1960s, connecting him to hits including *Dr. Jekyll and Mr. Hyde* (1930); *The Mark of Zorro* (1940); *Blood and Sand* (1941); *Silk Stockings* (1957),

38 Bennett Thomas Oberstein, "The Broadway Directing Career of Rouben Mammoulian" PhD dissertation Indiana University, 1977, 70.

French as "an eloquent oratorio," while others felt the writers had overly focused on sex, rather than the sordid consequences of colonialism.[39]

Regardless of what critics thought, the public loved the play and Broadway was abuzz with the story of Thi Linh. People stood in line for tickets and waited weeks for seats. The play became one of the most successful of the season, running for 137 performances before closing on March 23rd as the cast prepared to take the show on the road.[40]

Just as the depression hit, Harry was called to Hollywood. Now, he was certain there would be a new incarnation for *Congai*. He was already recognized as the successful screen writer of two other films centered on fascinating women: *Devil's Dancer*, starring Gilda Gray, the girl who gave America the dance sensation, the "shimmy"; and *The Cheat*, starring Tallulah Bankhead, who shocked the public in a scene where she reveals her lover branded her. That 1931 film was released just before new film censorship codes went into effect, which would dramatically restrict what Americans could view in their theaters. In the end, it was censorship that stopped Thi Linh's journey to the silver screen.

For years, Harry touted a film version to producers who joined him in his struggle to gain approval. But Thi Linh's graphic life was too far beyond the pale. Not only was sex her tool to control men, she didn't die for her sins but actually triumphed. She never allowed herself to become a victim, instead emerging unscathed as a heroine. This was in direct contradiction to "the formula" censors followed; for the sake of public morality, codes decreed that "scarlet" women had to repent and die miserably. Not only was this incongruous with Thi Linh's character, her creator would never allow it—he, too, was an unrepentant sexual outlaw living "immorally" with his male lover.[41]

---

39 Percy Hammond, "New York Theaters," *Los Angeles Times*, January 27, 1929. "The Theatre: *Helen Mencken in Congai*" Wall Street Journal, December 4, 1928; "The New Mencken Play," *The New York Times* October 28, 1928. "Helen Mencken in 'Congai' at Belasco," Washington *Post*, April 7, 1929.

40 Ngyen, Margaret. (2011). *Colonial Vietnam and Early Twentieth Century America: Melodrama, the Hybrid Body, and the Time of Revolution*. (Doctoral dissertation). Robert Marks to Laura Bragg, December 5, 1928, Laura Mary Bragg Papers, SCHS. The author acknowledges Barbara Bellows Rockefeller for bringing this to his attention. For information on Mammoulian's early life and its impact on *Congai*, see Mark Spergel, *Reinventing Reality: The Art and Life of Rouben Mammoulian* (Methuchen, NJ: The Scarecrow Press, 1993). The play itself is discussed pp. 78-83. See also Gerald Bordman, *American Theatre: A Chronicle of Comedy and Drama, 1914–1930* (New York: Oxford University Press, 1995), 369.

41 Sam Harris to Will H. Hayes, May 6, 1929, *Congai* MPAA/ PCA file, of Academy of Motion Picture Arts and Sciences Margaret Herrick Library. Other letters in this file discuss the problems with censors and making of the film.

Thi Linh had another black mark, literally, against her, in the eyes of the censors. She was a half-caste child of a mixed race relationship, a woman who, in Harry's words, had "dark blood." The "code" ruled out any mention of sex between Caucasians and those of another race. "[I]t would never do to have dark …triumph over white," he realized sadly.[42]

To his credit, Harry stayed true; he did not betray, sell out or desert Thi Linh as other of her "lovers" did. Harry would never give up on Thi Linh, even though she never appeared on the screen.

In *Congai*, he had described how Thi Linh helped all the men who possessed her, some of whom even expressed gratitude. Harry was among the thankful ones, for he knew it was Thi Linh who attracted producers and film makers to him. When he realized she would never appear in film form, he began to slyly sneak her persona and psyche into other characters. He wrote new stories that revolved around strong women who saved their men. These heroines, simultaneously saintly and seductive, were brought to life by actresses like Anne Harding in *Prestige* and Loretta Young in *The Devil's In Love*. For each, he shared the gifts he had given to Thi Linh: "the body of a courtezan and the soul of a nun."

If Thi Linh's ghost hovered over all his leading women, it manifested most in Harry's most important film—still considered a classic of American cinema—the 1932 *Shanghai Express*. Directed by Joseph von Sternberg, it starred Marlene Dietrich, a woman who, in the film, changes her name from Magda (derived from the Biblical Magdalene) to Shanghai Lily. Harry wrote the story that was the basis of the film just before the new censorship codes were enforced. Indeed, it was he who prompted the line Dietrich is still known for, a phrase Thi Linh could have comfortably delivered as well: "It took more than one man to change my name to Shanghai Lily." Like Thi Linh, Lily seduces men as she saves them, maintaining her spiritual chastity, if not her virginity. She stays loyal to her first love and true to her own higher morals as she moves immorally among men. Asian actress Anna May Wong appears in the film as a sort of a *congai* herself, but it is Dietrich's' character that approximates and sublimates Thi Linh.

Shanghai Express was Harry's Hollywood peak;[43] he'd never surpass

---

42 "The Gossip Shop," *The Bookman*, Volume LXIV number 5 (January 1927), 649 - 650.

43 The film was nominated for best picture and won an Academy Award for Lee Garmes' cinematography. Hervey's scenario, long overlooked in critical discussion of the film, was so well written it was cited for its excellence decades later in a text books. Warren Bower, ed., *How to Write for Pleasure and Profit* (Philadelphia: J. B. Lippincott Co., 1951), 179–180.

that success, and as was so often the case with American writers, the place's excesses and his own accelerating alcoholism almost did him in. Dogged by the IRS, in debt, and the victim of a man blackmailing him over a sexual liaison, Harry had to flee. He and Carleton pawned their possessions just to get out of town. Ultimately it was Harry's long suffering mother Jennie, still working at Savannah's DeSoto Hotel, who took them in.

In Savannah, Harry and Carleton lived together as a committed couple (or as author and "secretary") for another twenty years. Never able to get out of debt, Harry was forced to come to terms with what his life had become. The boy who dreamed of exotic adventures while growing up in hotel lobbies was reduced to a man who sat in one, spinning tales of past exploits to cadge cigarettes and drinks from transitory guests.

But like his heroine, Thi Linh, he survived; the world could not totally crush him. He, like she, had other triumphs. He wrote several more popular novels that garnered critical acclaim. One of his most captivating, *The Damned Don't Cry*, centers on heroine Zelda O'Brien, who in many ways resembles Thi Linh. Zelda's only mistake is being born on the wrong side of the tracks; "civilized" Savannah society expects only one role of her, and shows no interest in her purity or courage. Like her sister in Saigon, she has an early love affair resulting in an illegitimate son who returns to bring on her tragic end, again mirroring the life of Thi Linh. Harry had been condemned for exposing the hypocrisy of French colonialism more than a decade earlier; similarly, his scathing exposé of Savannah society would render him infamous in the town for years.

Harry loved Zelda, as he loved Thi Linh. "I often wonder what became of her," he'd muse. "At times I think I know. And I am urged to put it into a novel, as a means of saying to those who read her story, 'See—this is the triumph of Zelda O'Brien....' But I probably never shall; instead I'll be content to hold shadowy and intimate trysts with this tarnished heroine."[44]

And what of the original inspiration for the sisters Shanghai Lilly and Zelda O'Brien? She also returned to haunt him. "Thi Linh, an Indo-Chinese half-cast.... She too asks me to tell what became of her and sometimes I am tempted. But I prefer to remember her as I parted with her—a courageous woman who had lost everything but herself, and who

---

44 Harry Hervey, "Stories I Shall Never Write," clipping from unidentified Atlanta newspaper, November 30, 1941.

rose head and shoulders above the men who defeated her...."[45]

She remained a bracing vision to Harry. Like her, he was also trapped by circumstances beyond his control. Barely 50 years old when he was diagnosed with severe throat cancer, he went to New York City for treatment. There he suffered a series of gruesome and painful surgeries, dying in debt on August 12, 1951, with Carleton at his side. National journals and newspapers carried his obituary, but he was forgotten soon after he was laid to rest in Savannah's Bonaventure cemetery.[46]

Nearly 90 years have passed now since the hot summer day in Saigon when Harry first saw the elegant woman step out of the café and into her limousine. In a way, we are in that moment again, staring at her spellbound, along with all those idlers at their tables, as the woman who lost everything but herself sweeps majestically not just out of the Continental Hotel, but out of her author's and her own past. As to what new successes and incarnations lie in store for her we can only pause, admire, and guess.

About the biographer

Harlan Greene was born and educated in Charleston SC. He has served as assistant director of the South Carolina Historical Society, director of the North Carolina Preservation Consortium, director of Archives at Avery Research Center for African American History and Culture, at the College of Charleston, where he is now Senior Manuscript and Reference Archivist of Addlestone Library's Special Collections. He has received awards for his archival and historical work and for his fiction. Some of his publications include *Mr. Skylark: John Bennett and the Charleston Renaissance*, *Slave Badges and the Slave Hire System in Charleston, SC, 1783 – 1865* (with Harry S. Hutchins, Jr. and Brian E. Hutchins) and the novels *Why We Never Danced the Charleston*, *What the Dead Remember*, which won the Lambda Literary Award, and *The German Officer's Boy*. He is a frequent contributor to scholarly and popular journals on topics related to Charleston history, and is the author of a forthcoming biography of Harry Hervey.

---

45 Hervey, "Stories I Shall Never Write"

46 Carleton Hildreth outlived Harry, dying in 1977. Harry's mother, Jane Louise Davis Hervey, lies next to her son at Bonaventure Cemetery.

Youth in Search of High Adventure

by Albert J. Duffy [1]

The Hartford Courant—April 7, 1929

FIVE years ago a 17-year-old boy ran away from his home in Savannah. Georgia. With a youth but a scant five years older than himself he set out on an expedition to find traces of a lost race.

Deep in the tangles of the fever infested jungles of Indo-China they found the crumbling ruins of a lost civilization —ruins whose beauties had first been described to the older of the two young men by a drink palsied beachcomber in a waterfront saloon in Singapore.

The results of the expedition were two books, a novel and a travel narrative, and a play, *"Congai"*, which was one of the outstanding dramatic hits of the present season with Miss Helen Menken [2] as its star.

Let us suppose that you were a young man still in your very early twenties and had to your credit a New York dramatic hit. Would you put behind you the ease and adulation that New York is always ready to give to the successful and deliberately set out to find the most exacting and difficult job obtainable? Of course you wouldn't. Neither would I. But Carleton Hildreth did and that is why we find him in Hartford playing juvenile roles with the Fox Players, gladly assuming the monotonous and nerve-wracking routine of

---

1 Evidence compiled by Hervey biographer, Harlan Greene, contradicts some items reported in this promotional article. Readers are encouraged to consult his research for the facts.

2 Helen Menken (Dec. 12, 1901–Mar. 27, 1966) made her theatrical debut on Broadway as a teenager in 1917; by the mid-1920s she was an established actress. On May 20, 1926 she married another lesser known Broadway actor…but Helen certainly had an eye for acting talent. The American Film Institute later ranked her husband as the "Greatest Male Star of All Time"—his name was Humphrey Bogart. The couple's wedded bliss, however, was short-lived; she divorced him on Nov. 18, 1927 so they pursued their acting careers separately. Menken continued acting on stage and radio, and also worked behind-the-scenes on Broadway productions, as illustrated by Hildreth's account. While she never made the transition to film, some of her most famous Broadway roles were recreated by other actresses, including Janet Gaynor and Betty Davis.

Helen Menken in the starring role of Thi-Linh in the Broadway production of *Congai*.

the stock player with ten performances a week and long hours of study and rehearsal.

Best Way to Learn Theater.

"But why shouldn't I be playing in stock?" he asks. I have had all too little actual experience in the theater so I must get back to work and learn how to act all over again. I want to continue successful in the theater and to do so I must know the theater. Stock is the best school of the theater I know, so I am here and I'm learning something new each week.

"New York has a very short memory you know," Mr. Hildreth smiles. "There are too many men there now trying to live on the reflected glory of a single success. I don't want to do that. I want to follow up my first success with other hits. That's why I'm here, in the grammar school of the theater, learning my A B C's as any novice should."

Carleton Hildreth as born in Georgia—in a little town with a soft, musical name but a name, withal, that is hard to remember. Indeed, this interviewer has already forgotten it.

The Hildreth family moved to Savannah soon after Carleton was born and he grew up in that city. He attended the grade schools there and was graduated from high school. Immediately he turned to the absorbing work of the theater, working in stock companies in Savannah and with the Municipal Theater, a civic Institution. It was in a Municipal Theater production that Hildreth first met Harry Hervey.

Hervey, a young novelist who had recently come to live in a suburb of Savannah, agreed to play one of the roles in the Municipal Theater's production of "*Outward Bound*," Sutton Vane's dramatic story of the journey of a group of souls from the shores of the living to the unknown land of the dead.

Hervey's Travels.

Hildreth too, was cast for the play and he and Hervey soon became fast friends. In countless talks over midnight lunches after rehearsals and performances Hervey recounted his experience in the far places of the earth. He told of trips to the Far Fast, to India, China and Japan, and his stories were enormously interesting to his new friend, a fair haired soft voiced Georgian who had never travelled across the border of the United States and who had spent most of his life in the sleepy southern quiet of Georgia.

Then, one night, Hervey told his tale of Singapore.

Hervey was idling along the wharves of Singapore one stifling hot day a year or more before. A bedraggled figure separated from the crowd and shuffled up to his side. It was a beachcomber—a derelict of humanity, sodden with drink and dope, floating listlessly with the swirling tides of life.

"Buy me a drink, Guvnor? My throat's as dry and as hot as hell!"

Hervey took him to a cafe nearby, a drinking place frequented by the motley crews off the tramp steamers that made Singapore a port of call. After the derelict had slaked the first frenzied demands of his parched throat they sat and talked—this novelist and a drunken beachcomber. Across the damp, sticky table top reeking with the drippings of thousands of drinks, the drunkard told Hervey an amazing story.

The Derelict's Story.

He had been a civil engineer before the tropics and an insatiable desire for liquor had reduced him to his lowly estate. At one time he had worked on a surveying job in Indo-China. Far tip in the interior, he said, he had seen the ruins of the key city of the lost race of the Khmers. It was a beautiful city of palaces, the derelict said, and his bloodshot eyes lit for a moment with a faint fire of rekindled interest.

The city had been built on terraces and on the topmost terrace was the temple—the "holy of holies." On the walls of the temple, the beachcomber said, the history of the Khmers was told in a series of exquisite carvings in bas relief.

Hervey said that the rambling, drunken tale of the beachcomber had the ring of truth to it and, solely on the strength of his story, Hervey was planning a trip into the Interior of Indo-China in search for the lost city of the Khmers.

"Then I'll go along with you, too!" young Hildreth cried impulsively. They talked into the early hours of the morning, making feverish plans for the expedition. Hildreth was to go along as Hervey's secretary and companion—a white man could never make the trip Into the interior alone with only the natives for company.

Hildreth told his parents of the plan for the expedition in and was quickly informed that he could not go. A 17-year-old boy go trekking off into the wilds of a heathenish jungle to find some crumbling old ruins? It was unthinkable!

Answering Adventure's Call.

This parental disapproval was a hard blow to young Hildreth, afire with the spirit of adventure. His mind had been intrigued by the soft cadence, of strange, mysterious sounding names—Saigon, Angkor, Stung-Treng—names filled with all the glamor of glorious romance.

He ran away. Off to New York where weeks were spent in preparation for the trip. Visits to doctors, physical examinations, blood tests, vaccinations, more examinations, the injection of anti-this and anti-that serums: passports, visas, and, finally, the departure.

A long, lazy voyage; days spent in devouring every available word written about Indo-China and its people; nights of dancing on the deck under the stars to the languorous rhythm of a waltz floating softly from an orchestra on the forward deck.

Indo-China. The Quai Frances Garnier, Rue Catinat, the Hotel Continental. Saigon!

Indo-China is French territory and the few whites there are mostly French Officers attached to the garrison of the Tirailleurs Annamites, managers and executive heads of the territorial branches of Industrial and banking companies. There are but few Englishman and fewer Americans.

Hildreth and Hervey spent some time in Saigon absorbing the atmosphere and spirit of the place. They were welcome additions to the small colony of whites that clung tenaciously to the practices of civilization in this small clearing on the edge of the jungle.

A New World.

All of the social functions of the colony were carried on with the strictest formality. Men and women dressed formally for dinner and afternoon attire was prescribed for the tea-dansants at the Continental, the gathering place of the colony.

It was a new world to Hildreth; a new and glorious world. A world of gayly decorated bazars, of rickshaws drawn by swift, barefooted coolies, a world of marching Tirailleurs, dressed in dark tunics and spiked straw helmets; a world where white men desperately lonely, thousands of miles away from their homes and families, sought—and found—happiness with native women.

"*Congais*," they called these little native common law wives of the French colonies. "*Congai*," to quote Charles Brackett,[3] is the Indo-Chinese word for a young woman who is no better than she should be. The *congai* had their distinct social station. They were above the ordinary natives and below the few white women who had braved the tropic heat to be with their husbands.

It was this common practice of taking native girls as common law wives that inspired the writing of "*Congai*," Hervey's novel which was later dramatized by Hildreth and Hervey into the present successful play.

"Was the character of Thi-Linh, the little native *congai*, drawn from life?" we eagerly asked Hildreth.

Character from Life.

"Of course Thi-Linh is the dramatic counterpart of the *congai* of the head of the Saigon branch of a French banking company. She was a striking figure and lorded it over the other *congais* in Saigon in the grand manner. Her name was Marie Sanh and she was known as *Madame la Panthère* to the officers of the Tirailleurs garrison. You will

---

3 Charles William Brackett (Nov. 26, 1892–Mar. 9, 1969) was an American novelist, screenwriter, and film producer. He was a frequent contributor to *Collier's*, the *Saturday Evening Post* and *Vanity Fair*. He relates to this article because he was a drama critic for *The New Yorker* from 1925 to 1929.

**"...the opera—that last pitiful attempt at preserving the refinements of civilization."
Saigon Opera photo :Montague Archive.**

remember that in our play Thi-Linh changes her name to Marie Linh when she comes to live in Saigon."

"And was Marie Sanh—this *Madame la Panthère*—as intelligent and as civilized as you have made Thi-Linh in the book and the play?"

"No," Hildy smiled a reminiscent smile. "Marie Sanh, the Thi-Linh of real life, was an F. Scott Fitzgerald heroine—beautiful, but dumb."

The color of life in Saigon soon pales and Hildreth and Hervey grew impatient to start their expedition into the interior. They told their plans to the French colonists and were rewarded with polite but faintly amused smiles. Undiscovered ruins, indeed! Would not the gallant French soldiers have found such ruins if they existed? *Certainment!* But these Americans! One must humor them.

Undismayed, the pair pushed forward their final preparations for the trek. Days were spent in purchasing supplies at the bazars along Rue Taberd and Rue Paul Blanchy. Native guides were interviewed and long, acrimonious debates ensued before the natives were convinced that they were not doing business with inexperienced babies and reduced their prices to the prevailing level charged for such services.

In the evenings, when the parching sun was hidden and a freshening breeze waited under the awnings of the sidewalk cafes, Hildreth and Hervey continued their social contacts with the French colonists.

Found the Ruins.

They danced at the Continental, they sipped aperitifs at tables in the sidewalk cafes, they attended the opera—that last pitiful attempt at preserving the refinements of civilization—and heard fourth, yes, fifth and *sixth* rate companies murder the glorious music of the masters. The colonists did not go to the opera in Saigon to enjoy the music. They went because it was the thing to do, because they could dress and sit in boxes—there to see and be seen.

Finally the young adventurers completed their preparations and, after bidding goodbye to their new friends, they set out—seekers after a lost race!

This is not the place to tell the story of their exhibition. Harry Hervey has told it completely and vividly in *King Cobra*, his thrilling, narrative of the trip.[4] It will suffice here to say that after long, arduous days and nights in the jungle fighting off the dread threat of fever, they found the ruins of the City of Terraces, the lost city of the Khmers.

Throughout this trip, Hervey and Hildreth kept complete notes of their experiences and explorations and they took many interesting pictures of the ruined palaces and the temple of the Khmers. They also made an exhaustive record of the story of the Khmers found carved on the crumbling walls of the temple.

Just after they had started on their return journey through the jungle to Saigon, Hervey, who had been careless in taking his daily doses

---

4 In 2013, DatAsia Press released an expanded edition of *King Cobra*, with foreword by travel writer Pico Iyer, a profile of Hervey by his biographer Harlan Greene, and lavishly illustrated with more than 140 period photos of Indochina by Hervey himself and from Asian archivist Joel Montague.

King Cobra, original 1927 dust jacket.

of quinine, succumbed to fever. On Hildreth, therefore, fell the full responsibility of directing the natives on the trip and caring for his delirious companion.

Subject of Two Books.

They finally reached Saigon and lingered there while Hervey recovered from his illness. There Hildreth assembled and arranged their notes on the expedition and, in his leisure hours renewed his friendships with the colonists. He also met some of the Indo-Chinese royalty who were immensely interested in the results of the expedition.

It was while they were delaying their departure from Saigon that Hervey became interested in the life of the *congais*. He was intrigued by the majestic grace of *"Madame la Panthère"* and visualized her as the central figure of a novel set in Indo-China…a novel that would catch the spirit of the Annamite natives and the French colonists far better than it ever could be captured by a travel narrative.

Hildreth and Hervey left Indo-China to return to America by way of Singapore und Egypt. But before they left the tropics Hildreth fell victim to an attack of fever, making a quick recovery, however, on the open sea and, under the tender care of the English crew of their ship. They stopped off in Singapore and in Egypt and, before they sailed for America, they visited Paris and London. By the time they had returned to New York the first rough draft of the novel, *"Congai"* had been completed. Hervey polished off his work and the book was accepted for publication and received very favorable reviews as an interesting story set in an authentic background.

With *"Congai"* published Hervey, still assisted by Hildreth, began work on *"King Cobra,"* the story of the expedition to the Lost City of the Khmers, and this book, too, was eventually finished and accepted for publication.

How *"Congai"* Was Written.

And now, Hildreth, back in America once again, grew restless and longed to get back into the theater. He had sensed in Marie Sanh— *"Madame la Panthère"*—a truly dramatic figure and he suggested to Hervey that they dramatize *"Congai."* But before he pressed his suggestion Hildreth told Helen Menken of his idea and asked her what she thought of it. He wanted to be more sure of himself for he had not been in the theater for more than two years. When Miss Menken agreed with him enthusiastically and expressed a desire to create the role of Thi-Linh, Hildreth again approached Hervey, this time with more confidence in his own idea, and they started the dramatization.

The play finished, there began the tedious task of peddling it from one producer to another. Most managers today are looking for plays with small costs and requiring only one set. It is almost foolhardy for an unknown playwright to attempt to interest a producer in a play of many scenes and requiring a long cast of principals and extras as *"Congai"* does.

However, one manager saw possibilities in the play and took a short option on it. He had a heavy production schedule and did not get around to *"Congai"* and the option expired without any request from

Helen Menken in her starring role as Thi-Linh with Ara Gerald playing her ambitious mother, Mama Thi-Bao (Vera G. Hurst also appeared in that role).

the producer that it be renewed. The job of peddling the play started all over again.

Helen Menken as Thi-Linh.

Sam Harris read the play and liked it. He called in the playwrights and, after several conferences, bought the piece for immediate production. He also signed Helen Menken to create the role of Thi-Linh. Rehearsals were started as soon as the cast was completed. Incidentally, in picking the cast and effort was made to secure Robert Ames of Hartford, to play one of the roles but when Mr. Harris and Mr. Ames could not reach an agreement on salary, another actor was chosen.

Hildreth, during the rehearsals, gave his attention to the scenic and costume details of the production. Indo-China was a new country to the New York stage und it was necessary to work with the scenic designers and artists and with the costumers to see that all their work was authentically Indo-Chinese.

The period before a play opens in New York is a nightmare to everyone connected with the production. Last minute changes are always necessary and it seems that the whole world is conspiring to defeat the attempt to get the play opened on schedule time. Let Mr. Hildreth tell you about it himself:

"We took the play to Philadelphia for a tryout and everybody had their friends at the Philadelphia opening to pass judgment on the play. After the performance the entire audience seemed to troop backstage to tell us what was wrong with the play. So eloquent were some of the would-be critics that we completely rewrote the ending of the play three times before we left Philadelphia and, when we opened in New York, we reverted to the original ending.

Period of Uncertainty.

"After the New York opening the opinion of the critics seemed about evenly divided and there was a time for a week or so after the opening when no one was sure whether *"Congai"* was a hit or a flop. Then business picked up rapidly and we all began to breath freely again. We had a hit on our hands.

"I get heaps of enjoyment out of sitting in the theater and watching the reaction of the audience to the play. It is never exactly the same. Oftentimes French people, thinking we have been rough on the French colonization plan, hiss the play. As a matter of fact I think we have treated the French colonization plan very fairly. It has its evils and its weak spots, of course, but they are no weaker nor more evil than America's colonization practices in the Philippines or that of the English in India.

"Quite often though, when Thi-Linh, seeing her native lover march off to war with the Tirailleurs Annamites, scornfully bids them to 'March Annamites, march! Spill your blood for the white men who

SAM H. HARRIS THEATRE

226 West 42nd Street
Telephone Wisconsin 6800
SHUBERT THEATRE CORP., *Lessee . . . Direction of* LEE *and* J. J. SHUBERT

FIRE NOTICE: Look around now and choose the nearest exit to your seat. In case of fire, walk (not run) to that exit. Do not try to beat your neighbor to the street.
JOHN J. DORMAN, Fire Commissioner.

WEEK BEGINNING MONDAY EVENING, MARCH 4, 1929
MATINEES WEDNESDAY AND SATURDAY
Evenings at 8:50

SAM H. HARRIS
PRESENTS

"CONGAÏ"
A New Play
BY HARRY HERVEY AND CARLETON HILDRETH
FROM A NOVEL OF THE SAME NAME BY HARRY HERVEY
——WITH——

HELEN MENKEN

PRODUCTION DIRECTED BY ROUBEN MAMOULIAN
SETTINGS BY CLEON THROCKMORTON
PROGRAM CONTINUED ON SECOND PAGE FOLLOWING

AFTER THEATRE, DINE AT

The Nation's Host *Childs* from Coast to Coast

21 Restaurants in the Theatre District
OPEN ALL NIGHT

Congai was one of Broadway's most successful plays of the season with 137 performances between November 27, 1928 and March 23, 1929.

have civilized you!' and builds the speech up to a tremendous climax for the second act curtain, she has been hissed. It is amusing."

"Have you written any other plays?"

"Yes, we have finished two and now we are working on a third. One of the plays is a story of the sea and one is something after the manner of 'Fata Morgana,'[5] If you remember it. We have had two opportunities to sell this latter play but I am determined not to sell it until the producer will accept me to play the leading part. You see, the role was written with me in mind and I'm darned if I'll sell the play until I find someone with enough confidence in me to agree to let me create the part. That's one of the reasons I'm working here in Hartford, you see, polishing off the rough edges on my acting."

"And now, before we end his interview, I want you to tell me about some of your privations and troubles,"

"Privations? Troubles? I haven't had any privations or troubles. I've had five years filled with wonderful experiences and filled with fun. Then, to make it more wonderful, my five years of work with Mr. Hervey were climaxed with a real success. If you're looking for trouble come around sometime next week and watch me trying to play Jimmy in "*The Trial of Mary Dugan*." [6] There's trouble for you!"

---

5 "A Fata Morgana is an unusual and complex form of superior mirage that is seen in a narrow band right above the horizon. It is an Italian phrase derived from the vulgar Latin for "fairy" and the Arthurian sorceress Morgan le Fay, from a belief that these mirages, often seen in the Strait of Messina, were fairy castles in the air or false land created by her witchcraft to lure sailors to their death." (Wikipedia)

6 "The melodrama concerns a sensational courtroom trial of a showgirl accused of killing of her millionaire lover. Her defense attorney is her brother, Jimmy Dugan. It was first presented on Broadway in 1927, with Ann Harding in the title role, and in London in 1928 with Genevieve Tobin. Two American films were based on the play, one in 1929 directed by Bayard Veiller and starring Norma Shearer, and one in 1941 directed by Norman Z. McLeod and starring Laraine Day. During the play, the audience was addressed as if it were the jury." (Wikipedia)

Angkor, April 20, 1912 by André Joyeux—*La Terre de Bouddha*, DatAsia Press, 2013.

Francophilia: Harry Hervey's Homage to French Authors

By Kent Davis

> The ruins of Angkor! I remember so well a certain evening of April,
> a little overcast, on which as in a vision they appeared to me....
> There was one picture at which I stopped with a kind of thrill—of
> great strange towers entwined with exotic branches, the temples of
> mysterious Angkor! Not for one moment did I doubt but that one
> day I should see them in reality, through all and notwithstanding
> all, in spite of prohibitions, in spite of impossibilities.[1]

In 1865 fifteen-year-old Louis Marie Julien Viaud made the above
vow; thirty-six years later he realized his goal. In 1912, he published
Un Pèlerin d'Angkor (A Pilgrim to Angkor), soon followed by an English
translation. By then Viaud was far better known by his penname, Pierre
Loti, and his books were already inspiring many adventurers to head to
Asia…including a young American named Harry Hervey.

After his 1925 visit to French Indochina, Hervey himself became one of
the few American writers to focus on that part of the world, publishing
two major works about the region: *King Cobra*, a non-fiction account of
his trip; and *Congai*, a novel about a young Eurasian girl who becomes
the mistress to a series of colonial Frenchmen. This article examines and
clarifies Hervey's French literary references in both books, the majority
of which are unfamiliar to Anglophones because few of the works cited
or alluded to have been translated into English.

Using direct quotes from Hervey's text we will learn how Francophonic
literature influenced the author, briefly profiling specific authors he
mentioned. We'll discover how Hervey drew key elements—from
cultural subtleties to detailed scenes—from the existing genre of
French Indochina literature to enhance his own books. In its totality,
the evidence will demonstrate how French writers inspired Hervey

---

1 Pierre Loti, *Siam*, the English translation of *Un Pèlerin d'Angkor* by W. P. Baines, (Philadelphia:
McKay, 1913), 3-4. The title is a bit misleading because Angkor, previously under the political control
of Siam, had reverted back to Cambodia under the French Protectorate in 1905.

from his youth, greatly influencing his style and destiny, and how he returned the favor by bringing rare French history and ideas into the English language.

Part 1:
The Flowering of French Colonial Dreams

A ghost of childish fancy in me is stirred by even the suggestion of colonial troops. It takes me back to those luxurious days when I read *Le Roman d'un Spahi* and *Rarahu*. Consequently, these barracks drowsing in sensuous shade bring to life pages of romance, and wandering past them I am able to invest the stupid Annamite sentinel with the dignity of an iniquitous rascal or to find in the glimpses of khaki-clad soldiers, permitted by open doors and windows, a hint of something decadent and definitely improper.

I am convinced, for the moment, that all of them have native mistresses—for haven't I read and believed *Le Roman d'un Spahi* and *Rarahu*?—or, if not, at least they go every night to the Botanical Garden, which is conveniently near the barracks, to tryst with rice-powdered *congaies* who do not blacken their teeth with betel [*King Cobra*, 10].[2]

Harry Hervey dreamed of adventure, craved adventure, and even invented adventure long before he made it a reality in his life, which began quite modestly. On November 5, 1900, he was born into a middle class family that operated small hotels in the southern United States. As his biographer, Harlan Greene, observes, "it's easy to picture the dreamy boy sitting in palm-decked lobbies, perusing 'piles of books' and 'yellowed geographic journal[s] containing pictures of far-off places and people.' "[3]

Among those books, the works of Pierre Loti were clearly among the first to ignite Hervey's imaginative quest for excitement.

---

2 All page references to *King Cobra* (2013) and *Congai* (2014) refer to DatAsia Press editions.
3 Harlan Greene, "Harry Hervey: The Charmer Behind the Cobra," in *King Cobra*, 290.

Pierre Loti (Louis Marie Julien Viaud)

Pierre Loti (Louis Marie Julien Viaud)
Jan. 14, 1850–June 10, 1923

> Loti's shadow was inevitable, lying over all colonial or exotic novels.
> These abound in more or less explicit inter-textual references to the
> master's work—elegant literary pirouettes or *mises en abîme* before
> the term was ever coined.[4]

Pierre Loti wrote more than forty books during his career, filled with his vivid descriptions of travel, adventure and romance in the exotic Near and Far East that captured imaginations worldwide, and inspired countless people to realize their own dreams of Oriental travel. A century before Jennifer Yee wrote her opening quote, contemporary critic Edmund Gosse (1849–1928) described Loti as "unquestionably the finest descriptive writer of the day."

Born in Rochefort, France on January 14, 1850, Louis Viaud enrolled in the naval academy at Brest at the age of seventeen to pursue a career as an officer. As the quote on page 264 reveals, he did this to fulfill what he saw from a very young age as his destiny. Angkor first cast its spell over him when he found an engraving of the temple among some papers belonging to his older brother who had served in Indochina. Next to the illustration, he saw words that never left his memory: "In the depths of the forests of Siam, I have seen the star of evening rise over the ruins of Angkor."[5]

But decades of global travel and adventure preceded the fulfillment of his boyhood dream. Viaud's naval duties took him to Istanbul, the South Pacific, Senegal, Tonkin, Japan, Morocco, Algeria and elsewhere. Many of these exotic ports of call resulted in popular books, and more than a few romantic encounters. His first exploits in the Near East inspired *Aziyadé*, which was published anonymously by editor Calmann-Lévy in 1879. The book went unnoticed by the public.

The determined author then sent his publisher a second manuscript, *Rarahu*, a semi-autobiographical tale of South Pacific romance. The publisher showed this work to one Madame Adam, an editor seeking material for the periodical, *La Nouvelle Revue*. She enjoyed the story

---

4 Jennifer Yee, *Clichés De La Femme Exotique: Un Regard Sur La Littérature Coloniale Française Entre 1871 Et 1914*, (Paris, France: L'Harmattan, 2000), 21. Translation by Pedro Rodríguez.
5 Loti, *Siam*, 6.

and shared it with Alphonse Daudet (profiled below) who was taken by its power and originality. One more ingredient was needed: a compelling *nom de plume*. Viaud chose "Loti," a nickname meaning "flower" bestowed on him by the Tahitian Queen Pomaré. His career had begun in earnest. *Rarahu* was published under his new penname in 1880, followed in 1881 by *Le Roman d'un Spahi*, a colonial drama of love and death in French West Africa. During his lifetime, Loti's genius produced more than three dozen additional imaginative works.

For the quality of his prose, the Académie Française—the prestigious 40-member body presiding over the French language—elected Loti as its youngest member in 1891. A decade later, in November 1901, his ship anchored in Indochinese waters; Loti at last seized the opportunity to fulfill his childhood vow. Through the jungle he travelled to the temples of Angkor.

In 1910 Loti retired from a lifetime of service in the French navy to complete *Un Pèlerin d'Angkor*, the book that eventually drew Hervey to Asia shortly after the French adventurer died on June 10, 1923. At least two other prominent Indochina authors credit Loti for their Asian inspiration; Roland Meyer (1889–?) and Marguerite Duras (1914–1996). Meyer (profiled below) considered Loti's books the spur that drove him to Cambodia and Laos, where he wrote extensively about local cultures. Duras, who was actually born in Saigon, began writing about colonial life in the 1940s. In 1984, she released her most successful title, *L'Amant* (*The Lover*); a semi-autobiographical account about her youthful , interracial romance in Indochina. In 1984, *L'Amant* was awarded the prestigious Prix Goncourt, and became an award-winning feature film in 1992. Even in our modern world, Loti's inspiration bears fruit.

Pierre Loti was buried with state honors on the Île d'Oléron, near his Rochefort birthplace, where his home is today a museum.

Part 2:
Hervey's French Foundation

And by his tone I understood I had won the confidence of Gilbert
Filleau de Saint-Hilaire. "And I like poetry, too," he added, very
wistfully; then murmured, "Lamartine and Daudet, Gautier, Loti,
Baudelaire and Anatole France. Their names are like poetry, eh?"
[*King Cobra*, 136.]

Other than Loti, it is impossible to know all the French authors that
Hervey studied before visiting Indochina, but he does give us hints. He
was a voracious reader of adventure books, including those of Robert
Louis Stevenson, Joseph Conrad and Rudyard Kipling. In his 1925
semi-autobiographical novel, *Ethan Quest*, Hervey relates his love for
Loti's works: *Siam, The Romance of a Spahi*,[6] and *Rarahu*.[7] It is likely that
he came to know other popular French authors through translations.

The quote shows how Hervey's familiarity with and admiration
for French authors worked in his favor, enabling him to interact
intelligently with French locals, who were only too happy to discuss
their culture with the young traveler. This section profiles the sequence
of authors Hervey mentioned above, followed by a group from *Congai*.

Alphonse Marie Louis de Prat de Lamartine
Oct. 21, 1790 –Feb. 28, 1869

Il y a une femme à l'origine de toutes les grandes choses.

There is a woman at the beginning of all great things.

Histoire des Girondins, 1847.

One of the first of the French Romantic poets, Lamartine later became
an Orientalist after travelling in the Middle East in the 1830s.

At the age of 26, he had perhaps the most formative experience of his
life when he fell madly in love with a woman named Julie Charles.

---

6 Pierre Loti, *The romance of a Spahi*, (New York: Brentano's, 1914).
7 Pierre Loti, *Rarahu*, (Paris: Calmann-Lévy, 1879). An English translation by Clara Bell was
published as *Rarahu, or, The marriage of Loti* (New York: W.S. Gottsberger, 1890).

Their courtship ended abruptly, little more than a year later, when Lamartine travelled to see her only to learn of her unexpected sudden death from tuberculosis. It was due to the intense love, hope and loss of this relationship that Lamartine credited the inspiration and power of his early works, which became iconic in establishing what became known as the Romantic Movement.

In 1820 Lamartine married Elizabeth Birch, an English woman, and moved into a career in the diplomatic service while continuing to write poetry and pseudo-philosophical books. His interest turned increasingly to politics, so much so that in 1839 he stopped publishing poetry altogether and became a key founder of France's Second Republic. As a pacifist and supporter of democracy, he was instrumental in the abolition of both slavery and the death penalty in France.

Napoleon III eventually drove Lamartine out of politics. He spent his premature retirement writing a series of histories, eventually dying a broken man, exhausted, in debt and alone.

Alphonse Daudet

May 13, 1840 – Dec. 16 1897

*C'est ça la gloire. Un bon cigare dans la bouche
par le côté du feu et de la cendre.*

**Such is glory: a fine cigar
with the lit, ashy end in one's mouth.**

L'Immortel: mœurs parisiennes, 1888.

Novelist Alphonse Daudet was born in Nîmes, France, into a bourgeois (upper middle class) family that later lost much of its wealth with the collapse of his father's silk-manufacturing business. It was perhaps the resulting family turmoil that troubled Alphonse during his education in Lyon, where he was a poor student who was habitually truant. In 1856 he moved to Alès, in southern France, to become, of all things, a schoolteacher. The position lasted only a year, but long afterwards he complained of nightmares in which he himself was still a recalcitrant student.

In 1857 Daudet moved to Paris to work as a journalist, but also composed his own romantic poetry, publishing his first book, *Les*

Alphonse Daudet, circa 1860 and 1885.

Amoureuses, in 1858. Next, he gained a more prestigious position by becoming secretary to Charles, Duke of Morny, Napoleon III's most powerful minister. Before his death in 1865, Morny helped Daudet make the right connections and gain public visibility. By 1868 Daudet had published his first novel, *Le Petit Chose*, a largely autobiographical account of his depressing childhood in boarding school. Hervey may have taken note of its English translation, *Little Good-for-Nothing*, since the subject so closely mirrored his own unhappy youth at boarding-school. (Hervey himself published his own semi-autobiographical book, *Ethan Quest: His Saga*.)

In 1872, Daudet published *Aventures prodigieuses de Tartarin de Tarascon* that, as author Alain Ruscio relates, made him "the father of one of the most famous characters in [French] Tropical/Colonial literature, Tartarin of Tarascon."[8] Like Loti, Baudelaire (profiled below) and

---

8 Alain Ruscio, *Amours coloniales: aventures et fantasmes exotiques de Claire de Duras à Georges Simenon : romans et nouvelles,* (Bruxelles: Editions Complexe, 1996), 41.

Hervey, Daudet also drew inspiration from international travels at a young age. In this case, it was his visit to Algeria when he was only 21 years old, ostensibly to cure tuberculosis but actually to conceal the effects of venereal disease from his new bride. In his book, Daudet follows the life of his eponymous title character, Tartarin, presenting a candid, at times critical, view of French colonial life.

Inspired by the popularity of his adventurous protagonist Tartarin, Daudet created two book-length sequels, with numerous derivative English translations following, such as *Tartarin of Tarascon: Traveller, "Turk," and Lion-Hunter* (1891), *Port Tarascon: The Last Adventures of the Illustrious Tartarin* (1891) and *Tartarin on the Alps* (1894). Though unmentioned by Hervey, these works seem to be of the exact style that he would have sought to read.

Daudet's writing career gained momentum and for the next two decades he put out nearly a book a year. Although few sold well, he was ultimately recognized as an important member of Parisian literary society. As his opening quotation suggests, however, he never felt part of it. Like Gautier (profiled below), Daudet was never accepted as a member of the distinguished Académie Française; he responded to their rejection in 1888 with his novel, *L'Immortel*, a scathing satire of the institution.

One other book by Daudet may have been on Hervey's desk, or more likely hidden under his bed. In 1884 he published *Sapho: Moeurs Parisiennes*, which appeared in English in 1899 as *Sapho: Parisian Customs*. Daudet dedicated the book "To my sons when they are twenty," and with good reason. *Sapho* is a graphically erotic novel set in the decadent and sexually liberated Parisian art scene in which Daudet himself participated. The story revolves around a promiscuous twenty-one year old model and demimondaine who, with many acquaintances, dabbles in the sensual pleasures of casual sex, with a dose of sadism, masochism and intoxication. Again, the book is unmentioned by Hervey; again, it seems likely that he would have read it.

Like Baudelaire (profiled below), Daudet's death, at age 57, was hastened by the syphilis he had contracted at a young age. He is interred at the Père Lachaise Cemetery in Paris.

Théophile Gautier
Aug. 30, 1811 – Oct. 23, 1872

Virginité, mysticisme, mélancolie,
 – trois mots inconnus,
 – trois maladies nouvelles apportées par le Christ.

Virginity, mysticism, melancholy,
 – three words hitherto unknown,
 – three afflictions introduced by Christ.

Mademoiselle de Maupin, 1835.

Pierre Jules Théophile Gautier was a French poet, dramatist, novelist, journalist, travel writer, and critic of drama and art. Today, he is valued for the quality of his work, for his passion for Romanticism, and for his accounts of the art world under the Second Empire. He also earned the respect of many prominent writers of his era, including T.S. Elliott, Ezra Pound, Marcel Proust and Oscar Wilde.

Born in Tarbes, in the Hautes-Pyrénées department of south-western France, Gautier's family moved to Paris when he was three. Two tropical tales influenced him from an early age: Daniel Defoe's 1719 tale, *Robinson Crusoe,* the story of a castaway sailor stranded on a remote Caribbean island; and Bernardin de Saint-Pierre's 1788 novel, *Paul et Virginie,* about two childhood friends on the remote French island of Mauritius who fall in love.

Even more influential was his childhood friendship with future novelist and poet Gérard de Nerval (1808–1855), who later introduced him to German literature and to his eventual mentor, Victor Hugo (1802–1885). As an adult, Gautier ranked Hugo with composer Hector Berlioz and painter Eugène Delacroix to form his "trinity" of ideal Romantic Art.

Gautier began writing poetry in his twenties, but his primary vocation was contributing articles on a wide range of topics to popular French journals. This gave him ample opportunities to meet influential people, and to travel to Africa, the Near East and Russia, which inspired works such as *Constantinople* (1853), *Trésors d'Art de la Russie* (1858) and *Voyage en Russie* (1867).

Théophile Gautier, circa 1850 and 1860.

In his thirties Gautier joined fellow writers like Charles Baudelaire and Honoré de Balzac at Paris's Hôtel Pimodan for "hashish sessions," or "fantasias," organized by Dr. Jacques-Joseph Moreau. Accounts appeared in Gautier's *Le Club des Hashischins* and elsewhere, adding to his reputation as an extravagant and creative eccentric.

Like Daudet, Gautier also benefited from royal favor. In 1868, Napoleon III's cousin, Princess Mathilde, appointed him as her personal librarian, thereby giving him access to the court. Despite his connections and three applications he never attained the one honor he craved; membership in the Académie Française. He did, however, become the founding chairman of the Société Nationale des Beaux-Arts. Gautier died of heart disease at the age of sixty-one and is buried at the Montmartre Cemetery in Paris.

Anatole France
Apr. 16, 1844 –Oct. 12, 1924

*La chair des femmes se nourrit de caresses
comme l'abeille de fleurs.*

**Womanly flesh feeds on caresses
like the bee on flowers.**

Le lys rouge, 1894

The son of a bookseller, Jacques Anatole François Thibault grew up surrounded by books and read voraciously as a child. He became a precocious poet as an adolescent, a young member of the Parnasse school of poetry, and a well-known Parisian bibliophile. He actually adopted his penname from the name of his father's Paris bookshop, the Librairie de France, where he worked for many years before becoming librarian of the French Senate.

France later began publishing literary chronicles for reviews, as well as features in the prestigious newspaper *Temps*, but real success came when he turned to fiction. His first novel, *Le Crime de Sylvestre Bonnard* (1881) was awarded the Prix de l'Académie Française, and established the classical, limpid, ironic style that he would employ throughout his career.

Like his friend and fellow novelist Émile Zola (1840–1902), France spent much of his time—and devoted much of his writing—to politics, humanism, and social causes. He called for an expansion of civil rights and signed the petition in support of Alfred Dreyfus, a French artillery officer unjustly accused of treason in a sensational public trial, later writing about the affair in his novel *Monsieur Bergeret*.

The Académie elected France into its ranks in 1896, and the Nobel committee awarded him the Literature Prize in 1921. The following year his entire catalog was placed on the Vatican's *Index Librorum Prohibitorum (List of Prohibited Books)*, a recognition that the author rather enjoyed. On the occasion of his death in 1924, the President of the Chamber of Deputies, Paul Painlevé, declared "The level of human intelligence fell on that night."[9] He is buried in the Neuilly-sur-Seine community cemetery near Paris.

---

9 "Le niveau de l'intelligence humaine a baissé cette nuit-là."

Charles Pierre Baudelaire
April 9, 1821–Aug. 31, 1867

*Mais qu'importe l'éternité de la damnation
à qui a trouvé dans une seconde l'infini de la jouissance?*

**But what is the eternity of damnation
to one who has known in an instant the infinity of joy?**

"Le Mauvais vitrier" ["The Bad Glazier"], *Le Spleen de Paris*, 1862

Though an enemy of the Enlightenment (i.e. the Age of Reason) and of "progress," Charles Baudelaire wrote some of modernity's most influential poetry, most notably the slim, 1857 volume for which he is best known: *Les Fleurs du mal* (*The Flowers of Evil*). His words drift between poetry and prose and, though tethered to a classical conception of rhythm, break free of reason so as to render sensation in the mind of the reader. And sensation is what Baudelaire seems to have always sought.

Born to François and Caroline Baudelaire in Paris, his father was thirty-four years older than his mother and died when Charles was only six. The next year his mother remarried a military officer, later a respected French ambassador, which changed Charles' life and outlook. While the marriage enhanced his mother's financial stability, he then had to compete with his new step-father for his mother's attention. The resulting pain of rejection apparently traumatized him, with the additional learned behavior of knowing that he could successfully beg his mother for financial support, a behavior he continued throughout his life.

Growing up a spendthrift, a perpetual debtor and a dandy, in 1843 Baudelaire discovered what he would famously call "artificial paradises." It all began with "green jam," hashish, which he tasted for the first time at the apartment of his friend and fellow poet Louis Ménard. In the following years he would (with Théophile Gautier and others) attend meetings of Dr. Moreau's medico-experimental Club des Hashischins.

Baudelaire's addiction to opium began in 1847, when a doctor prescribed laudanum for the case of syphilis that he had contracted years earlier, most likely from a prostitute named Sarah la Louchette.

His drug-induced adventures led to his 1860 publication, *Les Paradis artificiels*, an essay primarily about hashish and the morality of drug-taking that was influenced by his English opium-eating predecessor Thomas de Quincey, as well as the stories of Edgar Allen Poe.

Poe cultivated the young man's sense of the macabre, and he drew inspiration from his dark plots. Indeed, Poe was so great an influence that Baudelaire became his French translator. Perhaps this contributed to his fixation on the idea of being doomed from the start, the idea that our lives are like partly wilted flowers, even as they emerge from the bud.

But not all of Baudelaire's sensations came through the ingestion of chemicals. He sought temporary excitement as a fervent revolutionary, manning the barricades during the French Revolution of 1848, but the works of Poe, and of counter-Revolutionary philosopher and politician Joseph de Maistre, steered him in other directions. He thereafter focused on the decadence he saw in French society's general abandonment of the Christian notion of original sin, no doubt less for the doctrinal reasons of the Church than for the aesthetic sensation of it.

Baudelaire also had an eye for art, and became perhaps the most important French art critic of his time. He covered several Salons and defended, among other things, the Romanticism of Delacroix. He was also a keen critic of literature, seeing far more in the multitudinous morality tales of Balzac than a talent for description.

Inevitably, as many others who lived life to extremes, Baudelaire was destined to die young. Following years of opium and alcohol abuse he suffered a massive stroke in 1866, spending his final months in a semi-paralyzed state. He died shortly after his 46th birthday and is interred in the Montparnasse Cemetery in Paris.

Charles Pierre Baudelaire
1863 portrait by Étienne Carjat.

Thi-Linh's Literary Tastes

> Her days were very full. From the imprimerie on the Rue Catinat
> she was able to get the latest books, and she read most of the new
> novels; novels by André Gide, Claude Farrère, Paul Morand, Pierre
> Benoit and many others. But she was not satisfied with reading only
> novels; she read much about the history of her country and of other
> countries as well. [Congai, 132]

The classic French authors in the previous section follow examples
ostensibly presented to Hervey by Gilbert Filleau de Saint-Hilaire,
a fellow passenger on his boat trip up the Mekong River. Here, Thi-
Linh, his protagonist in *Congai*, endorses four more contemporary
authors who apparently caught Hervey's attention. The first three are
profiled below while Pierre Benoit appears later in this article. Perhaps
Hervey, too, was a customer of the *imprimerie* on Rue Catinet.

André Paul Guillaume Gide
Nov. 22, 1869 – Feb. 19, 1951

*L'aigle se grise de son vol. Le rossignol s'enivre des nuits d'été. La plaine
tremble de chaleur. […], que toute émotion sache te devenir une ivresse.
Si ce que tu manges ne te grise pas, c'est que tu n'avais pas assez faim.*

**The eagle is drunk with its flight, as the nightingale from summer
nights. The plain trembles with heat. […] let every sensation lead
you to inebriation. If what you eat fails to intoxicate you, then you
lacked the hunger for it.[10]**

Les nourritures terrestres, 1921.

Gide's immersive view of life echoes that of Baudelaire, especially when
compared to his posthumously published poem, *Enivrez-vous [Be
Drunk]*, as described in the next section. Born to an established middle-
class family in Paris, Gide comfortably pursued a literary career that
bridged the 19th and 20th centuries. He is particularly relevant within
the context of Hervey's work because, in the words of Robert Aldrich,
Gide was "…born with homosexuality [and…] came to represent it
for several generations (in a way that [Marcel] Proust never did), and

---

10 André Gide, *Les nourritures terrestres,* (Paris: Gallimard, Éditions de la Nouvelle revue française,
1921), 36. Translation by Pedro Rodríguez.

twentieth-century French literature is littered with tributes to Gide's role in restoring to gay men a sense of self-respect and reassuring them that they were not alone."[11]

Gide began writing at a young age, publishing his first novel, *Les Cahiers d'André Walter [The Notebooks of Andre Walter]*, in 1891 at age 22, quickly followed by four more titles in the next two years. In 1892, he traveled to Algeria where he experienced, and accepted, his initiation into homosexuality. Despite his realization, Gide still aspired to marry his first cousin, Madeleine Rondeaux, a union that the idealized object of his affection resisted, and one that was also opposed by his domineering mother. Following his mother's death in 1895, Gide convinced Rondeaux to marry him the next year, a marriage that remained intact—but apparently unconsummated—until her death in 1938.[12]

Gide continued to write, and helped found a literary magazine, *Nouvelle Revue Française [The New French Review]*, in 1908. The year 1916 was especially significant in his life; it was then that the 37-year-old Gide "adopted" fifteen-year-old Marc Allégret, who became his lover and muse. The two moved to London to flee Gide's wife (who burned his papers in his absence) and the relationship went smoothly until 1923. In a bizarre twist, or perhaps in pursuit of a new emotional experience, Gide asked for (and received) permission to impregnate a 33-year-old woman named Elisabeth van Rysselberghe (who, incidentally, appears in many paintings done by her artist father, Theo van Rysselbergh). Upon learning of the pregnancy Gide was as thrilled as Allégret was annoyed. The girl was simply confused, although Gide reportedly acted as a supportive, though distant, father.

In 1925, perhaps to rekindle their relationship, Gide and Allégret embarked on an extended tour of French colonial Africa—nearly concurrent with Hervey's travels through Indochina with his lover Carlton Hildrith. Gide also wrote of his experiences, publishing *Voyage au Congo: carnets de route* in 1927. His book presented critical views of how exploitative colonial policies adversely affected native populations in French Equatorial Africa, augmenting the development of anti-colonial sentiments in France.

---

11 Robert Aldrich and Garry Wotherspoon, *Who's who in gay and lesbian history*, (London: Routledge, 2001), 213.
12 Michael Lucey, *Gide's bent: sexuality, politics, writing*, (New York [u.a.], Oxford Univ. Press, 1995), 12.

He dabbled in communism in the early 1930s, initially expressing positive views of its ideology. Enthused by the support of such a distinguished writer, the Soviet Union of Writers invited him to tour their country as a guest. Their public relations attempt backfired because, when he saw the repressive reality, he reversed his opinions and publically denounced the system after 1936.

Gide spent WWII in Tunisa and then returned to France. He was awarded the Nobel Prize in Literature in 1947 and, in 1952, shared another exhilarating honor with Anatole France; his works were placed on the Vatican's Index Librorum Prohibitorum (List of Prohibited Books). Gide continued to write until his death in Paris at the age of 81.[13]

Frederick Charles Bargone (Claude Farrère)
Apr. 27, 1876 – June 21,1957)

> Farrere possesses to unusual degree that quality which Galsworthy terms "Flower of Author"—a remarkable personality is displayed between all his lines, a charm which causes the casual reader of one of his works sooner or later to become a careful reader of them all.[14]

Following in the footsteps of his father, a naval infantry colonel, Bargone enrolled in the French Naval Academy in 1894. Like Pierre Loti, who he briefly served under, Bargone traveled the world, accruing experiences that would fuel his vocation as a prolific writer under the penname Claude Farrère. Farrère's close associations with Pierre Loti, Pierre Louÿs and colonial French Indochina, and honest descriptions of sexuality in his works, make him an important writer to examine in relation to Hervey.

Farrère's literary career spanned half a century, but sadly even France has nearly forgotten him.[15] From 1902 until 1955 he averaged more than a book a year, with 77 fiction and non-fiction titles to his credit. Only a few have been translated to English. Though he admired Loti (at times even attempted to imitate him[16]), Farrère's style was less descriptive, more direct, and filled with dynamic accounts of manly men in dramatic situations. His topics included exotic global travel, romance,

---

13 For additional information visit www.andregide.org.
14 Jesse Lee Bennett, "Three new French novelists, Farrere, Harry, Binet-Valmer", *Poet Lore*,1916, 592.
15 See "Goncourt oubliés 1: Claude Farrère, 1905" by Guillaume Sbalchiero, www.lexpress.fr.
16 See Akane Kawakami's *Travellers' visions: French literary encounters with Japan, 1881-2004*. (Liverpool: Liverpool University Press, 2005), 65-72.

Frederick Bargone (Claude Farrère) aboard the frigate *Iphigénie*, circa 1896-97. The color cover the 1920 edition of *Les Civilises*, illustrated by Jacques Nam (1881–1974).

war, military history, the French navy, historical events, mysteries, fantasies and even science fiction.[17]

Farrère first gained public recognition with the 1904 release of his attention-getting second title, *Fumée d'opium* (literally "*Smoking Opium*" but appearing in English as *Black Opium* in 1929). His third title in 1905, *Les Civilisés* [The Civilized], was an even greater success. It received the Prix Goncourt, a prestigious award that had only been established three years earlier to recognize "the author of the best and most imaginative prose work of the year."[18]

Given its morally shocking, anti-colonial content, the award choice seems surprising, but the committee sought excellence over ideology. As described later in this article, René Maran won the Goncourt in

---

17 His 1921 novel, *Les condamnés à mort*, tells of a futuristic society where working class citizens are enslaved by automation, predating the similar theme of Fritz Lang's popular 1927 science fiction film *Metropolis*. In 1926, Farrère's book appeared in English as *Useless Hands*.
18 See www.academie-goncourt.fr.

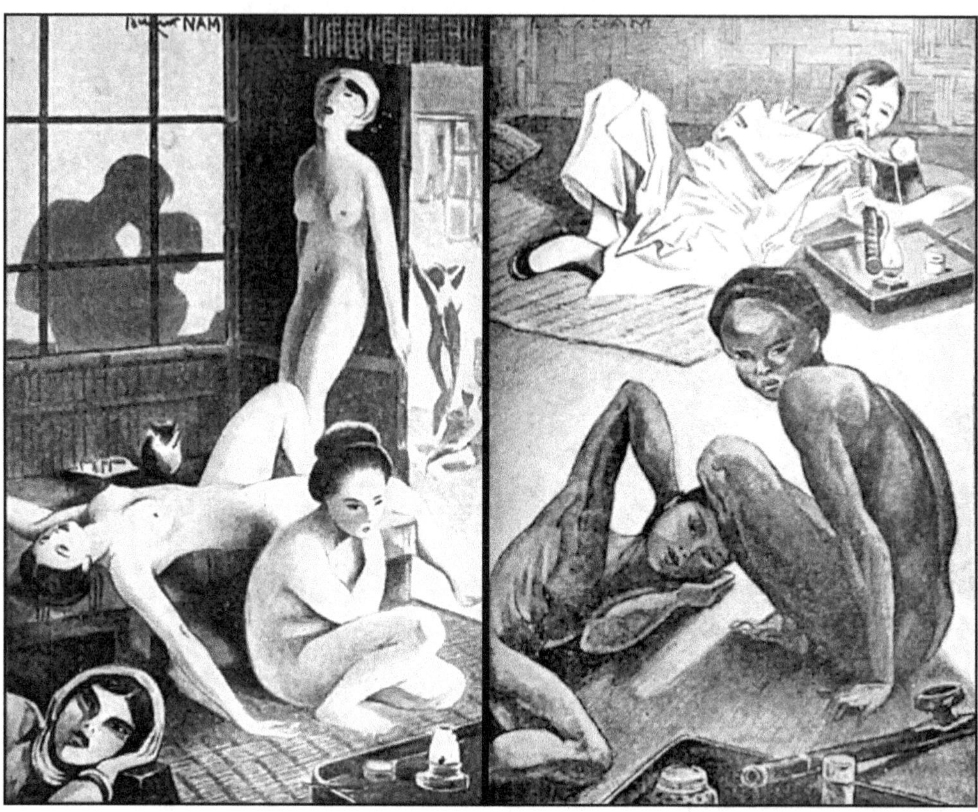

Illustrations from the 1920 edition of *Les Civilises* by Jacques Nam (pp. 49 & 138).
Despite the plot's primary focus on the immorality of French characters, there apparently was still room to cater to the reading public's more prurient vision of Asia.

1921 with *Batouala, veritable roman negre*, a novel that openly criticized colonialism in Africa and was soon banned in all the French colonies for its incendiary ideas.

Set in Saigon, *Les Civilisés* follows the lives of three Frenchmen indulging in women (and boys), inebriation and other pleasures of that colonial outpost. The book contrasts the behavior of "civilized" people, i.e. the "sophisticated" colonists, with "barbarians," i.e. the indigenous native population, who are described as people of good morals. The colonists don't fare well in the comparison, hence the book's critical reception in France. Though never translated to English, reviewer Jesse Lee Bennett offered this contemporary overview of the book in 1916:

> From an Anglo-Saxon point of view *Les Civilisés* is truly well calculated to startle. It is difficult to believe that it could ever be printed entirely unabridged in the English language, yet it is the most moral of books. It shows three over-civilized ultramoderns

exploiting life and life annihilating them—three men who have grasped, to the tiniest detail, Joseph Conrad's idea of an episodic spectacular universe with no continuity and who live with "minimum of exertion for maximum of pleasure."[19]

Modern scholar Jennifer Yee's takes her assessment a bit further:

> Indeed, the decadent young lieutenant's memories of his trip in *Civilisés* resemble a photo album, but one whose photographs are hardly the sort one would show to the young ladies of the time. An album with pictures of opium dens, certainly, but also a good number of pornographic images... The photo album thus becomes a metaphor for the collection of memories, and the travelogue can now take the form of a series of exotic snapshots.[20]

If *Les Civilisés* seems shocking, this is only due to the author's uncensored descriptions of the realities of colonial life. Also revealing is Farrère's humble dedication to Pierre Louÿs, who he directly credits with launching his career. The author effusively thanks Louÿs for writing the preface to his previous book, *Fumée d'opium*, and credits its acceptance and success to his involvement. In concluding his dedication, Farrère summarizes his gratitude to Louÿs:

> My dear friend, it was in reading *Aphrodite* that I saw it was possible in our day and age to write books that were both modern and old, classic and alive. Your example has paved the way for me. If I in turn have taken up a pen, you are not a little responsible—you, whose disciple I quite deeply feel myself to be. And thus I ask you today, my master, to accept my dedication of this book to you, for whom it was written. Will you like it? I haven't the slightest idea. Accept it regardless, as a token of my fervent admiration for your work, and of my friendship.[21]

Later, we will consider how Louÿs, and specifically *Aphrodite*, relate to Hervey's plot in *Congai*. Like Louÿs, Farrère also candidly wrote of lesbian and homosexual affairs with acceptance (for example, in *Les Civilisés*, 1905, and *Mademoiselle Dax, jeune fille*, 1907).

Farrère fought for France during World War I and, with 14 books completed, resigned from the navy in 1919, joining the newly formed

---

19 Bennett, *Poet Lore*, 592.
20 Jennifer Yee, *Clichés de la femme exotique: un regard sur la littérature coloniale française entre 1871 et 1914*, (Paris, France: L'Harmattan, 2000), 58. Translation by Pedro Rodríguez.
21 Claude Farrère, *Les civilisés; roman*, (Paris: P. Ollendorff, 1905), vi.

Association des écrivains combattants[22] [Association of Combat Writers]
the same year. Now able to devote his full attention to writing, he published
five books in 1920 alone. In addition to Indochina, Farrère also enjoyed
frequent trips to Turkey and Japan, resulting in a number of related titles.
Most of his works effectively contrasted Western values with those held in
other parts of the world, but his political views were less expansive.

Farrère was a nationalist and republican, whose sentiments rested
firmly with the extreme right. While his political views may have been
controversial, his bravery was unquestionable: at a book fair in 1932,
Farrère took two bullets trying (unsuccessfully) to prevent the assassination
of French President Paul Doumer. On March 28, 1935, he was elected to
the French Academy, defeating rival applicant Paul Claudel and gaining a
seat, despite rigorous objections from other members who objected to his
right wing sentiments.

He wrote until his death, publishing his last title in 1955, *Lyautey créateur*,
a profile of French Marshal Louis-Hubert Lyautey (1854-1934). In 1959,
the Association des écrivains combattants established the Claude-Farrère
Prize in his honor. Each year, it recognizes "a fantasy novel that has not
previously obtained a major literary prize."

Paul Morand
March 13, 1888 – July 24, 1976

Morand, who later became known for his clever novels and short
stories, was born into a life of art, wealth and privilege that evolved into
a diplomatic career. Through the connections of his father Eugène—a
painter, playwright and curator at the Louvre—the Morand home attracted
members of the social and artistic elite, including Auguste Rodin and
Oscar Wilde. Young Paul's tutor, later a lifelong friend, was Hippolyte Jean
Giraudoux, a writer and dramatist of renown who was six years his senior.

Despite growing up in a world that could create and enjoy art for art's sake,
without worry of financial needs, Morand also acquired his father's dark
pessimism, as well as his racism and prejudice (Jews were forbidden to
enter the family home). At the outbreak of World War I, Morand served
briefly before family connections relieved him of his obligations. This
enabled him to spend the war comfortably in England, Italy, Spain and
Paris pursuing things he found more engaging; fine dining, the theater,
pedigree horses, expensive cars and women.

---

22 www.lesecrivainscombattants.org.

From his youth, Morand maintained a friendship with homosexual writer Marcel Proust and, according to research by W. C. Carter, teased him privately about his persuasion.[23] While most people at the time, especially in artistic circles, accepted homosexuality, and homosexuals freely alluded to their tastes, it was a dangerous behavior to confirm publicly; as Oscar Wilde sadly found out years earlier in his conviction for "gross indecency." Morand broke from this etiquette by publishing an "Ode to Marcel Proust" in 1919, betraying his friend and publically impugning his "prowler side" as a gay man privately engaging in his own affairs. Despite this humiliation, Proust forgave Morand (after expressing his anger publicly and privately) and later wrote the preface to *Tendres Stocks*, described below.[24]

While Hervey was writing *Congai*, only three of Morand's novels were complete: *Ouvert la nuit*, *Fermé la nuit* and *Tendres Stocks*. The last title, later translated to English by Ezra Pound as *Fancy Goods – Open All Night*, related his wartime experiences from 1914-1918. As per the information above, the book primarily dealt with his sexual, rather than patriotic, accomplishments.

During World War II, Morand kept well away from the line of fire, but did find the time to seek election, unsuccessfully, into the Académie française in 1939 and 1941. In 1939, he was assigned to the French Embassy in London but, rather than support Charles de Gaulle and the Free French Forces fighting the Nazi invasion, he abandoned his post and moved to Vichy. There he swore allegiance to the collaborationist Vichy government, which was more in line with his anti-Semitic ideologies.

After the war he was charged with collaboration with the enemy but suffered no penalty beyond losing his government pension, which was no loss to the wealthy man. In 1958 he again attempted to gain a seat on the Académie française, losing to considerable opposition due to his wartime activities and a veto by Charles De Gaulle himself. Ultimately, at age 80, he was granted membership in October 1968, but was denied the formal ceremonies that normally welcome new members. In a parting gesture, DeGaulle, then in the last six months of his life, refused to receive Morand at the Elysée Palace.[25]

---

23 W. C. Carter, *Proust in love*, (New Haven, Yale University Press, 2006), 144-145.
24 Ibid., 145-146.
25 See www.xn--acadmie-franaise-npb1a.fr.

Part 3:
Hervey's First French Infusions

With the exception of Loti and Baudelaire, Hervey's cursory *King Cobra* mentions of the great French authors above prove little about his knowledge of the men or their works. It is not until later in that book—and most prominently in *Congai*—that we see Hervey actually working with the literature itself. This short section examines three initial examples of Hervey actually drawing from French content.

Sampling *Saramani*: Violation or Virtue?

> "Listen, I think I have a story. It is the life of the dancer, a life part romance and the rest ugly reality. I shall call this story '*Saramani, Danseuse Cambodgienne*'; you may call it what you like..."
> [*King Cobra*, 113].

In *King Cobra*, Hervey credits many of his insights into French colonial culture to his knowledgeable but unidentified friend, the "Tired Cavalier." Perhaps he cobbled his knowledge of local literature together from a series of French advisors, but the depth of his understanding and his command of the material suggest that he had at least one extremely well-read literary mentor in Indochina.

One of the most surprising examples is the third chapter of *King Cobra* entitled "Saramani – Tells of a King and a Few Concubines." Here, he relates a detailed story about the life of one former dancer in the royal palace of Cambodia. According to Hervey, his source is none other than the Tired Cavalier, so readers are led to believe that the tale is original to the book at hand. Indeed, this story exists nowhere else in the English language.

In 2006, I worked with Dr. Paul Cravath preparing his painstakingly researched 1975–1985 thesis on Cambodian dance for publication as *Earth in Flower*. [26] It was there that I first encountered the story of Saramani and learned that its true author was Roland Théodore Émile

---

26 Paul Cravath, *Earth in Flower: The Divine Mystery of the Cambodian Dance Drama*, (Holmes Beach, FL: DatAsia, 2007).

Saramani, Danseuse Khmèr, (Saigon: Imprimerie nouvelle A. Portail, 1919).

This rare photo shows Roland Meyer (lower right) on the steps of Angkor Wat in January 1918, one year before he published his epic novel *Saramani* in Saigon. His prestigious company includes (from lower left) *Résident-supérieur* of Cambodia Francois-Marius Baudoin and his daughter; Suzanne Groslier (four months pregnant, so her daughter Nicole is on her *first* visit to Angkor Wat), with her husband, author, artist and founder of the National Museum of Cambodia, George Groslier in pith helmet. At the top, looking a bit impatient with the photographer, is Albert Sarraut, then Governor-General of French Indochina, and soon to become the godfather of Nicole Groslier. Finally, next to Meyer we have the stylish, but unknown, Mlle Vibert. Photo courtesy Nicole Groslier.

Meyer, another Loti-inspired writer. In 1919, six years before Hervey's arrival in Indochina, Meyer published his book, *Saramani, danseuse khmère,* in Saigon. It was therefore an unexpected surprise to find Hervey relating the same plot under the same name in *King Cobra,* with no attribution to the original author or work.

At first I was annoyed that this cheeky American author liberally borrowed a French writer's creativity whole cloth. On examination, however, Hervey attributes the story to the Tired Cavalier, and merely records it. Whether Hervey knew such a book existed, or whether he trusted the originality of his source is unknown. What is significant is that Hervey's distillation of Meyer's epic 185,000 word novel is accurate, skillful and unique in the English language.

Meyer's sweeping look at Cambodian history, culture, geography, folklore, religion, flora, and fauna has hardly been recognized in the French language, and is nearly unknown in English, with only short mentions in a handful of recent academic papers. DatAsia Press has been working on the first English translation of Meyer's complete, unabridged book since 2008 with publication planned in 2015.[27]

Due to the sensitive subject matter on some topics, Meyer presented his original work as fiction. DatAsia's new research will reveal that much of the book—if not most of it—is in fact historically accurate. Hervey claims to have actually met the eponymous protagonist of *Saramani* herself, working as a shopkeeper in Phnom Penh. As it turns out, the real Saramani was, in fact, Roland Meyer's wife.

From this perspective, I now see Hervey's inclusion of Meyer's concept as a service to Anglophones that adds an important piece of evidence in documenting the actual life of the woman named Saramani. Here, and more extensively in *Congai,* Hervey shared French literary ideas and plots that readers otherwise would have never encountered.

27 Readers should note that Charpentier et Fasquelle (Paris) published a drastically (and badly) abridged edition in 1922 titled *Saramani, Danseuse Cambodgienne: Roman,* with more than 70,000 words deleted. Instead, see the 1919 original, *Saramani, Danseuse Khmèr* (Saigon: Imprimerie nouvelle A. Portail), pictured on the previous page, or the unabridged 1997 edition, *Saramani, Danseus Khmèr,* published by Kailash in Paris in three volumes: *1. Au pays des grands fleuves* ; *2, Le palais des quatre faces* ; *3, La légende des ruines.*

Hervey, Hedonism and Baudelaire in Indochina

> "Who was it," Malardier resumed, "Baudelaire, who said, 'Be always drunken! With wine, with poetry, or with virtue, as you will. But be drunken'? Only I pray you, Batteur, as a good Frenchman, not to be drunken with virtue! If you come to Indochina to know it, then become intoxicated with it—and the surest draught is a woman…. The *congai*, she is our symbol—the symbol of the ability of the Frenchman to mingle with the natives, whereas the Englishman only conquers them" [*Congai*, 10].

In citing Baudelaire's poem, *Enivrez-vous*[28] *(Be Drunk)*, at the beginning of *Congai*, Hervey sets the stage for embracing the French author's hedonistic ethos. Whatever your poison—drugs or women or philosophy—drink it, drink it until you are good and drunk, lest Time—or perhaps some more earthly creditor—lay its heavy burden upon your shoulders.

Hervey's characters all become drunk on something; alcohol, opium, lust, greed, religion, patriotism, love or life itself. As Malardier suggests, Hervey's male characters specifically fall under the intoxicating spell of Asian women, embodied in Hervey's *congai* heroine Thi-Linh. But through her Baudelairean education under French author, Justin Batteur, we learn that Hervey appreciated literary arts as well as hedonistic ones:

> Justin gave her many French books to read, some of them books of poetry. She liked the flowing lines of Lamartine and Baudelaire. Among these volumes were several French novels. They disturbed and excited her [*Congai*, 40].

Coincidentally, Hervey's life paralleled that of the great French writer in a number of ways. At the age of 20, Baudelaire's stepfather financed a voyage to India for him, trying to steer him away from irresponsible friends and toward a career in law or diplomacy. Hervey, too, took early and formative trips to South Asia and the Orient. Both authors amassed exotic experiences for later literary use, as did Alphonse Daudet.

Quite possibly the precocious Hervey even attempted to model his effusive literary style—mixing prose with poetic descriptions—after that of the great French writer. In his autobiographical book *Ethan Quest*, Hervey described the work of his doppelgänger/protagonist as follows:

---

28 *From Le spleen de Paris, ou Petits poèmes en prose,* published posthumously in 1869.

> Rhythms in color, he called them. He had even dared to send a
> few off to magazines. "Your work is very puzzling," the editor of a
> journal of poetry had written him. "It is not poetry nor is it prose. It
> is, I fear, simply inadequate expression. You feel color and emotion,
> but you cannot harness them in the necessary technique..." [123]

Like Baudelaire, one of Hervey's closest personal relationships was with his mother, Jennie Davis Hervey, and he frequently relied on her for financial and emotional support. Jennie indulged her son's dreamy ways, but it was also she who sent him to military academy to add discipline to his life. After graduating, Hervey's mother gave her son a place to live as he found his path in life.

Though Hervey did not fall victim to drugs or alcohol, his heavy use of tobacco did eventually kill him. Like Baudelaire, Hervey went through life as quite a dandy, as well as a spendthrift debtor. Joining Lamartine, the Romantic poet with such high ideals, all three authors died broken and penniless. In a final poignant parallel, it was Baudelaire's mother who championed her son's books for a few years beyond his premature death, as did Hervey's.

Of Chrysis, Courtesans and *Congaies*

> She brought with her several French novels, among them one
> that sent Thi-Linh's thoughts tumbling into dangerous patterns.
> It was by a man named Pierre Louÿs — *Aphrodite*. The story of a
> certain Chrysis, courtesan of ancient Alexandria. She and Nanette
> discussed the book at length.
>
> "When Monsieur Malardier gets tired of me," said Nanette, "I
> shall return to Hanoi—or perhaps I shall go to Saigon—and be
> like this Chrysis."
>
> "Isn't that dreadfully wicked?" asked Thi-Linh, excited.
>
> "Well, if one is going to be wicked then why not be as wicked as
> possible? Certainly I have no intention of being good—it is stupid...."
>
> "But to have so many men," Thi-Linh persisted, "and think only of
> getting money out of them is no better than being like girls who sell
> themselves for a night."
>
> Nanette smiled indulgently and wisely [*Congai*, 47].

Hervey again weaves a critical French language work into his plot to complement, inspire and expand upon the moral and intellectual dimensions of his characters.

Front cover of *Aphrodite: mœurs antiques*, (Paris: Librairie illustrée, 1909) with illustrations by Édouard François Zier (1856-1924).

Set in Ptolemaic Alexandria, *Aphrodite* is as much a love story as a crime story. Louÿs sets his tale of transgressive love in decadent, sensual and bejeweled classical Egypt—"in the world of the courtesans, a realm of beauty, luxury, and Sapphic indulgence, and some dark shadows as well."[29] There, the handsome sculptor Demetrios, favorite of Queen Berenice, falls for the well-to-do and beautiful blond courtesan Chrysis. Chrysis rejects Demetrios's advances, forcing him to commit thefts and even murder in an attempt to win her charms.

Sexually unconventional lifestyles were something that Chrysis, Thi-Linh, Nanette and Hervey all shared. Indeed, the original words of author Pierre Louÿs in his 1896 preface could equally be used to introduce Thi-Linh herself:

> Le personnage féminin qui occupe la première place dans le roman qu'on va feuilleter est une courtisane antique; mais, que le lecteur se rassure : elle ne se convertira pas.
>
> …Courtisane, elle le sera avec la franchise, l'ardeur et aussi la fierté de tout être humain qui a vocation et qui tient dans la société une place librement choisie; elle aura l'ambition de s'élever au plus haut point; elle n'imaginera même pas que sa vie ait besoin d'excuse ou de mystère : ceci demande à être expliqué.[30]
>
> [The feminine personage who occupies the principal place in the romance whose pages you are about to turn, is an antique courtesan; but be reassured: she will not convert herself.
>
> …Rather she will be a courtesan, with all the frankness, the ardor and the pride of every human being who has a vocation and who holds in society a freely chosen place; she will aspire to raise herself to the highest point; she will not even imagine a need for excuse or mystery in her life.][31]

Pierre Félix Louis (Louÿs)
Dec. 10, 1870 – June 6, 1925

Erotic author and poet Pierre Félix Louis was born in Ghent, Belgium but moved to Paris to study at the École Alsacienne. He would spend the rest of his life in France. At school, he forged a lifelong friendship with bi-sexual author and future Nobel Prize of Literature winner,

---

29 Adapted from www.sacred-texts.com.
30 Pierre Louÿs, *Aphrodite, moeurs antiques*, (Paris: Société du Mercure de France, 1896), iv-v.
31 Pierre Louÿs, ed. Willis L. Parker, *Aphrodite: ancient manners*, (New York: Three Sirens Press, 1932).

André Gide. Though Louis was a heterosexual, he freely accepted (and avidly promoted) sexual diversity, and was welcomed in homosexual circles. Heterosexual and lesbian eroticism were, however, his key interests and by age 18 he was writing erotic poetry and prose, often in the context of the classical Greek culture that he admired for its appreciation of art and personal freedoms.

Around 1890 he adopted his penname Louÿs and in 1891 published *Astarte*, an anthology of his early works. In 1895, he released *Les Chansons de Bilitis* [*Songs of Bilitis*]; a collection of 143 prose poems with a lesbian theme. He made his book even more sensational by claiming that the poems were original ancient Greek works written by a courtesan contemporary of Sappho herself; humbly submitted himself as merely the translator. Soon his fabrication was exposed but by then the book was so highly praised for its sensuality and sensitivity to feminine experience that this revelation only enhanced the author's reputation.

His first novel, *Aphrodite: moeurs antiques*,[32] appeared in 1896, selling more than 350,000 copies and establishing his reputation as an erotic author. By then Louÿs was frequently associated with homosexual writers Gide, Marcel Proust and Oscar Wilde (who dedicated *Salomé* to him in 1890), and he began distancing himself from his friends out of concern that people would assume he was also homosexual.

As one might expect from his literary interests, Louÿs was promiscuous and had many affairs with women and prostitutes. Like other artists of his era, he also habitually used alcohol, drugs and tobacco. In 1898, he (reputedly) fathered a son with paramour Marie de Regniér. The next year, in perhaps what was an apparent attempt to stabilize his life, he married for the first time; inexplicably, the bride he chose was Marie's sister, Louise de Hérédia. Louÿs soon withdrew into a more private life and stopped publishing his own works in 1901. In 1909 he was named a Chevalier in the Légion d'honneur for his contributions to French literature (later elevated to the rank of Officer in 1922). In 1913, his infidelity and financial irresponsibility led to the dissolution of his first

---

32   Pierre Louÿs and Antoine Calbet, *Aphrodite: mœurs antiques,* (Paris: Librairie Borel, 1896). Translated to English in 1906 as *Aphrodite: a novel of ancient manners* (Paris: C. Carrington).

marriage. In 1923, he married Alice Steenackers, already the mother of two of his children, with a third delivered after his death in 1925.

Like Baudelaire, Daudet, Hervey and many others his life ended badly: "Louÿs was convinced that he too would die at a young age[…]. This believe led him to focus his energy on the present moment; he devoted himself to pleasure and to art, squandering his resources and dying penniless…."[33]

Part 4:
A Rare Glimpse of Vietnamese Literature

"…she has read the *Lac-Van-Tien*—also the verses of *Thuy-Kien*, and others" [Mama Thi-Bao describing Thi-Linh in *Congai*, 29].

Early in *Congai*, Hervey mentions two strange Annamite titles in passing. I had skimmed over them many times without giving them any thought, beyond concluding that they were no more than random books Hervey mentioned to add local color. As Pico Iyer astutely observes in his foreword, "What I love about this book is how constantly it proved me wrong, and how deliberately it overturned my every expectation…."

Hervey's references to *Lac-Van-Tien* and *Thuy-Kien* are not random; they are, in fact, the most profound literary references he could have made to the local culture. Many scholars regard them as the two most important works in Vietnamese literature, actually forming a foundation for the resilience and national identity of that nation's people. Moreover, the two works deal with love, morality, friendship, gratitude, sexuality and the sacrifices—symbolic and actual—that one makes for one's family and country. In other words, both tell stories that resonate with the themes of *Congai* itself, and exemplify beliefs that contributed to making interracial and intercultural relationships a common occurrence in French Indochina.

---

33 Robert Aldrich and Garry Wotherspoon, *Who's who in gay and lesbian history*, (London: Routledge, 2001), 278.

19th century Vietnamese illustration showing Kiều Nguyệt Nga and Lục Vân Tiên.

Luc-van-tiên [The Tale of Luc Van Tien]

This epic tale was written in the second half of the 19th century by Nguyễn Đình Chiểu (July 1, 1822–July 3, 1888), a man who, in his lifetime, was considered the poet laureate of southern Vietnam. Blind and thus unable to enter combat, he fought the French colonial invasion with words. As the French controlled most printing presses, his vivid, anti-colonial poetry was largely circulated by word of mouth. His tales actually began orally, as the blind author dictated them to his students to record.

The Tale of Luc Van Tien, a poem of just over 2,000 lines, opens with a student at a Confucian school named Lục Vân Tiên. To complete his education and qualify as a mandarin, Tiên must travel to the capital to sit for civil service examinations. Along the way he encounters a beautiful woman, Kiều Nguyệt Nga, who had been kidnapped by bandits. He saves her life and her gratitude mixes with feelings of love. She offers her hairpin to him as a reward, which he refuses. She then offers him a poem, which he accepts, thereby beginning an exchange of poems, dreams and ideas between the two protagonists.

Tiên continues on his journey, but never sits for his examinations due to a series of unexpected, even tragic, events. Meanwhile, Nga returns to her home where her love for Tiên continues to grow. She receives false news that Tiên has died and bitterly takes a vow of chastity. Suitors persist in wooing her, finally driving her to attempt suicide to end her pain of loss, but Guanyin, the Buddhist Goddess of Mercy, intervenes. As both lives unfold, the narrator reminds readers that, though we may encounter many hardships in life, "the agents of mercy look after the virtuous." Ultimately, the deserving couple is rewarded with the fulfillment of their true love.

The poem affirms traditional Vietnamese virtues of bravery, justice, fortitude, loyalty and honoring true love. In many ways, Thi-Linh's determination and morality in *Congai* portray her adhering to these very same ideals.

Kim-Van-Kiéou [The Tale of Kieu]

This epic poem remains one of the best-known works of Vietnamese literature; its plot and content speak directly to Thi-Linh's story, and to the political symbolism of *Congai*. Written around 1800, it was written by Nguyễn Du (1766–1820), a scholar who spent much of the first thirty-five years of his life trying to survive a revolution between the ruling powers of his nation. Though loyal to the losing dynasty, Du was accepted as a scholar in the new court, where he unenthusiastically performed his duties for the last two decades of his life. It was at the beginning of this time that he wrote *The Tale of Kieu*, which is an autobiographical and political allegory as much as it is a tale of love and moral values.

The Tale of Kieu describes the tragic life of a talented, pure and beautiful young woman named Thuy Kieu:

> Her eyes were autumn streams, her brows spring hills.
> Flowers grudged her glamour, willows her fresh hue.
> A glance or two from her, and kingdoms rocked![34]

Like Hervey's heroine Thi-Linh, Kieu meets and falls in love with her soul mate at a young age, but likewise the happy future life she envisioned is doomed by fate. Kieu's father is threatened with imprisonment so the girl allows herself to be sold into a life of prostitution to save her family, selflessly sacrificing her love, purity and freedom. The story is provocative, heart-breaking and ultimately inspiring. As does *The Tale of Luc Van Tien*, it explores concepts of morality and of sacrificing personal beliefs and goals for higher ideals. Again, the lesson imparted is that those who are loyal and determined can survive the cruelest of circumstances.

In a brilliant, modern edition of Nguyễn Du's work, translator Huỳnh Sanh Thông offers insights that can equally be applied to Thi-Linh's life, as Hervey wove it in *Congai*:

> In the course of Vietnam's tormented history, the individual, like
> Kieu herself, has all too often become the toy of necessity, has
> been compelled to do the bidding of some alien power, to serve a
> master other than the one to whom he or she should owe allegiance.

---

34 Du Nguyễn, *The tale of Kieu: a bilingual edition of Truyện Kieu*, translated by Huỳnh Sanh Thông, (New Haven: Yale University Press, 1983), 3.

> Beyond its literal meaning, Kieu's prostitution is interpreted as a
> metaphor for the betrayal of principle under duress, the submission
> to force of circumstances.[35]

The first French edition, *Kim-Van-Kieou* translated by René Crayssac,
was not published until 1926, after Hervey's return to the US. This,
therefore, offers another indication that an accomplished French literary
scholar may have been guiding Hervey in his exploration of local
literature.[36]

Le Roman de Madamoiselle Lys

Though unmentioned by Hervey, a third contemporary Vietnamese
work parallels *Congai, Saramani* and other books of this genre in
significant ways, while offering another important account about early
20th century romance in French Indochina. *Le Roman de Madamoiselle
Lys (The Novel of Madamoiselle Lys)* by journalist Nguyễn Phan Long
(1889–1960) was published in Hanoi in 1921, making it one of the
earliest novels in French written by a Vietnamese author.

As in *Congai*, the author tells his story through a female protagonist,
Mlle Lys, who adopted the more sophisticated French name to replace
her given name, Thi-Hai. Miss Lys is a young, intelligent woman from
a wealthy, rural Vietnamese family who returns to her village after eight
years of study in the French school system of Saigon. Like children
of many upwardly mobile families, education has, for better or worse,
made her far worldlier, and given her far less traditional views than her
peers or her parents.

Mlle Lys immediately encounters problems fitting into her old way of
life. Her parents question her new ideas, she has little in common with
her childhood friends who have refined their traditional domestic skills
in her absence, and she is not at all interested in romantic advances from
local suitors who have no respect for her newly-formed independent and

---

35 Ibid., xl.
36 For more details, see Prof. John Swensson's research site, "The Tale of Kieu, Vietnam's Epic
National Poem," at www.deanza.edu. Also recommended is the 2013 book, *Kieu: the Tale of a
Beautiful and Talented Vietnamese Girl*, translated into rhyming verse by Michael Counsell.

pro-feminist attitudes. Now, her closest relationship is with her French piano teacher; the only person with whom she can intelligently discuss the French literature with which she has become so enamored. Perhaps inspired by the literary romances she adores, a real romance blossoms with a Frenchman, but ends badly, leaving Mlle Lys despondent.

To collect her thoughts, she travels to Angkor with her father, giving the book a wonderful interlude filled with historical information about the lost Khmer civilization, much like Meyer's *Saramani* and Hervey's *King Cobra*. The journey to the ancient ruins does little to improve her mood. Finally, Mlle Lys returns to her home where she undergoes a conversion, an epiphany that leads her to reject her Western education and embrace (the author's) traditional Confucian way of life, thereby discovering both her role in life and happiness.

In his extensive analysis of the text, Karl Britto, Associate Professor of French and Comparative Literature at Berkeley, describes the book as "above all a cautionary tale, a book that Nguyen Phan Long himself describes as [a book of ideas as much as a work of imagination]." [37]

In his preface, Long lays out a complicated political agenda that, in particular, seeks to embrace local tradition to protect Vietnamese women from corrupting French influences. At the same time he opposes nationalist and revolutionary movements and advocates collaboration with the French government— indeed, he dedicated his book to Maurice Long, then Governor General of Indochina.

His views espousing conservative and traditional roles for women are diametrically opposed to the liberated life Hervey gave to Thi-Linh in *Congai*, however his book is a fascinating look at the intercultural conflicts that influenced the evolution of French Indochina. [38]

---

37 Karl Ashoka Britto, *Disorientation France, Vietnam, and the ambivalence of interculturality*, (Hong Kong: Hong Kong University Press, 2004), 40.
38 DatAsia Press released a modern French language edition of *Le Roman de Madamoiselle Lys* in 2014 with an English translation underway.

Part 5:
Living the Romance of French Literature

Hervey has the distinction of being among the few Anglophones, and certainly one of the only Americans, of his time to have acquired sufficient fluency with French works about Indochina to weave them into his own narratives. Some may criticize him for borrowing French ideas; the reality was that French ideas were at the essence of the world he was writing about.

In that light we see the brilliance of grounding two novels about early twentieth century Southeast Asia in terms of the area's reigning culture. In *King Cobra*, Hervey touches upon the literature of France, but in *Congai* he immerses himself and becomes part of it. First, Hervey creates a male writer to work in the genre, actually creating a French book within his book. Ultimately, however, Hervey lives through his realistic female protagonist, Thi-Linh, sharing his appreciation, knowledge and craft with readers through her persona.

Thi-Linh: The Author's Author

> "What do you think of our native women?"
>
> Batteur's face, taut in the heat, relaxed into a smile; the reflected shimmer gave his eyes a curious effect of blurred and sleepy green.
>
> "Beautiful savages," he pronounced, still smiling.
>
> Father Mehry chuckled. "After a few months you won't call them savages" [*Congai*, 1].

Hervey opens *Congai* with secondary character Justin Batteur, who, like the author, was a young man newly arrived in Indochina and thirsty for adventure. A few pages later we discover that Hervey has given Batteur another shared quality: "'Monsieur is a writer…a distinguished man of letters in France'" (*Congai*, 29).

Hervey even gives Batteur dialogue from one his own most traumatic experiences in Indochina. In *King Cobra* (p. 257) Hervey nearly dies

Jean d'Esme's *Thi-Bâ: Fille d'Annam* has remained in print since its first appearance in 1920. From top left, the covers above show editions from: 1920, 1926, circa 1930s, 1932, 1932, 1954, 1956 and 2001.

of jungle fever, describing his hallucinatory memory of explorer Henri Mouhot's last words near Luang Prabang, Laos in 1861. Hervey survived, of course, but assigns Batteur a similar phrase to share as he dies: "*O pitié, mon Dieu...*" ["Lord, have mercy..."] (*Congai*, 62).

Hervey, however, only included Batteur to frame his actual protagonist—the true creative genius of his tale—the young Eurasian girl he named Thi-Linh. Even on the book's first page, quoted above, Hervey wasted no time setting the stage for her entrance.

In *King Cobra*, Hervey's Tired Cavalier nourished him on the genre of French romantic literature in Indochina, that had (and has) made almost no appearances in the English language. In *Congai*, Hervey reveals that it is in fact Thi-Linh who is the source of Batteur's ideas, just as Hervey works behind her. As Thi-Linh related,

> ...she understood him enough to know he wanted her to read books and discuss them with him; also to help him in his work without knowing too much about it. That she had a very definite part in the creation of his book she realized. Justin asked her many questions about the customs of her people and their legends. He had begun this book shortly after she came to live with him, and he told her that within another month it would be finished; he was writing swiftly, he said, "under an inspiration." The title was *Une Fille d'Annam*. [*Congai*, 45]

Une Fille d'Annam: Hervey's Book within the Book

> The manuscript of *Une Fille d'Annam* [*A Girl of Annam*] had been sent to France. He told her that very soon great machines would make many copies of it.
>
> "And when you see the book," he said with a smile, "you will find your name in the front. 'To Thi-Linh this story belongs,' it will say" [*Congai*, 52].

While the content of Batteur's imaginary book is glossed over in *Congai*, the concept mirrors a literary genre about East-West romances specifically in Indochina that attracted several important French and Vietnamese writers. As Hervey accurately portrays, local women often provided not only the inspiration but much of the essential content that shaped these books, even as some authors took full credit for their originality while hiding their female sources behind the scenes.

One early author who influenced, and perhaps initiated, the trend was Jean d'Estray. Born Jean Baptiste Marie Michel Rémy Marchadier in 1878, he became a French jurist, writer, journalist, traveler and war hero, who tragically died in 1940 during a World War II battle. In 1903 he published a collection of short stories: *Petits quarts d'heure amoureux d'Extrême-Orient* (which might be titled *Snippets of Love in the Far East* in English, but translates literally and luridly as *Quarter-Hours of Love…*). These candid, even prurient stories of Frenchmen seeking brief female companionship in the Far East were controversial at the time, and still attract the attention of modern critics. In 1906, d'Estray followed this with a travelogue of Southeast Asia, *Pastels d'Asie*, that had more appeal for general readers.

In 1911, d'Estray published the novel that truly defined the genre, *Thi-Sen: la petite amie exotique* (*Thi-Sen: The Exotic Little Lover*), a tale of civilizational clash and unrequited love. It opens with two French conquerors at Tonkin who have a young Vietnamese girl, Thi-Sen, brought to them from a village in revolt. One of the Frenchman falls in love with her, but she senses nothing and herself falls in love with a young native *tirailleur* (skirmisher or rifleman) named Meo. The ensuing interracial love triangle ends badly for all involved, a theme repeated in many of these accounts. His book won that year's Prix National de Littérature but, more importantly, defined a style that many, including Hervey, would write in to this day.

In 1919, Roland Meyer presented his own unique vision of Franco-Asian relationships with his voluminous work, *Saramani*, which Hervey drew from in *King Cobra* as described above. Given the length and complexity of this volume, and the quality of Hervey's distillation, it seems that he was guided by someone who knew its content intimately.

The next Hervey influence was Jean d'Esme, pseudonym for the aristocratic author Vicomte Jean d'Esmenard (1894–1966). D'Esme's French-boy-meets-Annamite-girl novel, *Thi-Bâ: Fille d'Annam* (*Thi-Ba: Daughter of Annam*), was published in 1920 and its title bears an obvious resemblance to Justin Batteur's imaginary book, *Une fille d'Annam*, in Hervey's *Congai*. Of all the books described in this section *Thi-Ba* has enjoyed the most enduring success, with frequent reprints over the past 90 years.

Hervey would have almost certainly noticed another book by d'Esme, his 1923 fantasy called *Les Dieux Rouges,* released the next year in English as *The Red Gods.* Set in the trackless jungles of Laos, the book describes a prehistoric lost race ruled by a mysterious sorceress in direct conflict with French colonial troops.

Not only does it explore an Indochina theme that would have appealed to Hervey, *The Red Gods* echoes a number of fantasy adventure stories that Hervey himself had published earlier, from 1920 to 1923, in pulp fiction magazines. Hervey almost certainly read d'Esme, but it is equally valid to ask if d'Esme also read Hervey? Separated in age by only six years, the two contemporaries had similar tastes and styles.

The year 1921 saw the publication of one of the more unique novels about East-West relationships: *Le roman de Mademoiselle Lys* (*The Novel of Madamoiselle Lys*). Its significance rests on the fact that it is among the first French language novels written by an Annamite, in this case Nguyễn Phan Long, within this genre. The book's relevance to Hervey's *Congai* is described in the Vietnamese literature section above, but we will again note that this male author also wrote his book in the first person style through his female protagonist, Thi-Hai, also known as Mlle Lys.

In 1922, perhaps weary of increasingly positive depictions of Asian women, Henry Casseville (1891–1962) contributed *Thi-Nhi, autre fille d'Annam* (*Thi-Nhi, Another Daughter of Annam*), a collection of vignettes about relationships, many of them decidedly negative.

All of the French titles cited above were published before Hervey's arrival in Saigon, but none have ever appeared in English. As a result, early 20th century romances in French Indochina were, and are today, as obscure to English readers as they were well-known to Francophones. Yet Hervey masterfully followed the French example and, in many creative ways, expanded upon their genre.

In that vein, Hervey was also not above giving *Une Fille d'Annam*, his "book within a book," a coveted honor shared by some of the titles above:

> "…the Académie Française has recognized my work. Do you know what that means? …It means that my books have a chance to live," he went on. "It means I have produced something of permanent value." (*Congai*, 54)

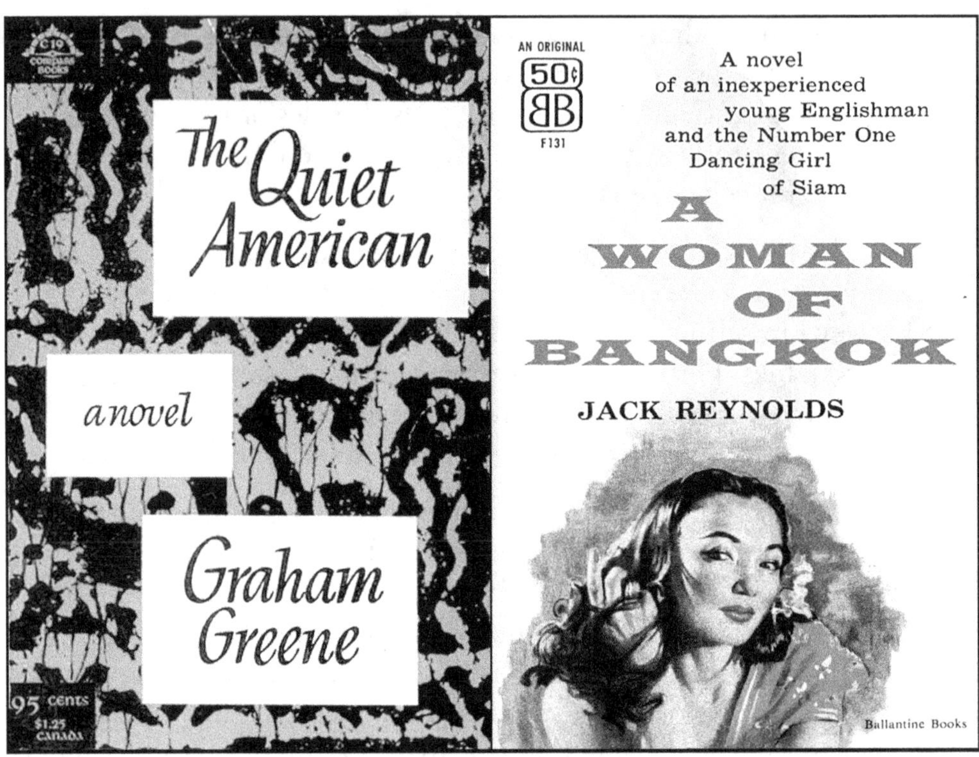

These classics reprised Hervey's *Congai* themes in 1956, nearly three decades later.

In preparing his foreword to *Congai*, Pico Iyer commented on Hervey's work saying "in truth I see this as one of the earliest and most interesting examples of a genre that has become huge, as you know: I think we mentioned how almost every contemporary novel in any bookstore in Bangkok could more or less be called *Congai*, and has a heroine strikingly similar to our own."

Indeed, as British and American interests in the region expanded— particularly with the advent of WWII and the American War in Vietnam—the English language collection of East-West romance books grew considerably. Graham Greene would follow with *The Quiet American* in 1955. In 1956, Welshman Jack Reynolds released his amorous Thai tale, *Woman of Bangkok*, mistakenly seen by many Anglophones as the "first" strong exemplar of the "White man– Southeast Asian girl" genre. The truth is that the French—and one American—had already mastered this game decades before.

Part 6:
Thi-Linh's Triumphant Tour of Colonial Literature

> Often he would invite friends to dinner—men of course—and beforehand he would tell her, "You must talk tonight—you must show them how clever you are" [M. Chavet to Thi-Linh in *Congai*, 131].

The ultimate showcase for Hervey's appreciation and knowledge of French colonial literature takes place at the dinner scene in *Congai*. His protagonist Thi-Linh is now a woman; a woman who has spent ten years living with French men, learning French culture and, most significantly, reading French books.

She has become mistress to one M. Chauvet, a wealthy executive running the Bank of Indochina, who holds dinner parties attended by the most prestigious persons in the federation of French Indochina. At this momentous affair, he introduces Thi-Linh saying "Gentlemen, I think all of you know my wise little peacock—all except Monsieur le Gouverneur." Like many Westerners, he had no idea how competent and determined to excel his "colonial subject" actually was. In the ensuing conversation Thi-Linh, and Hervey, would prove they enjoyed French authors…even more than some Frenchmen themselves.

The conversation opens with small talk of Chinese customs ("These Chinese are amusing devils…"). Then Hervey indulges himself with a cameo appearance as the officials lament the recent visit of a troublesome "American writer." The journalist, despite receiving "every courtesy," returned to America where he "wrote an article attacking the Colonial Government of Indo-China!" (*Congai*, 140). Hervey finishes by having the governor himself deliver the imaginary article's concluding line to the gathered guests:

> "'If the natives of Indo-China had a sense of humor, they would appreciate the elaborate pretensions of Frenchmen, and their convulsive laughter would completely unseat their masters, who, contrary to popular belief, are not at their best when the joke is of a personal nature!'" [*Congai*, 140]

Fatou-gaye, as depicted by artist Gaston Trilleau, in *A Spahi's Love-Story*,
the 1907 English language edition of Loti's book by Charles Carrington, London.

Touché, M. Hervey. Now that he has had his fun lambasting the bureaucrats (and promoting *King Cobra*), he turns the stage over to his literary protégée, Thi-Linh.

So we have a conservative group of powerful, colonial white men gathered for a formal dinner while drinking, smoking and gossiping among themselves. Into their midst Hervey introduces a confident, intelligent, self-educated, street-smart Francophonic Eurasian woman with an agenda to promote racial, cultural, sexual and, above all, *intellectual* equality. What could possibly go wrong?

Three Forbidden Loves: Pierre Loti's *Congai* Sisters

> Thi-Linh's mind was abnormally alert, and the quenching warmth of champagne seemed to multiply glittering words that ran from her tongue easily. [*Congai*, 140]

Thi-Linh was well aware of the racist attitudes her dinner companions shared. The far more controversial, and dangerous, aspect of colonial race issues, indeed the elephant in the room—or more accurately the *congai*—was the *mixing* of races, in beds, children and blood.

Thi-Linh was the embodiment of that forbidden subject: a half-French, half-Cambodian girl, now living openly with one of their own colonial masters. With that in mind she doesn't hesitate to evoke the idea of literary and literal miscegenation by quickly introducing one of Pierre Loti's female protagonists.

Fatou-gaye

> A young officer new to Indo-China was talking about Algeria…
>
> "You were long in Algeria?" she inserted deftly…
>
> "Two years, madame," replied the young officer.
>
> "I only know the country through *Le Roman d'un Spahi*" she said tentatively.
>
> "Which is, perhaps, inadequately," he returned. "For Monsieur Loti saw flowers where flowers were not." After a pause he added laughingly, "And I assure you, madame, that all officers do not consort with black Fatou-gayes!" [*Congai*, 141]

With the officer's remark the entire table fell silent and all eyes were upon Thi-Linh. She immediately knew "they were associating her with those African women, black creatures and mulatto wenches who were the mistresses of Spahis and other soldiers." The gauntlet was thrown down, but before hearing her rebuttal, let us examine the reference itself.

In 1881 Loti published *Le Roman d'un spahi*, the emotional novel about colonial love and loneliness that Hervey referenced in two of his own books. Loti's protagonist, Jean Peyral, is a peasant boy from the south of France who enlists in the army to serve as a *spahi*, i.e. a cavalryman in France's African army. In Senegal, homesick and yearning for his fiancée in France, the lonely Jean soon finds comfort, albeit socially unacceptable comfort, in the arms of a young black woman named Fatou-gaye.

Described in the book's introduction as "a negro girl, half goddess, half monkey,"[39] Fatou-gaye proves to be a loyal, dependable and sensually satisfying companion. She becomes his mistress (i.e. *congai*) and they live together for three years before Jean is ordered to Algiers. Instead, he chooses to take a leave from his military duties to remain with Fatou-gaye. With a growing awareness that their forbidden love is doomed, Jean finally choses to end the relationship. Afterwards, by chance, he meets Fatou-gaye again to discover that she has borne his son. In emotional turmoil, and with nothing resolved, Jean is suddenly ordered on a military campaign against a mutinous chief. Fatou-gaye secretly follows behind him with their son. Loti's conclusion is graphic, shocking and profound. Again, quoting from the original introduction above, "The black Venus has triumphed."

Returning to the dinner table in Hervey's tale, we find Thi-Linh coolly preparing her response.

> A well-poised cruelty balanced her emotions, and she assorted her words with the care of one choosing stones for a catapult
>
> "But in spite of seeing flowers where flowers were not," she pronounced evenly, "Monsieur Loti made savage music out of Africa—sometimes ironic music, with a little tremulous obbligato"—she smiled—"that, perhaps, is the loneliness of Frenchmen in exile." (*Congai*, 141)

After a momentarily silence, another guest attempts to dismiss Loti as "A young naval officer observing the world from the quarter-deck! A

---

39 Pierre Loti, *A Spahi's Love-Story*, (London: Charles Carrington, 1907), xii.

sailor with a penchant for exaggeration!..." Thi-Linh, wastes no time before moving in to redress this slight to her, and to Hervey's, hero.

> ..."Perhaps Loti exaggerated details," she said, "but not moods. In spite of being French, he was able to catch the nostalgic beauty of Asia. Indeed, in his habits he was extremely French—Fatou-gaye, Suleima, Aziyadé; how many were there?—but his reactions, when he put them on paper, were undeniably Eastern.

By mentioning two more of Loti's forbidden lovers—all of whom the men present would have been quite familiar with, most likely as objects of lust—Thi-Linh built her characterization of Frenchmen as serial philanderers engaged in promiscuity in every port of call.

Suleima

"Suleïma" is a short story in Loti's 1883 book *Fleurs d'ennui* (*Blossoms of Boredom*). It tells of two sailors, Loti and Plumkett, who know each other so well that they can practically read each other's thoughts, and of Suleïma, a teenage Algerian girl who enters their close relationship as a disturbing third wheel.

Peter James Tuberfield, in *Pierre Loti and the Theatricality of Desire*, describes it as a bisexual triangle, where Suleïma serves the dual function of injecting novelty into the sailors' monotonous, nearly identical lives, and of serving as a proxy in Loti's affections for Plumkett, the true object of his desires.

Aziyadé

Aziyadé (also known as *Constantinople)* was Loti's first book, published anonymously and to little recognition in 1879, but popular when appearing under his name following the success of *Rarahu* in 1880.

Aziyadé is semi-autobiographical, based on a diary Loti kept during his three-month stint as a French Naval officer in Greece and İstanbul in 1876. It tells the story of the 27-year old Loti's illicit love affair with an 18-year-old harem girl named Aziyadé. Although Aziyadé was but one of Loti's many amorous conquests, she appears to have been his greatest love; in fact, he would wear a gold ring with her name on it for the rest of his life.

Once again Loti presents us with a love triangle, this time through a friendship with a manservant named Samuel, of Spanish blood, Turkish culture and Jewish faith. Most critics believe, from the diary entries, that some sort of homosexual affair occurred between Loti and Samuel. Indeed, some believe that Aziyadé never existed at all and that the entire novel is the veiled story of a homosexual love affair.[40]

In the novel, Loti's affair with Aziyadé begins in Salonica, but he is called away to Istanbul, where the lovers find each other again and Aziyadé pledges her love. Loti briefly leaves her for another woman but returns. Then, receiving new orders to depart, he considers making himself a Turkish citizen to remain with his beloved, who warns that she will die if he leaves. He dismisses the idea and departs, later returning to Istanbul to learn that Aziyadé was cast out of the harem and, indeed, did die of a broken heart.

After *Congai* was published, Hervey may have seen the only known English translation of *Aziyadé* by Marjorie Laurie, available in many editions starting in 1927, but the reading is rather dry compared to the original as the work is bowdlerized in parts that relate to harem life, prostitution and homosexuality.

So by referring to three literary women—Fatou-gaye, Suleima and Aziyadé—Thi-Linh certainly made strong impressions on the guests. For another insightful view of their probable perspectives, we again quote Jennifer Yee, who draws from a contemporary source, saying:

> ...it is possible with women of certain races not too far removed from the European ideal to relive "the strange loves depicted by Loti; one can imagine oneself as Aziyadé's or Mme Chrysanthème's lover" [...]. To imagine oneself as the lover of one of Loti's exotic heroines: we might well consider this the theme of many a colonial story.[41]

---

40 In his biography, *Graham Greene: The Enemy Within*, (New York: Random House, 1994), 63-65, Michael Shelden presents a strikingly similar analysis of the relationship between Greene and Sergeant Chuchu in Panama, where the two men engage in highly charged sexual conversations with the help of an "imaginary woman."

41 Jennifer Yee, *Clichés De La Femme Exotique*, 21-22, quoting Charles Renel, *La race inconnue*, (Paris: Grasset, 1900) p. 142. Translation by Pedro Rodríguez.

In closing, Thi-Linh has the final word…and delivers her *coup de grâce*:

> "Now of course"—she paused, running her fingers over the stem of
> her wineglass—"he seems a bit archaic. For in these days Fatou-gaye
> doesn't kill herself, she gets another Frenchman."
>
> And she smiled deliberately and distractingly [*Congai*, 142].

French Literature in the Dark Continent

> Talk commenced at the other end of the table. She transferred her
> attention to the young officer from Algeria.
>
> "Speaking of Africa," she began, "there was a book—by René
> Maran—called *Batouala*."
>
> "*Batouala!*" burst out one of the Frenchmen near her. "Hot words
> written by a Negro! It is stupid—it is too bitter—it is merely
> ridiculous!"
>
> She was pleased, for she had thought that mention of *Batouala*
> would bring a heated reaction. [*Congai*, 143]

Racism, while perfectly acceptable among colonials, was one injustice
Thi-Linh chose to address directly, using literature as a perfect platform
to call the practice into question. She chose African subjects to provide
the strongest racial contrast, while alluding to the situation they all
shared in French Indochina. Did these men dislike the book, or the
color of the author who shared his ideas?

René Maran
Nov. 8, 1887 - May 9, 1960

French-Guyanese poet and novelist René Maran was born on a boat
headed to Fort-de-France, Martinique, where he lived until the age
of eleven. He next lived in Gabon—his father having been sent there
by the French Colonial Service—before attending boarding school in
Bordeaux. He later joined the French Colonial Service himself and
worked in French Equatorial Africa, the setting for many of his novels,
including the controversial *Batouala: A Negro novel from the French*, as it
was translated in 1922.[42]

---

42 René Maran, *Batouala: a Negro novel from the French,* (London: J. Cape., 1922).

As Thi-Linh's dinner companions would have known, Maran vigorously denounced French colonialism—indeed, its Baudelairean drunkenness—right from his preface, even while serving in its very administration. The following sample is provided so readers understand the volatility of Maran's ideas to the dinner guests at hand.

> For if the baseness of its everyday life were known, one would speak far less of this broad colonial life; indeed, one would not speak of it ever again. It is but a gradual debasement. Even among civil servants, rare are the colonials who cultivate their minds. They haven't the strength to withstand the environment. One grows accustomed to alcohol. Before the war many a European could by himself down fifteen liters of Pernod in the space of thirty days. Since then, alas, I have met one who has smashed every record. Eighty bottles of whiskey he was able to imbibe over the course of a month.
>
> Those subject to the worst sort of spinelessness are dragged down by these excesses and still others, all of them ignoble. And those charged with representing France cannot help but be disturbed by the depravity. It is they who must assume responsibility for the evils to which certain parts of the Negro countries are at present exposed. For if they hoped for promotion they must not have "had a history." To measure up to this frightful standard, they have abandoned all sense of pride, hesitated, temporized, lied and spun out their lies. They have shut their eyes and stopped up their ears. They have lacked the courage to speak out. And, adding moral asthenia to intellectual anemia, they have, with nary a regret, played their country false.[43]

Batouala nevertheless made Maran the first black writer ever to win the Prix Goncourt (1921). The milestone did not go unnoticed. In 1965 Jean-Paul Sartre, in his preface to Frantz Fanon's *The Wretched of the Earth*, mocked the French establishment's complacent self-congratulation that chose "for once, to award the Prix Goncourt to a black."[44]

Returning to the dinner conversation, though Thi-Linh was in deep literary waters, she appeased the men with some conciliatory remarks and a satisfying conclusion before moving on to her next African example.

---

43 René Maran, *Batoula : véritable roman nègre,* (Paris: Albin Michel, 1921) 14-15. Translation by Pedro Rodríguez.
44 Frantz Fanon, Jean-Paul Sartre and Constance Farrington, *The wretched of the earth,* (New York: Grove Press, Inc., 1965), xliv.

> "Its violence made it ineffectual," she said. "If Monsieur Maran
> had been a European instead of a Negro, his bitterness would
> have taken the form of satire. Or if he had had some French blood
> instead of merely a French education—" She paused, aware that
> she was spinning over fire, yet sure of herself. "Then," she finished,
> "he would have written with more artistic despair and less obvious
> purpose…"
>
> "Exactly," came Monsieur Chauvet's voice from the other end of the
> table.
>
> "Consider the other extreme," she continued, not satisfied; "that
> novel of Pierre Benoit's, *L'Atlantide*." [*Congai*, 143].

Here Thi-Linh introduces a clever new element to her debate. If the
Frenchmen reflexively reject "hot words written by a Negro" then surely
they must accept the words of an author and civil servant every bit as
French as themselves?

Pierre Benoit
July 16, 1886–March 3, 1962

Prolific French novelist Pierre Benoit was the son of a soldier, born in
Albi, southern France. He spent his early years and military service in
North Africa before becoming a civil servant and author. His first novel,
Koenigsmark, in 1918, was followed the next year by *L'Atlantide*. This
fantastic tale, later awarded the Grand Prix de l'Académie Française,
tells the story of two French officers captured by a lost tribe in the
Algerian Sahara. The tribe is ruled by, Queen Antinéa, a descendent of
Atlantis who periodically takes human lovers for amusement. The book
was translated into English and published in the United States in 1920
as a serial in *Adventure* magazine, a periodical Hervey certainly read.
In 1921, the novel appeared as a hit silent movie that was filmed on
location in Africa for the then-astounding cost of two million francs.

In October 1919, however, the originality of *L'Atlantide* was called into
question in when literary critic Harry Magden publicly accused Benoit
of plagiarizing ideas for his book from the novels *She* and *The Yellow
God*, by English adventure writer Henry Rider Haggard. Benoît sued
for libel and lost. The issue of plagiarism was never completely resolved
and the similarities perhaps represented literary "inspiration" more

Director Jacques Feyder spent 8 months filming *l'Atlantide* on location in Algeria with his cast and crew. The 3-hour epic also became one of the first films to portray the romantic, exotic flavors of the French colonial experience in North Africa.

than outright theft.[45] A similar situation of shared ideas exists in the similarities between Hervey's *Congai*, and Greene's novel, *The Quiet American*, published nearly thirty years later.[46]

In 1931 Benoit was elected to the Académie. His legacy would have been more appealing if not for the fact that he was a political right-winger, and an avid admirer of French fascist Charles Maurras. Worse, during the Nazi Occupation of France he joined the pro-Nazi Groupe Collaboration, whose membership included writer and politician Abel Bonnard, physician and chemist Georges Claude and writer Pierre Drieu La Rochelle. After the liberation of France, Benoit was arrested in September 1944. Although he was released within six months, his work remained on the blacklist of French Nazi collaborators for several years. He died in March 1962 in Ciboure, France.

The dinner conversation continues:

> "Merely a romancer, Benoit," pronounced the Frenchman who had been so vehement about *Batouala*.
>
> "But he is also very French," replied Thi-Linh. "For him, Africa is—well, grist for his literary mill. He is fantastic, his story impossible. Monsieur Maran is bitter, his story not impossible but improbable. There we have the two, native and Frenchman, both writing about a continent—and neither a great artist" [*Congai*, 143].

Next we see that Thi-Linh was merely toying with the man, providing two average examples before moving on to her next point. And so we come full circle, back to Pierre Loti who, as Thi-Linh testifies,

> "…is more artistic. And more truthful, paradoxical as that seems. He interpreted the moods of the East—of Indo-China as well as Africa—with passionate felicity—perhaps because, in spite of being born a Frenchman, he was, emotionally, a strange blending of both Oriental and Occidental" [*Congai*, 144].

Speaking through Thi-Linh, Hervey captures the essence of Pierre Loti's style; a style that to a great extent he adopted as his own.

---

45 See "The H. Rider Haggard Filmography" by Jessica Amanda Salmonson. www.violetbooks.com
46 See *Congai* appendix article, "Two Quiet Americans: Alden Pyle & Harry Hervey" by Kent Davis.

Was Hervey's Love for Loti More Than Platonic?

Is it possible that, in addition to their shared interest in exotic places, Hervey also sensed a shared a sexual orientation with the great French writer?

There has been much speculation in recent years that Loti was homosexual. This conclusion comes from the analysis of critics like Roland Barthes,[47] and scholars like Robert Aldrich[48] and Richard M. Barrong.[49] They argue that many of Loti's female characters are in fact proxies for the author to express his homosexuality.

Whether Loti was homosexual, bi-sexual or heterosexual is beyond the scope of this article. Our author Hervey, however, was an avowed homosexual and research by his biographer makes it seem quite probable that Hervey did use his own female character, Thi-Linh, as just such a proxy.[50]

Congai, after all, offers a detailed examination of the men in Thi-Linh's life—a catalog of masculinity that includes her several lovers, military officers, hedonistic government officials, bawdy soldiers on leave in cafés, native rickshaw pullers, young male prostitutes with made-up faces, and even a thoughtful and ambitious police prefect who ultimately coveted the *congai.* These men are variously described in sensual, intellectual and physical terms, always from Thi-Linh's perspective, and often within the context of their sexual relationships with her.

Hervey's mélange of men and women, in love and lust, offer true exhilaration to all types of readers. He owes much of his technique and inspiration to French masters, like Loti, who preceded him. But in creating Thi-Linh, Hervey has given us one of the most captivating and convincing heroines to ever grace the pages of colonial literature in French Indochina.

---

47 Barthes, Roland. *Writing Degree Zero.* New York: Hill and Wang, 2012.

48 Aldrich, Robert. *Colonialism and Homosexuality.* London: Routledge, 2003.

49 Berrong, Richard M. *In Love with a Handsome Sailor: The Emergence of Gay Identity and the Novels of Pierre Loti.* Toronto, Ont: University of Toronto Press, 2003. Internet resource.

50 See Harlan Greene's appendix article, "Through a Woman's Eyes: *Congaies,* Heroines & Harry Hervey," in *Congai.*

Part 7:
French Secrets of Travel Writing?

"You are a tourist," he said; and it was not even a question.

"I replied that I was a writer; for, aside from my perfectly healthy dislike for the word tourist applied to me, it would be technically incorrect because a tourist, in spite of popular opinion, travels to tell other countries about his own" [*King Cobra*, 6].

What journalist doesn't bristle at being called a mere tourist? Their rarified role is to penetrate the Zeitgeist, whereas, with few exceptions, tourists see what they are supposed to see and go where they are supposed to go. Tourists visit the same predictable sites that—through years of refinement —governments and businesses have carefully packaged for financial gain and the burnishing of national images. Short-term visitors hardly get a chance to experience local ways of life or sample local ideas. Indeed, such things are downright inconvenient, especially when language barriers and time constraints stand in the way.

Harry Hervey quite literally strayed far from the beaten path to interact with natives and colonial residents alike. Clearly he forged personal relationships with Frenchmen in accomplishing his task, and it is likely that others, in addition to his Tired Cavalier, guided him along the path of literary discovery. Though hints in *King Cobra* suggest that Hervey was less than proficient in French, he had at least read translations of French colonial adventure tales since childhood. And once he arrived in early twentieth-century French Indochina, he captured its subtle essence in myriad ways, despite the cultural and linguistic gulfs he had to cross.

In the end, Hervey joined that elite group of international writers who have transcended inter-cultural boundaries to share the lives, attitudes, traditions, hopes, fears and realities of locals. It is one thing to travel the world and quite another to explain what you've seen to those who weren't along for the ride.

Hervey's work epitomizes this style of travel, interaction and writing. He plunges into Asia like a native, and emerges to share thoughts and dreams that would otherwise seem unsharable.

So what did it take for Hervey to write as more than a mere tourist? The following six qualities seem to be essential ingredients:

1. Perception: Looking (and *seeing*) beyond what he was supposed to see. Noticing things that aren't obvious but, once identified, become unforgettable.

2. Empathy: Understanding that people who may have seemed entirely unlike himself experienced emotions and dreams just like his own, albeit through different filters of culture, place and upbringing. Empathy, says a Native American proverb, is the willingness to "walk a mile in another man's moccasins."

3. Intuition: Perhaps more innate than learned, Hervey's intuition gave him the ability to perceive, empathize with, and even feel the depths of other people's souls. His creation of Thi-Linh is a fine example.

4. Distillation: The volume of information one accumulates when visiting other cultures is infinite. As a great travel writer, Hervey gathered those strange cultural threads and wove them into something wonderful and useful.

5. Translation: Linguistic translation was essential, but Hervey's real challenge was *cultural* translation: sharing his foreign experiences and perceptions so that readers could not only identify with them, but embrace them as their own.

6. Transmission: The final act of conveying discoveries with "his own people" (e.g., readers, friends, compatriots). We all travel and have unusual experiences, but Hervey drew others in to share his sense of wonder, making him a writer for the world.

To these six, Hervey added one more rare quality in both his Indochina books: he wrote as a writer with a true appreciation and respect for other writers—French, Belgian, African and Vietnamese—while referencing their works in his text.

It is standard practice for writers to include some witty remarks from local literary luminaries to add color, but Hervey went far beyond this. His plots made multiple references to the huge body of works about the

French colonial experience in Indochina; works that were obscure even to most French readers, and were virtually unknown to Anglophones. While nineteenth-century Americans wrote of their Wild West, and the English described their Empire, French authors were living in their own extraordinary world of intercultural exchange. Only a handful of these French accounts have ever been translated to English, so the genre was, and is, relatively unknown to Anglophones, most especially to Americans who primarily relied on the English for their impressions of Asia.

Harry Hervey recognized the beauty of French prose, and became one of the few Americans to immerse himself in the tropical richness of French Indochina's colonial literature. He knew the unique genre that captured the passion and pain of relationships between Western men and Asian women, and understood it sufficiently to weave some of its most interesting texts into his own works. To his credit, Hervey honored the French writers who went before him, as he blazed the trail for English writers who would follow.

Congaies or Concubines?
Literary Views of Asian Women under Colonial Rule

Walter Jones

"A young Breton trooper follows [an Annamite] girl with an appraising look, taking in the back bandeau of her hair, her black lace tunic and the tiny black sandals that drop from her heels as she walks. He wonders if her teeth also are black. But that possibility is dispelled as she turns and smiles…The night is very soft…He will go to her father and make a bargain; then there will someone to keep his clothes in order, brush away the mildew.…Very simple.…And the map is changed." (*King Cobra*, 19)

In the sexual relationships of Western white men and Asian brown women of French Indochina, there existed an exploitive nature that paralleled the relationships between colonizers and their subjects. This paper examines this exploitation as described in several early English-language works, where the war of the sexes embodied—and in fictive works often symbolized—the political tensions that later erupted into the bitter Franco-Viet Minh War of the mid-1940s. Page citations in parentheses are detailed in the bibliography following the article.

The opening passage is quoted from the 1927 travelogue, *King Cobra: An Autobiography of Travel in French Indo-China* (19). Its author, novelist and adventurer Harry Hervey, became one of the first Americans to offer his impressions of how East-West relationships began in Indochina, and how this system worked as a means for French men to acquire women, known as *congaies,* for cohabitation.

In its most simple and beautiful form, the Vietnamese word *con gái* (transliterated here as *congai,* and plural *congaies*) simply means "young woman." A novelist of importance to this paper, Clotilde Chivas-Baron, compiled a set of Vietnamese legends in her 1920 book titled *Stories and Legends of Annam.* This quote from one of Chivas-Baron's stories, "Water Genie," illustrates the positive nature of the term *congai*:

> Every morning, before the sun reddened the horizon, and often again at eve, when the sky was streaked with long bands of purple and gold, Kam-Kong would go down the principle village street, the muddy street defiled with betel, encumbered with children, pigs and poultry. She went with elastic, somewhat cat-like steps, along the path bordered with cactus which winds down to the river. A bamboo on her shoulder sustained two brown earthen pots wherein the young *congai* was want to draw water (1, 2).

By 1885, however, the term *congai* had already taken on other meanings to foreigners, as demonstrated in this account by historian James George Scott in *France and Tongking*. Not only does he characterize native women as greedy and duplicitous, he blames them for the opium addiction that afflicted so many colonial residents:

> Unfortunately there are too many Frenchmen who indulge to excess. They learn the habit in the worst way, through the *Congai*, the "*moosmi*" of Annam. That damsel is one of the first things a Frenchman procures when he reaches the country, and prominent officials do not hesitate to announce in print that the language can only, and, as a matter of fact, is only, learnt through the *cocotte*. The girl is a regular piece of furniture, for she is bought from her family—at a very cheap rate too, for the Annamese are prolific; but nevertheless she usually takes command of the establishment. She is a not unattractive hussy, and makes the best of her time, for she is quite aware that comeliness, especially Oriental comeliness, is a very transient thing. She is therefore corrupt and rapacious in the extreme, and, the better to manage her plans, teaches her master to smoke opium. But it would be well if he only smoked in the company of his *chère amie*. He very often goes to much worse places. There is something peculiarly degrading in the spectacle of an officer in full uniform stretched at full length on the filthy boards of a stew, smoking himself into stupor. (316)

So, as French men began to colonize Indochina, the word *congai* took on darker meanings. In "Syphilis, Opiomania, and Pederasty" Frank Proschan interprets the word as changing from "'woman' to 'wife' to 'mistress' to 'whore'" (614). In "Eunuch Mandarins, Soldats Mamzelles, Effeminate Boys, and Graceless Women," he alters the definition slightly to substitute "concubine" for "mistress" (456). The idea of brown women as sexual possessions of white men is, however, represented in both terms.

In her essay, "Making Empire Respectable," Ann Laura Stoler describes the utilitarian view colonial governments had toward these temporary unions:

> Referred to as *nyai* in Java and Sumatra, *congai* in Indochina, and *petite epouse* throughout the French empire, the colonized woman living as a concubine to a European man formed the dominant domestic arrangement in colonial cultures through the early 20th century. Unlike prostitution, which could and often did result in a population of syphilitic and therefore non-productive European men, concubinage was considered to have a stabilizing effect on political order and colonial health—a relationship that kept men in their barracks and bungalows, out of brothels and less inclined to perverse liaisons with one another. (637)

Nicola Cooper expanded on the term *congai* in her book, *French in Indochina: Colonial Encounters*, creating the new term "encongayement" (154). This text hereafter uses encongayement to denote sexually-oriented partnerships between Western men and Asian women.

Encongayement as a concept is laden with the suggestion of the exploitation of women in Asian settings, where white men became conquerors, colonizers and masters of the native women they encountered. Cooper states that Asian women became an easy conquest for white men, with the *congai* representing "an Indochinese version of the traditional and mythologized indigenous woman: the compliant sexual conquest of the dominant white male coloniser" (154). To Cooper, the conqueror dehumanized the *congai* to the point that she became a "possession", a reward "due to the colonizing male" in a conquered country (155-57).

Frank Proschan, in "Eunuch Mandarins," elaborates on the slave-like nature of the *congai* system, suggesting how it abused the women involved:

> ...the concubine, despite her sexual nature, is seen primarily as a domestic, offering her services to the colonial just as any domestic provides services. "What good is it to speak of them?" asks [Oliver] Diraison-Seylor [in *Amours d'Extreme Orient* 1905] "Flesh domesticated by the conquerors....[And the name *congai*] becomes truly a mark of possession, of a 'thing' that belongs without restriction. It takes on in passion's legend, a meaning of passivity given to all sorts of sadism" (455-56).

Exploitive aspects inherent in the ownership model of the *congai* system are also described by Milton Osborne's in *Fear and Fascination in the Tropics: A Reader's Guide to French Fiction on Indochina* where he explains:

> …these were women, in a setting that for the most part offered no other female companionship, and so they were used for physical relief, as French writers frankly acknowledged. As early as 1896, in an autobiography published that year *Tonkinoiseries: Sourvenirs d'un officier* (*Things Tonkinese: An Officer's Memories),* Jean Lera established the conflict of emotions that would be repeated so often in later, fictional works: simultaneous lust for and a repulsion from the dehumanized image of a Vietnamese woman. Lera recalls how he purchased a <u>*congai*</u>; how he found himself drawn to her body but revolted by her red betel-stained teeth; and how finally he "succumbed to the brutish feeling of violent desire" (12).

In *Empire of Love,* Matt Matsuda further contends that the idea of the "possession of a native" became supported both in colonial laws approving mixed marriages and in colonial fiction, wherein writers such as Clotilde Chivas-Baron explored the mechanics and meanings of white-male and brown female relationships (139).

In addition to the potential for abusive behavior, two other negative elements of encongayement are the abandonment of native woman when the relationships end, and the creation of a half-caste race subject to rejection and discrimination on all sides. Cooper clearly explains the abandonment in terms of the colonizer's pattern of "landing, loving and leaving" (156). She explains that *congaies*, being "simple and inexpensive to keep…are abandoned as easily and rapidly as they were acquired" (155). Thus, for the native woman, the arrangement was a temporary one that left her without a husband or a lover once her white companion either returned to his homeland, or found another mistress. To Kathryn Robson and Jennifer Yee, in *France and "Indochina"*, the woman who married a French man was known only as a *"petite epouse"* (5). This term carries the connotation of a relationship of diminished and short-term value to the male colon.

Regarding the creation of an unwanted race, Milton Osborne observes in *Fear and Fascination in the Tropics*:

> Up to the Second World War, the pseudoscientific view of the inferiority of Asians to Europeans then prevailing among the French in Indochina sustained the idea that Eurasian 'half-castes'

[metis of colonial society] were necessarily less capable than those whose European blood had not been degraded by mixture with a local source (14-15).

Robson and Yee, in *France and "Indochina"* point to early twentieth century novels that deal with the mixed-blood situation: "From the 1920s onward, a series of novels analyze the shame and difficulties of the metis, the mixed-race child born to a white man and a native woman," and the two authors cite two imaginative works that reflect this unfavorable condition of the metis as being Herbert Wilde's *L'Autre race*, 1920 and Chivas-Baron's *Confidences de metisse*, 1927 (6).

Given the factual background on the existence and social conditions relating to encongayement, this narrative will now examine passages from five early novels that illustrate the *congai* concept. These fictive works include Clotilde Chivas-Baron's novella *Madame Hoa's Husbands*, one of three moderate-length works in *Three Women of Annam* (English translation, 1925); Harry Hervey's *Congai* (1927); Cosmo Forbes' *Where the Cobra Sings* (1932); Jean Hougron's *Reap the Whirlwind* (1953); and Graham Greene's *Quiet American* (1955).

Clotilde Chivas-Baron was an early twentieth century French feminist and activist (Lorcin), and an author of considerable accomplishment. Her 1920 *Stories and Legends of Annam* has been recently reprinted as one of Kessinger Publishing's legacy series. According to Matsuda in *Empire of Love*, Chivas-Baron received an award called the "Grand prix de literature colonial" in 1927, and is known for her own fictive works featuring strong and willful women (149).

Madame Hoa's Husband features two *congaies*, Hoa and Ginette, who are cousins. Both are involved in sexual relationships with French men, but they are quite different in their personalities. Whereas Hoa is temperate and accepting of her position in Vietnamese society, Ginette is hot-tempered, bitter and outspoken. Part of Ginette's discontent with life comes from the stigma attached to her for being Eurasian—the metis Osborne describes in *Fear and Fascination in the Tropics*. At one point in in the book Ginette vehemently describes her anger to Hoa, "I am a…half-breed! That means a creature held in contempt by both races to which I belong" (198). Further, in giving vent to her bitterness and to her view that, as *congaies*, she and her cousin are held in bondage,

Ginette becomes a symbol of rebellion against the injustices of the cohabitation system that has captured them. Once, accusing Hoa of being too complacent with her status as a *congai*, Ginette screams at Hoa, "You accept all the servitude, you accept all the humiliation… as for me, I cannot!" (199). Ginette's outburst reflects a feminism that was actually growing among Vietnamese women in the 1920s, an era when the revolutionary woman poet Bao Luong declared, "If men had prevented the French from coming in and brutalizing women, we'd have stayed home happily" (Tai 135).

Later in Chivas-Baron's work, at a moment when Hoa discovers that her French master has a fiancée in France, Ginette points out menacingly, "These are things that happen: they happen to us slaves… How many Occidentals, leaving behind them wife and children, choose young *congaies* for wives…while they are here?" (206). By giving Ginette such a strong voice against the colonial system of exploitation that had victimized her and her cousin, Chivas-Baron uses the fiery metis to reflect an actual sense of rebellion that was increasing among the native populations of 1920s Indochina (Robson and Yee 6).

As *Madame Hoa's Husbands* nears its conclusion, Ginette finally marries a wealthy French companion, promptly declaring her intent to use the Frenchman's financial resources to free her Vietnamese sisters from their bondage by establishing an education system that will give Indochinese women the ability to set themselves free. To Hoa, she exclaims:

> …I can contribute to the founding of schools; if half-breeds have, one day, a chance of living otherwise than by prostitution; if, one day, peasant women, feel in breathing the air of Annam…that they are breathing an air of freedom, I shall not have lived in vain! (262-63).

The second English-language novel to explore the social dimensions of the *congai* system in detail is Harry Hervey's 1927 work titled *Congai,* Based on his experiences traveling throughout Indochina, as he described in *King Cobra*, Hervey created an entire novel about the sexual liaisons between one Vietnamese woman and a series of French colonists. His plot was so compelling to the American public that, shortly after his book was released, he and his partner Carlton Hildrith received backing to turn the story into a successful Broadway play that later toured the US ("This Week's" xi).

Born in Texas in 1900, Hervey became a well-known adventurer, Orientalist, and innovative American writer of both fiction and non-fiction. In 1924, he "led an expedition into the interior of Indo-China" where he gained first-hand knowledge enabling him to write his novel about *congaies* (Marquis 395). *Congai* focuses on the life of a Eurasian concubine named Thi-Linh whose mother was an Annamite and whose father, whom she had never met, was a French medical doctor and scholar (12). Hervey gives readers insights into the mindset of the distinctive and intriguingly seductive *congaies* of Indochina by first describing Thi-Linh's aspirations forming in her childhood:

> Once when she was a little girl [Thi-Linh] had been sitting on the bank as a river boat passed on its long journey to Vien-tiane; and she saw on the deck a slender young woman in a tunic of flowered black tissue over yellow, with diamond earrings in her ears. Thi-Linh admired her air of aloofness toward the other natives on deck, implied in her very posture. Her face, pale with rice-powder against which her lips were scarlet as a grenadine flower, haunted Thi-Linh.... Later she told her mother about the bewildering creature on the river boat....Her mother nodded. 'She is the *congai* of Monsieur the Prefect of Police of Vien-tiane'" (12).

Later in the novel, Hervey underscores the transient nature of brown woman cohabiting with white men in a scene in which Thi-Linh, after becoming a *congai*, asks her mother about her French lover: "Will he leave me after a while?" To which her mother responds, "Probably" (26).

Continuing to build on the temporary aspect of the *congai*'s relationship to a Western male, Hervey uses Thi-Linh's friend—a second *congai* named Nanette—to illustrate how some women pursued self-preservation within the exploitive system. "Nanette," Hervey informs the reader, "in spite of her name, was a pure Annamite from Quang Tri," who had matured into "a restless little creature with incendiary thoughts" (46). Indeed, Nanette—hardened, realistic and outspoken like Chivas-Baron's Ginette in *Madame Hoa's Husbands*—becomes the *congai*'s voice of liberation and independence when she declares to Thi-Linh: "...I have no intention of being good—it is stupid. No Annamite would take me for a wife now, and French husbands do not last, so why not have many and get everything I can out of each?" (47).

Nanette, then, acknowledging a social stigma attached to the *congai* in Vietnamese society, and echoing the realization that marriage to a white man is only short-lived, becomes the rebel. Thus by refusing to be submissive and by declaring her own self-interest, she symbolizes in fiction a growing movement in reality toward revolution and the violent expulsion of the French male masters from Indochina in the mid-1950s. But colonial justice was harsh to those who sought to change the system, especially women. Hervey alludes to this in the fate he gives Nanette, who is later shot to death by the police.

The third novel in this discussion is Cosmo Forbes' 1932 work, *Where the Cobra Sings*. Cosmo Forbes is a pseudonym for Val Lewton, a Russian-born Hollywood producer who came to the United States with his mother in 1909 when he was five years old (Biography). He was working for MGM at the time he wrote *Where the Cobra Sings*, and his novel displays more of a Hollywood extravaganza than a realistic depiction of colonial life in Indochina. The book's characters are colorful and urbane: An American broker who flees San Francisco and buys a tea plantation in Cambodia; a Dutch tea-plantation owner; an unscrupulous Saigon businessman of murky European origin; a former British army officer who once served in a "smart" unit in India; and a beautiful *congai* from the island of Bali (67, 82, 84, 96). While *Where the Cobra Sings* clearly focuses on the idea of the *congai*, the plot rejects the concept of arranged, temporary, exploitive marriage between Western males and Asian females. As such, the novel deserves serious consideration.

Like Hervey, Forbes gives his own basically accurate description of the rationale for, and exploitive nature of, the *congai* system:

> Men came to the East to earn a living in the hard, killing climate. It was not to be expected that they bring white women with them into the topics. The system which permitted *congai*s was the result of their loneliness—easy marriages, binding only upon the girl and leaving the man free to go whenever fortune smiled or his work in the East was ended (83-84).

In his plot, the *congai* Amarah belongs to Jack Murgatroyd, the former British officer who has "few morals, no honor, drank recklessly and was willing to turn an easy dollar whenever the opportunity presented itself" (82). Here again, Forbes accurately reflects reality when he describes a master-slave relationship that exists between Amarah and Murgatroyd:

> Amarah never criticized what [Murgatroyd] did. She was his
> *congai*. It was the duty of a *congai* to obey. The white man could do
> as he wished, could even leave her when he pleased; but so long as
> he had paid the marriage fee to the broker and did not treat her
> too badly [but Murgatroyd often abused Amarah], she must stay
> with him….For the native, marriage was binding upon her, but not
> upon her lord and master (83).

In the end, however, Forbes' novel rejects the idea of the temporary
union of a native woman and white foreigner; instead, he has his
American protagonist fall in love with Amarah, finally taking her as his
legal wife (216). While this happy Hollywood ending to an adventure
story may seem superficial, it is precisely the focus on, and rejection
of, the *congai* system that makes the book valuable to consider. In
addition to the moral objection to encongayement raised by *Where the
Cobra Sings*, Forbes adds a note of warning regarding the ultimate fate
of many *congai*s by stating that in the end they will slide downhill to
become nothing more than inmates in Saigon's brothels (264).

The fourth novel under consideration is Jean Hougron's 1950 French
novel, *Tu récolteras la tempête*, which was translated to English and
released as *Reap the Whirlwind* in 1953 when French control of
Indochina was approaching its bitter and violent end. Although
Hougron never uses the term *congai* in this novel, his work graphically
reflects the brutality of the Franco-Vietminh War and casts yet
another chilling light on the relationship between French men and
their *congaies*.

Hougron had extensive experience in Indochina. Born in Normandy
in 1923, he migrated to Southeast Asia in 1947 to work as "a truck
driver, tobacco planter, beer salesman, and teacher," and finally for Radio
France-Asie before leaving Vietnam in 1951 (Yeager 208). His other
novels about Indochina include *Blaze of the Sun* (1954), *Fugitive* (1955),
Ambush (1956), and *Barbarian's Country* (1961)

The main character in *Reap The Whirlwind* is Georges Lastin, a violent
man who slit his wife's throat in France in 1942 before fleeing to
Indochina. Hougron describes his protagonist by stating "there was a
certain ruthlessness in Lastin's nature" (140). Developing Lastin's violent
tendencies toward women in general, Hougron gives his novel a tone of
misogyny as demonstrated by Lastin's reflecting upon his French wife's

death. Feeling no remorse about killing her, he blurts out that the world now has "one bitch less" (269).

In Indochina Lastin takes on a *congai*, an Indochinese woman named Lee who has set up "housekeeping" with her French lover (107, 224). Reflecting on the temporary situation of cohabiting with a white man, Lee constantly worries about Lastin abandoning her, a concern that causes her to secretly lace his food with opium in order to dull his desire for other women. Discovering Lee's action, Lastin reacts with a terrible but predictable brutality. After becoming filled with "cold rage"

> …he went home and beat her and beat her, careless of the neighbors who had come out on their doorsteps. He had beaten [Lee] until she lay limp and motionless at his feet. The next day without a word of explanation he beat her again (140).

While on a personal level this act of physical violence is clearly one of spouse abuse, it is symbolically and historically reflective of the coercion that colonial French masters resorted to in order to extract submissive obedience from their *congaies* and subjects. *Reap the Whirlwind* fully exposes the coercive use of brute force that formed a foundation of interpersonal relationships within the colonial framework of Indochina, where one race and gender were subjugated to the will of another.

The final novel to consider is Graham Greene's *The Quiet American*. First published in England in 1955, many regard it as one of the most skillfully written novels about Vietnam in the English language, evidenced by the fact it remains in print nearly 60 years after its debut. Greene prepared his book after spending time in Vietnam from 1951-1955, as detailed in *The Life of Graham Greene,* the second volume of his authorized biography by Norman Sherry.

Greene, like Hervey, incorporated many of his own personal experiences and political views in his novel. Unlike Hervey, he does not use the term *congai*, yet the novel's plot, characters and thematic framework are similar. His story revolves around the relationship between Phuong, an attractive young Vietnamese girl, who is kept as a mistress by Thomas Fowler, an aging British journalist working in Saigon to escape his unhappy marriage in England. As in *Congai*, an American unexpectedly enters the scene—in this case an American covert agent named Alden Pyle—upsetting the colonial relationship at hand.

One of *The Quiet American* tenets is expressed in Fowler's nihilistic attitude that everything in life is temporary. In reverse of the *congai*'s fear that her Westerner lover would leave her, Fowler feared that Phuong would inevitably leave him. As he contemplates a trip to Phat Diem, where a vicious battle rages between French paratroopers and the Viet Minh, Fowler asks himself why he wants to go to such a risky place. Perhaps it is:

> A chance of death? Why should I want to die when Phuong slept beside me every night? But I knew the answer to that question. From childhood I have never believed in permanence, and yet I had longed for it. Always I was afraid of losing happiness. This month, next year, Phuong would leave me. If not next year, in three years. Death was the only absolute value in my world (42-43).

Drawing from his own life, Greene uses his superb literary ability to reflect on the temporary nature of relationships, in this case the exploitive relationship between an older white man and a younger brown woman: cohabitation without the prospect of permanence. Fowler, an aging, married journalist much like the author, is about to be called home by his employer, so he fears losing Phuong (37, 59, 69). His fear becomes tangible at Phat Diem where the American declares his love for Phuong to Fowler. As the two men discuss the fate of Fowler's mistress, Pyle proclaims his desire to take Phuong as his legal wife, acting in her best interests. This causes Fowler to explode, "You can have her interests. I only want her body. I want her in bed with me. I'd rather ruin her and sleep with her than, than…look after her damned interests" (60).

Corollary to the idea of Phuong's being Fowler's temporary sexual possession, Greene explores the long-term result of trysts between Western men and Asian woman: the metis. Upon meeting an attractive metis in an opium-house in the north, Fowler remarks, "Across the way a metis with long and lovely legs lay coiled after her smoke reading a glossy woman's paper…" (167). Soon a French military pilot observes of this woman, "There is a girl who was involved [in the war] by her parents—what is her future when this port falls? France is only half her home…" (169). Here Greene makes it very clear that mixed-race people are condemned by the actions of their French fathers and *congai* mothers to a life of hardship and rejection.

At the novel's conclusion, Greene neatly ties up the plot by having

Fowler's Catholic wife in England agree to a divorce, thereby allowing him to continue his comfortable existence in Vietnam, sharing a bed with the young Phuong. When Fowler shares this news of divorce with Phuong, she immediately assumes that Fowler will now be free to marry her. Pointedly, Fowler makes no comment on whether he would move to this level of commitment (209-10).

Applying imaginative literature to real situations in French Indochina is productive because it allows people to delve into what Sandra Taylor, professor emeritus at the University of Utah and Vietnam War scholar, calls "meta-history" or "secret history." Her idea is that the combination of reading history texts and fiction assists researchers in garnering a more complete and accurate understanding—"complementary perspectives"—of the American conflict in Vietnam (68, 70). The basis of this study of encongayement is that Dr. Taylor's strategy of intertwining fact and fiction is valid, and that a serious reader can extend fiction about Western men in French Indochina to the events culminating in the Franco-Viet Minh War.

These rare English-language novels about French Indochina published before 1955 have much to offer in understanding the war that the United States met there once it began to commit American resources. The five novels presented in this narrative amply reflect one negative aspect of French colonial control that grew into a long and bloody conflict.

As Anton Chekov once stated, "Fiction is called artistic because it draws on life as it actually is" (Greene, ed. Pratt 402).

Citations

Note: Page references in the text refer to the modern DatAsia Press editions of Harry Hervey's *King Cobra* (2013) and *Congai* (2014).

"Biography for Val Lewton." Web (www.IMDB.com).

Chivas-Baron. Cl. "Madame Hoa's Husbands." *Three Women of Annam*. Trans. Faith Chipperfield. New York: Frank-Maurice, Inc., 1925.

Chivas-Baron. Clotilde. *Stories and Legends of Annam* Trans. E .M. Smith-Dampier. London and New York: Andrew Melrose, Ltd., 1920.

Cooper, Nicola. *France in Indochina: Colonial Encounters*. Oxford: Berg, 2001.

Forbes, Cosmo [Val Lewton]. *Where the Cobra Sings*. New York: Macaulay Company, 1932.

Greene, Graham. *The Quiet American*. London: William Heinemann Ltd, 1955.

— *The Quiet American*. Ed. John Clark Pratt. New York: Penguin Books, 1996.

Hervey, Harry. *Congai*. New York: Cosmopolitan Book Corporation, 1927.

— *Congai-Mistress of Indochine*. Holmes Beach, FL: DatAsia Press, 2013.

—*King Cobra: An Autobiography of Travel in French Indo-China*. New York: Cosmopolitan Book Corporation, 1927.

—*King Cobra: Mekong Adventures in French Indochina*. Holmes Beach, FL: DatAsia Press, 2013.

Hougron, Jean. *Blaze of the Sun*. London: Hurst and Blackett, 1954.

— *Reap the Whirlwind*. Translated by Elizabeth Abbott. New York: Farrar, Straus and Young, 1953.

Lorcin, Patricia, Rev. of The French Imperial Nation-State: Negritude and Colonial Humanism between the Two World Wars, by Gary Wilder. H-France Forum. 1.3 (Summer 2006): n. page. Web. 27 Jan. 2011.

Marquis—Who's Who. *Who Was Who in America*. Chicago: The A.N. Marquis Company,1963.

Matsuda, Matt K. Empire of Love: Histories of France and the Pacific. Oxford: Oxford University Press, 2005.

Osborne, Milton. *Fear and Fascination in the Tropics: A Reader's Guide to French Fiction and Indochina.* Madison, Wisconsin: University of Wisconsin, 1986.

Proschan, Frank. "Eunuch Mandarins, Soldats Memzelles, Effeminate Boys and Graceless Women: French Colonial Constructions of Vietnamese Genders." *GLQ: A Journal of Lesbian and Gay Studies 8.4* (2002): 435-67. Web. 17 Jun. 2011.

Proschan, Frank. "Syphilis, Opiomania, and Pederasty: Colonial Construction of Vietnamese (and French) Social Diseases." *Journal of the History of Sexuality* 11.4 (2002): 610-36. Web. 17 Jun. 2010.

Robson, Kathryn and Jennifer Yee, eds. *France and 'Indochina': Cultural Representatives*. Lanham: Lexington Books, 2005. Print.

Scott, James George. 1885. *France and Tongking; a narrative of the campaign of 1884 and the occupation of Further India*. London: T.F. Unwin.

Sherry, Norman. *The Life of Graham Greene,* 2 vols. New York: Viking Penguin, 1995.

Stoler, A. L. 1989. "Making Empire Respectable: The Politics of Race and Sexual Morality in 20th-Century Colonial Cultures", *American Ethnologist*, Vol. 16, No. 4, (November), pp. 634–660.

Tai, Hue-Tam Ho. Passion, Betrayal, and Revolution in Colonial Saigon: The Memoirs of *Bao Luong*. Berkeley: University of California Press, 2010.

Taylor, Sandra. "The Vietnam War as Meta-History." *Peace and Change: A Journal of Peace Research* 11.2 (1986): 67-79.

"This Week's Openings." *New York Times*. New York Times, 25 Nov. 1928. ProQuest Historical Newspapers.Web. 3 Feb. 2011.

Yeager, Jack A. "Jean Hougron's Indochina: Fantasy and Disillusionment." *France and 'Indochina': Cultural Representations*, Eds. Kathryn Robson and Jennifer Yee. Lanham Lexington Books, 2005.

About the Author

Walter Jones is a librarian, and Head of the Western Americana Collection at the Marriott Library at the University of Utah. From 1967-1971 we served in the US Army as a Korean linguist, followed by service with the Utah Army National Guard from 1976-1992. His research expertise includes early 20th century French Indochina, the Franco-Viet Minh and American wars in Indochina, and the Korean War.

This article is based on Jones' 2011 essay, "Gender as Colonial Exploitation in French. Indochina: Concubines in Selected Pre-1965. Novels Published in or Translated to English", published by the *War, Literature & the Arts Journal*. In 2004, *Dialogue: A Journal of Mormon Thought*, featured his first article about several American soldiers in the Viet Nam War, "MacDonald and the Jungle Monk." In 2012, Natrona County Public Library Foundation Press published his book about a once-notorious red light district: *The Sand Bar: A History of Casper, Wyoming's Controversial Lowlands*. Jones has been a featured speaker on Southeast Asia at five Vietnam Symposiums at Texas Tech University.

La Marseillaise vs. La Petite Tonkinoise

The Sound of Music in Hervey's Indochina

By Kent Davis

Les peuples sont comme le rossignol de la chanson;
Ils chantent bien tant qu'ils ont le cœur gai.

People are like the singing nightingale.
They sing well so long as they have cheerful hearts.

Anatole France

What was the soundtrack of early 20th century French Indochina? Harry Hervey, one of the few American authors to write extensively about the region, detailed not only what he saw, but what he *heard*. In *Congai,* and its non-fiction sequel *King Cobra,* he made nearly one hundred references to music that captured the region's unique ambiance, emotions and political climate.

But Hervey went beyond merely noting musical tastes and popular songs; he used music to illustrate interactions of colonial forces and local populations. This paper examines many of Hervey's references, and provides translations for two contrasting songs that embody the plot of *Congai;* the tale of Thi-Linh, a young French-Annamite woman whose life and fate are torn between two cultures.

In the 21st century, our daily lives are filled with—often assaulted by—music. Home entertainment systems, computers, car radios, cell phones and portable devices can give us our own background music, wherever we go. More frequently, however, others choose our music for us. Radio and TV producers hype the next hits. Advertisers assail us with catchy jingles that stick in our heads, as stores pipe in melodies to make us spend more money. Bars, clubs and restaurants create "ambiance" with volume levels ranging from "atmospheric" to "jet engine." At the beach or park, groups of revelers blast us with boom-boxes, and even passing cars with stadium-powered sub-woofers share the beat, whether we like it or not. Of course almost all of today's music is pre-recorded, so the supply is inexhaustible.

But things were different in early 20th century Indochina. Yes, gramophones were already ubiquitous, and Hervey even took one with him on his trip up the Mekong. In *Congai,* Thi-Linh notes, "after dinner they played the gramophone" (149). Also interesting is her analogous reference relating the technology to French behavior during the days of World War I:

> Whenever there was a great French victory Saigon whirled like the disk of
> a gramophone; and, like a gramophone, it soon unwound, to await another
> turn of the handle. (*Congai*, 98)

In *King Cobra*, Hervey says "Often I would play my gramophone for them, and in turn they would play on the *khène* [a mouth organ with bamboo pipes of varying lengths], and then figures would multiply on the shore" (239). So, while pre-recorded music was available in mid-1920s Southeast Asia, it wasn't the most popular medium and most of the music Hervey described was still performed live. Music was key to social events where families, friends, neighbors, travelers and tribes joined together to drink, dance, sing and frequently make music, rather than listening passively. Hervey documented the sounds of Indochina not only in the cities, but in the jungles, where natives and colonists alike made their own music, as they have for countless generations all over the world.

Music of the Countryside

Traditional Indochinese music was mysterious to most Western ears. Witnessing dancers in northern Cambodia at Angkor Wat, Hervey writes "as we sat down there came a clashing of barbaric music. This music rose from an orchestra half hidden in the crowd on the other side of the terrace. Tom-toms, primitive viols, and a long instrument that resembled a xylophone." (*King Cobra*, 66)

Deeper in the jungle, Hervey found music an integral part of native life. His local guides sang as they paddled his pirogue. Stopping in Mekong villages, they spontaneously shared their music with locals, even joining *bouns*, local festivals, already in progress:

> Presently one of the coolies got a *khene* and commenced to play. The gay fellow undulated his hips, and laughing, swung into a dance. One by one silent figures appeared in the surrounding darkness, and after a while, their shyness gone, they clapped their hands. There were about twenty Laotians, men and women, gathered on the edge of the clearing. The men sang; the women laughed, clinging to their babies which straddled their hips. (*King Cobra*, 231)

While colonials in the cities fixated on the latest Western hits, Hervey portrayed Frenchmen living in the countryside with a deeper appreciation for local culture. Gilbert Filleau de Saint-Hilaire, Administrator of Ta-Keo, explained:

> "Now in the interior it is different. Particularly along the Mé-Kong. You will like the Laotians—they are more like your Hawaiians; I have been in Honolulu once. They have not yet been rewarded with the white man's uplifting altruism. Singing, dancing, music of the *khene*; a gay, simple people. Sometimes I think it is the influence of the river. A great river, *la Mere Mé-Kong*. (*King Cobra*, 136)

He then translated lyrics while continuing his philosophic analysis:

> "A Cambodian *chanson*," the Frenchman volunteered. "Haunting music. Like the river. The name of that song is 'Si Nuon.' It says, 'Forget this affair, O my friend. It is but a little flutter of my heart.' Or something like that. It is typical of the Cambodians. Nothing very profound or lasting with them. Not even their religion." (*King Cobra*, 137)

It seems that colonists and natives alike were intrigued by foreign sounds. With her first French lover, Justin Batteur

> Thi-Linh too found contentment in those evenings. She would sing the few little French songs her mother had taught her and also many Annamite songs. Justin seemed to prefer the latter. (*Congai*, 35)

One song that Hervey included in both books is "*Clair de Lune*," a poignant poem written by Paul Verlaine in 1869, that Claude Debussy later rendered into music. In *Congai*, Thi-Linh wistfully remembers her mother singing the melody to her as a child, and she herself sang it to her Annamite lover, Kim Khouan, at the hidden jungle pool where they secretly met. In *King Cobra*, the *délégué* of Paksane sang the song during a night of revelry in his home on the banks of the Mekong. Even in that remote place, Western melodies could appear at any moment, as Hervey described upon his arrival in Laos:

> Instead of riding to the residence, we walked along the Mé-Kong, the charmingly Parisian aide and I. He said he knew an American song, and commenced to hum "Oh, You Beautiful Doll!" (*King Cobra*, 211)

Published in 1911, the ragtime love song was apparently still popular 14 years later and half-a-world away. Through music, Western influence penetrated deeply into the soul of Indochina.

Paris of the East

The colonial goal was to make Indochina, particularly the cities, into a facsimile of France. In the streets, shops, restaurants and buildings most frequented by colonists, French style and culture superseded native traditions entirely. In addition to food, drink, dress, laws, language and etiquette, this rule applied to entertainment.

Clearly, France was succeeding in its mission. When Hervey strolled the Rue Catinat in 1925 he heard one orchestra playing "Tea for Two," and later "I Want to Be Happy"; both songs recent hits from the play *No, No, Nanette* that opened in New York, London and Chicago in that same year.

Hervey opens *Congai* "at the Continental in Saigon, where Frenchmen listening to the latest music from Paris are able to forget for a moment that sun-weary land of exile." Later at the same venue, "the orchestra was jazzing 'Chanson Indoue'" (*King Cobra*, 34), and Hervey reports that orchestras played Western music non-stop from late afternoon well into the evenings. As an orchestra played in Saigon he observed local reactions as

> "…other natives, gathered in groups across the street by the opera-house, watched the people at the tables with an expression of perplexity. I could not help wondering what they thought, if they thought at all; whether they felt resentment or merely animal curiosity. (*King Cobra*, 8)

He also noted Cambodian reactions:

> When I returned to the hotel, the weekly afternoon *dansant* was at its languid height, and the rhythm of a French jazz orchestra stumbled out into

> the darkness where bewildered natives had paused to listen; while inside,
> the socially eligible of Pnom Penh were perspiring and simulating what
> they chose to call *la vie parisienne*. (*King Cobra*, 112)

While some natives may have been "bewildered"—just as Westerners were
bewildered by Asian ways—others were inspired to follow the French example, as
Hervey illustrates with Thi-Linh's character in *Congai*. Already imbued with French
blood from her long-vanished father, Thi-Linh's attraction began in her village. There,
her mother sang French songs to her, as the Catholic Church taught her its religioun
and the French language. When she finally moved to the now-French city of Saigon,
she saw a lifestyle that she was determined to embrace:

> On the Rue Catinat also were the main cafés.... These cafés! Whenever
> Thi-Linh passed them they started a little throbbing in her throat. Officers
> and women sat at marble-topped tables in an atmosphere electric with
> voices. In the later afternoon, orchestras made French music; and sometimes
> the people danced. (*Congai*, 68)

As Thi-Linh moved on to her second French lover, Captain Paul Lehrisson, music
and its emotional implications remained central to her life:

> There was a piano in the house. He swore at it and the climate every
> time he touched it. But Thi-Linh, who enjoyed the metallic vibrance of
> Annamite orchestras, thought its music beautiful. Weeks would pass when
> he did not play; then he would sit down, browse over the discolored keys
> and break into music that pounded the air into fury. When Paul played, all
> that sultry discontent seemed to rush out of his fingers into the piano and
> leave him exhausted but happy. (*Congai*, 80)

Gradually, the siren call of French culture, and the romance it represented, became as
irresistible as the music:

> "...among them that young Scandinavian who had taken her to the *dansant*
> at the Continental.... Her first *dansant* ...music pouring over her, the warm
> drench of lights...." (*Congai*, 129)

Hervey went on to single out the formal appreciation of music, regardless of its
quality, as a hallmark of Western culture in Saigon:

> Here stands the municipal opera-house, evidence of France's determination
> to be thoroughly cultured even though thousands of miles away from
> Paris; and here, at irregular intervals disreputable troupes of singers torture
> Puccini and Verdi for the benefit of bored colonial audiences....
> (*King Cobra*, 34)

Inevitably, the author added the opera to Thi-Lihn's lifestyle when she became
mistress to the wealthy, but aging, Monsieur Urbain Chauvet. Through her, Hervey
again criticized the reality he saw, but his protagonist still couldn't help being swept
up in the emotion of Western sounds:

> And when the opera came to Saigon she had a box. Most of the Frenchmen
> said the troupe sang very badly, but she observed that in spite of that they

never missed a performance. One did not go to the opera to hear music, she learned, at least not in Saigon; one went because the socially eligible would be there. Nevertheless, she enjoyed the singing. One performance, particularly, aroused her tremendously. It was about a Spanish dancer. Castanets shrilled through it, and the music welled up like blood, making hot revelry in her brain. (*Congai*, 132)

Music of Intoxication, Violence and War

Many Frenchmen were intoxicated by their colonial experiment; both figuratively, by their dominance over docile natives, and literally, by the tobacco, alcohol and opium that was part of everyday life. Hervey illustrated this with music, ranging from the camaraderie of colonists gathering to drink and sing, to the more ominous implications of music as a symbol of social, military and political agendas.

As soon as he arrived in Saigon, Hervey noted that "Until long after midnight the tables are occupied, and quite frequently, when a group of officers drifts in, lusty and ribald songs send their echoes out over the river." (*King Cobra*, 23) In his novel, Thi-Linh observes the same scene through Asian eyes:

> Sometimes they were very ribald, these officers. Usually that was when a number gathered about a table in the Hotel de la Rotonde, and shouted mad songs over glasses that were filled and refilled. The French were very noisy about their singing, Thi-Linh thought. (*Congai*, 85)

In the following pages, however, Hervey wove music into his plot to convey the oppression and violence he saw as the basis for the colonial administration of these Asian peoples.

> A serried panorama of khaki, creased with the glint of rifles, formed a background for sabers that suddenly became whirring flames; and white-mustached generals pinned decorations upon officers and kissed them. Always the brazen flood of "La Marseillaise" drenched those scenes. (Congai 85)

Through Thi-Linh's eyes, he described the colony's mood during World War I, when so many Annamese, Cambodian and Laotian men were recruited to travel to Europe to fight, and often die, for the distant land that "adopted" them:

> And now Saigon moved to a military cadence that mounted like savage drums.

> France at war—France at war. Words spun like knives in the hands of experts. So much talk about France, the Mother, and Indo-China, her adopted child. It was as if the engraving on the piaster notes had come to life: France, the Protectress, embodied in a big-jointed woman wearing a cap, with her arms affectionately about an Annamite girl and boy. (*Congai*, 88)

As the war became part of life in Saigon, Thi-Linh witnessed military parades, changes in behavior, and the underlying violence that France had brought into their world. Hervey then dramatically interspersed lyrics from the French national anthem with Thi-Linh's thoughts, building toward a dramatic final statement:

> *"Allons, enfants de la patrie… .*Brazen flood of "La Marseillaise" drenching the Rue Catinat. (*Congai*, 89)

> Now those officers with black braid and gold on their collars hurried about the government buildings. At night when they rode in rickshaws they had a tired, nervous air; and when they gathered around the tables in the hotels their songs clashed like sabers. (*Congai*, 89)

Like America's "Star Spangled Banner," "La Marseillaise" is a song born of war, inspired by the needs of war. Music is a powerful tool that governments and military organizations use to attract attention, to intimidate, to inspire and, as shown here, even to convince people to sacrifice their lives for nationalistic causes that may not even be their own.

Through Thi-Linh's eyes, Harry Hervey saw the senselessness of it all quite clearly. Sadly, violence did not end in Southeast Asia with this war. Or World War II, the French battles that followed, or the American War in Vietnam that followed that.

It is easy to read history, or even set it to music, but it is much harder to learn from our mistakes.

> Civilization is spinning on a flame. Forget those jests of white men who called you niggers. Forget their bastards who ferment your purity! It is the way of them, to joke like that.

> This Civilization is yours! It has given you Government and God! So up, Annamites! Tremble with hate for the enemies of France! Fill your bellies with the wine of it! Let your thighs run limp with the venom of it!

> They will rape your women, they will make armies of your men, they will rob you of your lands! The tablets of your Ancestors and the crests of France are one!

> Listen to the drums! Beating—beating. Let them fill your veins! Let them swell to the rupture of drums! Let them burst in the splendor of death for freedom! Sing, Annamites, sing! …Red music of marching men. Sing, brothers, sing! All together now, in one voice:

> *"Aux armes, citoyens! Formes vos bataillons! Marchons, marchons!"*

> Words like knives in the hands of experts. Thi-Linh felt them thud and quiver about her. (*Congai*, 90)

La Marseillaise

Painted by Eugène Delacroix in 1830, *La Liberté guidant le peuple* captures the spirit of "La Marseillaise" while featuring Liberty, the female symbol of France.

The French Assemblée Nationale offers this succinct history of "La Marseillaise":

> "Mr de Lisle, write [sic] for us a song that will rally our soldiers from all over to defend their homeland that is under threat and you will have won the nation," proposed Dietrich, the Mayor of Strasbourg on the evening April 25th 1792, to one of his guests, Rouget de Lisle. The painter Isidore Pils (1813-1875) immortalized the moment. It was a tumultuous period in history : five days after France's declaration of war on Austria and Prussia the French needed a marching song that could galvanize the troops of the Rhine Army. As a result, the highly successful French national anthem was born.
> (www.assemblee-nationale.fr)

Additional details about the composer, and a photo of the 1849 painting by Isidore Pils, are available on the site. The following French language lyrics are from the official site of the French Presidency (www.elysee.fr/la-presidence/la-marseillaise-de-rouget-de-lisle/) with the English lyrics adapted from Wikipedia.

La Marseillaise

Allons enfants de la Patrie,	Arise, children of the Fatherland,
Le jour de gloire est arrivé !	The day of glory has arrived!
Contre nous de la tyrannie,	Against us, tyranny's
L'étendard sanglant est levé, *(bis)*	Bloody banner is raised, *(repeat)*
Entendez-vous dans les campagnes	Do you hear, in the countryside,
Mugir ces féroces soldats ?	The roar of those ferocious soldiers?
Ils viennent jusque dans vos bras	They're coming right into your arms
Égorger vos fils et vos compagnes !	To slaughter your sons, your companions!

Aux armes, citoyens, — *To arms, citizens,*
Formez vos bataillons, — *Form your battalions,*
Marchons, marchons ! — *Let's march, let's march!*
Qu'un sang impur — *That a tainted blood*
Abreuve nos sillons ! — *Water our furrows!*

Que veut cette horde d'esclaves,	What does this horde of slaves,
De traîtres, de rois conjurés ?	Traitors and conspiring kings want?
Pour qui ces ignobles entraves,	For whom are these vile chains,
Ces fers dès longtemps préparés ? *(bis)*	These long-prepared irons? *(repeat)*
Français, pour nous, ah ! quel outrage	Frenchmen, for us, ah! What outrage
Quels transports il doit exciter !	What fury it must arouse!
C'est nous qu'on ose méditer	It is us they dare plan
De rendre à l'antique esclavage !	To return to the old slavery!
Aux armes, citoyens...	*To arms, citizens...*

Quoi ! des cohortes étrangères	What! Foreign cohorts
Feraient la loi dans nos foyers !	Would make the law in our homes!
Quoi ! Ces phalanges mercenaires	What! These mercenary phalanxes
Terrasseraient nos fiers guerriers ! *(bis)*	Would strike down our proud warriors! *(repeat)*
Grand Dieu ! Par des mains enchaînées	Great God ! By chained hands
Nos fronts sous le joug se ploieraient	Our brows would yield under the yoke
De vils despotes deviendraient	The Vile despots would become
Les maîtres de nos destinées !	The masters of our destinies!
Aux armes, citoyens...	*To arms, citizens...*

Tremblez, tyrans et vous perfides	Tremble, tyrants and you traitors
L'opprobre de tous les partis,	The shame of all parties,
Tremblez ! vos projets parricides	Tremble! Your parricidal schemes

Vont enfin recevoir leurs prix ! *(bis)*
Tout est soldat pour vous combattre,
S'ils tombent, nos jeunes héros,
La terre en produit de nouveaux,
Contre vous tout prêts à se battre !
Aux armes, citoyens...

Français, en guerriers magnanimes,
Portez ou retenez vos coups !
Épargnez ces tristes victimes,
À regret s'armant contre nous. *(bis)*
Mais ces despotes sanguinaires,
Mais ces complices de Bouillé,
Tous ces tigres qui, sans pitié,
Déchirent le sein de leur mère !
Aux armes, citoyens...

Amour sacré de la Patrie,
Conduis, soutiens nos bras vengeurs
Liberté, Liberté chérie,
Combats avec tes défenseurs ! *(bis)*
Sous nos drapeaux que la victoire
Accoure à tes mâles accents,
Que tes ennemis expirants
Voient ton triomphe et notre gloire !
Aux armes, citoyens...

(Couplet des enfants)
Nous entrerons dans la carrière
Quand nos aînés n'y seront plus,
Nous y trouverons leur poussière
Et la trace de leurs vertus *(bis)*
Bien moins jaloux de leur survivre
Que de partager leur cercueil,
Nous aurons le sublime orgueil
De les venger ou de les suivre
Aux armes, citoyens...

Will finally receive their reward! *(repeat)*
Everyone is a soldier to combat you
If they fall, our young heroes,
The earth will produce new ones,
Ready to fight against you!
To arms, citizens...

Frenchmen, as magnanimous warriors,
Bear or hold back your blows!
Spare those sorry victims,
Who regretfully bear arms against us. *(repeat)*
But (not) these bloodthirsty despots,
But (not) these accomplices of Bouillé,
All these tigers who, mercilessly,
Rip their mother's breast!
To arms, citizens...

Sacred love of the Homeland,
Lead, support our avenging arms
Liberty, cherished Liberty,
Fight with thy defenders! *(repeat)*
Under our flags, shall victory
Hurry to thy manly accents,
That thy expiring enemies,
See thy triumph and our glory!
To arms, citizens...

(Children's Verse)
We shall enter the (military) career
When our elders are no longer there,
There we shall find their dust
And the trace of their virtues *(repeat)*
Much less jealous to survive them
Than to share their coffins,
We shall have the sublime pride
Of avenging or following them
To arms, citizens...

✧ ✧ ✧

La Petite Tonkinoise

Sheet music for Polin's original 1906 presentation appears above left. In 1907, the song debuted in the US with entirely different English lyrics by James O'Dea.

Although Hervey did not mention hearing this song in Indochina, its popularity in France makes it a relevant artistic portrayal of the transient "land, love, leave" nature of most French relationships with Indochinese women. In 1905, Georges Villard penned a poem about the travels of a French sailor called "Le Navigatore" ("The Navigator"). Vincent Scotto, a young Marseilles composer set the poem to music, then offered the tune to Marsalès Pierre-Paul, a popular actor known for portraying a comic soldier named Polin. The actor liked the music, but not the words. He introduced Scotto to his friend Henri Christiné and together they spiced up the lyrics by describing a typical romance of French Indochina.

"Polin" added the song to his comedy revue in 1906. It soon became a hit that many other singers covered, including Maurice Chevalier. In 1907, a female version of the French lyrics was added so women, like the French star Mistinguett, could sing the song in the first person. That version achieved lasting success when American-born singer Josephine Baker made it her own in 1930.

The lyrics have, not surprisingly, been a topic of academic criticism in recent years. In her 2008 doctoral dissertation, *Putain de colonie! Anticolonialisme et modernisme dans la littérature du voyage en Indochine (1919-1939)*, Dr. Emanuelle Radar provides the most detailed analysis. Other researchers who comment are Maryse Bray and Agnes Catalyud, Emmanuel Mansutti and Alain Ruscio. The French language lyrics below are from multiple sources with the English translation original to this paper.

La petite tonkinoise

Pour qu'j'finisse
Mon service
Au Tonkin je suis parti
Ah! Quel beau pays mesdames
C'est l'paradis des p'tites femmes
Ell's sont belles
Et fidèles
Et j'sui dev'nu l'chéri
D'un' p'tit' femm' du pays
Qui s'appell' Mélaoli

Refrain:
Je suis gobé d'un' petite
C'est une Anna, c'est une Anna, une Annamite
Elle est vive elle est charmante
C'est comm' un z'oiseau qui chante
J'l'appell' ma p'tit bourgeoise
Ma Tonkiki, ma Tonkiki, ma Tonkinoise
Y'en a d'autr's qui m'font les doux yeux
Mais c'est ell' que j'aim' le mieux.

L'soir on cause
Des tas d'choses
Avant de se mettre au pieu
J'apprends la géographie
D'la Chine et d'la Manchourie
Les frontières
Les rivières
Le fleuv Jaun' et le fleuv' Bleu
Y'a mêm' l'Amour, c'est curieux
Qu'arros' l'Empir' du Milieu

Refrain
Très gentille
C'est la fille
D'un mandarin très fameux

To complete
My tour of duty
For Tonkin I set out
Ah! What a lovely land, my ladies
It's a paradise of tiny gals
They're pretty
And faithful
And I became the sweetheart
Of one little country girl
Whose name was Melaoli

Refrain
I'm smitten by a little lady
She's an Anna, she's an Anna, an Annamite
She's vivacious and charming,
She's like a songbird who sings
I call her my little missus,
My Tonkiki, my Tonkiki, my Tonkinoise.
Others bat their eyes at me,
But it's her I love the most.

When evening falls we chew the fat
About all kinds of things.
Before I go to bed
I give lessons of geography
Of China and Manchuria
The borders
The rivers
Like the Yellow and the Blue
Even the Love, oddly enough,
Flows through the Middle Kingdom

Refrain
Sweet as can be,
She's the daughter
Of a famous mandarin

C'est pour ça qu'sur sa poitrine
Elle a deux p'tites mandarines
Peu gourmandes
Ell' ne d'mande'
Quand nous mangeons tous les deux
Qu'une banane c'est peu coûteux
Moi j'y en donne autant qu'elle veux

Refrain
Mais tout passe
Et tout casse
En France je dus rentrer
J'avais l'cœur plein de tristesse
L'âme en peine
Ma p'tite reine
Était v'nue m'accompagner
Mais avant d'nous séparer
Je lui dis dans un baiser

Ne pleur' pas si je te quitte
Petite Anna, p'tite Anna, p'tite Annamite
Tu m'as donné ta jeunesse
Ton amour et tes caresses
T'étais ma p'tite bourgeoise
Ma Tonkiki, ma Tonkiki, ma Tonkinoise
Dans mon cœur j'garderai toujours
Le souv'nir de nos amours.

Hence, upon her chest
She has a pair of little mandarins
She's not greedy
She doesn't ask for much,
When we're eating together,
She asks only for a banana—it's not costly
So I give her all she wants

Refrain
But all things pass
And all things fall apart
To France I must return
I have a heart full of sadness
A heavy soul
My little queen
Came to see me off
But before we parted ways
I said to her with a kiss

Don't cry if I leave you
Little Anna, l'il Anna, l'il Annamite
You gave me your youth
Your love and caresses
You were my little missus
My Tonkiki, my Tonkiki, my Tonkinoise
In my heart I'll forever keep
The memory of our love.

Two Quiet Americans:
Alden Pyle and Harry Hervey

By Kent Davis

A journalist, most especially an Anglo-American travel writer, will run the risk of disappointing his editor if he visits Saigon and leaves out any reference to quiet Americans....

—Christopher Hitchens
"Graham Greene: I'll be Damned,"The Atlantic, March 2005.

In 1951 English novelist Graham Greene, then 46 years old, made his first visit to French Indochina. Four years later he published *The Quiet American*, a complex tale of political and romantic intrigue set in that exotic locale. With the onset of America's war in Southeast Asia, thousands of books on the topic would follow, but *The Quiet American* has remained among the essential works about twentieth-century Vietnam.

Worldcat.org, the most comprehensive online record of library holdings, lists nearly 250 entries related to Greene's novel, including unique editions, translations, study guides, critiques, commentaries and dissertations—this in addition to the 285 books and dissertations it lists under "'Graham Greene' biography." Meanwhile, a Google search generates half a million hits for "*The Quiet American*," and nearly a million for Greene himself.

Despite this preponderance of analysis, one thing seems to have eluded discovery: 28 years *before* Greene released *The Quiet American,* a young, now obscure, American author had *already* published a similar novel about French Indochina. His 1927 work also featured a European in Saigon keeping a young Asian woman as his mistress. It too made cogent observations about politics, colonialism, violence, war, discrimination, sexuality, nationalism and regional change. It too included the unexpected, violent death of a key character, a death that resulted directly from the protagonist's actions. And this earlier work also introduced an intelligent, personable French police detective who led the investigation...and ultimately opted to ignore the protagonist's involvement in the crime.

These and dozens of other similarities beg the question: Are such parallels in plot, characters and content to be expected in two novels set in the same region in nearly the same era? Perhaps, but one conspicuous coincidence stands out from the others. Among the French, English and Asian characters that one expects to find in 1927 Saigon, our young author inserted an unusual antagonist: a young, virile, rather naïve American—and it is the *American* who upsets, in every sense, the comfortable, established milieu of colonial life. He offered the young mistress a chance for true love, as he simultaneously embodied and expounded the American ideals of democracy, capitalism and freedom which, in that time and place, were both rocking the boat and sweeping the world.

It all seemed more than coincidental.

Graham Greene's Quiet American — Alden Pyle

Greene tells his 1955 tale from the perspective of a middle-aged, self-absorbed British reporter named Fowler who, in fleeing an unhappy marriage in England, has repaired to what is for him a far more comfortable corner of the world. In Vietnam Fowler dispassionately reports on the violent clashes of various factions vying for independence from France and control of the country. In Saigon he finds solace and sensual pleasure in the arms of a young Vietnamese woman, whose fate concerns him as little as the fate of Vietnam itself. He uses her youth for his transient carnal satisfaction, knowing he cannot offer her marriage, children or a stable future.

Greene was well aware of local politics. Indeed, while writing his novel from 1951 to 1954 he reportedly engaged in espionage there for the British government. As French colonial rule weakened, Vietnam became increasingly unstable, with multiple forces competing for influence. Expanding its role as a world power, America began stepping in to the previously French affair. It would thus seem rather shrewd of Greene to have inserted an idealistic young American into his plot. Alden Pyle is sent to Vietnam to promote vague— and arguably unrealistic—economic and political agendas on behalf of the US government. When he first meets this naïve new arrival Fowler's first instinct is to protect him, but he senses the risks. "Innocence," he says in his first-person narration, "always calls mutely for protection when we would be so much wiser to guard ourselves against it: innocence is like a dumb leper who has lost his bell, wandering the world, meaning no harm."

Greene came under fire for characterizing American policies as clumsy, or even reckless, but his novel is perhaps more profitably understood as a cautionary tale than as a mere critique of America. His American, Pyle, does indeed upset political—not to mention romantic — relationships in the plot. People die from his "innocent" meddling, and one fatality is Alden Pyle himself, thereafter becoming the eponymous "quiet American" of the book's title. Soon, America would also upset all relationships in the region and a great many Americans would die in Southeast Asia, along with a great part of America's idealism. There is prescience in Greene's novel.

But, then again, not every American in the Far East was an Alden Pyle.

Two American Authors in French Indochina

French writers naturally dominated local literature, but two American writers made substantive literary contributions. The first was Titanic survivor Helen Churchill Candee, who traveled to Southeast Asia in 1922–23 at the age of 64. Her resulting book, *Angkor the Magnificent*,[1] remains one of the most eloquent and evocative English language accounts of Cambodia and the Khmer civilization ever written.

As Candee was publishing her book another American, Harry Hervey, was just setting out for Saigon. Unlike the aging Candee, Hervey was a precocious 24-year-old writer who creatively contrived an unlikely expedition to seek an ancient Khmer temple lost in the jungle. Already recognized as an author and Orientalist, Hervey sold his idea to *McCall's* magazine and secured the funding for his adventure.

Today Hervey and his works are even more obscure than the lost temple he sought to find, but in the first half of the twentieth century his dramatic tales of mystery, scandal and romance captivated millions of Americans, and garnered praise from critics of literature, stage and screen. As the '20s got roaring, pulp fiction magazines featured Hervey's gritty, graphic short stories as he pioneered the noir fiction genre. Five of his early books dealt with Asian adventure travel, fictional and non-fictional, and he established a reputation as an expert on the mysterious Far East.

After touring French Indochina in 1925 he released two of his most successful titles: *King Cobra*, a first-person account of the region and its people, and *Congai*, a provocative novel about the political, social and romantic implications of France's colonial venture. He and his partner, Carleton Hildreth, even scripted *Congai* into a successful Broadway play that starred renowned stage actress Helen Mencken, Humphrey Bogart's first wife. That drew Hollywood's attention, and soon Hervey's ideas, books and screenplays were being turned into films with the likes of Marlene Dietrich, Dorothy Lamour, Bob Hope, Bing Crosby and Anthony Quinn in the leading roles. In addition to his film and magazine work, Hervey published twelve books of fiction and non-fiction in his lifetime.

---

1 In 2008, DatAsia Press published an expanded edition of *Angkor the Magnificent*, including the first published biography of the author [www.AngkorSecrets.com].

By 1951, however, Hervey's fame, finances and health had faded. That summer he traveled to New York City to seek treatment for throat cancer. After a series of gruesome and painful surgeries he lost his voice and finally his life. He died on August 12 of that year, at age 50. Days later, he was laid to rest in Savannah's Bonaventure cemetery with only a handful of brief obituaries marking his passing. But as one author faded away another made his first visit to Vietnam, and a more famous "quiet American" would soon appear.

The Lure of Far Eastern Literature

In fact, my deepest astonishment in reading *Congai* came with seeing how much it anticipates perhaps the greatest and most evergreen foreign novel about modern Vietnam, *The Quiet American*, by Graham Greene—a book that urchins outside the Metropole Hotel in Hanoi still tout to visitors (in pirated editions), and the one that every wise newcomer to the country still consults.

—Pico Iyer (foreword to *Congai*, 2014 edition).

I share Pico's admiration for Greene's literary accomplishment. From the moment I arrived in Bangkok in 1990, until my residency ended in 1995, I felt at home with the people, culture, food, climate and lifestyle. Asia was engaging, dynamic, challenging, frustrating, mystifying and enlightening… often all on the same day. *Every* day was like an adventure I had waited my whole life to have. Reading the experiences of those who preceded me was a natural response and I encountered Graham Greene's *The Quiet American* early in my stay. His prose felt so close to my soul that it seemed not to originate from the page, but from some wellspring within. This impression has only grown stronger the half dozen times I have read it since. I knew exactly what Fowler was talking about. (So, I discovered, did many others like Pico Iyer, who describes Greene's spell in *The Man Inside My Head*.)

Like Fowler, I too was called home by a job, but where he found a way to stay in the Far East, I returned. It was only after I left that I realized the extent of my fascination with Asia.

Back in the West, I began reading and collecting antique books about the region, the vast majority of which were written by Europeans. I first consulted the English, who wrote about Siam and Burma (now Thailand and Myanmar) as they looked beyond colonial India, the "jewel in the British crown." Following my first visit to Angkor in 2005, my attention shifted to Khmer history, which had primarily been the domain of French scholars for the previous 150 years. By crossing Thailand's southern border into Cambodia, I had also entered what was once French Indochina.

While the English had *ruled* their colonies (with quintessentially stiff upper lips) the French had *interacted*, and thus their written accounts of Cambodia, Vietnam and Laos were often far more captivating. French authors had steeped themselves in local art, culture and history, assimilating them as their own. Inevitably, many succumbed to the charms of local women and told of their experiences. As Pico Iyer observes in his foreword to *Congai,* "by day, after all, many Westerners imagined they were ruling the people they were in charge of; by night, in all kinds of ways, the empire struck back."

Harry Hervey's 1927 travelogue of Indochina, *King Cobra,* was one of my first acquisitions from the antiquaries. At any given time there are usually a dozen copies for sale on the used book market, and Worldcat.org lists 114 libraries worldwide that retain copies. The front matter of *King Cobra* listed Hervey's prior works, including his novel *Congai.* Although more difficult to find, I soon acquired a copy; the story it told was totally unexpected.

Over the previous five years my work had increasingly focused on French authors in Indochina, including George Groslier, Roland Meyer, Makhali-Phal, Guillaume Monod, André Joyeux, Pierre Rey, Pierre Loti, Henry Casseville, Jean d'Estray and Jean d'Esme. Hervey mentioned a few French works in *King Cobra* but here, in the pages of *Congai,* was a 24-year-old Harry Hervey winking at me as he proved his familiarity with the very authors and genre I'd been working so hard to understand. (A separate appendix article, "Francophilia: Harry Hervey's Homage to French Authors," details his references.)

I was struck by the depth of *Congai's* plot, by the accuracy of its local details, and especially by the veracity of its female protagonist, a Eurasian girl named Thi-Linh. Hervey's observations on politics, colonialism, militarism, sexuality, discrimination and human nature in French Indochina were astute. In many ways *Congai* expressed more profound truths than *King Cobra.* But the real shock was seeing so many similarities between this book and one of my favorite books about Southeast Asia: *The Quiet American.* I typed up some comparisons on Nov. 2, 2011, and then forgot about them for nearly two years.

During that time I worked on expanded new editions of *King Cobra* and *Congai,* and began exchanging frequent emails with Harlan Greene, senior archivist at the College of Charleston, who was preparing a comprehensive biography of Hervey. Our publishing projects being so complementary, we collaborated to expand our understanding of Hervey's works and life. As the new Indochina editions took shape we agreed that getting a prominent author to write the forewords would help restore recognition for Hervey's forgotten but significant literary talents. A number of names came up, but it was during a conversation with Walter Jones, a librarian at the University of Utah, that I realized who the perfect person for the job was: essayist and travel pundit Pico Iyer. On April 29 I wrote to Iyer, explaining the situation and inviting his involvement:

> You and Harry have something quite extraordinary in common: the ability to immerse yourselves in exotic locales and to witness—and ultimately express—subtleties of culture that lead others to a more profound emotional and intellectual understanding. That is your gift and that was his….
>
> An academic view from the Southeast Asian perspective would be too dry and limited. A literary critic would miss the importance of his American glimpse of Asian culture and sexuality, as well as his views of the colonial system.
>
> It was when I came across an article about your foreword to an anniversary edition of your namesake book *Siddhartha* that the light bulb went off….

Pico immediately expressed interest—and surprise that he had never heard of Hervey or his works—and agreed to write the forewords. The first step was for him to read the books, so I sent him my original copies of *King Cobra* and *Congai*. We exchanged numerous emails over the following weeks, as Pico asked myriad questions while crafting the two essays. By July 3 he had begun his work on the *Congai* paper, and wrote:

> And in truth I see this as one of the earliest and most interesting examples of a genre that has become huge, as you know: I think we mentioned how almost every contemporary novel in any bookstore in Bangkok could more or less be called *Congai*, and has a heroine strikingly similar to our own. Indeed, I think Graham Greene may have drawn on Harry for his masterful *Quiet American*, not only my favorite novel in the world but also the most enduring and revered foreigner novel ever written on Vietnam, I suspect.

It was rewarding to hear an expert compare Hervey's book to one I also considered a masterpiece on Asian life, but it also triggered a memory. I ran to find my long-forgotten notes from 2011 that made a similar observation.

In 1955, Graham Greene was at the peak of his literary career, and *The Quiet American* is almost universally lauded as one of the definitive social and political statements on twentieth-century Vietnam. To compare it with the work of a young, unknown author seemed presumptuous, yet the facts were compelling. More than 24 years before Greene ever set foot in Indochina, Harry Hervey had already spun a hauntingly familiar tale from similar thread.

Seeking Answers in Greeneland

> Greeneland is real. No European writer since Conrad has put the hot, poor
> and foully governed places of the earth on paper as vividly as Greene.
>
> —John Spurling
> *Graham Greene,* London and New York: Methuen, 1983, p. 74.

Could an exotic place and culture inspire two writers to craft strikingly similar
stories decades apart? Do great literary minds think alike? To find out I
clearly needed to learn more about Graham Greene.

As already noted, Greene's works and life have generated a huge number
of publications. I read news articles, commentaries, critiques and obituaries
on Greene, and acquired two major biographies: *The Life of Graham Greene:
1939–1955*, the second volume of Norman Sherry's authorized and expansive
biographical trilogy; and *Graham Greene: The Enemy Within*, a probing, candid
and clearly unauthorized biography by Michael Shelden. Both provided
valuable background information, but becoming a Greene expert overnight
was too ambitious a goal; I decided that the best course of action was to
consult prominent Greene scholars about the similarities between Hervey's
and Greene's novels.

I began by drafting a cordial letter of inquiry to recent speakers at the annual
Graham Greene festival (www.grahamgreenefestival.org). For those who
responded, I sent this detailed description of my situation, but did not name
Hervey or mention any dates of publication:

DATASIA PRESS NEW BOOK MANUSCRIPT OVERVIEW

A manuscript I am now preparing for publication struck me due to its
similarities to Graham Greene's book, *The Quiet American.*

The question I'm trying to answer is whether or not this is merely
coincidence? My problem is that both authors are dead so approaching
literary scholars like you is my most viable approach.

It is important to state that this new book does not directly mirror Greene's
prose or word choices in any way (my concern was such that I ran analysis
software as well as doing my own text comparisons). Nor does it mention
or credit Greene's work in any way. Nor can I find any connection between
Mr. Greene and the author (but they have things in common).

This book will be presented as a unique, independent and original literary
work, but I am curious about a possible connection between the works that
I have missed.

The list below outlines 20 key elements of plot, settings, characters, literary techniques and symbolic content that appear in this book. Every single one of these items also appears in *The Quiet American.*

I will be grateful for your view of this matter and any insights you can offer. Thank you for considering my request for your help.

1. The story is set in Vietnam under French colonial rule.

2. The author presents the story from the protagonist's viewpoint.

3. In fact, the author has so much in common with his protagonist that he weaves real events, experiences and issues from his own life into the plot.

4. The plot revolves around an older European man keeping a much younger Asian girl as a mistress for his personal comfort.

5. Most of the action is set in Saigon and the suburb of Cholon. Side trips into the Vietnamese countryside are used for key dramatic scenes. In Saigon, a number of significant scenes take place at the Continental café. A particular opium den on Rue d'Ormay is mentioned. The mistress frequently goes to the cinema and dance-halls.

6. Frequent opium use by colonial residents (and key characters) to endure their lives in Asia is an important plot element. Specifically, opium is described as a technique Vietnamese mistresses use to control their Western lovers.

7. French culture and language are central to the theme, e.g. specific mention of *La Marseillaise,* quotes from a Baudelaire poem, French books, etc.

8. The division between the lifestyles of colonials and natives is emphasized. The demeaning attitudes and behaviors the colonial ruling class exhibits towards the native population are central to the story.

9. Although set in a Buddhist land, Catholicism has a major influence on the plot, as well as the lives and viewpoints of primary characters.

10. Dream sequences of the protagonist are used for dramatic plot effects.

11. The phoenix bird, reborn from its own ashes, prominently appears as an icon of Vietnam and symbol of the resiliency and struggle for freedom by the female protagonist and her compatriots. [NOTE: In *The Quiet American,* Greene only mentions the phoenix once on his first page. However, he gave his female protagonist the name Phuong (which he explains means "Phoenix") thereby carrying the concept throughout his book.]

12. The story closely examines the young woman's mental attitudes toward love, family, relationships and local tradition. Male European characters conclude that she does not experience these things in the same way as Westerners and that their self-serving behavior ultimately will not do her any harm.

13. The young mistress adapts to European culture, imitating and then truly appreciating many aspects of its food, fashion, language and entertainment. Ultimately, she aspires to see the world beyond Vietnam.

14. Elder Vietnamese women take a more mercenary view, inducing the young mistress to take advantage of her situation. Their advice is for her to use her youth and charm to secure as much personal wealth and future stability as possible by selecting the best partners for her liaisons.

15. A naïve American, unfamiliar with local mores, unexpectedly appears on the scene, upsetting the status quo of the primary relationship between the older European lover and the young girl.

16. The American is used symbolically to personify and verbalize the (unwelcome) influence of American values of democracy, freedom and capitalism on the colonial scene.

17. One key character is murdered, with the protagonist (i.e. the first person narrator) implicated in the crime.

18. An intelligent, educated and personable French police inspector investigates the crime, threatening the fate of the protagonist.

19. The French police inspector finally decides to ignore the protagonist's possible involvement with the crime.

20. With the police inspector's absolution, the story ends happily, with the protagonist able to resume a normal life as before the murder, negating any problems caused by the American.

P.S. I'm still finding connections between the two texts, but these details initially stood out. Thank you for considering my request for your help.

Replies from Greeneland

The facts of a person's life will, like murder, come out.

—**Norman Sherry, Greene's authorized biographer**
(**quoted in the** *International Herald Tribune*, **Paris, September 15, 1989**).

While many of the scholars did not reply to my initial request, those who did were forthright and helpful. All agreed that the number of similarities seemed too great to ignore. "Too close for comfort," wrote one. Another cautioned that I might be opening myself up to legal trouble if I published the presumed "new" book. With every scholar who did write back I divulged all the background information and engaged in point-by-point discussions.

None of the scholars knew how Greene had researched his works about foreign countries. It is well established that Greene would travel to the locations he wrote about, but the extent of his background reading is unknown.

Hervey's two books about Indochina—the non-fictional *King Cobra* and the less popular novel *Congai* —were published in the US in 1927. Both books were then released in London the next year, where they were promoted by the distinguished British publishing house of Thornton Butterworth. In UK, *King Cobra* appeared as *Travels in French Indo-China,* and *Congai* appeared under the same title. Copies of *Congai* remain in the British Library (London), the University of Oxford (Oxford), Trinity College (Dublin), the National Library of Scotland (Edinburgh) and the National Library Board (Singapore). It would have been quite easy (and logical) for Greene to read either or both of Hervey's works before heading to Indochina himself.

Hervey biographer Harlan Greene queried the Graham Greene Birthplace Trust (www.grahamgreenebt.org) and was told that no works by Harry Hervey were in the Greene library, but this neither proves nor disproves anything. Greene's biographies all describe him as a former spy, master of deception and serial adulterer; if he *had* drawn from *Congai* his library is the last place one would expect to find a copy of one of Hervey's books.

Should We Expect Common Elements in Novels about Vietnam?

Individually some plot elements listed above are mundane and predicable, but taken together they seem to indicate a connection. I have found no other books from the region that use so many identical descriptive elements, so similarly arranged.

The French wrote extensively about their colonial experiences, real and imagined, in the early twentieth century. Almost none of this work has been translated into English. Dozens of French novels describe East-West romances, and even love triangles between Westerners and Orientals, but my research has unearthed none that contain the similarities seen between *Congai* and *The Quiet American*.

Suppose the twenty plot elements above were bones. It would be one thing for a paleontologist to infer a single species from a pair of similar bones found in different places. But when the bones pair up skeleton to skeleton...?

Ah, but Greene spent four winters in Vietnam and is known to have woven his own experiences into his works. Aren't these simply the elements *any* visitor to the Far East would notice?

Suppose I were writing a book about mid-twentieth-century America seeking prominent settings for the action. I might go with Chicago or San Francisco or Boston, but let's assume I chose New York. There, I might select the Empire

State Building and the 21 Club, or the Metropolitan Museum of Art and Katz's Delicatessen, or the Statue of Liberty and Barbetta, or the Chrysler Building and Delmonico's…. The options are various. Well, if one were writing about Vietnam, an entire country, the options would be equally various.

Hervey selected Saigon and Cholon, with dramatic trips into the countryside. He set a number of scenes at the Continental Café and mentioned an opium den on rue d'Ormey. Greene, it so happens, set similar scenes in the very same locations, despite the many other locations available in Indochina and Saigon.

The characters and their interactions add yet more similarities. An American appears out of nowhere in Saigon, disrupting a local East-West romance while symbolizing and verbalizing American political influence. There is a murder, an investigation by a French detective and, ultimately, an unlikely exoneration of the protagonist.

To return to my imaginary New York plot above, what if a *Peruvian* suddenly arrives to break up a love triangle and a murder ensues; a tough New York cop investigates and decides to give the implicated protagonist a pass. Then *another* book comes out and hits the same beats. Coincidence begins to seem less likely.

The twenty-five episodes of the brilliant BBC TV series *Foyle's War* feature an engaging British detective, with faithful assistants, solving crime mysteries. The plots mix British, German, Russian and even American characters, who fall in love, cheat on one another, murder or get murdered, roam the English countryside, inhabit stately homes, dine at pubs and restaurants, and so forth. Sherlock Holmes hovers like a specter over all British mystery fiction, yet not once during the run of *Foyle's War* did I think: "Hey! That's the same plot Arthur Conan Doyle used in…."

It might seem a perfectly logical assumption that the more we restrict setting and era, the more likely we are to repeat someone else's story, but the truth is different. There are in fact an infinite number of ways to tell any story, even the same story. Ask two people to tell a story about 20th century London… are they *really* going to tell the same story?

But perhaps Greene drew his ideas from *several* novels about Vietnam, in addition to his own experiences.

Unfortunately, before 1951, when Greene began writing his Indochinese tale, there was very little else in print on that topic. In his essay "Congaies or

Concubines? Literary Views of Native Women under Colonial Rule in Asia,"[2] Walter Jones examines the most prominent early works, including *Congai* and *The Quiet American*. None of the other plots are similar. Before the American war, Vietnam was a rare topic in English. In fact, anyone seeking English-language books about French Indochina in the first half of the twentieth century would have quickly and inevitably encountered the two works of Harry Hervey at the top of the list.

Did Graham Greene Plagiarize?

No. In my understanding of the term, plagiarism is the wholesale appropriation of words, not of ideas. I have compared the texts by hand and with software. No such appropriations of Hervey's words exist in Greene's text, and the writing styles are entirely different. As Pico Iyer observes in his foreword, Hervey's early novel is "humid, sometimes overwrought," as might be expected from an exuberant, 24-year-old author. Greene's is the dry, controlled, profound work of a seasoned writer approaching the age of 50. This is certainly not an example of plagiarism, but perhaps it is one of unaccredited inspiration.

Why hasn't anyone noticed this before now?

The skeleton of the books may be the same, but the flesh is so different.

—Harlan Greene, biographer of Harry Hervey.

One mundane explanation for this critical silence is the obscurity of *Congai*, a book that, until now, had been out of print for 87 years. And yet after the sensation caused by *The Quiet American* in 1955, one would think that *someone* would have noticed—if not for one, subtle but enormous difference between the works.

We have all, at some point, heard two friends relate the same incident to vastly different effect. We have all seen courtroom dramas with two witnesses doing the same. I propose that the biggest reason no one until now has noticed the similarities between *Congai* and *The Quiet American* is the diametric opposition of perspective between their two protagonists.

The power and originality of *Congai* rest in the story being told through the eyes of a young Eurasian mistress kept by older European men. As a young homosexual in the early twentieth century, Hervey doubtless suffered his share of discrimination. Perhaps his own experiences enabled him to so vividly

---

2 Included in the appendices of the 2014 DatAsia edition of *Congai*.

and convincingly express the sensibilities of a Eurasian woman; conveying the trials of her life under a colonial regime, the indignities and prejudice she suffered due to her mixed blood, and the contempt she incurred by defying sexual mores.

The Quiet American, on the other hand, is told through the eyes of a middle-aged British reporter who has fled an unhappy marriage in England to find comfort with another woman in Vietnam, where he salves his wounds with opium and leads a comfortably escapist life. Greene's power comes not from originality but from his actually having *been* a detached, middle-aged British reporter who fled an unhappy marriage in England, repaired to the Far East and there indulged his own passions, addictions and fantasies on a path of self-discovery.

Greene wrote *The Quiet American* from his own intimate perspective; Hervey did something more imaginative in writing *Congai* by speaking through the character of a Eurasian girl. Greene gives the man's perspective, Hervey the woman's. Hence the "he said, she said" contrast between these two accounts. Each has its independent existence. Each presents convincing characters through whom readers can experience the plot, albeit from diametrically opposed viewpoints.

Could Similar Observers See Similar Things?

Once I introduced the Greene scholars to the reality of the situation, all of them raised this possibility, and in many ways I agree with it. Talented writers intuit the world. They see the emotions, hopes and fears that lie beneath the surface, even in a foreign land. Hervey and Greene both had this gift and applied it to the Asian world they had entered. It is certainly possible that these two men shared a vision of Asia.

In 1927 Hervey wrote:

> And yet would all this vitally change Annam? Only in certain physical and political details. Still the peasants would work the soil with buffaloes yoked to wooden plows; would sow and harvest the rice-fields, half-naked and thigh-deep in the ooze. That peasant, she realized, was the symbol of a changeless Annam; a spirit that moved on impervious to the alterations in style and government [*Congai*, 183].[3]

In 1955 Greene made the same observation:

> If I believed in your God and another life, I'd bet my future harp against

---

3 *Congai* page references are from the 2014 DatAsia Press edition.

your golden crown that in five hundred years there may be no New York or London, but they'll be growing paddy in these fields, they'll be carrying their produce to market on long poles wearing their pointed hats. The small boys will be sitting on the buffaloes [*The Quiet American*, 95].[4]

Hervey imagined the dreams of his young Eurasian protagonist:

As she read, she passed out of the room into the pages of the book. She had become a little girl in Annam, the daughter of a mandarin [*Congai*, 59].

Greene used the same detail to shade his female character:

I remembered that Pyle had once criticized the elaborate hairdressing which she thought became the daughter of a mandarin (*The Quiet American*, 12].

Our father was of a very good family. He was a mandarin in Hue [*ibid.*, 43].

Hervey expressed the European view of Asian women, while expressing the woman's view of how emotionally inaccurate this viewpoint actually was:

"You native women are so sensible about the whole thing," he went on. "French women haven't learned to believe in inevitability. We men come and go, marry and leave, and you women continue as though nothing had happened."

How little he knew! So arrogantly blind. But one thing he had said was true. Belief in inevitability [*Congai*, 82].

Greene, like many other writers, expressed a Western view of Asian women:

"She's no child. She's tougher than you'll ever be. Do you know the kind of polish that doesn't take scratches? That's Phuong. She can survive a dozen of us. She'll get old, that's all. She'll suffer from childbirth and hunger and cold and rheumatism, but she'll never suffer like we do from thoughts, obsessions—she won't scratch, she'll only decay" [*The Quiet American*, 133].

Hervey had his protagonist reflect on her inescapable fate:

Herself she did not pity; her acceptance of the inevitable was complete. That, and the richness of experience, seemed all she had gained from those years of contact with the world [*Congai*, 114].

Greene did the same:

This month, next year, Phuong would leave me. If not next year, in three years. Death was the only absolute value in my world. Lose life and one would lose nothing again for ever [*The Quiet American*, 44].

Two talented authors used their intuition to create characters and situations. Perhaps only by coincidence one did so long before the other.

---

4 *The Quiet American* page references are from the 1980 Penguin Books paperback edition published in the United States.

Clues in the Unusual Openings?

> A guilty conscience needs to confess. A work of art is a confession.
> —Albert Camus, *Notebooks 1935-1942*.

I had never thought about Harry Hervey's unusual book opening until Pico Iyer noted how "its unorthodox form and tone, is so strikingly similar to Greene's…." Indeed, on the first page of his 1927 book Hervey directly addresses his protagonist, concluding with the words:

> Perhaps, *Madame la Panthère*, you will accept this inadequate testimonial of my belief in the integrity of your cleverness… [*Congai*, facing the book credits].

Similarly, Greene preceded his text with a most unusual dedication to his friends in Vietnam (italics added):

> Dear Réné and Phuong,
>
> *I have asked permission to dedicate this book to you* not only in memory of the happy evenings I have spent with you in Saigon over the last five years, but also because *I have quite shamelessly borrowed the location of your flat* to house one of my characters, *and your name, Phuong,* for the convenience of readers because it is simple, beautiful and easy to pronounce, which is not true of all your countrywomen's names. *You will both realize I have borrowed little else, certainly not the characters of anyone in Viet Nam.* Pyle, Granger, Fowler, Vigot, Joe—these have had no originals in the life of Saigon or Hanoi, and General Thé is dead: shot in the back, so they say. Even the historical events have been in at least one case rearranged. For example, the big bomb near the Continental preceded and did not follow the bicycle bombs. *I have no scruples about such small changes. This is a story and not a piece of history*, and I hope that *as a story about a few imaginary characters* it will pass for both of you one hot Saigon evening.
>
> Yours affectionately,
>
> Graham Greene [*The Quiet American*, facing the book credits]

What an odd way to open a book! Greene seems to be falling all over himself to show what a humble, considerate, grateful and, above all, honest author he is…and all this for merely (but "shamelessly") borrowing a humble apartment as a dramatic venue and one name. Yet, his pleas make him seem *quite* concerned that someone might *not* think his book 100% original. But as he repeatedly states, aside from a setting or two and a name, it is *all* from his imagination. He has "borrowed little else, *certainly* not the characters." He then carefully lists the characters and describes *exactly* what he *did* borrow. Finally,—just in case anyone missed his point—Greene closes by reiterating that this is just "a story about a few *imaginary* characters."

One of my proofreaders happens to have spent his career in law enforcement. After proofing *Congai,* he volunteered to read *The Quiet American* when I told him about my inquiry. The day he received the book he quickly called me and said: "Kent, I haven't even made it past Greene's dedication and he's already confessing! *No one* talks like that unless they have feelings of guilt."

I found his spontaneous reaction and professional perspective interesting enough to share. Clearly his observation is not conclusive, but a quote by Ralph Waldo Emerson immediately came to mind:

"The louder he talked of his honor, the faster we counted our spoons."

Conclusion

My admiration for *The Quiet American* has not changed a bit during this intriguing, admittedly inconclusive, investigation. My publishing goals are equally unchanged: restoring important but forgotten works of literature back into print, especially those that illuminate that wondrous part of the world known as Southeast Asia.

With this modern edition of *Congai,* new generations can experience Harry Hervey's pioneering vision of love, life and politics in French Indochina. The fact that the young American author conceived an original plot that, nearly three decades later, resonated in one of Graham Greene's greatest works is an exciting discovery, regardless of how that happened.

Certainly some Greeneland residents may choose to believe that the similarities were *all* mere coincidence. I sincerely invite those scholars to share any other pair of books by different authors about the same location that parallel one another to the extent seen here. If this is, in fact, a literary "Black Swan" type of event, it truly offers a fascinating topic for academic analysis.

If, on the other hand, Greene was inspired by Hervey's work, the results speak well of both men. They shared similar intuitions and gifts as they wove a similar story from opposing viewpoints. *The Quiet American* will always stand on its brilliance. And now the brilliance of Hervey's creation in *Congai* is once again available for consideration and comparison.

Harry Hervey Bibliography

by Kent Davis and Harlan Greene

This chronological bibliography documents Harry Hervey's major creative works. More detailed information will appear in Harlan Greene's forthcoming biography of the author.

Books

1922

Caravans by Night: A Romance of India

New York; The Century Co.

An exuberant first novel. A tale of jewel thieves and political intrigue in India, Burma, and Tibet. Along the way, the heroine, Dana Charteris, is torn between two men, Arnold Kent and Euan Kerth.

1923

The Black Parrot; A Tale of the Golden Chersonese

New York; The Century Co.

Based on his earlier short story, "The Black Panther," the book describes the exploits of adventuress Lhassa Camber in the wilds of Borneo, the Malay peninsula and Southeast Asia. Lhassa is kidnapped by Stephen Conquest and becomes involved in a plot to steal the priceless Emerald Buddha, along with other twists and turns along the way.

1924

Where Strange Gods Call; Pages Out of the East

New York; The Century Co. Illustrated by Christopher Murphy.

An account of the author's travels in Hawaii, Japan, China, the Malay Archipelago, Indonesia and the South Seas with vignettes portraying the exotic people, sights and cultures he found there. The book is based on two Pacific voyages Hervey made.

1925

Ethan Quest : His Saga

New York; The Cosmopolitan Book Co.

This tale's namesake and artistic hero hails from Savannah, GA and moves to Tennessee to attend Sewanee University. There, he loses his closest male friend and leaves his wife, before embarking to travel the world. Prophetically paralleling the life the author adopted for himself, the protagonist is joined by a male companion at his side; a native Hawaiian named Illio. Ethan never quite becomes the artist he wanted to be, but never gives up his idealistic quest for romance. In the United Kingdom the book was published under the title of *The Gay Sarong,* exemplifying Hervey's fascination with exotic fabrics.

1927
Congaï
New York; The Cosmopolitan Book Co.

London; Thornton Butterworth – 1928.

An emotional novel of a young French-Cambodian girl seeking survival as the mistress to a series of increasingly powerful French colonial men. This culturally and historically accurate novel provides unique American perspectives of the often painful interaction between French colonialism and Southeast Asian lifestyles. The book is the basis of the successful Broadway play of the same name, co-written with Carleton Hildreth, that cast Helen Menken (Humphrey Bogart's first wife) in the starring role.

King Cobra; an Autobiography of Travel in French Indo-China
New York; The Cosmopolitan Book Co.

London; Thornton Butterworth – 1928.

Hervey's non-fiction account of his travels in French Indochina with vivid descriptions of colonial Saigon, a French prison camp in the Vietnamese Highlands, the temple of Angkor Wat and a trip up the Mekong river to search for the "lost" ruins of Wat Phu to help him decipher the mystery of the disappearance of the Khmer civilization. In the United Kingdom the book was published as *Travels in French Indo-China.*

1929
Red Ending
New York; Horace Liveright, Inc.

A tale of two brothers, Belano and Dominy Farrell, during the jazz age in Charleston, SC. Contriving a "not quite romance" with a young flapper named Marianne, Belano tries to escape his mother, his Charleston life, and the fiendishly handsome Charles Semprez. It's a bleak view of a decadent culture where appearances are more important than the truth that lies beneath.

1931
The Iron Widow
New York: Horace Liveright. (Re-released as *She Devil* in 1953)

Delphine—a half-caste, sexually voracious woman—wreaks havoc on the men imprisoned in a French prison camp. Captain Lesesne, the dashing new administrator, resists her wiles, and is instead drawn to the same young boy, Jacquot, whom Delphine desires. Originally written as a play, it's overstated homoerotic overtones prevented production, so Hervey rewrote it as a novel. Published as *The Red Hotel* in the United Kingdom.

1939
The Damned Don't Cry
New York; The Greystone Press.

Born on the wrong side of the tracks in Savannah, Zelda O'Brien grows up unsullied in a dismal and sordid world. She falls in love with the aristocratic Dan Carter, and nearly succeeds in breaking with her squalid past until it catches up with her. Years later, she returns to the city to try to get her revenge, with tragic consequences. Powerful in spots, this naturalistic novel upset Savannah and has recently been returned to print.

1941
School for Eternity
New York: G. P. Putnam's Sons.

Lives and fates intertwine on a fateful Easter weekend on a Caribbean island. A band of disparate characters are suddenly invited to accept the hospitality of a mysterious count, who lives in a mountaintop mansion overlooking the city. While some characters are more types than individuals, the novel is highly polished, witty and well written. This was among Hervey's best received and best-selling works.

1947
The Veiled Fountain
New York: G. P. Putnam's Sons.

Two brothers in the Kimberly family, a composer named Brian and an English civil servant named Buzzy, inadvertently pursue the same mysterious woman with tragic results. Set mostly in India, the novel explores Eastern mysticism and is infused with music. A sophisticated tone offsets some of the soap-opera like plot twists.

1950

Barracoon

New York; G. P. Putnam's Sons.

Set in mid 19th century Portugal and Southwest Africa, the story revolves around Maria de Castro's realization of her husband's brutal role in the horrors of slave-trading. It is, as noted on the dust jacket, "the case history of a crime, but… also the story of a tender love and a spiritual victory over the powers of darkness."

Short Stories

In the 1920s, Hervey sold dozens of short stories to publications of the "pulp fiction" genre. While he returned to many of these themes in his novels, his early efforts—most hard to track down being in ephemeral publications that have not survived—should be counted more as his juvenilia rather than serious attempts at fiction.

The Parisienne magazine.

(Title and plot unknown). When Harry was only 16 and still attending school, renowned author and critic Henry Louis Mencken purchased one of his short stories. Mencken was editor and publisher of prestigious literary magazine, *The Smart Set*. The story he purchased from Hervey, however, actually appeared in his less prestigious, but more popular, "sister publication" *The Parisienne*. Mencken's co-editors soon used this formula to launch two other pulp magazines; *Spicy Stories* (1916) and *Black Mask* (1920).

The Drums of Doom. The first of Hervey's many works focusing on the devil, damnation and doom. (publication date unknown)

Black Mask magazine.

From the first issue of *Black Mask* (April 1920), Hervey was a regular contributor with eight stories published between then and July 1922.

Piracy. A tale set in Burma with an American college boy becoming involved with a stowaway and pirates. April 1920, pp. 65-78.

The Black Menace. "A complete novelette of romantic adventure...in the African wilds...in the manner of Rider Haggard's famous stories." June 1920, pp. 3-37. Henry Rider Haggard (1856-1925) was an English writer who specialized in African adventures.

More Deadly than the Viper. A mystery set in Tibet with an American trying to help a friend who is trapped by a vampire-like woman seducer who dooms her male victims to oblivion by tossing them into the Valley of the Vanishing Men. August 1920, pp. 49-64.

Daughter of the Pigeon. An intrepid sailor arrives at the Marquesas Islands of French Polynesia, determined to explore the mysterious interior of the isle of Taoha: "In the days before the Christian God came, when Po, the Power of Darkness, ruled the islands, the sea-robbers of Tahati used to hide their treasures there—somewhere near the High Place and the Vale Where Dead Men Walk...." September 1920, pp. 61-71.

Two Bells. "At two bells The Boy determined to commit murder..." Set on the "two-masted, square-rigged vessel" *Libertine*, this murder mystery unfolds a brutal tale of conflict, treachery and survival among a mixed group of sailors, thrown together by fate in the exotic waters of Australia and French Polynesia. November 1920, pp. 97-113.

Can This Thing Be? Plot unknown. February 1921, pp. 95-110.

Mr. Sin (Complete Mystery Novelette). A London-based mystery with "Scotland Yard detectives, séances by an Egyptian girl, an opium addicted baronet, a brother and sister set, a hunchback, a man named Quest, switched bodies, and a turbaned Hindu." March 1921, pp. 3-42.

The Devil at the Helm (Complete Mystery Novelette). Another tale with a demonic theme. July 1922, pp. 3-23.

The Follies magazine (successor to *The Parisienne*).

Devil's Business. A romantic adventure in Siam with a hero similar to the partially autobiographical protagonist in *Ethan Quest* and a temple similar to Cambodia's Angkor Wat. Published circa 1921.

Saucy Stories magazine.

The Lonely Heart. An American traveller explores London, including the city's seamier sides where love is sold by the hour, despite warnings from a local friend at Scotland Yard. Of course there's a woman... "For a full moment she hovered in the aperture, her thin face revealed in all its pallor, her luminous eyes upon me. Such pallid cheeks! Such pallid hands! And the speechless aching of a million years in her young eyes! She seemed a dim dream that hung there an instant and was gone. But her eyes were not gone...." May, 1919.

Monsieur Satan. Set on Bluebeard's Typhoon Island, Hervey's heroine later became the basis for one of his most famous characters, Shanghai Lilly, whom Marlene Dietrich later portrayed in the 1932 film, *Shanghai Express.* May 1921.

Fascinating Fiction magazine.

The Black Leopard. Plot unknown. Circa 1923.

Other short stories:

The Young Men Go Down. A young man watches beautiful men pass him in droves. He follows their path, to discover "the Golden One," a half-caste Magdalene who teaches him a different sort of salvation that changes his life. Edward J. O'Brien included this in *The Best Short Stories of 1924* and became the basis for the film *The Devil Dancer. The Nation,* January 30, 1924.

The Heavenly City, An Idyll of Aiko-san in Kioto. In the role of travel correspondent, Hervey takes readers on an unusual tour of the ancient Japanese city of Kioto (Kyoto). In addition to detailed descriptions of the city and area, he also gives insider impressions of his guest house, a Buddhist temple, restaurants and a private performance at a geisha house. At the Buddhist temple, the head monk befriends Hervey and invites him to witness a private dawn blessing ceremony. Even more interesting are his experiences with the geishas. Hervey gives detailed descriptions of the rituals of tea, music and dance, including Japanese terms. He also finds romance, of a sort, with the teenage waitress Aiko-san...who he discovers waiting for him in his hotel room one night. An entertaining read, to be sure. *Century Magazine,* September 1924.

The Lover of Madame Guillotine. In a remote French prison camp in Indochina, the commander's wife unexpectedly joins him and begins an affair with another officer. Based on Hervey's experience visiting the Lao Bao camp during his trip described in *King Cobra*, this story provided the basis for Hervey's film script for *Prestige*. *McClure's*, January 1927. [Included in the appendices of this book.]

Pulaski Adventure. In this cross between a rumination and a short story, Hervey rewrites history in a love story set in the environs of Civil War era Savannah, GA. *The Georgia Review,* Vol. 5, #2, Summer 1951, pp. 157–161.

On the Wall. Told in a hotel bar in the Far East, this weaves the tale of the unfaithful Marcia Cleverdon, whose husband tries to punish her by making his suicide seem like murder, framing Marcia as the primary suspect. Published posthumously. *The Georgia Review,* Vol. 7, #4, Winter 1953, pp. 390–402.

Movie Scripts

1927

The Devil Dancer (story). This silent film with screen play by Alice Duer Miller, is now lost. Miller based the film on Hervey's short story, "The Young Men Go Down," but changed much of the narrative, making the film into a vehicle for actress Gilda Gray. Gilda is credited by some for the invention of the dance, "The Shimmy."

1931

The Cheat (screenplay). Originally produced twice as a silent film by screenwriter Hector Turnbull, Hervey adapted the concept into a talking film. He added his own touches to the story of a woman who loses at gambling and borrows money from a mysterious Oriental. Her benefactor surmises he was cheated and punishes the woman, played by Tallulah Bankhead, by actually branding her. Released just before the 1931 Hollywood censorship codes were enforced, the shocking film was withdrawn and unavailable for years. It has been re-issued as a "Pre-Code" classic.

1932

A Passport to Hell (story). About to banished from an English colony in Africa, the story's heroine, played by Elissa Landi, marries a German, who is sent off to into a remote part of the continent, leaving her to drive other men to their doom. It was also released under the name *Burnt Offering* and *Dangerous Lady*.

Devil and the Deep (story). Charles Laughton made his American film debut in this film playing a naval submarine commender who is insanely jealous over his wife, played by Tallulah Bankhead. He incorrectly suspects her of having an affair with his subordinate, a lieutenant played by Cary Grant. His irrational and abusive behavior instead drives her into an affair with another lieutenant, played by Gary Cooper, leading the commander to plan a violent act of revenge.

The Wiser Sex (screenplay, co-written with Caroline Francke). Based on the Clyde Fitch play, *Her Confessions*, the plot centers on a woman framing a man for a crime he did not commit while another woman, knowing the evil women can do, tries to exonerate her victim.

Shanghai Express (story). A jilted woman in China, played by Marlene Dietrich, becomes a "coaster" known as Shanghai Lily, who earns a reputation as a notorious adventuress. Then, on a train to Shanghai during the Chinese civil war, she meets her past lover as other lives and fates intersect. Directed by Erich von Stroheim, the film is considered a cinema classic. Many people collaborated on the film, and although Hervey's contributions are clear, his work has largely been ignored in critical discussions. The film was remade twice, first as *Night Plane from Chunking* (1943) and then as *Peking Express* (1951).

Prestige (story). Partially based on Hervey's short story, "The Lover of Madame Guillotine." Therese Verlaine travels to the French prison camp run by her husband, the commandant, to find that his morals have degenerated. As in the original short story, she plans to flee with another man, but her plans fall apart in unexpected acts of violence. Her husband is then challenged to stabilize the situation, which will only be possible if he can regain his discipline and his personal prestige.

1933

The Devil's in Love (story). A wholesome young missionary woman, played by Loretta Young, becomes involved in the case of a dissolute outcast of the French Foreign legion when he is unjustly accused of a murder he didn't commit.

1934

His Greatest Gamble (screenplay). In an unusual twist for Hervey, this plot centers on male protagonist instead of a *femme fatale*. The central character, unjustly jailed, escapes prison to help his daughter who was raised to be neurotic and weak. Her father's positive influence restores her strength, but then he must decide how to deal with his own status as a fugitive.

1936

A Son Comes Home (story). A woman running a San Francisco chowder house rushes to defend her son when he is accused of a crime. She soon realizes it was another woman's son, and not her own, who is charged with the crime. As she works to clear the other boy, she encounters a moral dilemma when she realizes that her son was, in fact, complicit in the crime.

1940

Green Hell (additional dialogue). Hervey assisted his friend Frances Marion, once one the few leading women Hollywood screenwriters. The film's plot is of a woman wreaking havoc among adventurers seeking Incan treasure in the jungles of South America.

Road to Singapore (story). This was the first Bob Hope and Bing Crosby "Road" movie, a successful formula that became a series. Although Hervey originally intended this as a legitimate drama, the comedy duo played for laughs in the exotic setting, acting in playboy roles while oogling the glamorous Dorothy Lamour.

1942

So's Your Aunt Emma! (story). Also know as *Aunt Emma Paints the Town* or *Married to the Mob,* the plot features an unsophisticated country woman (played by Zazu Pitts) who comes to town to save her prize fighter nephew, who has become involved with big city crooks. She is mistaken as another mobster while fighting the criminals with her innocence.

<u>Critical Biographical Studies of Harry Hervey</u>

<u>**1954**</u>

Harry Hervey, Savannah Novelist

Anna C. Hunter. *Georgia Review,* Vol. 8 #2, Summer 1954, pp. 151–156.

<u>**1958**</u>

Harry Hervey: a bio-bibliography

William B. Richardson. Master's thesis, Florida State University, 80 pgs.

<u>**2014**</u>

The Life of Harry Hervey. (Final title to be announced)

Harlan Greene.

Forthcoming from the University of South Carolina Press

Exotic Visions of French Indochina

A 1925 adventure in Angkor.
ISBN: 978-1934431023

A jungle temple trek of 1912.
ISBN: 978-1934431900

Paintings of 1920s Indochina.
ISBN: 978-1934431917

Antique postcards of Cambodia.
ISBN: 978-9744801197

Exotic Visions of French Indochina

Exploring the Mekong in 1929.
ISBN 978-1-934431870

A romance of colonial Cambodia
ISBN: 978-1-934431-94-8

Fantastic folktales from ages past.
ISBN 978-1-934431-21-4

A lost-race romance of Laos
ISBN: 978-1934431764

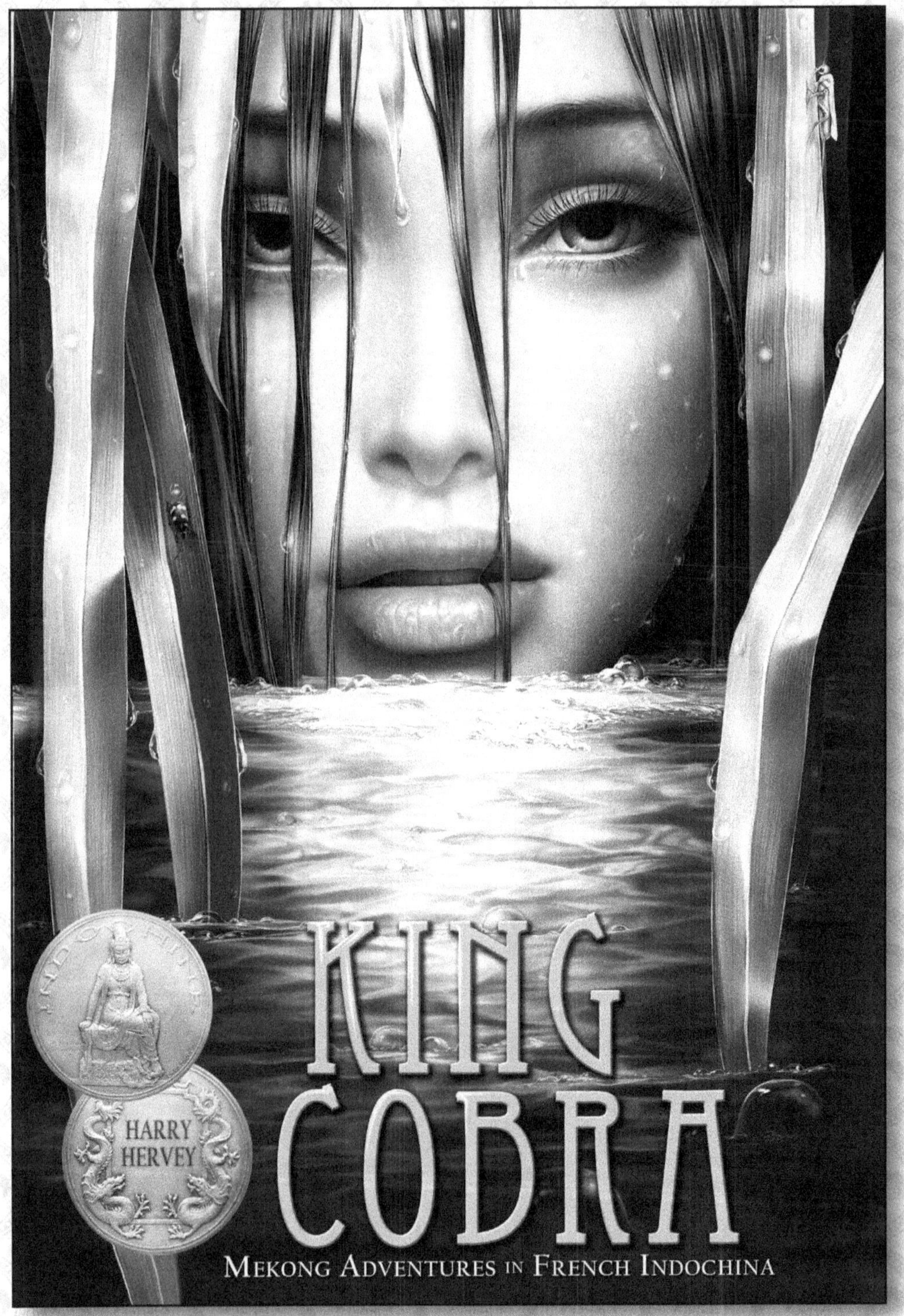

Harry Hervey's non-fiction sequel to *Congai*

"King Cobra imparts all the tremendous excitement of coming upon a hidden treasure in the jungles of Indochina. Once I began to surrender to Hervey's spell, I started—as, perhaps, he did—to lose all sense of where fact ended and fiction began."　**Foreword by PICO IYER**